Royally IN Trouble

USA TODAY BESTSELLING AUTHOR

MEGHAN QUINN

Prologue

NEW PRINCESS, NEW PROPOSAL

The editors of the highly esteemed Torskethorpe Daily *are pleased to announce that we had the distinct pleasure of sitting down with Her Royal Highness, Princess Lilija, and our soon-to-be Prince, Keller Fitzwilliam, about their recent engagement, their loving relationship, and the future of Torskethorpe. From our perspective, Torskethorpe is in good hands.*

TD: Thank you so much for sitting down with us. We want to first offer our congratulations on your recent engagement. If you can't tell already, the country is ecstatic and has been celebrating for the past four days. I know our readers want to know the details, but let's get started with how you met.

HRH: Thank you. We're excited too. It all feels so surreal, but then again, so has this journey. One day, I was in Miami, selling bathing suits while in a bikini when Keller came up to me and said . . . I'm the last heir to the throne in a country called Torskethorpe. It was the beginning of a fairy tale for us.

TD: So, Keller, you're the one who went to retrieve our treasured Princess Lilija?

KF: Yes. I was working for King Theodore at the time as his private secretary. He trusted me not only to retrieve Princess Lilija but also to educate her about our country and culture.

TD: That must have been a culture shock.

HRH: To say the least. But with every day that passed, it felt like I was coming home. I kept having these flashbacks to my mom and the traditions we shared that I had no idea belonged to this country. I might have been an outsider, but truly, on the inside, this country was running through my veins.

TD: We love that. And the people of this country can see it. You're such a warm, welcoming soul, and you truly are an embodiment of King Theodore and Queen Katla. And from what we've heard, they're more than thrilled about your engagement. Tell us a little bit about it.

HRH: I'll let Keller tell that story. He planned it, after all.

KF: When we first brought Princess Lilija to Torskethorpe, we had to keep her a secret because we didn't want to get the country's hopes up about a possible heir. We took her to Harrogate. This is where we stayed for weeks, educating the princess on the country and its culture.

HRH: And where I fell in love with not only Torskethorpe but also with Keller.

KF: When I decided to propose, I knew there was only one place I wanted to take her. I told her about an art exhibition at Harrogate and took her down to the castle, only to surprise her with a rooftop proposal, one of the first places I knew Princess Lilija was meant to be in my life forever.

TD: Princess Lilija, were you surprised?

HRH: Very much so. I had no idea. I thought we were going to go watch people paint the castle and landscape, and when Keller took me to the roof, I immediately started crying. It was an easy yes for me. I couldn't imagine marrying anyone else.

TD: Do you have a wedding date yet? I know it's soon, but the readers will want to know.

HRH: Not yet, but I believe the wedding will be sooner rather than later . . . at least that's what I've been told.

KF: [Keller kisses the back of Princess Lilija's hand] The sooner the better for me.

TD: Are you planning a traditional Torskethorpian wedding?

HRH: I plan on honoring this country as much as I can when it comes to our marriage and what my future role has for me.

TD: And are you ready to take on your future role? The Queen of Torskethorpe?

HRH: [gazes lovingly at Keller] I know with Keller by my side, I'll be ready for anything that comes my way.

I toss the paper to the side, disgust on the edge of my tongue.

"Going to be ready for anything that comes her way? Doubtful," I say as I glance up at Pickering, my assistant. "I need you to get me in touch with Magnus."

Pickering's eyes widen in question. "His Royal Highness Magnus?" he asks.

"Yes." I lean back in my desk chair. "Something needs to be done about this engagement, and I know he's the exact person to help me."

Pickering nods, turns away from my desk, and heads out of my office. I stare at the happy smiles of the newly engaged couple. Lilija looks just like her mum. It's almost sickening how close they resemble each other. And Keller . . . how was he able to wiggle his way into the future queen's pants?

Seems convenient.

Seems calculated.

Seems like I have no other choice but to do something about it.

Because over my dead body will Keller Fitzwilliam lead Torskethorpe.

Chapter One

LILLY

"Princess Lilly," Runa says, entering my room for the third time. "I must insist. It's time that you get up."

Grumbling into my silk-covered pillow, I say, "But I don't want to work out this morning."

"I understand, but since King Theodore's health scare, he's adamant the palace staff and family participate in at least thirty minutes of exercise every day."

When I lift my head from my pillow, my long blonde hair drapes over my face, clouding my vision. I blow a strand of hair off my eye and ask, "Did you do your thirty minutes of exercise today?"

"I did. A few ladies and I take brisk morning walks with weights on our ankles."

I flop my head back on my pillow and mumble, "Of course you did. You're perfect at everything."

Just then, a knock on my door continues the onslaught of

early morning barrages. No one rests in the palace. Can't a girl at least sleep in on the weekends?

Runa, the best right-hand lady to ever exist, answers the door, and I don't even have to turn around to know who it is. His large, domineering presence soaks up all the oxygen in the room with one clearing of his throat.

"Lilly," his commanding voice calls out.

"What?" I snap while pulling the pillow over my head.

"Lara is waiting for you. We have a meeting with Theo and Katla this morning about the wedding, so there is no time for you to give Runa issues about working out."

My future husband, everyone.

He sleeps in my bed but wakes up at some ungodly hour to do his two-hour workout, read about the monarchy—*as if he doesn't know everything about it already*—shower, and then help around the palace with whatever needs to be done. He's a machine. Always working, always assisting, always freaking nagging me.

"I'm not giving her issues," I say right before the blankets are torn off my body, leaving me curled on the mattress as naked as the day I was born. It's nothing Runa hasn't seen since she insists on getting me dressed. It's a part of her duty, and I've learned quite quickly that telling her she doesn't have to help me is more of an insult than anything. So, yeah . . . Runa helps me slip on my underwear every day. Not sure I'll ever get used to that.

And on Runa's end, I'm not sure she's ever going to get used to seeing a world of hickeys and bite marks all over my breasts and inner thighs. She learned quite quickly that Keller is ravenous. She doesn't even mention it now.

"Get up, love. Get dressed. Don't keep Lara waiting."

I want to shout into my pillow.

I want to bang my hand against the mattress and demand that everyone leave me alone so I can get my sleep.

Instead, I lift up, leaving my hair cascading over my face, and sit on the edge of the bed, arms loose by my side.

"Fine. I'm up." And then I drag my hair from my face and peer up at Keller. "May I have a moment with you, though?" His brow raises in question, so I add, "Please?"

He sighs and turns to Runa. "Give us a few minutes." Runa nods and leaves my room, clicking the door shut behind her.

With a soft smile, Keller closes the space between us and kneels in front of me. Hands on my thighs, he says, "Here's your moment. What do you want?"

"You," I say as I slip one of my legs over his shoulder.

"I don't have time, Lilly."

"Please, Keller. I woke up from a sex dream with you, and now I'm all hot and bothered, and I need some release."

His smirk grows wider as his hand smooths over my leg right before spreading it wide. "What was I doing in this dream?" The wicked look in his eyes assures me that I'll get exactly what I want.

I love this man so much.

"I was strapped down to the bed, and you were using that new toy on me."

He slowly nods and reaches over to my nightstand, pulling out the clit sucker he purchased for me. "This one?" He holds up the purple device between us.

I wet my lips, my body tingling in anticipation. "Yes, that one."

He pushes me back on the mattress to lie flat. "You have one minute to come," he says right before bowing his head between my legs and running his tongue along my clit.

"Yesssssss," I moan as my hands find my breasts. I start tweaking my nipples, rolling the hard nubs between my fingers.

This is the way to wake up, with Keller between my thighs. Not by Runa.

7

Not by having my blankets stripped off me.

And not with the demands of the day.

Just like this, with my fiancé's tongue lapping at my clit.

And fuck is he good at it. He knows just the right pressure, just the right amount of tongue, just the right pace.

And he's a perfectionist. He's learned my body, studied it, understands what drives me crazy, what revs me up, and what doesn't do much for me.

Right now, he's offering me long, solid strokes of his tongue, a sure-fire way to create a burning inferno at the base of my stomach. If he wants me to come fast, this is the way to do it.

My body tingles with each stroke, my legs widen with every ounce of pressure, and my pleasure tightens up with every repeat of the motion, bringing me to where I need to be quickly.

But then he pulls away, and I'm about to gasp in frustration when he says, "Thirty seconds, I better see you coming."

With that, he presses the toy to my pussy and turns it on. Immediately, a wave of soft air suction stimulates my clit.

Oh my God, yes.

My back arches off the bed, the sucking sensation overpowering. I clamp my mouth shut to keep from moaning too loud.

Keller twists my nipple ring, just the way I like it.

Yup, fuck this feels too good.

Unreal.

I slam my hands into the mattress, my neck straining as a guttural moan barely slips past my lips. I try to swallow it back so Runa doesn't hear me, but it comes out gargled.

"Fifteen seconds," he says. "If you don't come now, you won't until tonight."

God, please no.

My chest heaves with fear and excitement.

Thankfully, the suction is so stimulating that my legs start to shake. Tingling, numbing sensations float from my stomach to my limbs, and my pussy tightens in the best way, pulling every last ounce of focus right to where my clit is being sucked.

"Ten, nine, eight," he says.

"Fuck," I cry out. *Come, Lilly, don't hold on to the feeling. Just come.*

"Six, five, four . . ."

"I'm, I'm going to . . ." My mouth drops open, and just as I tip over the edge, he shuts the vibrator off and replaces it with his tongue and starts lapping.

It sends me over the edge, and I'm coming violently over his tongue, my hands threading into his hair, my legs clenching around him as my entire body shakes with pleasure.

"Fuck . . . me," I cry out as my orgasm rips through me, wave after wave, sending me into a tailspin of pleasure until nothing is left inside me.

My muscles relax, and Keller spreads my legs wide, his tongue licking my pussy, around my pussy, and around my thighs until he places a soft kiss right between my legs.

He lifts up as I remain motionless on the bed.

I open my eyes, my chest still heaving, and I look up at him. He has a satisfied look on his face, and an unsatisfied bulge in his pants.

"Put your dick in my mouth," I say. "I'll take care of it."

"We don't have time for that," he says as he moves to the bathroom, I'm sure to try to calm himself down.

I don't know how he can do that—get worked up, horny as hell, then just walk away without relief. I would combust. Not him. He's done it so many times. It's almost as if he loves torturing himself. While I'm over here, ready to cry if I don't come.

His discipline is unlike anything I've ever seen.

Also, how he can go from playful sex god to serious in seconds is something I'll never understand. Runa will walk in here soon, and I won't be able to hide the fact that he just pleasured me to completion.

Taking a deep breath, I sit up and push my hair out of my face just as the door to my room opens, and Runa slips in. Her eyes narrow on me, and I try to give her my best smile, but her lips purse to the side as she folds her arms at her chest.

Pretty sure she heard me.

"Good, you're here," Keller says, coming into the room, no erection in sight. How the hell did he do that? "Runa, I'll assume you'll take it from here. She has five minutes."

"Don't worry. She'll be ready."

Without a parting kiss, Keller is out the door.

That man is something else.

Runa's eyes fall to the mattress, and she says, "You could at least hide your devices before I come in here."

I glance down at the mattress where the bright purple clit stimulator is in full view.

With a nervous laugh, I pick it up, only to slip it into my nightstand. "How did that, uh, get out here?"

Runa just sighs and takes me by the hand, pulling me toward the bathroom.

Needing to break the silence because that was awkward, I ask, "How are you able to be up this early, work out, and still have the energy to deal with me?"

"Well." Runa directs me to the toilet, where I take a seat and do my business. "I don't stay up all hours of the night with a man."

Good point.

After I wipe and flush, I move toward the sink where I wash my hands. "It's not all hours of the night," I mumble. "Just a few."

"Just a few at night . . . and in the morning." My cheeks heat. "Ah, and from the handprint on your bottom, I can assume we engaged in some spanking last night?"

A smile pulls at my lips, and I brush my hair from my face. "Why, Runa, you never comment on my marks."

"That one is hard not to comment on." Growing serious, she asks, "Were you an equal participant?"

I roll my eyes and grip her shoulders so she's looking me square in the face. "For the last time, any mark you see on my body was encouraged by me. I like it rough, Runa."

If only there'd been time for Keller to nibble up my legs this morning . . . God, I love his teeth.

"Yes, that much is obvious."

She moves me over to the dressing area of the bathroom where she's laid out a pair of leggings, a sports bra, and a long-sleeved running shirt. Because my workout clothes are skintight, she holds off on helping me dress, thank God. No one wants to be shoved into spandex by someone else. When I'm all done, she sits me in front of the mirror and picks up a brush to attack my hair.

"What did you have for breakfast?" I ask, always interested in Runa's life. "Please tell me a pastry of some sort, maybe a cheese Danish, or a muffin."

"Eggs and toast with some cut-up berries."

Just like every morning.

"You know, Runa, it's okay to venture out of the box."

"I like routine." She pulls my hair back into a high pony-tail, the way I like it. "It's why I like what I do. My entire day has a routine, and I appreciate it. Makes me happy."

"Sooo . . . when I lie about in bed and don't get up right away, does that throw off your routine?"

"No," she answers and tightens my ponytail. "I've learned to build your reluctance of getting out of bed and your early morning extravaganzas into my routine." She smirks and then helps me out of the chair.

"Aren't you charming?" I head into my bedroom and straight to the settee where socks and shoes wait for me. I swear, if this princess thing doesn't work out, I'll have a rude awakening when thrust back into the real world. Everything is done for me now.

"Have a good time exercising," Runa says with a rueful smile.

I pause as I head toward the door. I'd much prefer to burn calories and work up a sweat while riding Keller's masterful cock. *Why isn't that considered* enjoyable *exercise?* "Runa, it almost seems like you get pleasure out of my pain." *And not the Keller-inflicted kind, sadly.*

"Never, Princess." But from her smirk, I don't think that's the case.

I open the door to my bedroom to find Lara walking down the hall toward me. Lara is my bodyguard. A toned and fit blonde babe, she's always on alert. She's become a very close confidante, and I couldn't imagine going through this major change in my life without her by my side.

She clasps her hands together with a huge smile on her face. "Ready?"

It's annoying how excited she is about working out. When I was staying in Harrogate with Keller, Lara, and Brimar—the traitor—I had to work out with them every morning as well, but she was nicer then. Now that I'm sure to take the crown, she's taken it upon herself to torture me.

"Am I ready?" I ask, stretching my hands above my head. "No, but I assume you don't really care, do you?"

She smirks. "Not so much, but if you have time for an orgasm, you have time to work out."

I gasp and whisper, "How did you know?"

"I saw the satisfied look on Keller's face as he walked out of your room."

The devil himself, giving away my personal business.

"Also, I could hear you down the hallway."

Oh dear God. I'm sure my face goes white.

"We need more privacy in this place," I say with a firm tone.

"Good luck with that," Lara says, then places her hand on my shoulder. "And don't worry about the workout. I have everything set up in the courtyard. We're doing stations today."

Great.

Stations.

Also known as thirty minutes of pure torture.

"You know . . . some might say exercising my right to a passionate moment with my fiancé would qualify as a workout."

"Not a good enough one."

"Felt good to me," I mutter as we turn the corner.

She chuckles and guides me to the courtyard where the torture happens.

"I'm just going to put it out there and say there is no way in hell I'm doing burpees today." I'm not in the mood to jump up and down after the orgasm Keller just gave me. Things are still . . . sensitive down there. "My fragile lady bones can't handle them."

"Don't pull that fragile lady bone stuff on me. Might work with Keller, but not with me." She tugs my arm. "Come on."

Ugh, nothing gets by her.

We head down the stairs, past the great hall, and with every corner we turn and long hallway we walk down, I make sure to say good morning to all the staff. I'm slowly learning their names, but it's taking me longer than I care to admit. Stombly, the large and ornate palace, has so much history within the walls that it takes a considerable staff to keep it running.

When we make it through the arched corridor to the courtyard, shrouded in beautifully manicured shrubbery and covered by a domed glass ceiling, I notice the workout setup.

Jump rope.

Foam boxes.

Dumbbells.

Yoga mats.

Ugh.

"Lara," I groan, the need to pout and stomp my foot at the forefront of my mind.

She laughs and nudges my shoulder. "Trust me, one day you'll be grateful I've pushed you this hard. Now, let's get to our warm-up. You have a meeting today you can't miss."

―――

"ARE YOU LIMPING?" Keller asks as we head toward the sitting room for our meeting with Theo, Katla, and the wedding planner.

I grip his hand and hold on to him for stability. "You try going through Lara's sadistic torture with a sensitive clit and attempt to walk in heels after." I pause and take a deep breath. "If I ever become queen, this mandatory thirty-minute health thing is over."

"It's good for you, Lilly."

I glance up at him and give him my most stern of looks. It does nothing to him. All he does is pull me closer.

"Are you nervous?" he asks.

"About the wedding planning? Why would I be nervous? It's a wedding. We have to pick out flowers and a cake and a dress. Doesn't seem like a big deal."

"Maybe for the average person, but for the future queen of Torskethorpe, so much more goes into our special day."

"I mean, sure . . . I'm going to have to wave a lot, but that's not *that* big of a deal."

"Are you really going into this that naïvely?"

"Well, you know, the uptight, headstrong clod who trained me didn't get to the chapter on royal weddings." I smile lovingly up at him.

"Watch it," he says sternly, although it's a fake stern.

14

"What are you going to do?" I ask, growing closer so I can whisper. "Spank me?"

"Lilly," he warns, causing me to smirk. I love pressing his buttons. Nothing is more satisfying than watching my stodgy, by-the-book fiancé grow irritated from my natural inclination to disobey him every chance I get.

Before we reach the red room where we're meeting everyone, Keller turns toward me and grips my shoulders so I look him in the eyes. "I don't believe I need to mention this, but just in case, since you've been slipping recently, you're to portray yourself with a sense of decorum in there."

I roll my eyes. "Honestly, Keller. You act like I'm some sort of rabid dog about to drag my hindquarters all over the two-hundred-year-old rug. I know when to joke and when to be serious."

"Says the woman who talked about her bra strap at her last public appearance."

"Uh . . . it was my underwire, not a bra strap. And if you had a thin metal rod poking you in the tit, you'd have something to say about it as well."

"Don't say tit."

"Tit. Tit. Tit," I whisper. His jaw grows tense, so I pat his chest. "Ease up, Fitzwilliam. I got this under control." And then I turn away from him and head toward the door where it's opened for me by the footmen.

"There she is." Katla, my grandmother, walks up to me, looking decadent in a hunter-green wool dress and matching jewelry. Katla is the epitome of class and poise. She's not the kind of lady who says tit. That's what I'm for, bringing the fun into the royal family.

Theo, or King Theodore Strom as the world knows him, wobbly stands from where he's sitting, beaming with pride as Katla takes both of my hands, and after I curtsy, she offers me a kiss on each cheek. Then she turns to Keller and does the same.

I step to the side and curtsy for Theo before he pulls me into a hug, his large arms circling me with a sense of comfort I've grown to love emphatically.

When he releases me and greets Keller with a handshake, I turn toward the wedding planner and offer her my hand. "Hello, I'm Lilly, and this is my fiancé, Keller. It's so lovely to meet you."

The tall blonde decked out in a red two-piece skirt suit with a brilliantly bright blouse and chunky red necklace smiles back at me. "It's such an honor to meet you, Princess Lilija. My name is Adela Anderson. King Theodore was just telling me about your adventure from Miami to Torskethorpe. I'm truly impressed with your courage and bravery."

"That's so kind. Thank you," I answer. "I finally feel at home now."

"I'm so glad to hear it."

"Let's all take a seat," Theo says as he sits down carefully and then lifts a glass of water to his lips. Keller mentioned that he thought Theo was looking weak again the other day, just like the day before Keller left Torskethorpe to find me. Obviously, the thought of losing Theo terrified me, so thankfully when I asked Katla about it, she said Theo was just fine, still recovering from a terrible case of pneumonia but doing much better. He's going through some physical therapy and working hard at building up his lung stamina. According to his doctors, he'll make a full recovery.

Keller takes a seat next to me on one of the red-and-gold couches positioned in a conversational circle. Instead of keeping his distance, he takes my hand in his, rests it on his leg, and remains as close as he can be.

For a time after the training in Harrogate, when we first arrived at Torskethorpe, he was adamant about not showing affection toward me in front of others, despite the king and queen approving of our relationship. But after he lost me, and we spent a few weeks apart, he hasn't once let up on showing me just who I belong to.

And I love every second of it.

"Since we haven't had a royal wedding in a while, I believe we'll need you to guide us through this, Adela," Katla says.

"It would be my pleasure. I hope you don't mind, but would I be able to bring my assistant in to take notes for me?"

"Of course," Katla says.

Adela turns toward the footman and says, "Would you please let Cornolia into the room?"

The footman nods and opens the door. A rather petite woman walks in, wearing a pair of dark-rimmed glasses with short brown hair and thick bangs that show no trace of her forehead. With a notebook clutched to her chest, she curtsies, then stands behind Adela's couch with her pen poised.

"My dear, please take a seat," Theo says. "No need to stand the whole time."

Cornolia nervously pushes her glasses up on her nose and sits on the couch next to Adela but remains silent. Pretty sure the girl wants to climb into the wall and never be seen again.

Adela opens a folder on her lap, shuffles through some papers, then looks up at all of us. "Just to be clear, we're going for a traditional Torskethorpian wedding, correct?"

"Yes," Theo says while glancing toward me. "I know you're not quite sure what that entails, Lilija, but I'd hope that you would be open to our traditions."

"Of course," I say, holding my hand to my chest. "I want to honor this country every chance I get. I'm open to everything that comes with a traditional Torskethorpian wedding. I want to do it all."

"That's wonderful to hear," Theo says with a prideful smile.

I'm not sure what a traditional Torskethorpian wedding entails, but I do know that my grandfather's smile means more to me than anything. After losing both of my parents, I didn't think I'd ever have someone look at me with such pride the way Theo does. But then my life changed one day, and now not only do I feel closer to my mom, but I have a support system around me, when I didn't have one when I was in Miami.

I will do just about anything to make them happy.

So if I have to carve a fish out of wood the size of Keller as part of the tradition, I will.

If I have to embroider my own veil, my God, I'll let my fingers bleed.

And if I have to choke down a bunch of their favorite fermented cod cakes, then . . . then I'll stuff some in a napkin and make it look like I ate them.

"Well, then, if we're performing a traditional Torskethorpian wedding, we'll be looking at a Friday winter wedding."

"Friday?" I ask. "Aren't weddings usually on the weekend? Especially a big wedding?"

"In our culture, we believe Fridays are the best day to get married because that's Frigga's day," Adela responds.

"Who is Frigga?" I ask, feeling confused. Where the hell was Frigga in the hour-long "training" sessions I had with Keller? Missed that one, did ya?

Calmly, Keller says, "Frigga is the goddess of marriage. Friday is the day of fertility and love." Of course he chimes in.

"Oh. Fertility and love." I nod. "Well, that's kind of cool. So a Friday wedding, how fun."

"It'll be an all-day event," Adela continues. "The schedule of events will go as follows. Maidenhood rituals will begin on Thursday." What the hell is that? "The wedding ceremony will take place at ten on Friday morning." Errr, what? "Followed by a parade where you'll be driven through the streets on the golden cod carriage." Golden cod carriage? That can't be real. "Where you will end at Strombly. Here you will take pictures with your groom and family. And from there, after official wedding pictures for history, you will get changed for your first reception." First? There's more than one? "There will be two following. Afternoon reception with just friends. And then of course our dignitary reception where you will be received by every guest." Adela glances up at me with a smile. "Did I get that right?"

Uh, I would say no—

"It's perfect," Katla says. "Just like what Theo and I had when we got married."

That's a long-ass day.

"It sounds exciting," I say even though a day with that much planned seems a touch overwhelming, but I'm not going to complain. "What uh, what are these maidenhood rituals you speak of?"

"Oh that's a surprise," Katla says with a smirk. "But don't worry, it'll be a lot of fun."

Note to self, google maidenhood rituals when alone.

"And of course, I'll have all the pre-marital requirements written down and handed to your personal secretaries so those can be taken care of before the wedding," Adela says.

"Oh, what would that entail?" I feel like such a fish out of water with all of these questions.

Theo sets down his water glass and says, "I don't believe you have anything like it in America." He rubs his chin. "If I had to compare it to another culture or class, I would say something like in the Catholic religion where they hold Pre-Cana classes for soon-to-be newlyweds. It would be like that, but it includes physical examinations and couples sessions to make sure you're both on the same page. I'll also be working closely with both of you on your future responsibilities. Since you're the heir to the throne, we need to make sure both you and Keller are ready to take on the responsibilities that coincide with such a title change."

"Oh, makes sense." I pause for a second and ask, "What if we fail?"

"We won't fail," Keller says with confidence.

"Well, I'm not saying that we will, but are there consequences? Like is there someone who will say we can't get married?"

Theo and Katla glance at each other, and before they can answer, Keller squeezes my hand tighter. "That's not something you need to worry about because it's not going to happen." He lifts my hand to his lips and places a light kiss to my knuckle. "We'll be getting married this winter."

"Okay," I say quietly, trusting him implicitly. If I know one thing for sure, it's that Keller is my rock, my everything. I can rely on him to tell me what's right and what's wrong, and if he says we can pass whatever this pre-wedding course is, then I fully believe him.

We spend the next hour going over the schedule, picking out flowers—which I was surprised about since I assumed that would be in person, but Theo wouldn't have anything but lilies —invitations—with gold foiling and embossing—and some other essentials like the cake that's a traditional kransakaka cake. It's the cake served at every wedding, tiered rings of almond-flavored pastry, served with a dripping of icing over every ring.

The entire time, Henrik, our secretary, and Cornolia furiously wrote every detail in their notes.

"Now, let's go over a date," Adela says. "We don't want anything too late into the winter season out of fear of frostbite for our constituents, so I'm thinking we will need to have the wedding in four weeks' time."

"Four weeks?" I nearly shout and then realize that reaction was way too loud. I smooth my hand over my dress and laugh nervously. "Wow, four weeks, that's quick. Are you sure we'll be able to get everything done in time?"

"Of course," Adela answers with unbridled confidence. "The country will stop everything to make your wedding arrangements happen."

"And I would have to agree with the timing," Katla says.

"The weather won't get better, and if we want to make sure our people are comfortable while waiting to see you two parade the commons, then we need to make this a very quick engagement."

Quietly, Keller says, "Is that going to be a problem?" From the insecurity in his voice, I quickly turn toward him.

"No, not at all. I want to get married. I was just surprised is all." I turn to everyone. "Four weeks it is."

"Lovely." Adela marks it down in her diary. "Well, that means we need to pick our wedding venue, so I'll set up a time immediately. And I'm sure Henrik will keep you up to date on appointments, interviews, and public appearances. We'll work closely with your office to ensure we don't inundate you with too much, but we'll need to act quickly. Thankfully, we've already hashed out some choices right here."

"What about a wedding party?" I ask. "I haven't really heard you mention anything about one."

"Ah," King Theo says, stepping in. "We don't have wedding parties here in Torskethorpe. Traditionally, the focus is on just the bride and the groom. Now, if you require a wedding party, we could possibly break tradition."

I shake my head. "Not necessary. I was just wondering if I had to ask Timmy to stand by my side."

"Who is Timmy?" Adela asks.

"My best friend," I answer. "He lives in Miami still. He's the one I shared the bikini truck business with."

"Ah, okay, well if you want him involved in any way, we can see to it."

"That's okay. I think he'd prefer to just take it all in. I'm sure I'll be the same way."

"Well, then, you let us know if you change your mind. This might be a day for the country, but this is also your special day, and we want to make sure we're meeting all of your expectations."

"I appreciate that," I say, then turn to Keller. "Do you have anything you need?"

"Just you," he says, his eyes on me.

My God . . .

If we weren't in a room with the king and queen and a wedding planning committee, I would mount this man right here, right now. Those committed eyes of his, fixated on me and only me, and the conviction in his voice displaying exactly what he wants, send shivers through my body, reminding me just how lucky I am.

I'm going to give him the blow job of his life tonight!

"There's one thing I know for sure," Adela says as she stands from the couch. "The country will be enamored with the new couple. I know just sitting here in your presence, I am."

With Adela wrapping up her meeting, we all stand, shake her hand, and she takes off with her assistant, leaving a tidal wave of to-do lists in her wake. When the door shuts, I let out a deep breath and sink back into my chair.

"Wow, that was a lot."

Keller takes a seat next to me and puts his arm around my shoulder, bringing me into his chest. He kisses the side of my head. "We'll get through it together."

"Yes, you will." Theo takes a seat as well. "Which brings me to a few things we need to talk about. First of all, Lilija, your friend Timmy has been cleared to stay with us for however long he wants. I'm sure Henrik has already reached out to him with some appropriate dates, and he'll work in some visiting time."

"Really?" I ask, perking up. It's been a while since I've seen my friend Timmy, the only true friend I had in Miami.

"Yes. Also, we've spoken to Pala, your aunt and the Queen of Marsdale. She's quite thrilled about the engagement and has made it a point to come back to Torskethorpe to meet you. She wants to bring her daughters as well. They are both around your age."

"Wait," I say, perking up even more and now sitting on the edge of the seat. "You mean I'm going to meet my aunt and my cousins?"

Pala is Theo and Katla's firstborn. She met a man in college, Clinton, and they fell in love. Turned out he was the only heir to the throne of Marsdale. Pala abdicated her position with Torskethorpe to be with him. At the time, it wasn't a big deal because she had three other siblings, but once her siblings started dropping like flies, it became a huge problem. Hence the position I'm in.

"Yes, we haven't finalized the plans," Katla says, her hands twisting in her lap. "But they're coming. It's been quite a while since we've seen them, so we're all a bit nervous." Katla is probably the most nervous since her relationship with Pala was strained when Pala chose to abdicate.

"It'll be wonderful. I've never had cousins, so this is . . . this is magical." Feeling like I'm on cloud nine, I ask, "Is there anything else?"

Theo tenses and nods. "One more thing." He directs his attention toward Keller and clears his throat. "Given we're sticking to the Torskethorpian traditions of this engagement and marriage, we need to address one thing."

"What is it?" I look between the two men, and I have the general sense that Keller knows what Theo is about to say.

"One of the traditions that dates back for generations is that the bride is to be a virgin."

I snort loud enough for the footmen outside the door to hear me.

For the walls to rattle.

For the curtains to be blown up into the air from one hard exhale from the nostrils.

He's joking, right?

"A virgin? Yeah, okay. Sorry to say but that ship sailed long ago." From my obnoxious outburst, Keller tenses next to me. "What?" I ask. "It's true, and it's not like they can turn me back into a virgin . . . right?" My voice dies as I look up at Katla and Theo. They exchange a worried glance between them as Keller shifts next to me. Uh . . . what do they know that I don't know? "Wait, can you turn me back into a virgin?"

"No, dear, of course not," Katla says. "I believe what Theo is trying to convey is that we would appreciate it if you two, as a couple, practice celibacy until your wedding night."

"Celibacy?" I ask, my eyes nearly popping out of their sockets. "Like . . . no sex?"

Katla nods. "That would be the definition of celibacy."

"But we sleep in the same room. Don't you think that would be a touch hard?"

Hard . . . Keller is always hard.

Hard at night.

Hard in the morning.

Hard when I get out of the shower.

Hard when funnily enough I'm brushing my hair.

There's no way we can be celibate, not with the virility running rampant through that man. Not to mention, I'm a rabid beast, frothing at the mouth, waiting for his next command. It's positively impossible.

We are sex fiends!

I need his mouth.

His hands.

His rock-hard cock.

I need him penetrating me all the time.

Thrusting.

Pulsing!

I need to be spanked.

Told that I'm a naughty girl.

Choked! Oh God, he won't be able to choke me. How will I ever live?

24

How the hell am I supposed to go on with my daily royal business knowing that when I retreat to my room at night, I won't be held down by the throat while my man uses me as his own personal fuck toy?

Nope, it can't happen.

I won't be able to survive!

Theo leans forward and says, "We're going to have Keller move into the sapphire room. As we speak the staff is collecting his items."

Well, there's a way to throw a wet blanket on a hard dick.

He's serious.

Celibacy.

Sorry to say it, but these Torskethorpian traditions are a load of crock.

"That's not necessary," Keller speaks up, his voice commanding, yet ready to appease. "I can take my old quarters."

Theo shakes his head. "You're a soon-to-be prince. That means you remain in Strombly. It will be best you remember that, Keller, moving forward." Ooo, look who just got put in his place.

"Yes, sir," Keller says, giving in right away. Don't blame him, Theo is a tough one to disobey.

But then it hits me. Keller will be sleeping in another room. Away from me. Far, far away, so far that . . . wait, where is the sapphire room? Is it close enough that I could at least peek in on him when he's showering?

"Wait, hold on," I say. "Does that mean I don't get to spend any time with him? Our days are busy enough, so the nights are what we save for each other. I don't want to be pulled away from Keller before we get married. I need him."

"And you'll have time with him. You can retreat to your room at night, all we ask is for the sanctity of our traditions to be honored. That just means keeping your clothes on." Theo raises a brow at me.

Oh God, reprimanded by my grandfather to keep my clothes on. That's not right.

He knows I'm a rabid sex fiend.

That's . . . problematic.

"It won't be a problem," Keller says. Of course he would say that. He's never one to challenge authority, but that means four weeks of no sex. Can he even handle that?

No sucking on his balls.

No twisting my nipple rings.

No flicking my clit.

No deep-throated cock sucking.

No bent over a bed, butt play . . .

Does he not realize that?

For the love of God, butt play, Keller!

Earth to my fiancé, we're going to have a case of deep-rooted, almost irreversible blue balls walking down the aisle.

"Thank you," Theo says with a sense of relief. Glad he finds relief in all of this. Someone has to. "I know it's something our gothi will be grateful for. It'll make his job easier."

"Gothi, who is that?" I ask, forgetting my mourning of butt play for a second.

"He's like a priest," Keller answers. "He doesn't have any religious affiliation. He's more spiritual than anything, but he's the man who oversees all marriages and pre-marriage classes."

"Oh . . . so is he going to ask us if we've had sex? Because since we're being honest, Keller and I have had a lot of sex."

"Lilly," Keller says under his breath.

"What? It's true. We have. I mean . . . a lot, more than I've ever had in my whole life, and probably not something I should be announcing to my grandparents, let alone the king and queen of a country, but I have to put it out there . . . just so much sex that I would have to have a true re-birth in order to be considered a virgin again."

"Jesus," Keller mutters.

"We understand the passion you have for each other,"

Katla says with a humoring smile on her lips. "And Gothi Elias will ask you if you've had pre-marital relations, so the answer you need to give him is yes, you have, but since your engagement, you've remained celibate."

"That won't be a problem," Keller says, all professional.

"But that's not true. Since the engagement, we've had even more sex, like . . . so much sex that I had a hard time walking—"

"It won't be a problem," Keller repeats, shutting me up real quick with a subtle squeeze of my hand.

"I'm glad to hear it." Theo places his hands on his thighs. "Are there any questions you might have? I know this is all very new to you, and the next month will fly by. I want you to know that we're open books, so if you need to ask us anything, we're here for you."

"Thank you," Keller says as he rises. He buttons his suit jacket. "I look forward to our conversations about what the future entails." Ew, God, suck up much, Keller?

"You'll be working closely with me," Katla says. "As the person who supports the crown, I believe I can offer you some valuable insight."

"I look forward to it," Keller says and lends me his hand. I take it, allowing him to help me to my feet. "I hate to cut this short, but I believe we have another engagement. An interview in the four-season glass patio."

"Ah, yes, you do." Theo rises and leans in to hug me.

We exchange goodbyes, and then with my hand in his, Keller guides me out the door and down the hallway once again.

After we're a few feet away, I ask, "Are you okay?"

"Yes," he answers curtly.

"You don't sound okay. You actually seem quite tense. Would that be because you can't play with my nipple piercings anymore?"

He stops and takes a deep breath before addressing me. "Lilly, what have I said about that mouth of yours?"

"To use it to swallow your cock?" I smile up at him, but I'm greeted with a furious set of eyebrows.

Huh, not in the joking mood.

Gripping my hand tightly, he diverts me to a room off the hallway and shuts the door behind us, only to pin me against it. With his voice so quiet, I almost can't hear him, he says, "These next four weeks are going to be hell, so I suggest you don't press my buttons by mouthing off. Got it?"

I know what other women would be thinking. "How dare you let him talk to you like that?" But the thing is, I like it. I like when he turns into a moody, commanding bastard. I like the way it feels when he tries to control me, and I enjoy testing him, seeing how far I can push him past his irritated point.

"Uh-huh," I answer while my eyes fall to his lips. "But why were you so willing to just give me up back there?" I ask, my hands lifting to his chest to play with his exposed skin from the top few buttons undone on his dress shirt. "You acted as if not having sex with me will just be some easy task to check off your to-do list."

"What did you want me to do? Hump your leg in front of everyone and beg them to reconsider?"

"I would have at least felt cherished with that." I glide my finger along his heated skin.

His hand cups my cheek, and he lowers his face close to mine. His irritation fades as he intimately says, "You know I cherish you. You're my everything, Lilly. But it's important for me to respect Theo and Katla's wishes, and if that means keeping my hands off you, then so be it."

"But . . . aren't you going to miss me?" I ask.

"What the hell do you think?" He sucks in a sharp breath as his nose runs along my jaw, sending a wave of chills down my arms and legs.

"I want to say yes you'll miss me." His nose moves up my

cheek, his lips trailing. "That you'll miss my mouth, my kisses . . . my cunt, but now I'm questioning everything."

"Lilly, stop," he says, his voice so dark that it turns me on even more. His hand slides up my side, right below my breast. "Don't make it harder than it has to be."

"Are you hard now?" I ask, bringing my hand to the front of his pants where I can feel how stiff he is just by being this close to me.

"Don't." He hisses as he takes deep breaths. "Don't tease me. You know I won't disobey Theo."

"Just tell me what you'll miss the most."

His eyes connect with mine as he says, "Being inside you. Nothing is more real, and nothing beats the feeling."

I lean my head against the door and groan. "This isn't fair."

"It's not, and you must know I want nothing more than to put all of this—the planning, the interviews, the classes—aside and just be married to you. If we could elope, I would. But that can't happen because you're the future of Torskethorpe, and the people of this country want to celebrate that."

"I know. But from that meeting alone, I can already tell this is going to be stressful, demanding. And these classes? Do you really think we need them?"

He shakes his head. "No. I don't, but once again, it's something that Theo and Katla would appreciate we take part in."

"Theo and Katla mean a lot to me." I sigh, my shoulders drooping in defeat. "Which means I'll do anything they ask." I run my hands up the lapels of his suit. "I just don't want to lose you in the process."

"You're not going to lose me," he says. "If anything, this will make us stronger."

"Promise?"

He leans forward an inch more and presses a light kiss to my lips. "Promise."

Chapter Two

KELLER

"Thank you for meeting with me," Theo says. "I know it's late."

"It's fine. I had nothing planned but some light reading," I answer. Some light reading and some dirty thoughts about Lilly from this morning that I planned on using while jacking off in the shower.

But plans changed.

Theo asked me to meet up with him in his bedroom, which I've done many times when I was his private secretary, so seeing him in his pajamas is nothing new to me.

"Katla is enjoying a nice long bath, so we have some time to ourselves." Theo runs his hands over his lavish bedding while I lean forward in the chair I pulled up in front of his bed. Last time I was in this position, he was asking me to find Lilly, so my heart is racing, wondering if what we're going to talk about has as much impact as that conversation had. His eyes lift to mine, and he asks, "How are you feeling?"

"How am I feeling?" I ask, not quite expecting that to be the conversation starter.

"Yes, I know that it's been an onslaught of meetings and decisions since you came back from Harrogate. I wanted to make sure you were doing okay."

"Oh, yeah." I shift uncomfortably. "I mean, it's been fine."

Theo studies me. "Why don't I believe you?"

Probably because you've known me since I was a child, and the role I'm currently in is one I would never have expected.

"Just need some time to get used to it is all. There's an adjustment period."

He nods. "You know, Katla had an adjustment period too. It takes a moment. It can be uncomfortable for someone to be thrust into the limelight who is not used to the attention."

"It is, but I know it'll get easier as time goes on."

"And the wedding planning and requirements, you seem to guide Lilly through them so easily, but as I watched you take it all in, I noticed you were tense."

Probably because I can't sleep with my girl, my lifeline, the one thing that puts me at ease.

"Just a lot of changes," I answer.

"You understand why we're asking these things of you, correct?"

"Yes, sir," I answer.

"Because it's important to me, to this country to follow our traditions."

"Yes, sir. It's important to me as well," I answer. "This country means everything to me."

"Good, because this country is going to need you, Keller." He picks up the glass of water that's on his nightstand and takes a sip. "Can I be frank with you?"

"Please," I answer.

"I know taking on this responsibility is a huge step for you, and it's one of the reasons you ran away from Lilly initially." I grind my teeth together, hating that I ran away, hating that the moment I got scared will forever be a part of my history with Lilly. I'll never fully forgive myself for putting her in so much pain. "But I need you to step up, Keller. I need you to fit into this new role. I need to be able to rely on you for carrying the traditions of this country. You know I love my granddaughter, but she's still learning about Torskethorpe, and it will take time to mold her into a version of herself that represents this country properly. Until then, I'm going to rely on you to take the lead."

"Of course. You can count on me."

"This is very important to me, Keller," Theo says in a serious tone, probably the most solemn I've ever heard him talk. "I'm not sure how much longer I'm going to be around, and I love that my blood will carry on in this country, but you're also the key to making sure our traditions and values continue. You know them better than anyone."

I swallow hard, feeling the weight of his request. "I understand."

"Which means you push back when you need to push back. She might be queen, but you also have a say in this role. Just like Katla has kept me in line, I expect you to do the same with Lilly." Theo reaches out and presses his hand to my cheek. "You've always been a son to me, Keller. Seeing you in this role brings me so much pride. I know you'll do excellent things, and you'll honor this country the way it was intended to be honored."

"Thank you," I say.

"Now tell me, tell me you promise you'll carry on these traditions. You won't let the past haunt you, but instead move forward and create a life of your own with Lilija."

"I promise," I say, the weight of that promise resting heavily on my chest.

Theo has given me an incredibly fulfilling life, peerless opportunities I'm forever indebted. Without Theo taking me under his wing, teaching me how to act professionally, understand the royal way of life, I would never be where I am today. So this promise . . . it's something I'll never break.

"Good." He pats my face. "Now, I have to talk about one more thing that'll be uncomfortable, but it needs to be said." He once again smooths his hands over his comforter. "I expect you are aware of your other responsibility."

My brows draw down. "I'm not sure what you might be talking about."

Theo shifts uncomfortably. "It'll be your responsibility to make sure Lilly gets pregnant."

Oh, Jesus.

"We must carry on the legacy, Keller," Theo adds.

"Uh . . . yes, sir. I don't believe that'll be a problem." Especially after four weeks of not being able to share a bed with her. I'm pretty sure my pent-up frustration will impregnate her on our wedding night.

He nods. "Good." Then his eyes meet mine, and he holds up three fingers. "At least three children. Being a single child myself, having the weight of this country solely on my shoulders was not easy to handle. I want your kids to be a support system for each other. And I'll need you to facilitate that support. Teach them about this country, about our value of family. It's something I didn't do with my own children, and see what happened?" He sighs and shakes his head. "I wish I could take it all back, those early years."

"With your children?" I ask.

He nods. "Yes, I wish I could do it differently. I wish I wasn't so strict. I wish I gave them more love. I wish I paid more attention. Maybe they wouldn't have all left me."

"They didn't leave you," I say. "All of their situations were so different, mainly based on love. You can't control who someone falls in love with. That's something you can't protect your children from unfortunately." I push my hand through my hair. "Look at me, for instance. Would I have ever considered to be in the position I'm in? The future Prince of Torskethorpe?" I shake my head. "Never. But here I am, because I found the person I was supposed to be with, and her trajectory in life led us to this position, just like your children were led to different journeys."

Theo nods slightly. "I appreciate that, Keller." He grips my shoulder. "You're a good boy. Your parents would be very proud of the man you've become."

From the mention of my parents, my heart rate picks up. I don't like talking about them or thinking about them that much either. Their tragic death lives in my nightmares, and any mention of them can switch my brain from resting at night to terror at twilight.

"How do you feel about your parents not knowing Lilly? Being here to welcome her as your bride?"

Leave it to Theo to ask the hard questions without even a second thought about it.

"Uh . . ." I clear my throat. "Fine."

"Doesn't seem like you're fine," Theo answers. "Actually feels like you're more tense than the conversation about getting Lilly pregnant."

"I just don't like to talk about them, is all."

"But they're a part of you."

"Not anymore," I answer.

"Now you look at me, son," Theo says with a commanding voice. "Just because they're no longer in your present life doesn't mean you would disregard them. Is that how you're going to act when I leave this earth one day?"

"No." I shake my head. "It's just too painful." Slowing down, I try to explain to him exactly what I mean. I clasp my hands in front of me and say, "Thinking about the way they passed, stuck in their room, fire blazing around them, smoke seeping into their lungs, it's too . . ." My throat grows tight. "It's too hard. It's all I can think about when they're brought up. Not the fun memories, not the love, not the moments supposed to mark a childhood."

"I see." Theo is silent for a second. "Well, for what it's worth, I know they'd be proud of you and the man you are today. You might be taking on a different role, but don't forget where you came from. You're a product of your parents and should be very proud of that."

"Thank you," I say, staring down at the floor in fear that I might grow emotional from this conversation. "Um, if that's all, I think I should go to bed. Early morning wake-up call."

He doesn't answer right away. Instead, I can feel his eyes on me, staring, waiting for me to say more, but I keep my mouth shut. The mention of my parents will do that.

"That would be it," Theo says, which gives me permission to stand from my chair. I move it back to its accompanying desk and walk over to the door where I grip the handle and turn toward Theo.

"Thank you for taking the time to talk to me. I won't let you down, Theo."

"I know you won't." Theo smiles at me. "I love you, son."

I wet my lips and quietly say, "I love you too," then I'm out the door, my heart racing, my feet pounding across the soft carpet, propelling me as far away from that conversation as they can get.

⊏══⊐

"HOW ARE YOU FEELING THIS MORNING?" Ottar asks.

Ottar is my new security detail, something I'm not sure I'll ever get used to. The man is just as tall as I am and maybe has about ten more pounds of muscle on him, but I'm building up pretty close to his size with the workouts we've been doing every morning.

"Good," I answer, despite feeling restless the past few nights. King Theo's conversation with me still floats around in my head, making its mark.

The weight of his requests.

The need to fit into my new role despite how uncomfortable I am.

The responsibility of acting as Lilly's consort.

"It's been three days."

"I'm well aware of how long it's been," I say as I pick up my towel and wipe the sweat off my brow with it.

Three days without fucking Lilly while trying to mentally take on all the changes. Three nights when I haven't curled my body around her beautiful naked form. Three nights when I haven't made my girl come or heard her scream my name. It's been absolute torture.

"Just checking in, because you're doing a lot of grunting today."

I glance over at him, brow raised. "You know, it was easier when you didn't talk. Lara has softened you." Lara and Ottar are a couple. They don't show it when on duty. The only reason Lilly and I know is because we're close to them.

"Lara made me realize that you don't have a lot of people to talk to and that maybe I should try to get you to open up."

"Uh-huh," I say while I move back over to the bench where my weights are racked, ready for me to lift. "And tell me exactly why bringing up the fact that it's been three days since I've been able to sleep with my fiancée is a smart thing to talk about?"

I lie down and place my hands on the bar as Ottar helps me lift it off the rack.

"Because it's healthy to talk about how you're feeling."

I don't answer him right away, because I'm focused on my breathing and not dropping this weight on my chest. After the sixth rep, I rack the weight and sit up, letting my tired arms hang in front of me.

"You want to talk about feelings?" I ask as I catch my breath. "How about we talk about the date you took Lara out on."

"Okay," he says so easily, as if he wasn't this mute giant that followed me around only last week.

I've known Ottar for a decent amount of time. He's been on staff for a few years now, and since Brimar was incarcerated for treason, he's stepped up his duties. There's no doubt he's the best I've seen, besides Lara of course.

"You go first, and then I'll talk about Lara."

I stand from the bench and turn to face him. "Is this how it's going to go? We're going to open up to each other . . . have more of a relationship than bodyguard and subject?"

He shrugs and re-racks the weight. "Nothing wrong with that. It works for Lara and Princess Lilly. Seems like it's something we need to do."

I give him another quizzical gaze.

Even though I hate to admit it, it would be nice to get some of this heavy shit off my chest, the shit I'd never tell Theo or Katla about . . . or Lara, for that matter, because even though she's one of my best friends—besides Lilly—I doubt she wants to hear about my manly urges and needs to be close to my fiancée.

"Okay, sure." I point my finger at him. "But whatever we say to each other stays between us. You can't tell Lara."

"And you can't fucking tell Princess Lilly," he counters.

"Tell Lilly you and I communicate about emotions and shit?" I shake my head. "That's the last thing I need. For all she knows, we work out together in silence. That's it. If she knew we spoke, she would never let me live it down. She would berate me with question after question. She's not hearing a damn word from me."

"Best leave it that way."

"Good." We head to the barbells together and each pick up a set of forty for bicep curls. "How am I feeling?" I ask. "Not fucking well."

"You don't say?" Look at that, the man even has some sarcasm up his sleeve. Who would have known?

Weights at my waist, I flex one up and switch to the other arm. Ottar does the same. "Not being able to be with Lilly at night doesn't sit right. I feel itchy and not because I have to . . ." I glance at him. "I know I'm talking about the future queen, so excuse my language."

"How about we just treat her as your girlfriend, future queen not in the mix."

I nod at that. "I would say it's not like I have to fuck her every night to feel right, but not having her near me when I wake up and when I go to bed makes my skin crawl with a combination of aggravation and need. I feel like I can't protect her the way I want."

"I can understand that feeling." We both set our weights down and head back to the bench. "It's like you're unsettled until you have eyes on the person you're supposed to protect."

"Exactly," I say. "And now with the popularity of the engagement and the wedding planning, the past three days have felt like a whirlwind that I couldn't stop. I feel out of control."

"Have you spoken to King Theo?"

After a drink, I set up on the bench again for another set. Ottar racks me up. "I haven't. I thought about asking him if I could stay with her and promise not to be intimate, but I know how that will go. I don't believe either of us will be able to behave. Especially Lilly. She has a hard time following directions, which of course turns me on in some fucked-up way."

"I see." When I lie down and pick up the bar, Ottar rubs his hand over his face. "Seems like you're going to have to just deal with the hand you were dealt."

I puff out a few breaths, push the bar up and down three more times, and then I set the bar on the rack. Staring up at the ceiling of the gym, I say, "Yeah, I was afraid of that."

I hate feeling out of control. I like to be able to have my eyes on everything, everything that matters to me. I realized that when I first started dating Lilly. I'm more comfortable when I know where she is, what she's doing, and that she's protected at all costs. The anxiety I feel when I don't have that under control brings me right back to the day I watched my parents' living quarters burn down with them inside.

I couldn't control the situation.

I couldn't get them out.

I just stood there, completely helpless.

We switch positions, and while Ottar gets ready, I say, "What about you and Lara? She won't say a word to me about your date. Did it not go well?"

Ottar is a large, behemoth of a man, bald, built out of steel, has a bicep almost as big as his head, and as Lilly has put it, he can crack a walnut with his ass. But the moment I mentioned his date, I saw him transform into a puddle of a man.

"No, it went amazing." He lifts the bar, and I know he doesn't really smile, but as he raises the bar up and down, the slightest of smirks crosses over his lips. So light that if I wasn't paying attention, I would have missed it.

When he's done, he stands from the bench and doesn't say anything else. Instead, he moves us back over to the barbells.

"Uh, is that it?" I ask.

"Yup," he answers.

"You're not going to say anything else?"

"Nope."

"How the fuck does that track?"

"It doesn't," he answers and then hands me some barbells. "Now get to work. You have an appointment in an hour, and you still owe me pushups."

Jesus Christ, does everyone in my life know how to play me?

"IT'S SUCH a pleasure to meet you," Gothi Elias says as he takes a seat in front of us.

After my workout, I made it to my room for a quick shower. When I exited my bathroom to get changed, Lilly was sitting on my bed, dressed in a beautiful yellow dress, her hair curled, looking so goddamn edible that I almost pushed her back on the mattress to remind her who she belonged to. I asked her what the hell she was doing, and her simple answer was waiting for me.

Doubt that was the truth. She was trying to entice me, and it was working, especially when she asked if her boobs were too revealing in her dress. She knew damn well they weren't too revealing, but that didn't stop her from hinging at the waist and pushing her breasts together for me.

Irritated, I quickly dressed and then escorted her to the ancestor room where we'll conduct our meetings with Gothi Elias. Not only is the room covered in portraits of royals from the past, but it's draped in elegant ivory curtains, low-hanging crystal chandeliers, and it offers soundproof anonymity and peace from any prying ears. Bright and cheerful, yet safe and secure. Just the way I like it.

"The pleasure is ours," Lilly says while folding her hand on her lap. "And please, just call me Lilly."

"As long as you call me Elias," he counters.

"Deal." Lilly smiles.

"Well, first, I must say congratulations. As I'm sure you probably know already, the country is bustling with excitement over the announcement of your engagement. It's been quite some time since we've had a royal wedding that we're due for a jubilant celebration."

"Thank you, we're quite excited." Lilly places her hand on my thigh, and I quickly shift my legs to knock her away. Knowing her, she'd smooth that hand right up my thigh to dangerous territories. The girl gives zero fucks.

Elias must notice the move on my end because he directs

his attention toward me. "Keller, you seem a bit stiff. Are you uncomfortable?"

Yes.

Very.

I've heard about these sessions. They like to dive deep into the personal lives of the betrothed. They pick apart the relationship. They are brutally honest, and I'm already uneasy with not being able to sleep in the same room as Lilly—or touch her, for that matter. And to top it all off, I don't like talking about my personal life or feelings with people I don't know.

And I don't know Elias.

"Just anticipating what today will be about," I answer.

"Ah, well, I can understand that. Today, I'd like to get to know both of you. Although you are the future queen of Torskethorpe, I'm afraid my knowledge of who you are is lacking, Lilly. And Keller, despite being the personal secretary to the king, that's about as much as I know as well. It'll serve me best if I get to know you both better. Let's start with you, Keller."

Of course.

"Nothing too important," I answer. "My parents used to work for the palace. My dad was part of the kitchen staff, and my mom helped preserve the artwork around Strombly. I haven't known of a home outside these walls. They lost their lives in the Strombly fire, and I stayed here to serve. Worked my way up to the position of the king's private secretary. That's about it."

Short.

Simple.

To the point.

"I see," Elias says. "That was rather quick, don't you think?"

"Efficient," I answer.

Lilly pats my thigh. "He's not much of a talker. Me, on the other hand, get me going, and I'll never stop."

41

She could not be more right about that.

"I think it's best that we dive deeper into Keller then, don't you think? If he's not much of a talker, there may be things you don't know about him."

There goes my idea on efficiency.

I shift on the couch. "I'm not very comfortable with diving in too deep."

"And why is that, Keller? Are there things you haven't told Lilly?"

Lilly turns to me, those bright blue eyes staring up at me. "Are there?"

"No," I answer, feeling my entire body wanting to squirm away from this conversation. "I just don't like revisiting the past."

"The past is what defines us," Elias answers with such a calming tone that it actually makes the hairs on the back of my neck stand to attention.

"The past is what shapes us," I reply. "Not defines us."

"So how would you be shaped?"

When I don't answer, Lilly says, "Well, he was actually sort of adopted by King Theo and—"

"Lilly," I snap at her, causing her to startle.

"What?" she asks, looking in my direction.

"That isn't public information."

"But he's Gothi Elias, he doesn't count. We're supposed to tell him everything."

"She's right, Keller," Elias says. "I've been sworn to secrecy, so what's said in this room stays in this room. I'm just here to help facilitate conversation between you and Lilly, to make sure you two are ready to take on the important commitment of marriage. And this isn't just any marriage, this is one with high stakes. A public marriage."

I move my mouth to the side, not happy with any of this. I don't like discussing my private life with anyone I don't know.

He might be a gothi of Torskethorpe, but that doesn't give me the reassurance to be open about my adoption.

Lilly notices the tension bouncing through me, so she turns to Elias and says, "May I have a private moment with him?"

"Of course." Elias stands and moves out of the room.

With the click of the door shutting, Lilly fully turns toward me and places her hands on my leg. "Keller, you can't snap at me like that. He's going to think you're some sort of commanding asshole, and then he won't let you marry me."

"That's not going to happen," I say, glancing away.

"Either way. You can't snap. You have to be open to conversation."

"I'm open. I told him about my life. There's no need to dig further into it. He doesn't need to know everything. He just needs to know the bare minimum."

"It doesn't seem like he does. This appointment doesn't have a timeframe. I think we're supposed to get it all out there."

"I don't want to get it all out there. I'm a private person, Lilly. You know that." I turn toward her. "And I don't need you talking for me, telling him some of my most private information."

"I'm sorry. I just thought you needed a little encouragement."

"I need this to be over with. I'm not talking about the adoption. I'm not talking about my parents. You know what you need to know about that part of my life. I don't need to tell some facilitator about it."

She nods. "Okay, so then what do you want me to do?"

"Tell him you already know that side of me and that it doesn't need to be repeated."

Her lips roll together. "Keller, don't you think that's counterproductive?"

"No," I answer. "You already know everything. He doesn't need to be a part of that conversation."

"Okay." She turns away, and I sense she's not satisfied with that answer, so I tug on her hand to face me again.

"Lilly. This marriage, it's between you and me, no one else. We might have to go through these courses and sit through these meetings, and give up nights together, but at the end of it all, this marriage, it's you and me. So let's protect that."

She nods and then leans in and presses a light kiss to my lips before standing from the couch.

"Where are you going?"

"To get Elias."

"Sit down," I say to her as I stand. "Another thing you need to realize is the world revolves around you. You don't beckon people."

"Keller, don't be ridiculous."

"I'm serious, Lilly. Theo and Katla would tell you the same thing. A protocol needs to be followed." I move toward the door and invite Elias back into the room.

When we're all seated, he smiles between us and asks, "Everything okay?"

"Yes," Lilly answers. "I spoke briefly with Keller, and I believe there's nothing we need to revisit when it comes to our backgrounds. That's something we've already hashed out when we were in Harrogate."

Elias tenses, and I can tell this isn't how he normally handles his conversations with soon-to-be-married couples. But given that Lilly just told him how she feels, he succumbs.

"Well, then, tell me how you two became a couple."

"Now that's a long, drawn-out story," Lilly says. "And trust me, it didn't take forever because of my lack of trying. Just look at the man. I wanted a piece of him as soon as I could get it."

Here we fucking go . . .

Chapter Three

LILLY

"Are you really mad at me?" I ask as we head down the second-floor hallway toward my room.

"Keep your voice down," Keller says as we march into my room, and he slams the door right before gripping his forehead in frustration.

Yup. He's mad.

Okay, after the whole adoption slip, I found it like a breath of fresh air to talk about our relationship and how we became a couple. Apparently, Keller wasn't too pleased about how that conversation went, either.

All I said was that he was training me.

We spent a lot of time together.

I thought he was hot as hell and flirted.

I might have mentioned being topless with him in a hot spring and him groping me, but that's neither here nor there.

The real point of this is that we had an honest conversation with Elias, which helped him ease off questioning about

Keller's background. I could tell he wasn't happy about not diving into Keller's past.

Arms folded, I ask, "Are you just going to stand there annoyed, or are you going to talk to me about what I did this time that put you in such a grumpy mood?"

"I'm not in a grumpy mood," he says, looking up at me. "Just frustrated with you."

"Well, that much is obvious. Care to explain why?"

"You just . . . fuck, you divulge too much information."

"I was telling him the truth."

"You don't need to go into details, like how I had a goddamn hard-on in the hot springs while playing with your nipple rings."

My cheeks flame, an odd feeling for me because I rarely feel embarrassed. It's usually only when someone shames me.

"He found that to be an intricate detail. He asked if that's when you first started to fall for me."

"Yeah, because he thinks I'm some sort of pervert who falls for a girl with nipple rings."

"Oh my God, that's not what he thought."

"You don't know that. He asked me if it was something I liked. Jesus Christ, Lilly, that's not something a gothi should know."

"Well . . . do you like them?"

He gives me a hardened look that nearly scares me right out of my heels. "Don't fucking start right now." He pushes his hand through his hair. "I need to go for a walk."

"Why?" I ask as I move toward him. "You can't go for a walk. We're talking."

"I think you've done enough talking."

He heads for the door, but I move in front of him. "Keller, stop. You're being sensitive. That was barely a thing. We even laughed about the hard-on."

"You don't get it, Lilly. I don't talk about that shit . . . ever. I barely talk to Lara about what I like, how I feel. I don't need my personal life waved like a flag in front of someone else. Someone I don't know. Someone I don't trust."

"What the hell did you expect would happen when we went to these classes?" Did he honestly think we were going to skate through them? I'm new to these types of things, but what I gathered from what I was told, we would have to do more than skim the surface of our relationship.

"That we were going to talk about communication and move on. I didn't think we would get into anything too personal. Or get into the details of our anatomy. It's asking too much from us to share that information with a stranger."

"He's a man of the clergy."

"No, he's not," Keller says. "He's not religious at all. He's not a priest, pastor, or anything like that. He's a man who has been certified to go through these classes with couples. That's it."

"Wait, he's not a man of God?"

"No, Jesus Christ, Lilly. You thought he was a man of God, and you're talking to him about your nipple piercings?"

"Just be happy I didn't tell him about the clit piercing." I try to offer him a cute smile, but it falls flat.

"You're saving that for the next session." He reaches for the door, but I stop him again.

"Please don't be mad at me. Okay? I'm sorry. I just get a little babbly when I'm nervous. Now that I've met him, I'm sure everything will be fine now, okay?"

When he doesn't say anything, I move between him and the door and place my hands on his thick, hot chest.

"Please, Keller. I'm sorry. I didn't mean to embarrass you or give away your private information. Please forgive me. I can't stand it when you're upset with me."

Looking toward the ceiling in frustration, he heaves a large sigh before meeting my gaze. "You drive me fucking crazy, Lilly." The tension and the anger have moderately faded while he pulls me into a much-needed hug.

Snuggling in close, I ask, "Do I make you crazy, or . . . do I keep you on your toes?"

"Both." He presses a kiss to the top of my head. "I'm still going for a walk. I'm tense and I need to walk it off before dinner tonight."

"Okay, but promise me you still love me."

He tilts my chin up so our eyes meet. "I'll forever and always love you. There's no changing that, even with your wild, unstoppable mouth."

"Good." I stand on my tippy-toes and press a kiss to his jaw. "I'll love you forever and always as well . . . my king."

He lets out a deep groan before gripping my neck and moving his mouth to mine where he blisters my mouth with his hot kisses. Yes, this is my happy place, when he has command over my body and gives me exactly what I need, his heart, his soul.

If I know one thing for sure, no matter how angry we might be at each other, this right here, this is our happy place.

This is where we belong, in each other's arms.

I'm about to wrap one leg around his when he pulls away and lightly whispers, "Mine," in my ear.

I melt, right there, in front of him.

Heart full, I glance up at him, and as he presses his hand to my cheek, I lean into his touch. "Always yours, Keller."

"Good girl," he says right before placing a sweet kiss on my forehead and gently moving me to the side. "We'll talk tonight." Then he disappears down the hallway.

That man, lord help me. Not sure I'll get over the fact he chose me.

Knowing I have some time to myself—for once—I leap onto my bed, kick off my shoes, and grab my phone so I can text Timmy.

Lilly: *Please tell me I'm going to see you soon.*

I'm about to filter through some of the wedding emails

that have been sent to me from Adela when Timmy texts back.

Timmy: *Three weeks! I'll be there for the wedding. I had some loose ends to tie up around here before I could come up.*

Lilly: *Three weeks? Ugh, that's depressing.*

Timmy: *I know. I wish it was sooner. But I have some DJ commitments to see through first.*

Lilly: *I understand.*

Timmy: *Everything okay? How was your first marriage session today?*

Lilly: *A disaster. Keller acted like he was up for anything when we were going over the requirements of our wedding, but then when we get to the actual marriage session, he clams up and gets pissed if I say anything too personal.*

Timmy: *How can you not say anything too personal? Isn't that what the classes are all about?*

Lilly: *THANK YOU! That's what I thought. But you should have seen him. He was all jittery and angry. When we were done, he confronted me about it.*

Timmy: *He's a prideful man, Lilly. I've never met him in person, but even I know this about him.*

Lilly: *I know, but we're talking about marriage classes here. I don't want anything to mess up this wedding for us and him not talking might just do that.*

Timmy: *Is that what they said?*

Lilly: *No.*

Timmy: *Maybe bring it up to Theo and Katla.*

Lilly: *You realize when you're here, you're going to have to call them Your Royal Highness.*

Timmy: *Trust me, I know. That Henrik guy sent me a thirty-page document on decorum and structure.*

Lilly: *I got the same one. A real snooze fest, right?*

Timmy: *Is that how you should be talking about the country you're going to reign one day?*

Lilly: *If I can't say it to you, who can I tell?*

Timmy: True. Question. How cold is it up there?

Lilly: Well, let's just say your nipples won't defrost until you leave.

Timmy: Color me intrigued.

Lilly: And your nuts might fall off from frostbite.

Timmy: One less thing to have to shave.

Lilly: This is why I love you. I need this inappropriateness in my life. Ever since I've come up here, I've had to be so proper. I need to talk to someone about nuts freezing off.

Timmy: Don't worry, babe, I'll be there in three weeks, and we'll have all the fun.

Lilly: I'm holding you to that.

⸺

"NOW, as I said, we have two choices where you have your wedding." Adela opens her folder. We're currently in a palace car, I presume, driving to the destination choices. The cars have two rows of seating in the back with the seats facing each other for better conversation. I'd never seen anything like it until I arrived here, and dare I say, I really like them.

Theo stayed behind at Strombly, but Katla joined us, and of course, she looks as beautiful as ever in a tweed, forest-green suit and matching leather gloves. I'm starting to notice a trend with her style and mimicking it the best I can, but it's taking me a second to develop a style that fits my personality and speaks to my future role.

Continuing, Adela says, "We have Frigga's Sanctuary to view and of course the prestigious Norse Temple." The car pulls up to a stone entrance. "Which we're at right now."

Lara and Ottar climb out of the car in front of us in their matching black suits, and I can't help but think how cute they are together, even when they're on the job. Ottar stands by the stone entrance while Lara opens the door for us. Keller is the first to exit and holds his hand out for every woman, with Katla being the last to exit.

"Right this way." Adela walks through the wooden door under the stone arch. Keller takes my hand in his and we enter a dark stone corridor straight into an ornate cathedral with gray stone vaults, matching stone flooring, and gorgeous stained-glass windows on every side, emitting a rainbow of sunlight.

"Wow," I say, taking in the entire space.

I've never seen such intriguing and time-honored architecture. The carvings seem so alive and intricate, and rich fabrics hang from the walls and decorate the stone floor. *It's incredible.* It's a temple made for royalty, that much is obvious.

"Now this of course is where Queen Katla and King Theo were married, as well as Prince Sveinn." Adela directs our attention to what feels like half a mile-long aisle. "Chairs will obviously fill either side of the aisle where there are no pews, so they'll extend to the entrance. We didn't enter through that way for privacy reasons, but you can get the idea of how long your walk down the aisle will be."

I gulp. "That's, uh, that's pretty long."

"Enough room for a large train. If that's what you want. This is all your choice," Katla says.

"Did you, uh, have a long train?" I ask.

"Twenty feet," Katla answers.

"Twenty feet? My God, how did you walk?"

"With precision and the help of my father." She glances at me, and her smile fades. "Whoever you decide to walk you down the aisle will also help you."

"I can," Keller says, his hand growing tighter.

"But you should be at the altar waiting for me," I say.

"Or we can walk together," he states matter-of-factly. From the tip of his chin and the affirmation in his voice, he's asserting I don't have to do this alone. It's one of the many reasons I love him.

"Something we can figure out further down the line." Adela brings us to the "altar," and she says, "This is where everything will happen. The acoustics are great in here, so when you do your love chant, the congregation will be able to hear you."

"Uh, pardon me." I hold up a finger in question. "What's a love chant?"

"Oh, it's a beautiful tradition," Katla says. "Quite lovely, actually. In front of all of your family and friends, you sing to each other about your undying love."

Say what now?

"But . . . I don't sing."

"Oh, none of us do, dear. That's the fun of it."

Can't quite imagine how singing in front of the entire country—off key—is going to be fun, but hey, I'm here for the experience . . . and to marry Keller of course.

"Now, will you add the traditional length to your hair?" Adela asks.

"What's that now?"

Katla turns to me with an understanding smile. "Here in Torskethorpe, the hair of the bride is more important than the dress, which means, we spend a great deal of time perfecting it. One of the things we do is add length to it. Traditionally, the length would be horsehair, but other brides have also used artificial lengths."

"Horsehair?" My nose slightly curls. I try to stop it because I don't want to be offensive, but . . . horsehair? "Are you . . . are you killing these horses for their hair?"

"Of course not." Katla dismisses me with her hand. "All horsehair is properly harvested."

Properly harvested? What the hell does that entail?

"The reason I ask is because if it's synthetic and long, we might want to forgo the candles or opt for fake ones," Adela says, but sorry, I'm still caught up on the horsehair.

How are we harvesting horsehair?

Does PETA know about this?

I can't imagine they've given the thumbs-up on harvesting horsehair.

"I believe King Theo will want her to have horsehair, just like I did and his mother before him. I believe we still have our wedding lengths in the vault. We could dust them off and give them a try," Katla announces with pride.

Age-old horsehair? This has got to be a joke.

Imagine the smell.

Musty.

Dusty.

Horsey.

Like dipping my head in a hay bale.

I don't want to be rude, but . . . I'm shivering over here from the thought of ancient horsehair being threaded with mine.

"Uh . . . something we can think about." I offer a solid smile because what else can I really do at this moment? Can't quite curl my nose in distaste. This is hand-me-down, some-thing-borrowed horsehair, a tradition that dates back for generations. "Maybe just to be safe, we do fake candles. I know Pottery Barn makes some great ones . . . errr, you don't have a Pottery Barn here, do you?"

"Not quite." Katla smirks. "But Adela will be able to get us anything we need."

"That's right. I'll start looking into fake candles." She moves around the altar. "This has plenty of room for the sword ceremony as well."

"Sword ceremony?" I ask. "Don't tell me Keller and I are going to battle it out. Trust me when I say there'll be blood-shed on his end." I joust my hand toward Keller, who doesn't even flinch. "I'm coming for you, you big oaf."

He just stares at me, unmoving.

God, not even a crack of a smile.

"I believe it." Katla pats Keller on the arm. He continues

his silence, just stands there, observing. What I wouldn't give to know what's going on in his head.

Probably thinking what a lunatic I am.

Also . . . how does he feel about the horsehair?

Would he lusciously run his fingers through it on our wedding night?

"The sword ceremony is a grand tradition at the end of the wedding where you exchange swords, indicating your commitment to each other to provide for and protect each other and your family," Katla says.

"Ah, I see." I nod. Sounds kind of sweet. "How big are these swords?"

"Seven feet," Keller replies, finally coming to life.

"Seven freaking feet?" I nearly yell. Where does one even purchase a seven-foot sword? "Is anyone going to give me a crane to lift the thing up?"

Katla takes my hand in hers, a smile on her lips. "He's teasing you."

My eyes dart to my stone-faced fiancé. "Oh, you going to be like that?"

"Maybe if you paid attention more during my training in Harrogate, you would know the answers to your questions."

"We never went over weddings. I would have remembered that."

"We did. You passed out twice while I was reciting the information you needed to know."

I prop my hands on my hips. "Well, whose fault is that? The student is only as good as the teacher."

The vein in his jaw ticks. It's the only response. Ugh, freaking frustrating man.

I turn back to Adela. "Glad to hear the swords aren't seven feet. That's a relief because it would have been a real show, seeing me yank a seven-foot sword around, horsehair dangling near fire-burning candles, twenty-foot train tangling in my legs. Could have felt more like a circus than a wedding."

"NOW THE ONLY reason we're going to Frigga's Sanctuary is because I feel like it could fit more of an ancestral vibe rather than what we've used in recent years," Adela says as we drive through one of the very few forests in the country.

"It's beautiful but not big enough," Katla says.

"Agreed, but we could do some finagling. It would take more time and precision with planning, but I do believe we could make it work."

I stare out the window, taking in the fading greens of the trees and the fall colors starting to bloom. Green moss still covers the ground, while little red berries are scattered throughout the picturesque scenery. As if someone took the land where fairies live and imported it in the middle of Torskethorpe, it feels like a fantasy rather than reality.

"Have you been here before?" I ask Keller.

He shakes his head as he stares out the window as well. He's been silent most of this trip, quietly taking everything in. Discussing the sword exchange was the only time he's really opened his mouth.

I reach over and take his hand in mine. He offers three squeezes, our secret sign to tell each other "I love you," and that little gesture eases the tension growing in my chest. There are moments when I have a difficult time reading him, if he's happy, angry, sad . . . turned on. They all mesh together. So having him tell me he loves me so subtly shows me that he might be quiet, but he's okay.

"Ah, here we are," Adela says. "This is as far as we can go with a car."

Lara opens our door, and Ottar stands to the side, alert.

Keller once again steps out first and helps Katla, me, and Adela. I cling to his side, and before looking toward the building, I lift on my toes and press a quick kiss to his lips. From his gentle smile, maybe he needed that as much as I did.

He wraps his large palm around my back and pulls me in close just as we turn to face Frigga's Sanctuary.

And wow . . . consider my breath stolen.

In the middle of tall birch trees is a glass structure, angled like a cathedral but completely transparent, only held up by wooden beams.

Unlike Norse Temple, there's nothing extra to this building. There's no stained glass, no rich, luxurious fabrics, no precisely laid stone. It's Mother Nature and glass.

And it's positively stunning.

Unlike anything I've ever seen before.

We take the rock pathway toward the sanctuary. Moss overthrows the straight lines of the path, while freshly fallen leaves sweep up into the air with the briefest of gusts from the wind. Crystal-clear glass gives us an unobstructed view from one end of the sanctuary to the other. And as we approach closer, wooden benches carved from birch trees extend up the aisle, offering minimal seating, probably for no more than one hundred people.

"It's breathtaking," I whisper as Ottar and Lara hold the sanctuary doors open for us.

Silence falls as we all take in the space at the same time. The quiet cracks from the wind, the soft, gentle whispers of nature floating by, it's peaceful.

Calming.

A space I want to get married in.

Nothing about it is ostentatious.

It's real.

It's raw.

It's me and Keller.

"I love it," I say, looking around. "Absolutely love it."

"What is the capacity?" Katla asks.

"One hundred and seventy-five," Adela answers. "The guest list would have to be cut down immensely. But we could fashion something outside the sanctuary that would allow for more seats and wouldn't disturb nature."

"How many are on the guest list?" I ask.

"Around one thousand," Katla answers.

One thousand?

My eyes nearly cross at the thought of that many people.

I glance around the space. "There's no way you can fit them here."

"No," Adela answers. "But we could have them at Norse Temple, where we live-stream the wedding. And then here, we could fashion something more intimate."

"I find that odd," Katla says. "Don't you? To invite people to a wedding but not really have them at the wedding?"

"It is different," Adela says. "But there is a rich history here at Frigga's Sanctuary. It's why I offered it as a suggestion."

"I do love it," I say. "It feels less cold, more intimate. And if it snows, the trees could be flocked in white. It could be beautiful."

"Norse Temple isn't cold," Keller says, startling me with his deep voice. "It's full of tradition and history."

"It *is* where Theo and I got married," Katla replies. "And it is quite beautiful when decorated in flowers. It won't seem so cold then. And the acoustics when the choir sings, it's just the most beautiful thing you'll ever hear."

"I didn't mean to insult Norse Temple," I say, feeling awkward, especially since Keller doesn't seem to agree with me on this decision. I tread carefully. "I was just saying that Frigga's Sanctuary feels more intimate, probably because it's smaller."

"Understandable. They are both great places to get married," Adela says. "There would be more logistics that would have to be worked out here in Frigga's Sanctuary, especially with the camera crew and live-streaming the wedding, transportation, and also tenting since there isn't a bridal suite or anything like that. But all technicalities we could work out."

"No need for the trouble," Keller says. "Norse Temple will work just fine."

Uh . . . hello?

What happened to being a united front on making decisions?

Smiling, I grab Keller's hand and say, "Will you excuse us for a second?"

I pull him toward the altar where I turn his large back to Adela and Katla and then on a whisper, say, "What the hell are you doing?"

"What do you mean?" he asks, looking clueless.

"Keller, I love it here, this is where I want to marry you. Did you not get that from all of my comments and obvious gushing?"

"It's too small."

"Uh, but Adela said she could make it work."

"At what cost? Are you going to insult guests by not inviting them to the actual wedding?"

"I think a live stream in Norse Temple could be new-agey and fun."

"That's not what Torskethorpe is about. You should know this by now. We're a community. The country has invited you in, and to get married here, where only an exclusive number of people can be present physically, it seems like a slap to the face."

"I understand that it's not conducive to everyone's feelings, but this is also our wedding day, which means we should do the things we want. And I want to get married to you here. It's not as intimidating."

"And I want to honor the people who raised me, the community who took me in, and the place where . . ." His voice cuts off, and he places his hands on his hips. He clears his throat and says, "This isn't up for debate. Norse Temple is the obvious choice."

"Not up for debate? Excuse me, I thought this was my wedding too."

"It is. But I'm putting my foot down on this. We aren't getting married here."

"You're putting your foot down?" I ask, stepping back an inch. Color me shocked because I'm pretty sure we don't ever "put our foot down" at each other. "Should I be scared?"

"You should be respectful," he says and looks away, avoiding all eye contact with me, which isn't Keller. He's the type of man who, when he "puts his foot down," he owns it. He demands attention when he's forcing one of his commands on you. So why is he looking away now?

What's going on that I don't know about?

I get this overwhelming sense that he's hiding something. He was reserved and quiet at Norse Temple. And now here, he's stiff, unwelcoming to any suggestions, like he's made up his mind, and nothing can change that. It's unlike him. He's been different all day, and I can't quite put my finger on it. Is there a connection with Norse Temple that he's not telling me about?

I don't know what hurts more, his silence or his need to rule over me.

I run my tongue over my lips and cross my arms at my chest. "Care to say that again?"

"Don't test me right now, Lilly. Norse Temple is where we're getting married."

"And why is that?" I ask.

But he doesn't answer, just stares down at me for a few beats before he turns on his heel, and to my shock, he heads back down the aisle to Katla and Adela, where he announces, "Norse Temple will be the choice."

Pardon fucking me?

"I think that's a great choice," Katla says while bringing him into a hug. "That way, your parents can be there too."

Uh . . . what?

His parents?

I hold my breath, waiting for Keller to respond to Katla, but he doesn't. He only returns the hug and then walks out of the sanctuary and to the car where Lara is standing, leaving me in his wake, shocked and in disbelief.

What the hell just happened?

⸻

"CAN YOU STOP WALKING SO FAST?" I ask Keller as he strides double-time down the hallway to where we're meeting with Gothi Elias.

"We're going to be late."

"So we're late. I would really like to talk to you about the whole Norse Temple thing."

"We can talk about it later," he says before opening the door to the ancestor room where Elias is smiling brightly.

"Welcome," he says while spreading his arms. "How is the happy couple?"

"Great," I say with so much sarcasm that it floods the very carpet we walk on. I push past Keller, bumping into his shoulder on the way.

During the entire drive back to Strombly, I tried to gather his attention, tried to get him to talk to me. I even texted him several times, but he left them unanswered. And when we got back to the palace, he ushered us right to the ancestor room instead of stopping for one freaking second to discuss things with me.

It was such a brutal, unsuspecting switch in attitude and composure that I feel like I'm experiencing a serious case of whiplash. One second, we're telling each other how much we love one another, and the next, I'm trying to figure out why my fiancé is not only being a dick but why he's keeping things from me.

"Hmm, your answer has a hint of sarcasm," Elias says, concern etched in his brow.

Wow, Elias, so perceptive.

"Lilly," Keller warns under his breath, trying to compose me.

Ha, nice try, pal. You should have taken a second to talk to me.

"We seem to be having some miscommunication today," I say to Elias as I take a seat on the couch and cross one leg over the other while folding my arms across my chest.

"Oh, about what?" Elias asks as Keller angrily sits next to me, but instead of placing his hand on my thigh, he leaves at least a few inches between us.

Could he not be more obvious?

"We went to look at wedding venues today. The Norse Temple and Frigga's Sanctuary."

"Both beautiful," Elias says.

"I thought so, but I fell in love with the sanctuary. It was more intimate and smaller, but the wedding planner said she could make it work. When I spoke with Keller about it privately, he said he was putting his foot down and we were having the wedding at Norse Temple." He stiffly shifts next to me, and with that slight move, I can taste the anger simmering inside him. But that doesn't stop me from talking. "And then to my surprise, Queen Katla says something to him about his parents being there, something he never told me. So, you know, that's been our fun today."

"I see." Elias directs his attention to Keller. "What did Queen Katla mean by your parents being at Norse Temple?"

"Not something I want to talk about," Keller responds.

Shocking!

"Is it because you don't trust Lilly with that information?"

"Is it?" I ask, turning toward him.

"No." His brow turns down. "It's because I told her we would talk about it in private later. It's not something I'm going to talk about here."

"Why didn't you tell her while looking at the venues?"

Great question.

"Because she would have asked a million questions, and the wedding planner was there. I wasn't about to get into it. She doesn't understand that when I say I'm going to talk about it later, I mean it."

"You could have just told me quickly."

"Nothing is ever quick with you," Keller says in a frustrated tone.

Elias clasps his hands together. "You know, I think we need to loosen up a bit. Why don't we do a little exercise? It seems like tensions are high, and we could use a bout of fun to ease everyone into our meeting today."

"Sure, whatever you think is best," I say.

"Great. Let's stand. Keller, please remove your suit jacket."

Reluctantly, Keller stands and takes off his navy-blue suit jacket, revealing his tight-fitted white button-up shirt. And even though I'm mad at him right now, irritated . . . confused, it doesn't change the fact that my eyes eat him up every chance I get.

The white of his shirt is crisp and clean cut, framing his muscular build by clinging to his boulder-like arms and pronounced chest, stretching the buttons so you can almost see skin when he takes a deep breath. Not to mention the way his shirt tucks into his narrowed waistline. It reminds me that it's been over a week since I've been intimate with this man and how much I miss it.

Snapping me out of my ogling, Elias says, "Lilly, stand in front of Keller, but with your back to him."

I do as I'm told and wait for his next direction.

"Now, look me in the eyes. Do you trust the man behind you?"

"Yes," I say without even skipping a beat. There is no doubt that I trust him with my whole life. He's done nothing but protect me. Love me. How could I not trust him?

"So if you were to take two steps forward and then fall backward, do you believe he would catch you?"

"Yes, and then he would make sure I was okay after. He's very protective."

"And you're willing to say this even when you're mad at him."

"She's not mad at me," Keller interjects.

I glance over my shoulder. "Yes, I am."

"You're just irritated."

"Uh, pardon me, pal, but I would appreciate it if you didn't set back feminism fifty years by telling me how I feel. I'm angry with you, swallow it." I turn back to Elias. "Despite being angry with my stubborn fiancé, I know he would catch me. I know he would take care of me and make sure I'm never in harm's way."

"Okay." Elias smiles. "Fall backward."

Without even giving it a second thought, I extend my arms to the side and tip backward, only to be caught by two large arms. His grip is protective yet soft and gentle, and as he brings me back up, his lips caress my ear as he asks, "You okay?"

"Yes," I reply, irritated, because his voice sent goosebumps down my arm, and I'm trying to be mad at him.

He then fully stands me up, and I hold my hands out to Elias. "See. He would never let anything happen to me."

"That's wonderful." Elias nods at Keller. "Is that true? You would never let anything happen to Lilly?"

"Never," Keller answers with such certainty that it relieves me . . . only a smidge. I'm still mad at him. I'm still irritated he tried to control me, and I'm very much upset that he's not telling me something about Norse Temple.

"Good." Elias's smile grows. "Now switch places."

"Okay," I say starting to move, but Keller stays put and holds out his hand in confusion.

"Hold on, switch places as in you want me to fall into Lilly?" he asks.

"Yes," Elias answers.

Simple request, Keller. I move around him and push him forward. "There ya go, fella. Get into position."

"I'm not falling into her," Keller says, stiff as a board.

"Do you not trust her?" Elias asks.

"No, I do," Keller says. "This has nothing to do with trust and everything to do with the fact she's much smaller than me. I'll hurt her."

"Hey." I push at his back. "You know I've been working out. I can handle your body."

"Just trust the exercise," Elias says as Keller grumbles under his breath, and then I get in position, legs slightly bent, a touch of a lean forward to brace for impact. I rub my hands together, ready to catch this giant bag of potatoes. "Okay, Keller, I have to ask you again, do you trust Lilly?"

"Yes," he answers, exasperation in his voice.

"So then take two steps forward and fall backward."

Keller shakes his head. "Not going to happen."

"Why?" Elias asks.

"Because I told you, I'm too big for her."

"You're not. I can handle you," I say, growing annoyed. "Just fall backward."

Sure, he might be a foot taller and much, much bigger with pounds upon pounds of muscle, but I could still handle him. No problem.

Just watch me.

"I'm not falling backward," Keller says adamantly.

"Okay, besides the fact that you're taller than her, is something else propelling you to say no to trusting her ability to catch you?"

"I trust her," Keller growls.

"Not if you won't fall back," I say.

Elias holds his hand up to me. "Let me take a moment with him."

"Sure," I say, gesturing to Elias, knowing full well any psychobabble Elias throws Keller's way will go in one ear and out the other.

"Keller, there seems to be a mental block that occurred in our last session and is still evident in this session. From what I learned, you were open to taking these classes. I would assume that someone who is open would be a willing participant."

"To an extent," Keller replies.

"Can you explain?"

Keller lets out a sigh. "I know Lilly is the person I'm supposed to marry. I don't need a class to tell me that."

"That's not what these classes are about," Elias says. "These classes are to help you harness the tools you'll need in order to approach marriage with a healthy outlook. And I'm sorry to be blunt, but from what I've noticed already, you don't seem to have the tools you need, despite what you might think."

Ooo, now that was a jab. From the silent beast in front of me, I'm going to say he's not taking that comment very well. I can only imagine the frustration he's feeling, it probably matches mine. If only he would ease up and open up a smidge, it would make this process so much easier.

"Why did you feel the need to put your foot down in the sanctuary and not tell her the real reason you want your wedding in the Norse Temple? Is it because the memorial service for your parents was held at the temple?"

"What?" I ask, peeking around Keller's large body. "Is that true?"

"How the fuck do you know that?" Keller seethes.

Elias holds his hands in front of him, completely undisturbed by the venom dripping from Keller's tongue. He looks like a viper, ready to strike his prey. Poor Elias is in the line of fire.

"The king personally asked me to walk you through these courses. I take that responsibility very seriously, just like you take your job very seriously, Keller. Which means if you weren't going to tell me about your life and your background, I would have to find out for myself."

"You researched me?"

Ooo, bad move, Elias.

"Yes, I did. I read your palace file. Granted, it didn't offer much about your personality, but I can make assumptions on that based on our short interactions. You're private, loyal, a hard worker, and you're incredibly protective. You hold on to what matters the most to you, and when faced with adversity, you always do what's right, despite who it might hurt." Elias clears his throat. "You're in this class because you have a deep-rooted desire to not only follow the rules, but to listen to anything King Theo says without hesitation or discussion. You respect the man more than anyone . . . even your future bride."

"That's not true," Keller says.

"If it was King Theo behind you, rather than Lilly, would you fall?"

"No," Keller answers.

"What if King Theo demanded it?" Elias asks.

Even from where I stand behind him, I can tell Keller clenches his jaw.

"The answer is yes, isn't it?" Elias asks. "Your silence tells us everything. Which makes me believe you respect and trust King Theo more than you respect and trust your future wife."

And hell if that doesn't freaking sting.

Keller pushes his hand through his hair. Instead of sitting in the background, I move forward so I come into his view.

"Keller, is that true?"

He blows out a heavy breath. "No, you're just . . . you're different. I'm supposed to protect you."

"You're supposed to protect the king as well," I say. "There's no difference."

"Yes, there is," he argues with me. "I'm in love with you. You're going to be my wife. There is a layer of protection I don't have with King Theo."

"So then why trust him more?"

"I don't," Keller yells. "Jesus fuck." He pulls at his hair. "This is fucking ridiculous. Just because I don't want to crush you, you think I don't trust you?"

"It's not just that," I say. "Why didn't you tell me about your parents?"

"I told you," he says in frustration. "I didn't want to get into it with the wedding planner right there. I would talk to you about it later tonight, but typical Lilly, you can't just drop shit."

"Excuse me?"

"Why don't we sit down and talk?" Elias interrupts, clearly trying to defuse the bomb he set off.

"No," Keller shoots back. "She wants to catch me, then we're going to let her catch me."

"I'm not going to catch you when you say it like that, with spite," I reply, unsure why. My head is a jumbled mess, and self-preservation is at the forefront.

"Oh no, you're going to catch me. You want to see how much I trust you, then stand behind me."

"Not to prove a point, Keller," I snap. "I want you to want me to catch you."

"Fine, I want you to catch me."

"I don't believe you."

"You know, if we just take a seat, we can discuss this in more detail." Elias gestures toward the couches.

"So now you don't trust me?" Keller asks.

"Oh no, I trust you. Don't try to turn this on me. Do you want to see just how much I trust you?" Without warning, I spin around and toss my body backward. Because he's the man that he is, he catches me before I even get close to the floor. "See?" I throw my hands up in the air as he rights me to a stand. I do it again. I flop backward.

He catches me.

Props me up.

I twirl and fall backward again, Keller right there to prop me back up.

"Stop it," he seethes.

"Just proving a point," I say.

"It's proven."

"Great."

"Now catch me," he says. "Get behind me and catch me."

"Do you want me to catch you?" I ask.

"Yes," he says through clenched teeth.

"Why do I feel like you're just saying that?"

"Just catch me," he yells right before he turns and leans back.

It all happens in slow motion.

The eclipsing shadow of his large body.

The propulsion of his anger.

The rapid fall of his weight.

Before I realize I'm making a huge mistake, I scream bloody murder and step to the side, allowing Keller to fall to the floor, landing on his back with a loud plop.

The earth around us shakes.

The water on the coffee table rattles.

And a chilling air falls over us as my knees knock together in fear.

Dear God . . . I let him fall.

Deafening silence fills the room as Elias and I both stare at Keller on the floor, neither of us quite sure what to do. What to say.

But someone has to say something.

Someone has to bridge the silence.

Someone has to make this better, and since Elias can't seem to find his words, I step up.

Clearing my throat, I say, "Perhaps next time, you give a girl a warning?"

Keller scrambles to his feet and gives me the scariest look I've ever seen.

I shrink in place.

"Is, uh, is your butt butt okay?" Why did I say butt twice?

Probably because I've never seen Keller's eyebrows so dangerously pointed before.

Keller glances up at Elias and says, "We're done here," and then he takes off without me.

Well . . . I don't think that could have gone any worse.

Chapter Four

KELLER

A familiar body sits next to me at the island in the main kitchen. It's very rare to see someone from the royal family in the main kitchen since it's where all the food is prepped and served. It's why I find solace in it.

That and the booze they have on hand.

"Care to explain to me why Lilly is a bumbling mess in her room right now?" Lara asks as she steals my tumbler from my hand and sips my whiskey.

I press my face into my hands and lean on the island. "Fuck," I mumble.

"Ah, one of those days."

"Yeah . . . one of those days," I breathe out.

"Why don't you tell me what's going on."

What's going on is that my life feels like it's spiraling out of control, and I don't know how to stop it. Between my new responsibilities, the wedding, the marital classes, the invasion of my privacy . . . I'm losing my goddamn mind. It's all coming in at once.

After a few moments, I say, "I love her, Lara."

"I know you do," Lara says.

"But I didn't think it would be this hard."

"Tell me what's hard."

I push back and press my fingers into my brow. "You know me. I have a history. I have demons, things I don't like to talk about or acknowledge for that matter, and it seems like everyone is trying to get into my business and make me talk about the things that cloud my mind." I twist my tumbler in my hand. "It's dredging up memories, nightmares."

"You're having nightmares again?" Lara asks. "The same nightmares about your parents?"

I nod. "I haven't had one since Harrogate, and now . . ." I swallow hard. "They feel more real than ever."

"Have you told Lilly?" I shake my head. "Why not?" she asks. "You need to tell her when you're going through something like this."

"And show her how much less of a man I am?" I ask. "She's already marrying lower than she should."

Lara tilts her head in disappointment. "Keller, I thought you worked through those thoughts."

"I did."

"Doesn't seem like it when you say things like that."

Frustrated, I turn toward Lara. "You don't get it, Lara. You don't see the way people look at me when I'm next to her or when they want to get to know me. Lilly comes from this prestigious background—"

"Selling bikinis in the back of a truck in South Beach, Miami doesn't really scream prestigious."

"That's not what I'm talking about. Her blood is royal. Mine is not, and I've come to terms with that, but I don't need people like a gothi or a wedding planner digging into my background. I don't need them knowing about my demons, my fears, my inadequacies. This is a marriage, not a fucking full-on background check. King Theo has already approved of me. I don't need anyone else's approval."

"Is that what you think is going on here? That they're trying to decide whether you're good enough?"

I drag my hand over my forehead. "I don't know. It feels like it. It feels like the whole country has yet to make an opinion about me."

"I don't believe that's the case here, Keller. I think they're all just trying to help you and Lilly be well prepared for marriage. *Your* fears and anxieties are making you believe otherwise."

"That fucking gothi is not trying to help." I sip my whiskey, then hand it to Lara. "Did you know he looked me up? He knew all about my parents and that they were memorialized at Norse Temple. Not only is he creating a divide between Lilly and me, but that's also a huge invasion of my privacy. I don't want people knowing that I lost my parents in a tragic fire, or that they had their funeral service at Norse Temple, or that I'm inferior for my new role."

"You're not inferior. That's in your head. And that other stuff, do you not even want your future wife to know?"

"I was going to tell her," I groan. "Jesus Christ. She didn't even give me a chance." I drag my hand over my mouth. "You know Lilly and how demanding she can be. If I said anything in front of the wedding planner, she'd want more information, and there was no way I was saying it in front of the gothi because he would make it his mission to dissect my feelings on the matter. I don't want to do that. It's already fucking with my head. I just want to be married to Lilly and move on."

"If only it were that easy," Lara says. "But you're marrying a future queen, Keller. Nothing about this process, and I mean nothing, is going to be easy. I think you need to let that settle in. Until the day you say I do, you're going to be tested, tried, and questioned. The sooner you accept that, the better. If you don't, you're just going to cause friction between you and Lilly. Is that what you want?"

"No," I answer pathetically.

"Then give me that glass and go talk to your girl."

I grumble under my breath and stand from my stool. Before moving toward the exit, I say, "Did she tell you she let me fall to the floor during the trust exercise?"

"Yes," Lara says with a grin. "And I laughed my ass off."

I shove her shoulder and walk away. "Dick."

She laughs even harder, her voice echoing down the corridor toward the stairs.

━━

I DON'T BOTHER KNOCKING on her door as I know she won't answer it. So I slowly open the heavy door and fit my body through as I look around her room.

Not on her couch.

Not on her bed.

"Lilly?" I call out.

After a second, she responds, "What do you want?"

Her voice trails from the bathroom, so I make my way over there where I find her in a robe, washing her face.

I lean against the doorframe, arms folded at my chest. "Can we talk?"

"No," she answers.

"Please?" I say in a stronger tone.

"Why do you want to talk? So you can apologize for being an ass again?" She splashes water on her face, then dries off with a towel. When she lowers the navy-blue terry-cloth fabric, she says, "That was humiliating today, Keller."

"It was," I answer. "You didn't make it any easier."

She points at her chest. "I didn't make it any easier? Are you really blaming me?"

"No. I'm not blaming you for anything, hence why I want to talk about it."

After hanging her towel, she picks up the serum that's on her countertop and rubs it between her fingers before dabbing it on her face.

"Fine, talk." She picks up another bottle, swabs a dab of white cream with the back of her nail before putting it on her face as well.

"Can we go to your room?"

She rubs the cream all over her face, then wipes her fingers on her towel. When she's done, she moves toward her bedroom, her shoulder bumping me in the process.

Yeah, she's pissed.

I so hate that I've angered her. *She deserves better than that.*

She settles on the settee in the middle of her room, crossing one leg over the other while examining her nails.

I move over to the settee as well and take a seat.

"Can you look at me when I talk to you?"

Her eyes fall to mine. "You weren't talking yet."

"Well, I'm talking now." I press my hands down my thighs, shifting to get more comfortable. "This isn't easy for me, Lilly."

"What isn't easy?" she asks.

"Marrying you," I answer, causing her expression to fall.

"Then don't." She glances away. She's putting up a front.

"Stop, don't say that shit."

"Well, what do you want me to say when you tell me it's not 'easy' marrying me? This might be news to you, Keller, but women typically don't want to hear something like that."

"I meant the process is not easy. I wasn't speaking about you, in particular."

"What a relief." Her sarcasm will be hard to break through tonight. "So then, what exactly do you mean by that? Are you too troubled to go through the process? Like you can't handle it?"

"No," I answer. "I can handle it, but it's just hard, and I need you to know that."

"Yeah, well, it's hard for us both, Keller. You're not the only one having a difficult time with all of this."

"I know, but—"

"But nothing." She shakes her head out of frustration. "What's crazy to me is that you acted like everything was fine when we met up with Theo, Katla, and Adela. What changed?"

Yeah, what changed?

My past is knocking on my door, wanting to be invited to the conversations.

The pressure from Theo, the frank talk we had in his bedchamber.

Not to mention, Elias seems to have some sort of vendetta against me.

The control I like to have is slipping from my fingers.

I don't want to tell her about the conversation I had with Theo because that was a private moment with him. Bringing up Elias might be a sore subject, so I go with the last option. "I don't like people diving into my past, knowing things about me that should be kept private. That makes me uncomfortable. And with every new interview, every new appointment and outing, I can feel that control I have over my history start to slip."

"Keller, there's no avoiding it, people are going to find out about you. Have you not seen the tabloids in America? Someone always finds a way to dig out information about a person. That's how it works. Unfortunately, that's what happens when you're tossed into the spotlight." She shifts as well, facing me more. "And when you came to apologize to me after we first broke up, you sat on this very settee and told me that you could handle this relationship. That you could be the man I need. Are you changing your mind?"

"No," I say, dragging my hand over my face in frustration. "That's not what I'm trying to say."

"Then what are you trying to say? Because all I learned today was that you value Theo more than you value me, and perhaps . . . perhaps maybe we aren't as close as I thought we were." Her voice tightens, and she looks away, but that doesn't prevent me from seeing the tears welling in her eyes.

"Lilly, stop," I say, reaching for her hand, but she steals it away, keeping it close to her body. "We're close. And I don't value Theo over you. You're the love of my goddamn life."

"Yet you're not telling me everything."

"I told you, I was going to talk to you after we got back from our class with Elias. How many times do I have to say that? You just couldn't wait."

"Or maybe, you should have told me about your parents before we even left. Of all people, you must have known which places were options for the ceremony. You know this land and its traditions. So you had time to talk to me about this. If I'd known Norse Temple had a deep-rooted connection for you *before* we went, I wouldn't have even gone to see the sanctuary. But you're keeping these details to yourself and then throwing out your alpha, controlling attitude in front of everyone else. All that's doing is pissing me off."

"I . . . I didn't want to bring it up. Katla was the one who forced me to say something."

She slowly nods. "And that's supposed to make me feel better how? I should know everything about you, Keller, but ever since we got engaged, it's like you've become this closed book, and I don't get it."

"I'm protecting you," I say. "Shielding you from trivial things—"

"Getting married in the same temple where you farewelled your parents is not trivial, Keller. That's pretty monumental. And it hurts me that you don't think I would want to know that."

"You have enough on your plate."

"Why don't you let me be the one who decides that?" She leans in. "And yes, I have a lot on my plate, but do you know what always comes first in my life?" She pokes my chest. "You. You will always and forever come first. Over this country, over this responsibility that rests on my shoulders. You, Keller. You matter more to me than anything."

I glance away, staring down at my hands in my lap because I don't know how to respond to that. I've never had anyone so passionately love me like Lilly, and sometimes, it takes my breath away, confuses me, sends me into a whirlwind of disorientation. It's just been so long since I've had such . . . *focused* love. Perhaps that's the downfall of having . . . *then losing* such wonderful parents.

"Did you hear me?" Lilly, the feistiest girl I've ever met, pokes me again. "You matter more to me than anything."

"Yes," I answer.

"Then respond. Christ, Keller."

When I look up at her, I feel at a loss of words. "I . . . I don't know what to say."

"Oh, I don't know, maybe that I come first in your mind as well. Maybe thank you. Maybe something along the lines of I'm sorry, Lilly, for making this difficult. I'll try better."

I sigh and reach for her hand. This time, she lets me take it. "I'm sorry, Lilly. I'll do better."

"How will you do better?" she asks. I should have known it wouldn't be that easy.

"How do you want me to do better?"

"Talk to me," she begs. "Tell me what the hell is going on in your head because you're starting to scare me."

"Scare you how?" I ask, rubbing my hand over her knuckle.

"Like . . . like you would run out on our wedding, not show up, like this is all too much for you."

"I would never do that," I respond with certainty. "You're

mine, Lilly. We will be married. Nothing in this world will take that away from happening."

She moves in closer so her leg presses against mine. "Promise me."

"I promise," I say, cupping her cheek. "Nothing will prevent me from walking down that aisle with you." Another tear falls down her cheek, and this time, I wipe it away. "I'm sorry about earlier. I didn't want to say anything to you because there's a lot going on, but I've had some nightmares recently and they've hit harder than I care to admit. They've thrown me off."

"What?" she asks, concern growing in her expression. "Like the one you had in Harrogate?"

I nod. "Yeah. I, uh . . . that's why I didn't want to talk to Elias about my family. It's why I've been tense lately. Just a lot of memories that aren't sitting well."

"Keller, you need to tell me these things."

"I know."

She runs her hand up my chest and then straddles my lap. *God, I've missed this woman.* This. Us. Our sexual relationship. I've missed this. Being close to her, loving on her . . . *getting lost in her.*

"Lilly," I say softly. "We can't . . ."

"I won't," she says as she cups either side of my neck. "I just need to be close to you." She leans in and presses a kiss to my cheek. "I'm here for you, for whatever you need."

"I should be the one who's helping you," I say, feeling inadequate.

"It goes both ways. You don't always have to be the hero."

"I'm not trying to be a hero. I'm just trying to be the man you need, the man you deserve. Showing weakness is not a part of that."

"Showing weakness is what makes you human, Keller."

There's a knock on the door right before it opens to reveal

Runa. When she catches the position Lilly is in, she offers a very disapproving sneer.

"What are you doing?" she asks.

"Don't worry," Lilly says, "we were just talking. That's it. Nothing to worry about."

"Okay, well, I need to get you ready for bed."

"Go on," I say while placing a kiss on her cheek. "I should retreat to my room anyway."

I stand, but Lilly joins me and grips my shirt. Speaking quietly, she says, "We're not done talking about this, okay? I'll text you."

"Okay." I press a kiss to her lips and move away. "Have a good night, Runa."

"You too," Runa says before closing the door behind me.

Feeling exhausted, I move down the hallway, past the three bedrooms that separate me from Lilly, and into my room. Draped in sapphire fabric and opulent furniture, my room feels more like a museum than a place that I would call home.

If I were to be honest, I miss my room back in the quarters. I miss the simplicity of it. Staying in this room, in the palace without Lilly by my side, makes me feel like an imposter, like I don't belong. Despite how much Theo, Katla, and Lilly tell me that I belong, I'm not sure that feeling will ever go away. It's not how I was raised. Being a prince was not how I pictured my future . . .

Jesus Christ, if only my parents were alive to see what was happening.

What would they say?

Would they be proud?

Would they be mad at me for crossing that line? The palace line that divides those who help and those who rule rich in their blood?

I honestly couldn't tell you what they would think, and that gnaws at me.

I move toward my en suite bathroom and remove my

button-up jacket. I begged Theo not to assign me someone to help with my daily activities in my room like Runa because it would mess with my head. Theo agreed but said once I'm married to Lilly, that will have to change.

So for now, I'll have the task of undressing myself. *It would be far more pleasurable if Lilly was undressing me. Cannot lie.*

I quickly get ready for bed. With my briefs still on, I move to my bed and slip under the rich covers, heavy and cool. Despite this bed being one of the most comfortable that I've ever slept in, I suffer greatly from a lack of sleep. It's damaging not to be with Lilly at night, but fuck if I'm going to complain about it. What kind of man would I be if I couldn't sleep alone?

I rest my head on my pillow just as my phone dings with a text.

Lilly: *Are you in bed?*

Settling in, I text her back.

Keller: *Yeah. You?*

Lilly: *I am. I hate being away from you.*

Keller: *I hate it too.*

Lilly: *I also hated today. I feel like there's distance between us, and I don't like that.*

Keller: *There's no distance.*

Lilly: *Feels like it.*

Keller: *Do you feel like that because we have to be separated at night?*

Lilly: *No, I felt like that when we were at the temple and sanctuary, like something was standing between us. And of course with Elias . . .*

Keller: *I don't like him.*

Lilly: *That much is obvious. Should I talk to Theo and see if we can get someone else?*

Keller: *No. It's fine.*

Lilly: *Are you sure? Because you sort of lost it today.*

Keller: *I lost it? You lost it. You were the one flopping your body around. What if I didn't catch you one time?*

Lilly: *I knew you would. It was nothing to worry about on my end.*
Keller: *Still.*
Lilly: *Still, what? All you had to do was fall back and trust me.*
Keller: *Much good that did me. My ass is still sore.*
Lilly: *I wasn't ready. I would have caught you if I was fully prepared and in the right position.*
Keller: *Still sticking with that?*
Lilly: *Yes. Now, how do we move on from here? I feel like everything is still up in the air.*
Keller: *I don't know.*
Lilly: *Is this how it's going to be, Keller? Tense and uncomfortable? This process should be fun.*
Keller: *I agree, it should be, but not when you're the future queen of Torskethorpe. Nothing will be normal again.*
Lilly: *So that's what I should expect from now on?*
Keller: *Yes.*
Lilly: *That's not really fair.*
Keller: *Nothing is fair when you're in the line of service, and that's what you're in. You serve your people now.*
Lilly: *I guess so . . .*
Keller: *You okay?*
Lilly: *Not really, but I guess it'll just be something I'll have to get over. I'm exhausted. I'm going to go to bed.*
Keller: *Okay. I love you.*
Lilly: *Love you too. Good night.*
Keller: *Night, love.*

Chapter Five

LILLY

"Which design do you like best?" Katla asks as we stare down at five different sketches of wedding dresses.

Trust me when I say I never thought picking out my wedding dress would be like this—with a designer displaying dress designs that they worked countless hours on only for me to judge them. I always assumed it would be more like finding a few bridal shops that I like, picking out some dresses, and putting on a fashion show. I also thought my mother would be here, and that I would be in America, not the future heir to the crown of a small country.

"Well, I think they're all beautiful," I say even though the one on the far right is a design I would never be caught dead in. Fringe sleeves with a turtleneck? What were we thinking on that one? "But I'm leaning toward the simple A-line with the lace bodice or the bohemian chic with the plunging sleeves."

Katla grips my hand tightly and coos, "That's what I was thinking as well, but I didn't want to sway you either way."

It's cute how excited Katla has been about this entire process. Even though I haven't known her long, *and we are so different*, every now and then, she says something a certain way, and I almost turn expecting to see my mom. Mom never really had an accent, but I swear I can hear my mother in my ear. *And, I'd be lost without that.* I've missed my mom in various ways over the years, but right now is a time I wish she was here the most. *Would she be happy I'm taking the throne? Would she love that I've returned to her birthplace?*

"Lovely," Parish, the designer, says. "I actually was thinking you would pick those as well, so I took it upon myself to sew a rough draft of each for you to try on. Would you be comfortable trying them on now?"

"Of course," I say, excited. "That would give me a better indication of what to expect and probably make my decision easier."

"Perfect." Parish squeezes her hands together. "Do you mind if I take a moment to set them up and give them a quick steam?"

"Not at all," Katla says. She turns to one of the footmen and says, "Please direct Miss Parish to the adjacent room to set up. We'll wait in here."

"Thank you," Parish says.

Once she gathers her illustrations and follows the footman to the adjoining room, Katla turns to me. "Are you really happy with the designs? If not, we can ask someone else. I don't want you to feel pressured into picking one."

"No, I love the two options. I could easily see myself getting married in them. I think I'm leaning more toward the bohemian one, but it will be good to see."

"Are you sure? Because I have no problem asking for more designs or asking someone else."

I shake my head. "No, really, these are great."

"Okay." Katla shifts her mouth to the side as if she doesn't believe me. "It just seems like . . . like you're not as excited as I thought you would be."

"Sorry," I say on a sigh as I lean back on the couch, slouching in my royal posture for a moment. "Things have been a touch rocky lately, so I'm feeling distracted."

"Rocky in what way?"

I don't want to worry Katla, not with everything she has on her plate, so I keep it simple. "Just little tiffs with Keller. I think the stress of the wedding is getting to us. But nothing that will rock the boat. Nothing to worry about. Just tired is all."

"Ah, I understand." Katla pats my leg. "Theo and I went through the same roller coaster when we were getting married. There are a lot of stressors that come with a wedding. Add the pressure of getting married in front of the public and it escalates emotions. It will all settle down when you finally have your special day and then of course your honeymoon. Any idea where you might want to go?"

"Oh, I guess I haven't thought about that."

"Do you know where you should go?" Katla says, growing excited. "Theo owns an island off the coast of Morocco. It's incredibly secluded, and few know about it. There's a vacation home he had built many years ago. A small cottage that offers the prettiest of views, an ocean so blue you'll never want to leave. We haven't been in years, but it would be the perfect getaway for you two."

"Sounds amazing," I say. "I'll talk to Keller about it."

"Knowing him, he's already thought about going there. He's been once before, Theo forced him to take a vacation and sent him down there. It's where he earned his pilot's license."

I pause and turn more toward Katla. "Excuse my shock, but Keller has his pilot's license?"

"You didn't know that?" she asks. "Yes, he wanted to learn in case he ever needed it. He's also an expert in combat battle, a certified marksman, and can drive any type of boat you put in front of him. He was adamant about learning all the attributes of survival and protection."

"Huh." I glance away, feeling foolish that I didn't know that about him. What else don't I know? Have I truly not taken the time to dive in deep with Keller? What does he not know about me? I worry my lip. "Do you think we're moving too quickly? Like, do you think I should get to know Keller more before we get married? I mean, I should have known that about him, but I didn't. I feel sort of embarrassed."

"Nothing to be embarrassed about," Katla reassures me. "I didn't know plenty of things about Theo until we were married. And even at that, I didn't find out until a few years down the road. That's the fun part of being married. You spend your life together, learning about one another. No married couple on this planet knows everything about each other before they get married. And you don't need to. You need to know the important things, and you and Keller already have that."

"Yeah, I suppose so." I let out a large sigh. "A pilot . . . God, that's really hot."

Katla laughs. "I'm sure just another thing to add to your list."

She's right about that.

━━━

LILLY: *Where are you?*
    Keller: *With the doctor.*
    Lilly: *Why? Are you okay?*
    Keller: *Yes, it's for my basic checkup.*
    Lilly: *Oh, duh. Did he feel your balls?*
    Keller: *Yes.*
    Lilly: *Jealous. Did you cough real good for him?*
    Keller: *Why are you like this?*

Lilly: Can't help it. What are you doing now?

Keller: Staring at a cup.

Lilly: That's weird, what kind of a cup?

Keller: A cup I have to jack off into.

Lilly: OMG! Are you serious? Why?

Keller: Part of making sure I can fulfill my duties as the man who needs to impregnate you.

Lilly: Stop, that's not true.

Keller: Why would I lie about something like that?

Lilly: I don't know. So you're for real? You have to jack off into a cup?

Keller: Yes. The doctor is waiting outside.

Lilly: Wait, where are you?

Keller: In my bedroom.

Lilly: Did he give you anything to make you hard?

Keller: No. He had magazines, but I didn't want them.

Lilly: Why not? I would have taken them. Stare at some boobies.

Keller: The only "boobies" I want to stare at are yours.

Lilly: Well, we can remedy that.

"Hey, Runa," I call out as she prepares my dress for dinner tonight.

"Yes?" she says.

"Can you give me like twenty minutes of privacy?" I smile at her, blinking my eyes.

She flattens her lips as she stares at me. "Why may I ask?"

"Private reasons." I smile even brighter. "Please just be a gem. Guard the door. Make sure no one comes in."

She heaves a heavy sigh and turns off the steamer she was using to erase some of the wrinkles at the bottom of my dress. "You have fifteen minutes."

"I can work with that," I say right before she takes off and shuts the door behind her. Lucky for me, I'm wearing nothing but a robe, so I undo it and prop my phone up on my nightstand where I FaceTime Keller, exposing my body for the camera.

After two rings, he answers, and when he comes into view, his brows quickly narrow. "Lilly, what the hell are you doing?"

"I have fifteen minutes," I say while I play with my nipple ring. "Make it quick."

"We're not supposed to be doing this."

"Uh, Theo said no fornication, technically, this is just playing around. Don't you want to play around with me . . . my king?"

He groans in frustration, his head falling back, exposing his thick, muscular neck. "Fuck, Lilly, don't say that."

"Come on, Keller." I sit up now and spread my legs, giving him a whole view. "Play with me." I twist my nipples, causing myself to moan.

When I glance down at the phone, I see his eyes intent on my fingers, so I encourage him more by moving my hand down my stomach and between my legs.

"Tell me what you want me to do," I say softly.

I see the moment he breaks because his tongue peeks out and wets his lips right before he stands from his chair and moves over to his bed where he sets the phone and cup down on the nightstand. He's propped the phone up to give me the perfect view of his waist where he undoes his pants and pushes them down along with his briefs, revealing his beautiful erection that stretches up toward his stomach.

"I miss your cock so much," I groan. I've never seen a more perfect man in my entire life, from head to toe. His brawny chest, thick pecs, and intricately carved, boulder-like arms, down his stacked abs and the V in his hips, the most deliciously large cock. Every time I see him with his clothes off, I yearn with need for him.

"I miss your greedy, warm cunt," he replies in a gruff voice just before he sits on the bed, giving me the perfect view of him stroking himself.

Long.

Thick.

Yearning.

His large hand circles the head and then strokes down his length, making me so fucking jealous it's not my hand, or mouth for that matter, doing the work.

I settle in for the show, so grateful I at least get to watch him when he says in a gruff voice, "Turn around."

Surprised, I ask, "What? But I won't be able to see—"

"I *said* turn around," he says in a dark tone.

Not sure where he's going with this, I lower my head and say, "Yes, my king," before turning around, offering him my back.

"Remove the robe," he says next.

I let the robe slide down my body until it pools on the floor.

"Good girl," he coos, his voice comforting as I listen to his every command. "Now, I want to see that delicious cunt. Get on all fours and press your chest to the mattress."

Oh . . .

A smile plays at my lips, and I prop my ass up, spread my legs just enough to give him the best view, and then lower my chest and face to the mattress. I position the camera so he has a full shot of everything, and the thought of him being able to watch me like this adds an extra layer of eroticism, making me that much more aroused.

"Perfect," he answers on a strangled tone. "So fucking perfect." He clears his throat. "Now, reach between your legs and play with that drenched pussy."

I massage two fingers over my clit. And fuck does it feel good.

"Yes, just like that," he says as he pumps his cock, the slick sound spurring on my own arousal. "Let me see that clit ring, tug on it."

I roll my teeth over my bottom lip, the mystery of not seeing him and only hearing his voice spurring me on more as I slip my clit ring between my fingers and give it a light tug. A sharp point of pleasure flies up my spine, causing me to moan.

"Again," he says.

And I listen.

"That's it, love," he says. "Make that pussy wet. I want to see you dripping."

I give the ring a few more tugs before I bring my fingers back to my clit and massage it where a hiss escapes my lips.

"I wish this was your tongue."

"Me too," he says. "I miss having your scent all over my face."

The thought sends a chill over my arms. He gives the best oral. Best I've ever had. There's something about a man who has no shame in driving his face between your legs and loving it.

"Remove your fingers," he says.

I pause. "Why?"

"Don't question me, Lilly. Just do it."

I remove my fingers, my pussy throbbing, wanting more attention, not as close as I want to be.

"Good girl. Now take one of the pillows, roll it, and put it between your legs." Not sure where he's going with this, I roll one of the softer pillows on my bed and stick it between my legs. "Good," he says through a soft hiss. "Now . . . rub that cunt on it. Hard."

My mouth waters as I realize what he wants me to do. He wants me to dry hump the pillow.

I grip the sheets below me, and I start rocking my ass back and forth, feeling the cool fabric of the pillow rub over my pussy. Immediately, my body lights up from the feel of it. Christ . . . I've done this one other time out of sheer desperation for release. I forgot how good it feels.

"Spread your legs wider," he says.

I do and the friction over my clit has me picking up the pace.

"Yes, fuck," I cry out, feeling my back tense.

"Slow down," he says. "I can see you're getting close. Give me long, slow, clenched strokes."

I bite down on my bottom lip and slow down, my head falling back, my back arching as I continue to move my center over the pillow. The debilitating pace takes away my control.

"Keller, I need more."

"In time, love," he says. "Let me just watch you drive yourself crazy."

I keep my pace so slow that tears start to threaten my eyes because I need to go fast, my nerves are begging for it, my muscles ready to fire off, everything is bunching up but not tightly, not where I need it, creating this edging feeling that's taking over my entire body.

"Goddammit, Keller," I cry. "Please."

"What do you call me?" he asks.

"My king, please," I cry out as my voice becomes breathless.

"Don't come yet, do you hear me?"

I nod even though I'm not there yet. I'm in a purgatory where my release simmers but is not ready to fall over the edge.

"I asked you a question. I need to hear your voice. Do you hear me?"

"Yes . . . my king," I answer as my heart rate picks up, my hips begging to move faster.

After a few more drawn-out sweeps, he says, "Stop."

I pause, my chest heaving, my body breaking out in a solid sweat.

"Remove the pillow and finger yourself. I want to see your luscious hole and your fingers slide inside."

I toss the pillow away and lean forward again to offer him the view he wants. I slide my finger inside me.

"Two fingers," he says.

I add another, and I groan as I try to hit the spot that I

need, but I can't reach it, not in this position. So once again, aggravation creeps up my neck. "I need more, my king," I say. "I'm . . . I'm edging in the worst way."

"Good," he says. "Fuck, you're so hot, especially when sexually frustrated. I want to eat you, fuck that pussy with my tongue."

"Please, I need it," I say as I continue to slip my fingers in and out, the sensation starting to spike my orgasm.

"We shouldn't even be doing this . . . but I can't deny you." His pace picks up, a grunt falling past his lips, the sexiest sound ever.

I dip my fingers some more, swirling and pulling out, waiting for his next command. And the more he grunts, the more my body reacts, and I start to edge closer.

"Are you close?" he asks.

"Yes," I answer.

"Then flip around and spread your legs wide. I want to see your cheeks flush as you come."

Thank God.

I turn back around, my eyes immediately fixating on my phone and his enlarged dick.

So hard.

Precum on the tip.

His stomach muscles contracting as he tugs feverishly.

From the strained look on his face and the veins in his neck, I know he's going to come any second.

I scoot closer to the phone and spread my legs wide, giving him a very X-rated view as I rub my fingers over my clit.

"That cunt . . . it's mine," he growls.

"All yours," I say.

"And those tits. Play with them, Lilly. Make me jealous, envious of what I can't have."

My fingers glide over my nipple rings, plucking, twisting, showing him everything that he would do if he were here. I even lower my mouth just above them and flick my tongue over the hardened nubs.

"Fuck . . . me," he calls out, his hand now moving so fast over his cock, it's almost a blur.

The strength in his grip, the power in his thrust, the strangle in his voice, it heats my body into an inferno, and before I know it, I'm panting his name.

"My king, please, I need to come."

He doesn't say anything at first, and I nearly shout at him as I move my fingers back to my clit and massage it, my orgasm right there, starting to tip me over the edge.

"Keller," I cry out.

"Come," he says just as he groans out.

I'm too overcome with my own pleasure to notice him catching his sperm in the cup. My eyes squeeze shut, blocking out everything around me, and as I come, all I can think about is how good this feels and how much better it would be if he was actually in the room with me.

When my hand slows down and I start to catch my breath, I bring my attention to the phone where Keller is nowhere to be found.

Body still thrumming, I sit up and grab the phone. "Keller?" I ask.

"Hold on," he calls out from a distance. So I wrap my robe around my body again, just in case my fifteen minutes are up with Runa. I honestly can't tell time when I'm in the middle of an orgasm, and when he comes back, I catch a light flush on his neck.

"Had to clean up," he says quickly.

"You good?" I answer.

"Yes." His eyes meet mine. "Thank you, love."

My heart melts from the term of endearment. "You're welcome."

He blows out a heavy breath. "I miss this, miss you."

"Same," I say. "So much."

He nods. "But we're not doing that again, so don't ask."

"What do you mean?"

"We aren't having phone sex. We shouldn't have even done that," he says. "It's against what Theo and Katla are asking us."

"Technically—"

"No, Lilly. Not again. Understood?"

Feeling the wind stolen from my sails, I nod. "I understand."

"Good girl." He glances to the side. "I need to go."

"Okay. Love—"

I don't get to finish as he hangs up the phone. I stare at the blank screen, jarred from the brisk end to our conversation. What the hell was that about?

Insecurity laces through me as I set my phone down, just in time for Runa to knock on my door and enter the room.

"Lovely, you're done. Let's get you dressed."

I guess I am done.

I put on a fake smile for Runa and follow her into the bathroom. The entire time, my mind is reeling about what just happened. *He's never done that before. Been so distant . . . especially straight after sex. Was he just using me so he could get off?* No. No, that's not Keller's style. And I could tell he needed me, needed to see me. Wanted me.

Is it just pre-wedding jitters? Should I just ignore that sick feeling in my stomach?

Is there more at play here than I realize?

Chapter Six

KELLER

"What's this meeting about?" I ask as I sit down at a conference table with Ottar, Henrik, and Lara.

Henrik places his hands on the table. "We wanted to go over security for the wedding. Since you're so protective of Princess Lilija, we thought you'd want to be a part of the conversation."

"Yes, I would," I say, but based on the avoidance of eye contact from Lara and the uncomfortable silence, I have the distinct feeling that I've been called in here for something else. "What's going on?"

Henrik clears his throat. "We also wanted to discuss a letter we received yesterday, unmarked by postage, delivered straight to the palace by a courier. When we asked who it was from, they said it came from an unmarked folder with instructions."

The hairs on the back of my neck stand to attention. "Who is it for?"

"You," Henrik answers.

I wet my lips and then hold my hand out. "Let me see it."

Henrik pulls a blue envelope from his leather portfolio and smooths it across the table until I grip it. "We took the liberty of reading it."

I flap the envelope open and pull out the thick cardstock paper. It's a rich texture with ribbing on the outer edge, a typed message in the middle. Unsigned.

This message is for Keller Fitzwilliam. We read your engagement article. It seems congratulations are in order. Working your way from the staff quarters all the way to the crown. Impressive feat. Unfortunately, we are not pleased. Not with you or with the future queen. So, your excitement will be short-lived, as we will alter that future. Consider this your warning. See you soon.

My jaw grows tight as I read it two more times.

When I'm done, I glance up at Ottar and Lara. "We need to double our security detail."

"Our thoughts exactly," Ottar says, a grim look in his eyes. "We're already training soldiers from the king's regimen. Been in service for the king for the past twenty years. Dedicated. Loyal. We'll be assigning them to you as soon as they're ready in the next few days."

"Me?" I ask. "I don't need security. I'm talking about Lilly."

Ottar's brows turn down. "Keller, this threat is aimed directly at you."

"It's aimed to hurt Lilly. Don't you see that? You and I can handle anything that comes our way. Not Lilly."

Henrik clears his throat. "We've spoken to King Theodore, and he has assigned a three-man group to your protection."

My eyes whip to Henrik. "I don't need three men watching over me. Like I said, I can handle my own. What I need to make sure is one, Lilly doesn't hear about this, and two, she's watched over every second of the goddamn day." I toss the letter into the middle of the table. "And we need to find out who the fuck sent that letter."

Calmly, Lara says, "It isn't up for debate, Keller. King's orders. You might believe you can handle your own protection, but you have a much bigger target on your back now, and the importance of your life has skyrocketed, meaning, you're no longer in charge of your own protection. You're now a protectee."

"I don't need—"

"Do you want Lilly to suffer?" Ottar asks, his voice stern, nearly menacing.

"Why the fuck would you even ask that?"

"Because you refused protection. If something happens to you, she suffers. I know this is different for you, and it will take some getting used to, but you will not go against the king's orders. That's final." Ottar rests his beefy arms on the table. "As for Lilly, she will be covered. Lara has mentored and trained the finest to be by her side. We are bringing you into this conversation as a courtesy because of who you are, who you're marrying, and the unmatched guard you have over your future wife. Don't lose that privilege by going against what we've been told to do."

I run my tongue over my teeth, letting his words sink in. As much as I hate to admit it, the man is right. I'm no longer in a position where I can participate in the intricate details like security and protection. And if Theo were here, he would be reprimanding me for turning down security detail. It's a tough pill to swallow, but Ottar has a point. I don't want Lilly to suffer, and if something happens to me, I know she'll never get over it.

I run my hand over my mouth and finally say, "Fine, I'll accept the added detail, but I would like to stay in the loop on the details when it comes to who is manning Lilly and myself as well as the investigation into this letter. I'm assuming it's being investigated?"

"We don't take threats lightly. You know that," Ottar says. "An investigation is already underway, and we have our top security detail on it. We will brief you when we know more. As for right now, whoever wrote this has been very cautious with covering their tracks, which brings us to the wedding."

Lara hands me a map with a parade route. "Due to the threat, we've cut the parade route in half. To avoid thinning our coverage of rooftops and the crowds, we're going to limit the route. King Theo wasn't pleased because he wants to celebrate your marriage, but he's also very wary about your safety, so he agreed that this is the best option."

I take in the map and trace the route with my eyes, looking for blind corners and high buildings. "Will we have spotters at Norse Temple?"

"Yes," Lara replies. "On top of the building as well as around it. And we'll also have drones flying over the parade route, looking for any suspicious activity."

"Good," I reply. "Are we adding protection to King Theo and Queen Katla?"

Ottar shakes his head. "He doesn't believe there's a threat to him, and we agree. But we have settled on extra security detail on the day of the wedding."

Henrik steps in. "According to their schedule, they don't have any outings until the wedding day, so we don't have to worry about them too much."

I nod. "Okay." Blowing out a heavy breath, I ask, "What are you going to tell Lilly? I don't want to frighten her."

"We're going to tell her the truth."

I shake my head. "No. Don't. It will scare her, and she's already dealing with so much. We can tell her it's protocol as we get closer to the wedding."

"I don't know," Ottar says as Lara presses her hand to Ottar's.

"I have to agree with Keller on this one. Lilly has been a ball of stress. I think we should leave it at a protocol issue. We don't want to scare her. If we tell her about the letter, there's no doubt in my mind that she'll overthink it, and it will affect her public appearances."

"She's right," I say. "Lilly wears her heart and expressions on her sleeve, and she won't be able to hide the fear if she knows. And I don't think Henrik wants a scared prospective queen at public engagements."

"It would worry the public," Henrik adds. "We don't want to give the public any inclination that she's having second thoughts because that's how it would be perceived."

Ottar drags his hand over his bald head. "Fine. We won't tell her about the letter. But if there comes a time when we need to, I make the executive decision. Got it?"

I nod as I stare him down, communicating that I appreciate him and the passion he has for keeping my girl safe. Because above all else, that's what matters most.

Lilly matters most.

⸻

"WE ARE SO pleased to have you at our school today," Carina Olsen, the head administrator at the playschool we're visiting today, says in greeting. One of the initiatives Lilly has taken on is early education since she's shown great passion for the subject. She used to volunteer with her mum at the local YMCAs in Miami, so when we asked her where she thought it would be best to spend her time, she was quick to answer. Not only does she love children, but she wanted to carry on the tradition that her mum instilled in her.

We actually had to have a sit-down with Theo, Katla, and Henrik and talk about what we would be focusing on when it came to our community outreach. Since Lilly doesn't have a vast knowledge of the country's traditions, she opted for something more universal like early education. I've stated that I would be more than happy to take on maintaining the traditions of the country, with Lilly by my side of course. We've been told that making public appearances together, especially right now leading up to the wedding, would be more favored than separate appearances. Fine by me. The more time I can spend with Lilly, the more comfortable I am in this new role. *This* I can do. With Lilly, without the pressure of anyone vying to uncover my deeply held pain. *This* feels right.

"We're honored to be here," Lilly says.

Dressed in a pair of brown tweed pants and brown turtleneck with a matching brown coat, she looks regal, nothing like the woman I picked up in South Beach. She's been choosing more sophisticated looks, and it's taking me a second to get used to it, but she looks good nonetheless, especially with her hair curled at the ends and just enough mascara on her eyelashes to make her blue irises pop.

With the extra security, the hallways seem infinitely smaller, and moving around is cumbersome, but as we established, it's necessary. When we told Lilly about the added security, she was completely unfazed and didn't even ask any questions. Then again, she hasn't been her normal self. She's lacking some energy as of late, and I'm blaming it on the recent demand with the wedding and the classes. There's an evident strain on our relationship too. She's been a little cold and not as affectionate. I haven't tried to make up for her lack of affection because I've been in my own head about the recent threats.

It will be fine, though. Once all is said and done and we're married, we'll be completely fine.

"Well, let me give you a tour. This is one of ten playschools we have in the capital. We tend to have smaller classes to allow our educators to have more one-on-one time with the students. Our students range from two to six years old and we're thirty percent funded by the government and the rest is paid for by the attending families." She walks us down a hall that's lit up with construction paper flowers cut and glued together, creating a kaleidoscope garden.

"How adorable is this," Lilly says while taking in all of the flowers. "Wait, are these lilies?"

Carina smiles proudly. "Yes, the kids and staff truly wanted to welcome you."

"That's so sweet." She observes the flowers some more and then turns toward me. "Aren't these beautiful?"

I nod, not much of a gushing man myself.

Cameras click from behind us as Lilly cutely smells one. "Ooo, they even have that lovely glue stick smell." The people around us laugh, and I just admire my girl for so easily capturing hearts with one simple comment.

After we take in the art projects in the hallway, Lilly making sure to stop and admire some of her favorites, we're brought into a classroom where kids in green-and-blue uniforms squirm on a round rug at the front of the room. They're sitting cross-legged, hands in their laps, huge smiles stretched across their faces.

When Lilly comes into view, they all start clapping and cheering. It's really fucking cute.

Two mini chairs sit at the front of the room. Chairs made for children, not adults, that we're directed to. Henrik advised that we'd read a book to the class, but he didn't mention the tiny chairs. With my hand in hers, Lilly brings me to the front of the classroom and takes a seat, tugging me to join her.

Christ.

Of course Lilly has no problem fitting her small ass in the chair. Me, on the other hand . . .

I maneuver my large body in front of the minuscule chair and then squat until my butt hits the surface. About six inches from the ground, my knees nearly kiss my shoulders as I attempt to make room for my body, but from the squirming kids inching closer, I have no room to stretch out.

So I hunch up and try to look comfortable.

From the smiles on the educators' faces, I can tell I'm failing tremendously.

"I'm so happy to be here. How is everyone?" Lilly asks.

The kids all shout together, their tiny voices filling the room in a high-pitched squeal that causes me to flinch.

Can you tell I haven't been around a lot of kids, or really any for that matter? I've spent my whole time working for the king among the palace walls, so being around this many kids is foreign to me.

I don't know how to act.

How to talk to them.

How not to look like a giant troll that resurrected himself from a bridge to sit on a chair entirely too small for his body.

Cameras flash as reporters take notes and hold out recorders while Lilly leads the room in a collective song about counting cods. I just sit there, trying not to break my back from the immense amount of pain I'm experiencing.

"And this is how the cod counts, the cod counts, the cod counts," Lilly sings next to me, clapping her hands.

I catch Henrik in the back, motioning for me to join in.

I smile through the pain and clap my hands with the kids as my lower back tenses, the fabric of my pants clinging tightly to my thighs. For fuck's sake, don't let my pants rip right in front of these kids.

"The cod counts, the cod counts, the cod counts." Lilly laughs and sings.

Jesus, how long is the cod counting?

She looks over at me, and I smile through my grimace, nodding my head. Yup, the cod is still counting.

She takes my hand and waves them in the air, and the kids do the same. "The cod . . . coooooounnnnnntttttssss," Lilly sings loudly, the kids shrieking, and then the song is over. Everyone claps, me included, glad that nightmare is over.

"Wow, you're such good singers," Lilly says. "Should we sing it again?"

NO!

"Yes!" the kids cheer.

Lilly raises her hands like an orchestra conductor. "This . . . is the way the cod counts . . ."

And I thought the nightmares of my parents' deaths were bad, this . . . this might be giving those a run for their money. Every second I'm forced to sit in this minuscule chair, my legs start to cramp up.

Sharp, intense jolts pulse down my thighs, straight to my knees.

I blame the leg day workout with Ottar this morning because fuck, the pain is intense.

"That's right, the cod counts this way, the cod counts this way . . ."

The pain throbs through my knees, creating a stiffening sensation that builds with every goddamn number the cod counts.

Fuck.

I glance in front of me to see if there is any space for my legs as I mind-numbingly clap my hands to the tune. Five kids all in the way, but directly in front of me, the main culprit of blocking any leg extension is a little girl with bright blonde hair and a huge bow that fills up the top of her head. She's the key to the release of this unyielding cramping. All I need is a few inches, just a couple, and there are enough inches for her to scoot over.

Maybe if I tap her on the shoulder and ask her to move, she'll oblige.

"The cod counts, the cod counts, the cod counts."

The fucking cod is going to be counting in my head until the end of time after this.

I lean forward an inch as the song wraps up, and I'm about to ask the little girl to scootch when Lilly says, "Who wants to hear a story?"

The kids all cheer, causing Bow Girl to move in closer to

me. And then to my horror, she looks up at me and offers me a toothy grin right before wrapping her arm around my leg and giving it a squeeze. A squeeze that she doesn't let up on.

Yup . . . my leg has now turned into her personal stuffy.

Lilly opens the assigned story book and immediately starts entertaining. I'm breathing heavily through my flared nostrils as the pain scorches up my leg to my hip and then back down.

I need some goddamn relief. Maybe Bow Girl won't mind if I scoot her hug fest an inch or so.

Knowing I won't be able to sit through this story cramped up like this, I very slowly edge my foot forward.

Wincing, waiting for her to notice, I hold my breath, but when Bow Girl doesn't notice, I go in for another push just as Lilly makes the kids laugh with some funny voice she uses for a character. The laughter grants me the perfect opportunity to push a touch more without the girl noticing.

Oh sweet fucking hell, that's better but not by much. Just enough to give me a momentary reprieve before the cramping rears its ugly head and comes back with a vengeance.

The pain is so strong that I'm nearly panting.

The sight I must be right now, breathing out of my goddamn nose like a bull ready to take down a red flag, my knees kissing my ears, and a child wrapped around my leg in a grip so tight, you would think she was using it as her own personal lifesaver.

Fuck.

Shit.

God Almighty.

My teeth clamp down on my inner cheek as the cramps jolt the muscles in my thighs.

Move, make any sort of adjustment, anything to end this pain.

I shift on my seat, moving one butt cheek across the seat, only for the other to hold up my heavy body. I consider spreading my legs even farther, but given the restriction of my pants, and the possibility of showing off a solid definition of my junk to the press and children in front of me, I think better of it.

All I can do is wait and hope for Lilly to read faster.

I glance over at her, my fists clenching, my nails digging into my palms as I try to counteract the pain. I examine the book and notice that she's barely made a dent in the pages. What is this? A novel?

Christ.

Maybe if I turn toward her, I could slip my leg under hers. Then again, not sure I could fit on this chair sideways since I barely fit on it normally. Might not be a good idea.

I take a deep breath, trying to cleanse out the pain and focus on something else, but fuck, it's not working.

It's excruciating.

Throbbing pain centralizes in my kneecap, creating such a tornado of cramps up my legs that a sheen of sweat breaks out on my lower back.

I roll my teeth over my bottom lip, tilt my head down, squeeze my eyes shut as I can't take it, and push my leg with Bow Girl on it forward one more centimeter. This time, the girl notices and looks up at me, a sneer in her eye.

"Don't push me!" she shouts to my horror.

Lilly falls silent as she glances over at me. And then every single pair of eyes in the room fall on me.

Uh . . .

I tack on a smile as a bead of sweat rolls down my temple. "I, uh, I wasn't pushing you," I say.

"Yes, you were. Your foot is on my butt."

"What?" I ask, eyes wide. "No, it's not." I glance up at the press. "My foot isn't on her—ahhh fffffffuuuuu . . ."

My mouth closes shut as my entire leg cramps up in one massive charley horse. My body separates from my brain, my muscles taking on a mind of their own.

I can't stop myself from what happens next.

My thigh involuntarily contracts, fueled by the pain, and propels my shin and foot forward at Mach speed, and before I can even shout a fair warning, my leg stretches out in front of me, knocking Bow Girl right over onto the lap of another boy.

"Ahhh! He kicked me!" she screams. "The big man kicked me."

I have no response as I mutter, "Fucking hell," right before crumpling forward like a giant falling from the beanstalk, right to the floor, toppling over children in front of me.

"Hey, get off me," shouts the boy Bow Girl landed on. "I don't want you on me."

"Ew, his shoe is on me."

"Ahh, he's touching me."

"I'm being squished."

"Why is the big man dead?"

"Oh dear," the teacher says just as my vision turns fuzzy.

"Ew, look, his underwear is showing!"

What? And that's when a breeze blows by my ass.

Children scream.

Cameras click.

Lilly places the children's book on top of my ass while my hand clenches my thigh. I am writhing in pain.

This could not have gone more wrong.

⸺

"WELL . . . THAT WAS DIFFERENT," Lilly finally says, breaking the silence as we drive back to Strombly together, Henrik doing damage control on his phone in front of us.

"We're not talking about it," I say, staring out the window, still blinded from the cameras flashing in my eyes.

"I just . . . I just want to know, did you have your foot on her butt?"

"No!" I shout. "Jesus Christ. I'm not some fucking creep, Lilly."

"Okay, okay, but you kind of kicked a girl today," Lilly says. "And from what I remember during our trainings, kicking the public, especially children, is frowned upon."

There's that sass that was missing earlier. Glad it could come back for my demise.

"Like I said, my leg cramped up from that fucking small-ass chair, and I couldn't recover."

"And the pants . . ."

"An unfortunate addition."

"Okay." I can hear the smile in her voice. "Just confirming."

"Confirming what?" I ask, glancing over at her.

"The story. I'm sure I'll be asked about it."

"You don't respond," I say.

At that moment, Henrik looks up. "He's right. You don't respond to anything negative, ever. If you're asked how your day is, you answer. If they ask you what you think about your aunts and uncles not being able to take the throne, leaving the task to you, you don't answer. You just smile and move on."

"Oh, I see." Lilly nods. "Keller kicking a girl into another kid's lap is a smile and move-on question."

"I didn't kick her," I shout.

But they both ignore me as Henrik says, "That's correct. This is a smile and move-on story."

"And the pants? Do I mention anything about that? I mean, thank God you were wearing underwear. Imagine having your crack out in front of children . . ."

"No mention of the pants," Henrik says and then looks up at me. "Might want to size up, though, they were very tight. Front and back."

My nostrils flare, but nothing comes out of my mouth.

"So we can't go the self-deprecating route?" Lilly asks, still on this. "You know, blame the man's lack of potassium?"

"I don't have a lack of potassium. I was sore from leg day and cramped up. There is nothing more to it," I say.

"Maybe we can throw in that his hydration levels have been low," she says. "Oh! Or maybe we can say something like he's been so emotional with the wedding planning that he's cried himself to dehydration." She taps her chin. "Oh yes, that has real potential."

I give her a deadpan expression. "We're not saying that."

"No, this is a good way to spin you kicking an innocent little girl. It will earn you sympathy."

I drag my hand over my face and groan, "I didn't kick her."

Getting into a public relations role, Lilly brightens as she says, "Just picture the headlines, emotional groom, dehydrated from tears of joy. Subline: accidentally boots girl with bow. We can explain how this whole process has been incredibly emotional for him, and it's unlocked the flood gates. We can end it with how the palace is working closely with the medical staff on properly hydrating the soon-to-be prince. There's nothing more real than dehydration. The entire world is practically dehydrated. And we've all been there when the water hasn't been consumed, and we can feel it seizing our bodies." She claps for herself. "Totally relatable."

Both Henrik and I stare at her, silence falling in the car.

"What?" she asks. "You can't tell me that's not a brilliant spin. Shows that he's human, an emotional one at that. Garners sympathy. Offers a brilliant explanation. And perhaps, a slight chuckle to round everything out. Ticks all the boxes."

"We're not making me into an emotional mess who has cried so much that he cramped up and kicked a girl."

"Aha!" Lilly points at me. "So you admit it, you kicked her."

"Jesus fucking Christ," I mutter as I turn back toward my window.

Chapter Seven

LILLY

SOON-TO-BE PRINCE, STIFF AS THEY COME

At one of their first outings since becoming an engaged couple, Princess Lilija and Keller Fitzwilliam visited one of the local playschools. Princess Lilija, eager to embrace a greater understanding of the Torskethorpian playschool system, shined like the day we first met her. Wearing a mono-chromatic matching trouser and turtleneck, she represented Torskethorpe royalty with heartfelt interest and a genuine smile. As for our soon-to-be prince? Well, let's just say he was stiffer than a dead cod dried up on the shore. Visibly uncomfortable, he struggled to keep seated in front of the children while Princess Lilija read them a story. Attendees said he was casually moving a little girl away from him until he fully booted her into another student and then fell to the ground, faking an injury. The tumble to the ground led the imminent monarch to split his pants in front of the children, offering a view of black briefs. The student was okay, and there was no harm done other than the less-than-welcoming groom's image . . . and questions about what underwear he wears. High bets are on Calvin

Kleins. Residents are worried. Is this the prince we should expect, or was it just a tragic first appearance? Only time will tell.

I wince as I close the article on my phone.

Pretty sure my hydration story would have been a hell of a lot better than that.

And for the record . . . they are Calvin Kleins. Great detective work, people of Torskethorpe.

"Your Highness? King Theo will see you now."

I glance up at the footman and nod before walking through the open door to Theo's private office.

Sitting at his desk, looking over articles himself, he appears to be stressed as he pulls at his gray hair, his eyes scrolling over a piece of paper.

When he spots me approaching, he looks up and sets the paper down on his large white oak desk.

"Lilija," he says as he stands and moves around his desk. He pulls me into a warm hug and presses a kiss to the top of my head. It's like that with every greeting. No matter what the situation, even if he just saw me moments ago, he always greets me with a hug and a kiss. I think it's because he's making up for lost time . . . that and he's a very loving man. "Please have a seat." He gestures toward the sitting area.

"I'm going to assume you saw the articles about Keller," I say.

Theo's lips thin as his brows draw down into a frown. "I did, unfortunately. They did not paint him in a good light. Have you spoken to him?"

I shake my head. "He was working out this morning and then had a meeting with Ottar and some of the staff about safety around the palace."

"Hmm." He smooths his hand over his cheek. "I'm sure he's seen this, and he's avoiding it. That would be his initial reaction. Ignore it and that means it didn't happen."

"That would be Keller," I say just as a staff member knocks on the door.

"Come in," Theo calls out.

The door opens, and a cart is rolled into the room with tea and fruit.

The staff member sets the tray between us and then pours us both some tea before leaving.

"You know, I've spoken with Gothi Elias," Theo says, his voice concerned. "He's expressed worry about your sessions. You haven't fully finished one yet, and Keller seems agitated and jumpy, not willing to talk, not willing to participate."

I heavily sigh as I attempt to hold back my emotions, because even though I've spoken to Keller about our sessions and the wedding planning, it hasn't eased the anguish I carry in my heart. With each passing day, he's growing more and more agitated, and we're growing further and further apart. Even with the whole incident at the school, I tried to lighten the mood with some fun banter, something I've done in the past, but he just turned away. Before all of this, he would have pulled me to the side, threatened me with a good time in the bedroom for my mouthy ways, and it would have been amazing. Instead, he went back to his room, leaving me feeling lonelier than ever.

"It hasn't been easy . . . or fun for that matter." I pick up one of the napkins and dab at my eyes. "Sorry, I don't mean to get emotional, it's just been . . . it's been hard recently."

"Lilija," Theo says softly as he leans forward. "Never apologize for crying. You're in a safe space, so feel free to show all of your emotions."

That just makes it worse as more tears try to escape. It takes me a few moments to gather myself, but once I do, I talk through a tight throat. "Is Gothi Elias not going to approve of our marriage?"

"I think he's just concerned is all," Theo says. "There are always growing pains with every relationship, and I believe you and Keller might be going through one at the moment."

"But I don't even know why," I say. "I'm so confused. It feels like this all came out of nowhere."

"Have you spoken with him?"

"I have, and whenever we talk, it feels like we keep going around in circles with no solution."

"What have you said to him?"

I stir my tea with a spoon, then lift the warm liquid to my lips, letting the bitter taste rest on my tongue before answering. "That I'm nervous he's not telling me everything he should. He's keeping things from me, his feelings, his fears. I'm afraid he's pulling away. I'm worried he might run. That this will all be too much for him."

"What has he said?"

"That it's not. That he'll never run. That we'll be married. He reassures me, but I've never felt more alone than I do now. We never seem to get to the bottom of all the tension. Maybe it's in my head. Maybe, like you said, it's just the stress of the time we're in, but everything feels off." I set my tea down. "And he also mentioned that he's been having nightmares again."

"Has he?" Theo says while picking up a piece of apple and taking a bite. "Well, I think we need to remember that with Keller, he's a creature of habit, and he's battling a lot of change at the moment. He might be moody and difficult to work with, but we need to keep pushing him because this is his new normal. He needs to get used to this public attention, and this responsibility. There will be growing pains, but as long as we're there, guiding him along the way and helping him out of his shell, then he'll get better over time."

"Do you think that's what this is about?" I ask. "The impending responsibility of what it is to be the prince of Torskethorpe?"

"Yes, I do." Theo eats some more of his apple. "Keller's entire life has been spent behind the scenes. And now that he's at the forefront of it all, I believe it's confusing to him. I think he still has reservations about it. When I spoke to Henrik about the school outing, he told me how visibly uncomfortable Keller was. It wasn't just the fact that he accidentally booted a little girl. It was that he wasn't in his element from the moment he stepped out of the car. And the closer we get to the wedding, the more that reality is setting in for him. This will be his life, and he needs to accept that."

"Oh," I say, feeling bad. "Do you think . . . do you think he can't handle it? Am I forcing him to do something that he's not cut out for?"

Theo shakes his head. "He can handle it. I know he can. He just needs to think about treating the people of the community the same as he treated his staff here at the palace. It's the same thing, just on a different level. He needs to have a change of thought, and that's something I discussed with Gothi Elias."

"You did?" I ask. "Is that something we're going to work on during our next session?"

"I'm not sure, but he's aware."

"So . . . do you think we'll be okay? You don't think he's going to decide in the middle of the night that this life isn't for him and take off?"

Theo shakes his head. "Never. If anything, Keller is loyal to his bones. He has pledged his life to us, to the crown, to you. There will just be some bumps and challenges we'll have to deal with along the way."

"Okay." I let out a deep breath, then lean back in my chair, my tears starting to fall again. "God, I'm sorry." I dab at my eyes. "It's just been tough, but this conversation has given me some peace. Thank you."

"You're welcome. Anytime you need to talk, I'm here for you."

"HEY," I say shyly as Keller comes up to me. He places his hand on my hip and pulls me into his strong chest. His woodsy cologne envelops me. *So good.* He presses a soft kiss to the top of my head, and the combination has me feeling dreamy.

And just like that, the worries, the stress, the frustration all melts away.

Quietly, he whispers into my ear, "You look beautiful."

I squeeze my eyes shut. Right now, it doesn't seem like there is anything distracting around us like cameras or assistants telling us where to be or what to do. It's just me and Keller, like when we were in Harrogate. I want to stay in this moment.

I smooth my arms around his waist and hold on to him tightly.

"I missed you today."

He wraps his arms around me as well. "I missed you too, Lilly."

I glance up at him and rest my chin on his chest. "You usually see me in the morning, or at least make the effort to."

"I was busy. It won't happen again." He lowers his mouth and presses his lips to mine. I hold on to him, on to his kiss for a moment longer, soaking him in. When he pulls away, he notices the tears that threaten to fall over my lids. "Why are you going to cry?"

"I just feel like things are so out of whack, and this moment brings me back to when we were in Harrogate, in your room, just holding each other."

"We did a lot more than hold each other."

That brings a smile to my face. I pinch his side and say, "That's what I'm supposed to say."

"Maybe you're rubbing off on me."

"I wish I was rubbing *you* off."

He rolls his eyes and kisses my forehead once again. "Come on, we don't want to be late for Elias."

"Hold on." I tug on his hand. "Can we talk about yesterday, what the media is saying?"

"No need. Everything is fine," he says, but in an instant, I watch him morph from easygoing and carefree to tense. I'm sure reading the articles hasn't been easy, and the mention of it doesn't feel good. I just want to make sure he's okay.

But I also don't want to push him. I know Theo said to help him, but pushing him to anger is not the way to do it, so I accept his answer. "Okay, but for what it's worth, they had it all wrong. You didn't kick her; it was a mere shove. Honestly, she was in *your* way."

That brings the smallest of smiles to his face.

"At least you've changed your perspective." He squeezes my hand, and Elias welcomes us into the ancestor room.

After taking a seat, Keller sitting closer this time, Elias sits across from us and rests his hands in his lap.

"Shall we talk about yesterday?"

Oh Elias . . .

"We don't really have to," I say.

"I cramped up," Keller says, surprising me. "I couldn't avoid it, and I accidentally knocked a girl with my leg. It was all a big mistake. I spoke with Ottar today, and we won't be doing any heavy workouts on days when we have engagements that require me to sit in tiny chairs. Nothing else to talk about."

Huh, at least he spoke to Ottar about it. Leave it to Keller to gain control of the narrative before I can even wake up and go to the bathroom.

"Well, that's a good problem-solving tactic. Well done, Keller. Although, I do wonder about how you handled your attitude before the incident happened."

Come on, Elias. Why poke the bear?

We were good.

We brought it up.

We took blame.

We found a solution.

Move on, you nitwit.

Keller shifts beside me, his telltale sign of being uncomfortable. "What are you talking about?" Now there's an edge to his voice.

See what you did, Elias? You stuck your nose where it shouldn't belong! Not the way to start these sessions.

"It was brought to my attention that before you sat down with the children, you were stiff and unwelcoming."

"I don't think that's true," I say and then give it a thought. "I mean, sure, he might have been a touch stiff, but he was wearing new, freshly pressed pants, which could have been touching him in a weird way. That could have made any regular old person stiff. I know when I'm wearing an uncomfortable bra or a thong that won't stop jamming up my crack—"

"Lilly," Keller reprimands.

Oh right, have class.

Class, class, class.

"Err, I mean . . . when my dress doesn't feel right, I become stiff as well. So it could have been the pants."

"Was it the pants?" Elias asks Keller.

"The pants were fine."

Come on, man! I threw you a lifesaver there with the pants. Take it!

"Is it because you just don't feel comfortable in your role yet?" Elias asks.

"I don't," Keller answers honestly, nearly blowing my skirt right over my head with shock. Well, not sure what he did this morning, but the man is much different from the other day where he was in full-on denial, ready to snap at any second.

"Care to elaborate?"

"I wasn't supposed to be in this role, so it's hard for me to accept."

"It seems like your fiancée is doing a great job accepting her new role."

"Hey now," I say, stepping in, not sure why Elias is trying to be so freaking rude. "That's different."

Elias crosses one leg over the other. "How is it different? You were living a completely different life in Miami, selling bikinis out of the back of a truck. You knew nothing of this country, yet you've been able to step up, learn our traditions, and adapt. And to add to it, you also lost your parents."

"Not at a young age like Keller," I say. "And to argue you, I felt like I was missing something in my life. I went searching for a connection, and that's what this role has brought me. Keller has known one thing his whole life, to serve the palace. He was taught at a very young age to stay out of the spotlight, that palace life wasn't for him, so he has to retrain his brain to be in this position. We differ because I felt like I was brought home, whereas Keller is being torn away from everything he knows."

Elias smiles. "Well, I can see that you're quite right, Princess Lilija. I'm glad that you were able to explain it so well to me." Elias looks at Keller. "Did she get it right?"

Keller's jaw works back and forth, his hands curling into fists on his lap. "Yes, she got it right."

"Wonderful. Understanding each other is a very important aspect of marriage. You could easily derail your journey if you don't understand each other properly. Which brings me to our next exercise."

Elias lifts a canvas duffel bag from the floor and sets it on his lap. Curious, I lean forward to get a better look as he unzips the bag and pulls out a phone, headphones, and cards.

What on earth?

He places everything on the coffee table in front of us and then sets his bag back down. "We're going to work on communication today. Now, communication isn't just about talking, but listening and reading our partners. The better you can read them, the better you'll be able to help them when you need them the most. Let's start with Keller. I'm going to put these noise-canceling headphones on you and play some music while Lilly attempts to read a sentence off one of the cards in my stack. You need to read her expressions and try to convey what she's saying to you."

"Oh, Jimmy Fallon plays this game on his show." When Keller and Elias both look at me with odd expressions, I add, "The late-night talk show host . . . really? You don't know who Jimmy Fallon is? I would have thought he's worldwide. Anyway, let's play."

Keller and I turn toward each other while Elias helps him with the headphones. When the music is turned on, Keller cringes. "What the hell is this?" He lifts the headphones off his ears, and it's loud enough that I can hear the distinct sound of yodelers.

"I thought it would be distracting so you won't hear what she's saying," Elias answers.

"It's very distracting," Keller says as he puts the headphones back on.

"Can you hear me?" I ask Keller.

"What? Are we starting?" he shouts.

"No," I say. "Just seeing if you can hear me?"

"Honey tree? Is that what you're saying?"

"No," I groan and then lift his headphones. "I was asking if you can hear me."

"I think we have our answer," Keller shoots back.

I snap the headphones on his head and receive a murderous look. I just return it with a smile.

Elias hands me a card, and I glance at the sentence I'm supposed to read to Keller.

Okay. This will be easy. All I have to do is enunciate well.

And if anything, Keller and I can read each other's minds.

He knows exactly what I need in bed, and I know exactly how to reciprocate.

When it comes to communication, his facial expressions give me all the evidence I need to know what he's thinking.

This game is child's play for us.

Watch and learn.

Mentally cracks knuckles

Staring Keller in the eyes, I speak very slowly as I say, "Love of my life."

"Lobster mitten," he shouts.

My brows turn down.

Lobster mitten?

Where the hell did that come from?

I shake my head and move my lips slowly.

"Love . . . of . . . my . . . liiiiiife."

"Love myself."

"Ooo, close!" I say. "You got the first one but not the second part. Really pay attention."

"You're speaking too fast. I can't tell what you're saying."

"I said you got the first one, not the second."

"What?"

"First one."

"Firstborn?"

"No." I shake my head. "First one!"

"What? First myself? First lobster? First mitten?"

"No, not first." I shake my head and hand. "Love is good. You got love." I give him a thumbs-up.

"Love glove?" His nose cringes. "Oh . . . a condom? We don't use condoms," he shouts so loud I swear the footmen can hear him.

I press my hand to my forehead and take a deep breath. "Okay, starting over." I erase the air to indicate a new slate. I then hold up my hand and show four fingers for four words.

"Four lobsters?"

"There are no lobsters!" I shout, tossing my hand in the air before reaching over and plucking his headphone off his head. "No lobsters, forget the lobsters, for the love of God!"

Silence falls, only the distant sound of yodelers fills the air as we both turn to Elias, who is charmed by our interaction.

I clear my throat and sit back down on my side of the couch. "Sorry about that." I straighten out my dress. "Just can't stand when people can't hear me is all. Now, shall we get—"

"Are you starting again? You're going too fast."

I stare up at the ceiling and whisper, "I think I'm dead inside."

━━━

"CINDY LAUPER, cyanide, Cybil Shepard, sill . . . windowsill. Wait, silo. The Silos! Chip and Joanna Gaines. Shiplap. Wait, is it shiplap? Ship . . . ship sales. Sailing ship. Come sail on my ship with me," I say. "No? Sail . . . uh . . . Sail . . . oh wait . . . Sail away with me!" I toss the headphones off my head, ridding myself of the yodelers. "It was sail away with me, wasn't it? See, I told you I would be good at this."

Keller stares at me blankly, ghostly white from my shouting.

Without saying a word, he slowly hands me the card he was reading from.

"Salami sandwich for two?" I look over at Elias. "What the hell kind of sentence is that?"

"It doesn't matter what the sentence says, what matters is how you two communicate." He folds his arms. "And it seems like you communicate by yelling."

"Nuh-uh," I say like a child. "We communicate just fine. No yelling involved. You saw yelling because we were trying to make sure we heard each other. Simple mistake."

"Let me ask you this. During the last argument you had, was there yelling?"

"No," I answer as Keller says, "Yes."

I whip my head around to look at him. "There wasn't yelling, was there?"

"There was."

"Well . . . if there was, it's just because we're passionate about what we believe in, not because we have an issue communicating."

"I'm not saying you have an issue communicating," Elias says.

"Then what are you saying?" I ask, folding my arms.

"I'm just pointing out flaws and bringing them to your attention."

"Ah, is that what these sessions are for? To make us feel bad about ourselves *and* our relationship?"

"Lilly." Keller places his hand on my thigh.

"No. I would really like to know what this is all about because it seems like Elias is trying to make us look bad when we actually have a solid relationship. As solid as they come. A relationship that was built on——"

"Sex," Elias says with conviction.

"What?" I ask, my jaw hitting the floor. "No, it wasn't."

"Yes, it was. That's what you told me. Your initial drive to be with him was because you found him attractive."

"Isn't that everyone's initial instinct? Attraction first, emotions later?"

"Some, but not everyone. A relationship built on the foundation of sex is much more likely to crumble than one built on friendship and trust."

"We already crossed the trust subject. We made it quite clear we trust each other. I mean, yeah, I might have let Keller fall to the ground, but that was because I wasn't mentally ready to catch his large frame. Watch, we can do it again, prove to you he trusts me." I push at Keller's shoulder. "Go ahead, stand up and fall into me."

"We're not doing that again," Keller grumbles.

"Why not?" I whisper-shout. "Let's show him what we got."

"Princess Lilija, can I please ask why you're getting so

defensive right now? This is a safe space. There is no need to prove anything."

"Yes, there is," I say. "Because clearly every challenge you give us, we fail, and I'm sick of failing. We shouldn't be failing. We love each other, we're supposed to be getting married, and every time I come in this room, it feels like . . . you make it seem like . . ."

"Like what?" Elias asks.

"Like . . ." My lip trembles. "Like we shouldn't get married."

I don't dare look at Keller because I can only imagine being met with anger and insecurity.

"Is that how you feel?" Elias asks. "That you shouldn't get married?"

"No," I say quickly. "But that's how you make me feel. And I don't like it. I love this man—"

"My intentions aren't to make you have doubts," Elias says.

"Doubts?" Keller says, and his eyes land on me, a scorching feeling of loaded questions.

I face him. "No, Keller. I don't have doubts." I press my hand against my forehead. "How do I explain this? I don't have doubts, but these meetings make me feel like I should . . ."

I don't get to finish because Keller stands, and without a word muttered, he moves past me and right out the door.

Fuck.

I stand to chase after him when Elias says, "Princess Lili-ja." I glance over my shoulder at him. "Give him space."

"No," I answer. "If I give him space, he'll take too much. Our relationship is already strained thanks to you, and I refuse to let him feel like I have doubts about our marriage, because I don't." I move past the door and chase him down the hallway. "Keller, wait."

He doesn't stop. He just keeps walking, so I pick up my

pace, despite staff members watching us. When I finally reach him, we're at the staircase that leads up to our rooms. I tug on his hand.

"Stop, please."

"Not here," he says under his breath.

And for one of the first times since we became a couple, I listen.

I know this is a moment that I need to walk carefully, and listening to his demands will be what's best.

In silence, we walk up the stairs, down the hallway, and to my bedroom where we're offered privacy.

It isn't until the door is completely shut that I turn to him and say, "Keller, I don't have doubts. I don't believe we shouldn't get married. You have to know that."

He pushes his hand through his hair. "But it seems that way, doesn't it?"

"What?" I ask, shocked.

"Hell, Lilly, we couldn't even do a simple task like read each other's lips. Doesn't that say something? Doesn't all of this say something?"

"No," I answer in a panic. "It means nothing. They're just stupid little tasks that don't make any sense. We pronounce a few things differently because we're from different countries. It totally makes sense that we couldn't read each other's lips. No, it's like they're trying to push us past our breaking point—"

"Well, it's fucking working." He walks over to the window and rests his hand on the sill, his eyes focused on the outside world. After a few short seconds, he says, "You know, I went into our session today, trying to put on a good show, trying to be positive, but I was met with the inability to communicate with my fiancée. How the hell do you think that makes me feel? I'm supposed to guide us, to protect us, to be the foundation for our relationship, and I can't even fucking communicate with you."

"Keller, that's not true. Look at what we're doing right

now. We're communicating. After every session, we've sat down and talked about it. That says more than some stupid lip-reading game." I go up to him and place my hands on his back. "I'm just as frustrated as you—"

"I'm not frustrated, Lilly," he says, pulling away. "I'm angry." He turns to face me. "Every time we go into that room, I feel more and more inadequate to hold your hand. I know that's how Elias sees me. That I'm not good enough to be with you."

"Stop it. That's not true."

"I know it's not true," he shouts back. "But it doesn't stop that prick from pointing out every goddamn flaw of mine."

"Everyone has flaws, Keller. It's what being a human is all about. No one is perfect."

"When I'm the guy marrying you . . . I need to be pretty damn perfect." He moves past me and heads straight for the door.

There he goes, leaving all over again.

It's the only thing he's known how to do recently, leave when things get tough. Is that how it will be when we're married?

Growing angrier by the second, I shout, "Don't you dare leave this fucking room, Keller."

He pauses, his back tensing as he slowly spins around to look at me. "Excuse me?"

"You heard me." I fold my arms across my chest. "You're not leaving this goddamn room. That seems to be all you know, to run away when things get tough. Not this time."

He runs his tongue over his teeth and then to my surprise, he takes his jacket off and tosses it on my bed before rolling up his sleeves, his eyes remaining on me the entire time.

"You have something to say?" he asks.

"Yes, we're going to talk about this because I'll be damned if you give up on us."

"I'm not giving up on us."

"You are when you run away every time things get heated," I say, gesturing toward the door. "That's not the way to have a conversation, Keller."

"I walk away because if I don't, I'm afraid I might say something I regret."

"Just say it," I shout at him, holding my arms out. "Fucking say it, because then at least we can get it all out in the open."

"Fine." His eyes scan me. "I hate that you're the future of this country. I hate that I fell in love with a princess. Despise it."

Uh . . . was not expecting that.

I back up from the venom coming out of his mouth, but he doesn't let me get far. He moves in close, pinning my hip against the bedroom wall. When my back hits the hard surface, my breath escapes me. I look up at Keller and see the anger in his pupils.

"Then . . . then why are you marrying me?" I ask. "If you hate it so much, why go through with it if you'll be miserable?"

He wets his lips. "Why do you think?" he challenges as his hand slides up my rib cage, right below my breast, confusing me.

Does he want me?

Is he angry with me?

He's giving me all kinds of mixed signals.

"Why bother being with me? I honestly can't answer that right now," I say.

The corner of his jaw throbs with tension as his grip grows tighter. "You can't answer that? Then you obviously don't know me like you should."

"I thought I did," I reply as his hand moves to the zipper on the side of my dress, his fingers toying with the small piece of metal. The thought of him undressing me sends chills down my legs. "But . . ." He unzips the dress, and my words get caught in my throat.

"But what?" he asks as he smooths one of the sleeves of the dress off my shoulder.

"But . . ." I gulp. "You're so moody. You're difficult to read. Like right now, you're stripping me out of my dress, but you're also angry. What is it, Keller?"

"Do you know why I'm so moody?" he asks.

I shake my head as he lowers the other sleeve, leaving my dress to pool at my hips. His eyes fall to the blue lace of my bra while his finger traces the underwire. My entire body is lit up with anticipation, waiting for his next move. Hoping and praying he isn't just teasing me. We've been put on a no-sex ban, but that doesn't mean we can't have fun in other ways, seek out pleasure with hands . . . mouths, anything to take this anxiety-ridden, chest-heavy feeling off us.

He leans down so his mouth is right next to my ear. "Because I fell in love with a woman who has a much more important role in this world than loving me back."

That steals my breath right from my lungs.

He thinks my love for Torskethorpe outweighs my love for him?

"Keller," I say as his lips find my neck. My hands find the back of his head and hold him tight. How could he even say that? My love for him will always be stronger than this country. I know that shouldn't be the case, but it is. I push at him so he has to look me in the eyes. "You know how you always say I matter most?"

"You do," he answers, his eyes not so angry, more resigned now. "Well, in my world, you matter most to me. More than this country, more than this role, and no matter what you say or do, that will always be the case."

His eyes search mine, and when I feel like he's going to say something, he pushes off the wall and turns his back to me.

With his hands on his hips, he stands still, most likely contemplating what I said.

Understanding races through me as I think back to what he initially said. That he hates that I'm the future of this country. The trouble he's had adjusting. How uncomfortable he's been since we started working our way around the country with interviews and engagements.

I move forward, pushing my dress down so I'm left in nothing but my thong and bra. I move to his back and slip my arms around his waist, and even though he's at least a foot taller than me, he leans into my embrace.

I press a kiss to his back. "I wish I wasn't the future of this country too," I whisper. "I wish that it was just you and me, living a simple life. I wish we could elope, express our love on a cliff, just us and the ocean setting the soundtrack for our love." I kiss his back again. "But unfortunately, this is the card we've drawn. And you can either love me for who I am and who I'm meant to be, or you can continue to fight against it and live in a world where your wishes and dreams prevent you from fully committing to me."

He turns in my arms and lifts my chin so our eyes are connected. "I've always been and always will be committed to you."

"Then let's get through this together," I say. "Please don't pull away from me."

He looks away. "You don't regret this? Regret me?"

"No," I say quickly. "Keller, the reason I'm here, able to take on this role, is because of you, because you're my backbone. I need you, more than you could possibly even imagine." I smooth my hand up his chest. "Whatever happens in those meetings with Elias, or whatever happens at an engagement or with this wedding planning, I need you to know that it won't change the way I feel about you. Ever."

He sighs, his shoulders slouching as he moves his hands around my waist and then under the elastic of my thong, palms pressing against my ass. He lowers his forehead to mine and takes in a sharp breath.

"I'm sorry I'm not the man you need me to be."

"But you are."

"I'm not." He lifts up and kisses my forehead before letting me go.

"Where are you going?" I ask as he picks up his jacket and shrugs it on.

"If I stay here, I'll fuck you."

"Maybe you need to fuck me, to remind yourself that you're good enough."

He shakes his head. "I made a promise to Theo."

"You also made a promise to me, to love me, to be there for me, to protect me."

"And I plan on keeping that promise until the day I die," he says as he walks over to the door, leaving me standing in my room, practically naked.

"Then why strip me down?"

"I needed to feel your skin." His ragged eyes meet mine. "Feeling you close eases the tension in my heart. I love you, Lilly."

"Prove it," I say.

He grips the back of his neck and says, "I will." And then he takes off, leaving me even more frustrated. This time, there's an extra component to that frustration with how he turned me on and then walked away.

I flop back on my bed and stare up at the ceiling.

I just want this to be over.

All of this.

The wedding.

The anxiety.

The stress.

I want to be married and moving on with other things. I want to lie next to my husband each night, touch *his* skin, kiss *his* lips, and know that everything is fine.

"I fell in love with a woman who has a much more important role in this world than loving me back." Oh, Keller.

"I'm sorry I'm not the man you need me to be."

How can that man feel that way? How can he doubt himself when he was the picture of confidence when I first met him? Loving him is . . . everything.

I sigh, my heart hurting, feeling so alone right now.

Thankfully, my aunt Pala and cousins arrive soon as well as Timmy. I dearly hope they won't create more waves but be a good distraction. *God knows we need that.*

Chapter Eight

"What's this?" I ask as Pickering sets a newspaper down on my desk.

"Some reading I thought you'd be interested in," Pickering says with a smile.

I pick up the newspaper and take in the headline.

SOON-TO-BE PRINCE, STIFF AS THEY COME.

I glance up at Pickering, a smile crossing my lips. "Please tell me this is what I think it is."

Pickering nods. "Princess Lilija and Keller were at a local playschool together. He was observed as stiff and unwelcoming. While Princess Lilija was reading to the kids, he ended up kicking one of the children. It's a great read. I suggest you enjoy a cup of tea with it."

"That's some of the best news I've heard in a while. I will enjoy it with some tea. How was Lilija observed?"

Pickering rolls his eyes. "Naturally, everyone loved her."

My lips twist to the side. "These fucking morons. Don't they realize she's just parading in a role that's not meant for her? When are they going to realize she's posing for the cameras and knows nothing about the responsibilities of royalty?"

"Hopefully soon. From what our source has said, she lacks decorum and has a loose tongue. I think only time will tell. Until then, you have a phone call with King Magnus in an hour. Is there anything you want me to do to prepare for that?"

I shake my head. "No. We're going over some final details." I stare down at the picture of Keller and Lilija sitting in front of a group of children, Keller visibly uncomfortable. *You will never take on the throne, Fitzwilliam. You'll be in a fiery grave, just like your pathetic parents.* "This almost seems too easy, doesn't it?"

"Once the logistics are ironed out, I think it will be quite easy. We have them just where we want them."

I nod and twist the paper into a roll, wishing it was Fitzwilliam's neck. "Ten days, Pickering. Ten days and we'll finally take back what was stolen from us. Torskethorpe belongs to us, and their attempt to bring in an outsider to save their country will blow up in their faces. And soon their farce will come to a rightful end."

"That it will," Pickering says with a large smile.

I shoo my hand at him. "Now get the hell out of here. I want some privacy while I read."

Chapter Nine

KELLER

"Are you going to do that whole groom's thing where you dig up a sword from an ancestor's grave?" Ottar asks as we make our way up to my bedroom where I'll be fitted for my wedding suit.

"Does it look like I'm the type of guy who digs up an old grave for a sword?" I ask.

Ottar chuckles next to me. "No, but you're a man of tradition, that's why I'm asking."

"The answer is no."

"Then what are you doing on the eve of your wedding?"

"Probably sitting in my room, counting down the minutes until I get to marry Lilly."

"Romantic."

I glance at Ottar. "Why? Should I be doing something?"

"Didn't know if you wanted company."

"Are you proposing you spend the night keeping me company?"

Ottar shrugs. "Lara thought it would be nice if I suggested it."

"So you don't really want to spend time with me, you're just offering because your girlfriend is making you?"

"Why are you being difficult?"

"Because I'm not in the mood for any wedding activities. I just want this to be over with."

"Pretty sure that's what every bride wants to hear," Ottar says as he nods toward a footman we pass in the hallway.

"Yeah, Lilly would probably have my head if she heard me say that." I sigh and then quietly add, "We got into it the other day, again." I clench my fists at my side, the only indication that I'm ready to blow up from my pent-up irritation. "I'm pretty sure we're on the verge of breaking."

"It might seem that way, but you have to know that's not the case. It's just the stress of it all. You have a week and a half left."

"Yes," I answer as Ottar reaches for the door to my bedroom where the tailor waits.

"Homestretch. Hang in there."

We head into the bedroom and are greeted by a thin man with a balding head. "Hello, I'm Jiminy, and I'll be fitting you today. Given the provided measurements, I hope we have a solid base already, but we'll make any adjustments you might need."

"Thank you," I say.

"I'll step outside while you get dressed. Let me know when you're ready."

Jiminy takes off, and I walk up to the suit, but Ottar pulls me back.

"What?" I ask.

"Just want to check it first."

I want to ask him if that's really necessary, but I know it is. If I were in his shoes, with the pressure that we're feeling, I would do the same thing.

"Have you made any leeway on the letter?" I ask.

Ottar shakes his head. "No, but we did receive another one."

"What?" I ask, on a growl. "Why haven't I been informed of this?"

"I was going to tell you this morning, but you've been in a shit mood. I was looking for a better moment."

My eyebrows pull together as I say, "Never hold back information like that. If I'm on my goddamn deathbed, I want to know what the hell is going on."

Ottar pats around on the suit and examines the fabric. "Fair enough." He stands tall, and from the inside of his suit jacket, he pulls out another blue envelope and hands it to me.

I flip it open and pull out the blue cardstock.

Ten days to go.

Ten days until we meet again.

Ten days until we gain our vengeance.

My mouth works from side to side as I stare at the menacing letter, my mind whirling, my heart pumping.

Vengeance? Who would need to seek their vengeance? This is personal, and for the life of me, I can't think who this could be. I've lived a pretty straight-forward life. I've stayed out of the way, I've helped the king, I've brought life back to this country by retrieving Lilly.

And if this person has a countdown, that can only mean this could be much worse than we're expecting.

"We have to cancel the wedding," I say.

Ottar shakes his head and hands me the pants before plucking the letter from my hand. "Theo won't have any of it. He trusts our security."

"He wants to go ahead with this wedding even though there's an obvious threat? Lilly could get hurt."

"Lilly is not the one they're after," Ottar says. "You are. It was clear in the last letter, and this one is obviously stating a past relationship. The only person who would have a past relationship in this country is you." He nods at me to change into my pants, so I unbuckle in front of him while he continues, "We're looking into Brimar and his connections."

That makes my head snap up from where I'm slipping on my pants. "What can he achieve from prison?" *For treason, the asshole.*

"It's easy to have outside sources do the dirty work," Ottar says. "You assisted in putting Brimar away, so him seeking vengeance, even if he has to pull some strings, makes the most sense."

I strip out of my suit jacket and button-up shirt, leaving my upper torso bare.

I could see Brimar wanting to seek revenge. He's been in prison for a few months now, which is well fucking deserved given what he did to us. But to be able to orchestrate something like this? I don't know.

"Does he have connections like that?" I ask. "I know he slipped up right in front of me, but I've known him my whole life. I wouldn't think he had connections outside our circle."

"Yes, but he also has a vendetta against you, and he's been in prison long enough to make connections. He's a valid concern, and someone we're monitoring."

I slip the dress shirt on and then my suit jacket just as there's a knock on the door.

Ottar moves past me to open it. "Lilly," he says softly, then steps to the side, revealing my girl in a light-pink blouse and white trousers. Her hair is pulled back into a high ponytail, and her lips are painted the same color as her top. She looks so fucking good, especially as her gaze falls to my unbuttoned dress shirt, straight to my chest.

"Hey," she says. "Uh, can I sit in on the fitting?"

"If you wish," Ottar says. "Let me give you a minute. I'll bring Jiminy in shortly."

Ottar shuts the door behind him as Lilly walks up to me. Things are still tense between us. Not sure they'll be normal until after the wedding, especially since we have to keep going to meetings with Elias.

Our last one was pretty simple. We had to write down the specific attributes we love about each other. There was no arguing, no fighting, and no walking out. It was an hour of us loving each other and just what we needed at that moment. As Lilly looked deeply into my eyes and told me she loved my confidence, loyalty, strength, leadership, body, heart, and soul, some of that anger and fear slipped off my shoulders. Not all of it, and now especially with another threatening letter, but her words somewhat soothed me. I believe it's one of the reasons Lilly can look at me with love in her eyes right now, like she used to look at me in Harrogate. Nothing between us. Nothing messing with our heads.

"You look really hot," she says as she closes the distance between us and smooths her hand up my abs. The feel of her warm palm against my bare skin sends a thrill up my spine. I've missed her touch.

"Thank you," I say softly as I lift her chin and press a kiss to her rosy-pink lips. "How was your meeting with Theo?"

"Good. Just going over everyday things. Nothing I want to talk about right now."

"No?" I ask.

She shakes her head. "No, I just want to admire my fiancé in his suit."

That brings a small smile to my lips even though in the back of my mind, I can't help but think about Brimar and his possible connection to the threats. But to avoid concerning Lilly, I keep my expression neutral. "Then take a seat, love."

She smirks then lifts up on her toes and kisses the underside of my jaw. "Don't mind if I do."

She moves toward the couch in my room and slips her shoes off before pulling her legs into her chest and staring at me.

"What?" I ask when she smirks.

"You're more cut, especially the V in your hip."

"Yeah?" I ask.

She nods. "Been taking some frustration out during those morning workouts?"

"You could say that."

"Well, it's showing. I can't wait to strip you down and drag my tongue up and down your body."

I wet my lips, the thought of that happening instantly arousing me. "Don't make me hard right before the tailor comes in."

She chuckles. "Why not? I think it would be fun for him to have to navigate around your enormous cock."

Just as she finishes her sentence, there's a knock on the door. Ottar opens it, peeking his head in before he opens the door completely, letting Jiminy back in.

"How does the suit feel?" Jiminy asks.

"Good," I respond.

"I think it looks incredibly good on him," Lilly says, rolling her teeth over her bottom lip. I want to shoot her a warning, to tell her enough with those looks, but since we're in front of company, I'm at a loss for controlling the situation. Instead, as I look into the mirror that Jiminy set up, I'm forced to see Lilly's reflection, her eyes roaming my body, hungry, needy.

It's a monumental effort to tear my eyes off her and focus on what Jiminy is saying.

"How does the crotch feel?"

Tight.

Growing with every time my eye catches Lilly's.

Desperate for the girl behind me.

"Good," I answer in a gruff tone that Lilly catches because the smirk on her face grows to a full-on smile.

"The butt looks good too," Lilly says while hugging her legs even closer to her body.

I raise my brow at her in the mirror, and it makes her

giggle. "Ottar, can you escort the princess out of here? She's ogling too much."

"It's my right to ogle," she replies.

"And far be it from me to argue with that," Ottar says as he stands next to the door, watching the interaction.

"Much help you are."

Completely oblivious, Jiminy asks, "How does the waist feel?" He moves his hand across my abdomen and quickly removes his touch, as if I just burned him. "My goodness." He adjusts the glasses he put on before working on his pinning. "I've never seen such a set of abs like this in person."

"Aren't they delicious?" Lilly asks, causing me to frown at her in the mirror. She just kicks her feet up in glee.

"They're rather magnificent. Well done, sir."

"Thanks, Jiminy," I answer awkwardly while he adjusts the waist, pinning it just a pinch tighter so they sit nicely and don't slide around on my narrow hips.

For the next ten minutes, Jiminy slides my clothes around, asking questions, making sure everything is in place. The whole time, Lilly stares at me, giving her input, telling me how great I look, and eating me up with those hungry eyes of hers. By the time Jiminy finishes, I'm ready to climb out of this suit and straight into bed with my girl.

"Well, that should be it. I'll give you some privacy to get changed. Please just be careful with the pins."

"Of course," I answer while Ottar leads Jiminy out of the room.

When the door shuts behind them, I turn on Lilly with a stern look in my eyes. "You."

"What?" she asks as she twirls the end of her ponytail.

"Do you realize the things I had to think about in order not to get hard while Jiminy was swooshing his hands all over my body?"

"Ooo, delight me."

I close the distance between us and lean over her, my arms propping me up on the couch. "You're going to pay for that."

"I hope soon." She wets her lips. "I'm wearing the batteries out on my flower."

My brows shoot up to my hairline. "Your flower?"

An evil grin spreads over her lips. "Mm-hmm, got myself a new toy." Her fingers trail down my chest. "And it might not be as good as your lips sucking on my clit, but it's pretty close."

My fingers dig into the back of the couch as my mind wanders with what she'd look like using a new toy. The blush in her cheeks, her hard nipples pointing toward the ceiling, her legs spread, her lips parted as she moans . . .

Fucking hell.

I push away from the couch before I do something stupid like shove my cock down her throat right here, right now.

"Tempted?" she asks.

I glance over my shoulder as I carefully remove the suit jacket and button-up shirt. "I'm always tempted by you."

"Good answer."

She stands from the couch, slips her heels on, then walks up behind me. Her hands wrap around my waist and travel up my abs, spending an exorbitant amount of time in the divots as she kisses my back.

"I miss this."

"Me too," I reply.

"Just a few more days. Are you nervous?"

"No," I answer as her hands slide down to the waistband of my pants.

"I think that session with Elias cleared some of the tension, don't you think?"

"Yes," I answer even though I still feel some at times, especially when we have to discuss anything of importance.

"I'm glad." She slides one hand down the front of my pants and cups me in her palm.

"Lilly," I groan.

"God, Keller," she says as I turn in her arms, releasing her hold on me. Her eyes beam up at me. "Please let me touch you."

"Not a good idea."

"I want you."

I run my hand along her cheek. "I want you too, but we made a promise."

"I know, but I want to break it."

"We're not," I say more sternly, causing her to pout.

"Ugh, why are you so loyal?"

I chuckle. "Sorry, do you want me to be the kind of man who goes against his word?"

"Occasionally, maybe, when it benefits me and my aching . . . wet . . . pussy."

I curl my lip to the side. "Stop it."

She cries out in frustration as I remove the pants and drape them over a chair, leaving me in only my briefs. Her eyes immediately fall to my slightly aroused cock and travel up to my gaze.

"I could get that at full mast in seconds."

"Trust me, I know." I reach for my regular pants and slip them on. "Now, shouldn't you be getting ready for Timmy to visit?"

"There's nothing to do, the staff has done everything. I just approved of what his bedroom looks like and the basket of goodies that they put on his dresser to welcome him."

"I mean mentally. You're going to show him around the palace, get him acquainted. And what about Queen Pala and Princesses Isabella and Marit? Aren't they arriving a day or so after Timmy?"

"I believe so. But once again, nothing to get ready."

I slip my dress shirt on and start buttoning it up, Lilly's face falling with disappointment. "Have you read up on them?"

"Should I?" She cringes. "Is that something people do?"

"Yes," I answer. "You should always read up on your guests so you have an idea of who they are, what they like, and conversations you can have with them. We've been over this."

"I thought that was just, you know, something you could do, not something that you should do."

I stare her down. "You should do it, especially as the future queen of Torskethorpe."

"So you want me to go read up on my cousins?"

"Yes."

"Are you just saying that so I leave you and your penis alone?"

"Yes."

She chuckles, then offers me a kiss, which I take. When she releases me, her hand trails down my stomach one last time, and she's walking toward the door and out of my bedroom.

When she's gone, I let out a deep breath. See, everything will be okay.

Everything is fine.

⸺

"HAVE A SEAT," Theo says as I walk into his private office.

After the fitting, I was summoned to Theo's office unexpectedly. I assumed it would be about the new threat we received, but as I spot my doctor to the right, I have a sinking feeling this has nothing to do with that letter and everything to do with me.

I take a seat in one of the wingback chairs across from Theo's desk. I unbutton my suit jacket and try to keep my hands from shaking as I nod to my doctor. "Everything okay?" I ask.

From the morose looks on their faces, I'm going to guess no.

Theo clears his throat and says, "We've gotten some test

results in, and your doctor wanted to talk to me about them before he approached you. Given the circumstances and the waiver you filled out offering me permission to your records, I allowed him to speak to me first."

"Should I be worried?" I glance between the two of them and of course, Theo continues to take the lead.

"Dr. Johansen has informed me that we've received the test results back that involve your sperm count." Theo places his hands on the desk and looks me directly in the eye. "They were low, Keller."

I swallow hard as sweat forms on my upper lip.

This isn't just news.

This is life changing.

They take that test to determine if you're able to carry on the bloodline. It's been written in stone ever since the technology has been available.

And my world is being flipped upside down yet again. Fuck.

The feeling of inadequacy takes over me. I knew a part of my responsibility in marrying Lilly was to produce an heir. Or several. To ensure she carries on the Strom bloodline. *And now, even providing her that might be impossible.* My gut twists. I did not expect this.

"Um . . . how low?" I ask, my voice shaking.

"Lower than normal," the doctor says.

Panic swallows me whole as I glance at Theo. "What . . . uh, what does that mean?"

With a worried look in his eyes, Theo says, "It means you'll have a hard time getting Lilly pregnant."

Fuck.

My throat immediately tightens.

I'm not good enough.

She could do better with someone else.

I'll never be able to live up to the expectations that coincide with marrying Lilly.

I'm letting Theo down.

I choke back my emotions the best that I can, but it feels near impossible as I realize exactly what this means.

I can't marry her.

Tears spring to my eyes from *that* realization, and I clench my teeth, attempting to hold back my disappointment. No, this isn't disappointment. *This is agony.* I understand grief, I've lived through it before. But this level of heartbreak is something I never thought I'd experience again. This . . . *there is no word to describe this.*

I nod. "I understand." I ball my hands together and lean forward. "How, uh . . . how should we proceed?" A tear from my despair falls down my cheek, and I try to nonchalantly brush it away, but Theo sees it.

"Dr. Johansen, I believe we're good for now. I'll call you if we need anything else."

Dr. Johansen stands, knowing exactly when he's been dismissed. "Of course." He bows to Theo and then he leaves the office, giving me and Theo much-needed privacy.

"Fuck," I say as more tears stream down my cheeks. I keep my head turned down to hide the pain ripping through me.

Because this is the end.

This is it.

If I can't get Lilly pregnant, then what fucking good am I?

"I . . . I feel like I can't breathe," I say as I gasp for air.

Theo, as quick as he can, makes his way around his desk and pulls up the other chair next to mine. His warm palm falls to my back as he comforts me.

"I love her, Theo. I can't fucking let go of her." I turn my head and through watery eyes, I ask, "Am I going to have to let her go?"

Theo lets out a sigh and shakes his head.

"What?" I ask, sitting taller. "Are you serious?"

"Yes," he says and then clears his throat, his voice sounding tight as well. "Dr. Johansen didn't say it was impossible, just that it will be difficult. And no way will I be able to tell Lilly or you, for that matter, that you can't marry. I'll lose both of you, and that's not something I can stomach."

"But . . ." I swallow down the lump in my throat. "What if I can't get her pregnant?"

"We'll cross that bridge when we get there."

I appreciate his confidence in the matter, but I know what's at stake here, so I level with him. "Theo, it is my job to provide her an heir. After Lilly, no one takes the crown, so if she doesn't have a kid, then the country goes to Arkham. Is that something you can stomach?"

Theo sits back in his chair and presses his hand to his forehead. "Like I said, that's something we can think about—"

"Please excuse me for cutting in, Theo, but it's not something we can think about later on. It's something to decide now. I can't marry Lilly on the off chance that I can provide an heir."

"You sure as hell can't call off the wedding," he says. "That'll break her. She will leave. And we'll lose to Arkham anyway."

"Then what the hell do we do?"

Theo thinks on it for a moment, pinching his brow. After a few seconds, he says, "IVF or sperm donation."

"What?" I ask.

Theo sits back in his chair and says, "If you can't get her pregnant naturally or through IVF, then we'll have to find a sperm donor." A donor . . . someone else to fulfill my duty. Rejection consumes me, and I can feel this sense of blackness start to take over, starting at the tips of my toes and traveling up my legs, all the way to my hollow heart. "Talk to me, Keller. What's going on in your head?"

I work my jaw, side to side, my entire worth crackling, tumbling to the ground in a matter of seconds.

A sperm donor.

I know it's the logical thing to do, but there's something about my wife carrying someone else's child that doesn't settle well. And yes, the child will know me as the father, but that doesn't negate the fact that I wasn't able to do my job.

Although, pushing aside the emotions of it all, it's logical. It's the solution. A solution that digs a black hole in the depths of my heart.

"Keller . . ."

I make eye contact with Theo and wipe at my nose before saying, "There's the solution." I stand from the chair and say, "I'll inform Lilly."

"I don't think that's necessary," Theo says. "You don't want to stress her out."

"I'm not about to marry the woman holding on to this information. It will be an out for her, if she wants to take it."

"Keller." Theo walks up to me, placing his hand on my shoulder. "This is not a moment to be a hero. If you're not okay with this—"

"I don't have a choice," I say. "It's either keep the option of a sperm donor open or say goodbye to Lilly. The latter isn't an option, not where I'm concerned."

"But will you be bitter about it?"

"Yes," I answer honestly. "If I can't get Lilly pregnant, then I'll damn well know I haven't lived up to the job entrusted to me. It won't settle well. I won't be bitter about the situation. I'll be bitter toward myself. I knew I wasn't supposed to be in this position, and this is a stark example of why."

"Your job is to love, protect, and serve Lilly," Theo says.

"And generate offspring. You even said it yourself. If I can't do that, then I'm not serving this country." *I won't be loving Lilly how she needs it either.* I know she loves kids. I saw that as clear as day at the playschool event. *But for her to get that, they won't be mine.* None of my bloodline will be continued. *It seems I'm even failing my parents. Again.* But Theo's right, and I've always trusted in his wisdom. If I leave Lilly now, she will most likely leave Torskethorpe.

What if I wait until after she's been enthroned? Arkham wouldn't win then . . .

I start to move away, but Theo calls out my name. "Keller." When I look at him over my shoulder, he says, "Don't let this make a mark on your special day. You never know . . . when it's the right time, you might still fulfill your duties."

Eyes on his, I say, "Only time will tell."

Chapter Ten

LILLY

Keller: *Where are you?*

Lilly: *In my room. Just got changed and I'm about to watch some Harry Styles concert videos. What are you doing?*

Keller: *I need to speak with you.*

Lilly: *Okay, are you coming to my room or do you want to meet me somewhere?*

Keller: *I'll come to you.*

I set my phone down and look up at the door. Why do I have this feeling that whatever he's going to talk to me about isn't going to be good?

Probably because I know he was called to Theo's office earlier.

And probably because he skipped dinner with me, saying he had to catch up on a few things.

And also because he hasn't texted me until just now despite me sending him a few texts, one in particular of a picture of the carved fish I've been working on. Something I knew he would comment on because he's been impressed with my whittling.

My stomach twists in knots as I keep my eyes fixated on the door, waiting for him to enter. We just found a neutral spot in our relationship. With all of the wedding planning going on in the background, and the demands of our schedule, we were able to sort out some normalcy, but now . . . now I feel like it's going to be flipped upside down.

There is a knock on my door, and I don't have to tell him to come in because he opens the door and fits his impressive body into my bedroom, closing the door behind him.

While I'm in a night set, tank top and matching silk pants, Keller is still in a suit, this one dark blue. But instead of his perfectly styled hair, it looks like he's been pulling on the strands, sticking them up in all different directions.

"Hey," I say as I scoot to the edge of the bed. "Is everything okay?"

As he moves toward me, he takes off his suit jacket and tosses it on the foot of my bed. He sits and positions his back against the headboard and then holds out his hand.

Concerned, I take it, and he leads me to sit on his lap. When I'm situated, he wraps his arms around me, buries his head against my chest, and squeezes me tight toward him. My hands fall to the back of his head, and I hold him close as well.

"Keller," I say softly, my nerves firing with fear and uncertainty. "What's wrong?"

He doesn't say anything.

He just holds me.

Not lifting his head.

Not rubbing my back.

Nothing but clinging to me as if I was his lifeline.

The sorrow I feel in this embrace grips me in a chokehold, tightening my throat and raising the hairs on the back of my neck because this isn't Keller. He's strong. He's protective.

He's a presence in the room, a presence that resembles courage, vitality. He's the rock, the one you lean on, and right now, that rock is crumbling.

I drag my hand over the back of his head, reassuring him that I'm here for him, for whatever it might be, and as I hold him, my mind whirling with possibilities of what might be happening, what has driven him to this moment, I feel the tell-tale sign of a tear hitting my bare skin.

I freeze.

My heart pounds rapidly in my chest to the point that my lungs feel like they're pulling harder for oxygen.

He's crying?

Why?

I wet my dry lips. "Keller, you're scaring me. What's going on?" I take that moment to lift his head, and that's when I'm confronted with the tears in his eyes, the wetness on his cheeks, the devastation in his expression.

I wipe at his eyes. "Please tell me what happened."

His brows pinch together but not in the stern way they normally do when he disapproves of something I said or did. This is more like a hurt puppy look, and it just about kills me.

"I . . . I love you, Lilly," he chokes out.

"I love you too," I say, my eyes wildly scanning him.

"But . . ." He chokes on his words, unable to get them out, which makes this so much worse.

"But what?" I ask. I turn so I'm straddling his lap now, and I push his back against the headboard with my hands on his chest. "Keller, you have to talk to me because I'm really starting to panic."

His head falls back and the muscles in his throat contract as he swallows. "Theo called me into his office. He . . ." More tears fall down his cheeks, and I try to wipe them away as quickly as I can. "He told me that, uh . . . that I have a low sperm count." He lifts his head now, and when his eyes connect with mine, I know exactly what he's going to say. "It'll be hard for me to get you pregnant."

Everything in me stills.

The blood pumping through my veins.

The air pressing through my lungs.

The thoughts running rampant in my mind.

Because I know exactly what this means.

"Keller," I choke out. "What . . . what are you telling me?"

He drags his hand over his face. "I'm saying what I've told you from the very beginning. I'm not the man you should be with."

"Stop it." I clutch his shirt. "Stop fucking saying that. You are the man I should be with. We can . . . we can figure this out. What did Theo say?"

"He said if I don't go through with the wedding, you'll leave. You won't go through with this role."

"Wait, hold on." I sit taller. "Are you saying you don't want to go through with the wedding? Do you not want to marry me?"

His tired, strained eyes stare up at me. "I love you, Lilly, more than life itself, but I also know your role and your responsibilities—"

"Fuck that," I say. "Fuck all of that. I told you, this is about you and me."

"I know, but we can't be naive. Being the queen of Torskethorpe is bigger than us. And when you become queen, you are responsible for carrying on the bloodline. You are responsible for making sure that our country isn't handed over to Arkham. And despite the way my world revolves around you, I can't let you disappoint Theo or the people of this country who have fallen head over heels in love with you like I have."

My throat tightens as I grip his cheeks. "I'm not going to become queen unless you're by my side. I can't do this without you."

"I can still be by your side, just . . . in a different role."

"As in a bodyguard or adviser?" I ask, and when he nods, I actually laugh. "You believe that you can disassociate your feelings from me and act like what we have isn't a once-in-a-lifetime love? You can stand by my side while I'm crowned queen, you can watch me date someone else, fuck someone else . . . marry someone else? You're telling me you can do that?"

His jaw grows tight, and he looks away.

"That's what I thought. But hey, if you're looking for a way out of this, then you can have it. If this is you trying to take the easy way out—"

"That's not what I'm doing, and you fucking know it." He stabs his finger into the mattress, anger now ringing in his voice. "It is my fucking job to make sure you're taken care of, that you are able to continue the bloodline. And I can't do that."

"You don't know if you can't. It will just be harder. You're giving up before even trying. How could you just give up like that on us?"

"I'm not giving up," he shouts. "I'm giving you the option to leave. To be with someone else, someone who could provide for you the way that you need."

"When are you going to realize that you are what I need?" I ask. "When are you going to see that? See the value in yourself?"

"I know my value," he says. "That's not the issue here. The issue is, I might not be able to give you what you need, and I'm letting you know, if you want to walk away, I'm not going to hold you back."

"Well, I'm not going anywhere," I say. "You're what I want, what I need. If it comes down to it, I'll get pregnant some other way, but not being with you is not an option."

"Maybe you should take some time to think about it."

"I don't need fucking time." I grip his chin tightly so our eyes meet. "I know what I want. It's you. Over and over again, it's you. This news, it's a speedbump, something we'll deal with when the time comes, but it's nothing that will tear you away from me." I lean in and press my forehead against his. "You're mine, Keller, and nothing will take that away. So don't try to push me away. This isn't the end of us."

His breathing picks up as his arms wrap around me, pulling me in even tighter.

"I'm sorry," he whispers, his voice full of sorrow.

"There's nothing to be sorry for. You can't control this. And we won't let this news control us either. I don't know much about what a low sperm count means, but I do know it doesn't mean it's impossible to get pregnant. And we have time, Keller. Let's not keep finding hurdles. We'll deal with this, as with *everything*, together when the time comes."

He brings his head to the crook of my neck, and that's where he holds me, never letting go until Runa comes into my room and tells him he has to leave. Even at that, he manages to pause before listening. When he left, though, it didn't feel quite right. He kissed me, hugged me, but then let go of my hand, keeping his eyes on me and walking out of my room without breaking eye contact. It felt like he was giving me one last goodbye.

It worried me so much that later that night, I sent him a text.

Lilly: *Are you going to leave me?*
Keller: *Never.*

A BLACK SEDAN pulls up in front of the palace. Despite the chilly day, the sun is out for a short amount of time, welcoming my much-anticipated guest.

Standing impatiently next to Keller, who is holding my hand, the car comes to a stop and the driver steps out.

Rounding the car, he opens the back passenger door, revealing a bronze god.

Timmy Tuna.

I release Keller's hand and run up to him. "Timmy!" I shout as I fling myself into his familiar arms.

"Holy shit, it's cold," he says as he squeezes me tight.

I chuckle and pull away, taking him all in.

"You have a beard." I smooth my hand over his jaw.

"Because I thought it would help prevent my face from freezing off while visiting you."

"Smart." He also dyed his hair brown instead of his usual blond tips, and he's wearing a big puffy jacket that I'm pretty sure he would never be caught dead wearing in Miami. "And look at you all bundled up."

"You told me it was cold. I came prepared." He looks me up and down. "Girl, you've come a long way since selling bikinis. You're so classy now."

I fluff my hair. "I prefer posh."

He chuckles, then glances over my shoulder, his eyes widening as his mouth breaks out in a large smile. "Uh, please tell me that's your fiancé behind you."

I smirk. "That's him."

"Holy mother of God, Lilly."

Chuckling, I grab Timmy by the hand and pull him over to Keller, who is patiently watching the interaction. "Timmy, I want you to meet my man, Keller. Keller, this is Timmy."

Keller lends out his hand and Timmy takes it in awe. "It's very nice to meet you in person finally," Keller says. "How was the trip? Hopefully pleasant."

Gobsmacked, Timmy just stares up at Keller for a few moments before saying, "Uh, yeah, it was pleasant."

"I'm glad to hear it." Keller threads his hands together. "I'd like to stay, but I have a meeting I must attend, but I'm sure you and Lilly want some time to catch up anyway. I'll see you later for dinner."

"Sounds great," Timmy replies.

Keller takes a step forward toward me and lifts my chin with his finger before placing a soft kiss on my lips. "See you later, love."

"Bye," I answer right before he takes off.

When he's out of earshot, Timmy says, "Jesus Christ, Lilly. I think that's the first time my penis got hard and shriveled up all at the same time. That man is living sin."

I burst out in laughter and loop my arm around his waist. "I'm so glad you're here."

———

"YOU KNOW, I believed it from the moment you told me about Keller's offer in Miami. But now that I'm here, standing in your family's palace . . ." He faces me and shakes his head. "I don't think I believe it anymore."

"How does that make sense?" I ask him as I lounge on the settee in my room, watching him take in every little intricate detail.

"It doesn't, but it just feels like I'm living in a dream right now." He turns toward me. "And you're about to be married in grand fashion. This is all so surreal."

"It does feel surreal, doesn't it?"

"Do you ever miss everyday life?" he asks. "When was the last time you went out in public and no one recognized you?"

"A while," I answer. "But I usually don't leave the palace unless it's a scheduled event."

"Really?" he asks. "So you're just sort of . . . trapped in here?"

"Trapped is not the right terminology," I respond as Timmy runs his fingers along the rich fabric of my curtains. "There is a lot of space here, lots of grounds to walk about, and it won't always be like this. We're just slightly restricted right now with the wedding and all of that."

"So when the wedding is over, you'll be able to go . . . grocery shopping, something like that?"

"Probably not." I laugh. "Not that I want to do that anyway. Does anyone really like grocery shopping?"

"I sure as hell don't. I get them delivered now because I can't be bothered."

"What do you have delivered? Fish sticks, tartar sauce, and clementines?"

He walks over to me, boops me on the nose, and says, "Precisely."

I sit up and take his hand in mine. "I've missed you so much."

"I've missed you too. Spraying down people in white T-shirts doesn't hit right anymore without you."

"I miss seeing all of those wet nipples, men and women."

"They miss you." He looks around my room. "But look at this, this is so much more, and not just because of the extraordinary circumstances where you're freaking rich, but because you're actually doing something that matters. You're making an impact on this world, in history. It's so crazy to me, and I'm still trying to wrap my head around it."

"You and me both," I say.

"Do you ever miss it?" he asks. "The normal life?"

"Yes," I answer. "Granted, this is all still very new to me, but I do miss being able to do whatever I want to do for the day. I miss being able to lounge on my couch and binge trashy shows. I miss the beach, the warm sun, and people watching. I miss being able to just let loose and not worry about who might see me and what I might have said to them that could be taken the wrong way. I'm very fortunate, in so many ways, but a slice of normalcy has been taken away, and I'm still trying to deal with that."

"Understandable," he says. "It's a huge change for you, but it seems like you're handling it very well. And you have a fine-as-hell man walking by your side." Timmy squeezes my hand. "If I had ovaries, they would have cried while I shook his hand."

I chuckle. "I'm sure he would love to know that."

"Don't tell him. I need to remain as composed as possible in his eyes."

"Why?" I ask.

"Because if he ever decides to leave you, I want to be there for him, open arms."

From the mention of Keller leaving me, I immediately feel my face fall flat, and Timmy notices.

"What did I say?" he asks. "I know that look. That's your worried look. What's going on?"

This is what I needed, someone who knows me down to my core. I love Lara. Not only has she been an amazing body-guard, but she's become one of my best friends here. But we're still getting to know each other. I don't think she'd pick up on my change of mood as quickly as Timmy or have the courage to immediately ask me.

"Things are still strained with Keller. He got some bad news that has put more of a strain on our relationship. I'm truly concerned whether he's going to be walking down that aisle with me."

"What kind of news?" he asks softly.

"Basically? That it will be difficult for him to get me pregnant."

"Oh." Timmy leans against the back of the settee. "I'm sure he didn't take that news lightly. From what you've told me about Keller, he's prideful and takes his job very seriously. As the future prince of Torskethorpe, he does have to help you continue the bloodline. I can't imagine what that information has done to his pride, to the value he offers you."

I stare at Timmy, completely shocked that he could so easily understand and reverberate Keller's emotions to me without truly knowing him.

"How do you understand him so well without knowing him?"

"You don't have to know him to understand the kind of man he is. It's written all over his face, the way he holds your hand, his stature. This is a painful blow to him, and I'm not surprised to hear that he's hurting from it."

"He is, badly," I say, thinking back to the other night when he was crying in my arms. "He actually told me that I could walk away."

"Of course he did." Timmy shakes his head. "He doesn't think he's good enough. Why wouldn't he give you the option to leave? What did you say to him?"

"That I would never. That he was it for me and we would figure this all out when the time came."

"Did he believe you?"

I let out a large sigh and stare up at the ceiling. "I honestly don't know. Before you arrived, we had another marriage counseling class. He felt stiff next to me. Nothing terrible happened like in the other sessions, but this time, he wasn't very vocal and just listened. I think he was going through the motions." I press my hand to my head. "I don't know, Timmy. I keep telling myself everything will be okay after the wedding, but I have this sickening feeling it's not going to be okay. That . . . that this is the beginning of the end."

Timmy's brows turn down. "I hate to diminish your feelings by saying that's crazy thinking . . . but Lilly, that's crazy thinking. I saw how that man kissed you before he took off. There is no way that kiss is any indication of the beginning of the end." He pats my leg. "This is all nerves. We just need to loosen you up. Get you to have some fun." A thought must pop into his head because he grins widely. "You know, I brought some wigs and things with me. Why don't we ditch the palace and go have some fun?"

I shake my head. "Lara would never let me. They've

upped the security since the wedding. Unfortunately, we're in for the night."

"Not if we sneak out," Timmy says.

"Timmy, we can't sneak out."

"Are you saying it's physically impossible, or it's not allowed? Because I could tell you right now these walls have some secret passages, so I bet we could easily sneak out."

I then recall the secret passageway behind the picture frame right outside my room that leads to the staff quarters. From there, it would be an easy way out to the local bar around the corner.

"There are secret passageways, aren't there?" he asks with excitement.

"I might know of one."

He claps his hands. "Let's do it. We can make you unrecognizable with a wig, give you some whorish makeup, maybe a mole here and there, really throw people off, and we can have a relaxing but fun night."

"I don't know," I say even though my mind has already fallen in love with the idea. "Keller would be mad. Lara would be furious. My security wouldn't be happy either."

"That's why we act like you have a headache, and when everyone leaves you alone, we sneak you out." He tugs on my arm. "Come on, you need this."

I do. I need the reprieve from the stress. From the constant pressure of my relationship on the brink of falling apart. One night to relax, that doesn't seem like it would be too bad.

I twist my lips to the side. "Okay, let's do it."

"Really?" Timmy asks.

"Really. But let me handle Keller and my security. They guard my door, so I'm going to need to slip out without them thinking I'm leaving."

"Okay, so . . . what's the plan?"

"Let me think on this, we have to execute this properly."

"Well, I'm all ears."

KELLER: *You sure you're okay?*

Lilly: *Yeah, just going to rest for a bit. Thanks for checking in on me.*

Keller: *Just want to make sure you're not avoiding me. I know I've been an asshole to be around recently. I'm working on it.*

Hell, now I feel guilty.

Lilly: *Not avoiding you. And just a few more days. Then this will all be over.*

Keller: *A few more days.*

Lilly: *Love you.*

Keller: *Love you, Lilly.*

With that, I place my phone in my purse, which I slip on my shoulder, before putting my robe over my entire going-out outfit.

The plan is as follows. I slip out of my room, telling the guards I'm going to Timmy's room for a quick second so they don't follow me. Once in his room, we put on the disguise and then head around the hall to the picture. It's risky, but I'm ready to take a risk.

On a deep breath, I clench my robe together and open my bedroom door. I smile at the guards who are standing off to the side. "Hey, I'm going to go to Timmy's room. He needs some slippers, his feet are cold." I hold up a pair of my fuzzy pink slippers.

They just nod, giving me the go-ahead to walk down the hallway to Timmy's room, which is right past Keller's. Quietly, I tiptoe across the carpet, and when I reach Timmy's room, I don't knock, I just let myself in.

He's sitting at the vanity near the window, brushing a long brown wig. When he sees me in the reflection of his mirror, he holds up the wig. "For you, my queen." He stands from the vanity, and I strip out of my robe, revealing a pair of jeans and a thick sweater. My shoes are tucked under one arm, so I let those drop to the floor, then I walk over to Timmy where he puts my wig on.

"Oh girl, you can rock the brown hair." He adjusts the bangs and picks up a ball cap, shakes it out, and slips it over my head. It's a plain faded green hat, but it does the trick because when I look in the mirror, it sits low enough on my head so you can't really see my eyes.

"Perfect," I say. "What about you?"

He reaches into his suitcase and pulls out a light blond wig that he slips on his head, the style reaching his jawline. He tops it off with a winter hat and then slips on a plaid fleece quarter zip.

My jaw nearly falls to the ground when I take him in. "You look so . . . butch."

He laughs. "I know. But I pull it off, don't I?"

"You honestly do," I answer. "You could fit in nicely here."

"I would consider it if I wasn't wearing three pairs of underwear to avoid any frostbite to my nether regions. Don't think I'll ever get used to this cold."

"You'd be surprised. It's starting to grow on me."

"Well, if I meet a strapping fisherman ready to rock my boat, maybe I'll consider it."

I roll my eyes. "Come on, let's get out of here before anyone catches on."

"Aren't we going to do your makeup?"

I shake my head. "I think it's best if I go natural. I wear makeup all the time. They won't be able to recognize me like this."

"As you wish." When I raise my brow at him, he says, "What? Not into the whole *Princess Bride* thing? I think it's quite fitting."

I tug on his hand and lead him to his bedroom door. "Be more creative."

He lightly chuckles and together, we head down the hall-way, around the corner, and toward the picture frame.

Whispering, I say, "We have to be quick with the picture, because the guards could catch us if we're not quiet."

"I'm nearly shivering out of my boots with nerves at this point. The quicker the better."

"This was your idea, remember?" I whisper.

"Yes, but you need to remember that I'm all talk most of the time."

"Oh my God," I hiss at him. "Don't chicken out on me now."

"I'm not," he says. "But I'm allowed to be nervous."

I pause, halting him right on the edge of the picture. We have to make a quick left turn and it will be right there.

"I'll go first, open the picture, and then you follow right behind me. No stumbling, no second-guessing."

"Got it."

On a deep breath, I peek around the corner. *No guards.* Yes! I whip around the corner, open the picture frame, and slip into the dark hole. When I feel Timmy right behind me, I step to the side, letting him in, and then I let the picture connect back with the wall.

"Jesus, my heart is beating a mile a minute," he whispers.

"Tell me about it." I pull my phone from my purse and turn on the flashlight, illuminating the long dark corridor.

"Well, it's not creepy in here at all."

"Come on." I tug on his arm, guiding him through the corridor and to the door that leads to the staff quarters. "We're almost there."

"You have to tell me if there are any cobwebs in my wig when we get out of this place. I can't be meeting fishermen looking like a damn corpse who just escaped his crypt."

I laugh, the sound bouncing off the stone. "Don't worry, I'll be sure to check out every fiber of your wig."

"It's the least you can do."

Chapter Eleven

KELLER

I rest my head against my bed's headboard and stare straight ahead, the book in my hands getting as much attention as it has for the past few weeks . . . just about none.

My mind won't stop racing.

I had another nightmare last night about my parents, calling out to me from the other side of a window, begging for my help, but I wasn't able to help them. I shot out of my bed in a cold sweat, my heart racing. I didn't go back to sleep after that. These are the moments when I miss Lilly even more. The comfort of her body was what I wanted. *Fuck, I want to hold her. I* need *to fuck her. Make love to her. Control her.*

I've spent every hour I haven't been with Lilly studying the parade route, checking in with Ottar and Lara about security, making sure we have guards posted on every corner and every rooftop.

When I'm with Lilly, I've tried to push past the weight of

my issues and continue to be present with her. Love her. Show her I'm still the man she fell in love with.

And when I'm in my room alone, I attempt to think of nothing. Nothing at all, but it feels next to impossible with my mind whirling, swirling with what-ifs.

On a sigh, I set my book on my nightstand and reach for the light when there is a knock on my door.

Lilly.

No one else would visit me at night.

I don't bother slipping a shirt on. Instead, I walk over to the door in my shorts and open it. But I don't see Lilly on the other side. Lara stands there with a grim look on her face.

"Is Lilly in here?" she asks.

"No," I answer, a scowl pulling at my expression.

"Don't mess with me, Keller. If she's in here, just tell me."

"She's not," I answer, red flags going off in my head. "Can you not find her?"

Lara shakes her head. "The guards called me, said she left to go to Timmy's room, and when she didn't return after half an hour, they went to his room. There's no one in there."

I let go of the door and go straight to my phone then pull up our text thread and shoot her a text.

Keller: *Where are you?*

After it's sent, I walk over to my closet and pull on a long-sleeved shirt, then slip on some socks and running shoes. *What the fuck is going on?*

"Have there been any breaches in the palace?"

Lara shakes her head. "We've checked all the cameras. Nothing out of the ordinary."

"Have you asked the staff? Are they in the kitchen? Maybe they went to get something to eat."

"All rooms in the palace except yours have been cleared. She hasn't been seen, neither has Timmy."

I grab my phone and then move past Lara, straight to Timmy's room a few doors down. That's where I find Ottar, searching the room, checking out the windows, and running a flashlight over all nooks and crannies.

"What do you have?" I ask him.

"Nothing. The windows are locked. There's no sign of forced entry. The only thing we have is Lilly's robe that was on the floor."

"Jesus," I mutter as I pull on my hair. "Have you checked her room?"

"Yes," Lara says. "Nothing."

"Was her phone in there?" Lara shakes her head. "Which means she should have it," I say. I flash my screen and unlock it before pulling up her location that she shares with me. My eyes narrow when I see exactly where she is. I grip my phone tighter, anger searing through me.

"What is it?" Lara asks.

"She's at the Crowned Cod."

"What?" Lara asks as I push past her, Lara and Ottar hot on my heels. I move down the hallway, straight to the painting that I know leads to the staff quarters. She used it to visit me before I was staying in the palace, so why wouldn't she use it again? When I come face to face with the painting, I see it. *Fuck. Slight scuff mark on the wall.* They went through here.

I fling it open and head down the corridor.

I don't bother with a flashlight.

I charge forward, knowing this corridor well. I used to use it with Lara and Brimar all the time.

"Keller, slow down," Lara says.

"No," I shoot back.

Nothing will stop me from pulling her out of that sleazy bar. With every step I take, my shoulders grow tense with anger, with worry . . .

Someone is out there trying to hurt us, hurt me . . . hurt her. And she's out in public, at a bar known for its fights, without guards, unprotected.

My fists clench at my sides, and when I see the door that

leads to the staff quarters, I push my hand against the door, flinging it open, startling a few people in the hallway.

I charge forward, headed right for the exit when a large hand pulls my shoulder backward and pushes me up against a wall. A beefy forearm shoves against my chest, holding me in place.

Ottar.

When my eyes meet his, he says, "You're not going anywhere."

"Unless you want this to be bloody, I suggest you let me fucking go," I say.

Lara comes up to the side and presses her hand to my chest as well, her calm voice breaking through the mania flying around in my head. "Keller, listen to him. I know you're angry. I know you're worried, but there are several reasons you shouldn't leave the palace."

Keeping my eyes on Ottar, I say, "Name them."

"For one, if you charge into that bar and grab Lilly, people will see you, they'll take pictures, they'll take videos. She might be in disguise to avoid attention, but you're not. The last thing the palace needs right now is another negative story about you," Lara says.

"Not to mention, there's someone out there trying to hurt you," Ottar says. "And I'll be damned if it happens on my watch."

"Let us do our job," Lara says. "We'll bring her back here and then you can talk to her. Until then, you need to wait."

I look back and forth between them, frustration that they're right ripping through me. I'd love nothing more than to go to that bar, grab Lilly by the arm, and drag her back here. But I know damn well that not only would Theo be angry that I risked myself like that, but Henrik wouldn't appreciate the negative publicity right before the wedding. *Especially since I don't have the best reputation at the moment.*

Irritated, I push at Ottar's chest to get him off me, and I

turn my back to them. Hand tugging on my hair, I say, "You have ten minutes. If you're not back in ten, I'm coming to find her." I then face them and add, "I'll be right here, waiting."

Lara and Ottar exchange looks and nod, before taking off down the hallway at a jog. If I can't retrieve her myself, then I wouldn't trust anyone else but Lara and Ottar.

Doesn't mean I like it, though.

I glance down at my phone, looking to see if she texted me, and when I see that she hasn't, I grip my phone even tighter. What if something happened to her? What if someone recognized her, kidnapped her from the bar, and left her phone there? What if they have her right now . . . and they're taking her somewhere we'll never find?

No.

That won't be the case.

Because if she was captured, I'll spend every waking hour of my life looking for her. I'll die before I let her be harmed.

Anxious, I pace the hallway, staff members passing by me, their eyes drifting, taking me in, watching my every strangled movement. No doubt there will be some sort of leak to the papers about the nervous prince, pacing the hallways right before the wedding.

I can see the headlines now.

But fuck if I care.

I'm not moving. Not until I know she's back in this palace.

And she's not leaving my sight when she gets back. I'll see to it.

I spend the next eight minutes driving myself mad with worry. *Why haven't they returned? What happened to her? Who could she have run into? What the fuck was she thinking?* And with every motion in the hallway, my eyes deceive me, thinking it's them returning when, in fact, it's just staff members moving around from room to room.

I want to shout at them not to fucking move. To stay where they are, but I bite my tongue and turn away, staring at the secret doorway that leads into the palace. That will be boarded up. Tomorrow. I will make sure of it.

"Keller." My back stiffens when I hear Lara's voice, and I whip around to find her standing behind me with Lilly dressed in a brown wig and baseball cap. Timmy is next to her, looking frightened to death as Ottar holds his arm.

Relief flies through me but is quickly replaced with white-hot rage.

"See that Timmy finds his way back to his room and that where he *can* go and where he *can't* go is explained to him." I grip Lilly by her arm and pull her forward without a word.

"Keller," she says as I bring her through the door to the secret corridor.

"I suggest you don't say a goddamn word." I push us through the painting, slamming it open against the wall, and when two guards startle from the noise, I say, "See that this is boarded up, immediately."

One of them takes off as I pull Lilly toward her room, open the door, and move her into the quiet, dark space. When I shut the door and lock it, I press my hand against the hard wood and take a deep breath.

She's safe.

Remember that.

She's here, with you, in her bedroom, safe.

When I turn around, I catch her removing the baseball cap and wig and dropping them to the floor. Her eyes remain on mine the entire time.

I push my hand through my hair. "What the fuck were you thinking?"

"I don't know," she says as she drops into her vanity chair. "I just got caught up in the prospect of having fun, without someone looking over me every two seconds."

"Those people who *look over you* are making sure nothing bad happens to you."

"Well, nothing bad happened," she says.

"Because you're fucking lucky," I shout at her. "Jesus Christ, Lilly. I know this country loves you, but there are some out there who don't, who are anti-monarchy, and if they had a shot at it, they would tear this palace down. They wouldn't even think twice about it."

"I'm sorry, I wasn't thinking."

"Damn right you weren't thinking." I rest my hands on my hips, my stomach twisting, knotting together, making me feel so goddamn nauseous that I need to take a second to breathe through the heaviness in my chest. "Do you know how fucking worried I was? How you made Lara and Ottar feel? Like their protection was an absolute joke? Going out tonight wasn't just some fun thing you could do with your friend. It has consequences. You lost trust with Lara and Ottar, you made me feel like a goddamn helpless human, and you sent the security detail on high alert. And fuck if we know what might leak to the press from what the staff heard or saw in the quarters. This was a huge fuck-up."

She twists her hands together, looking apologetic. "I'm sorry."

I shake my head, not sure what else I can say that won't be entirely too insulting. Anger rages within me, and to avoid letting my thoughts fly out of my mouth, I say, "Get ready for bed."

She walks up to me, attempts to put her hand on my chest, but I step away. "Keller—"

"I said get ready," I say through a clenched jaw, causing her to move away from me and to her bathroom.

When I hear the water running, I shoot a text to Lara.

Keller: *I'm staying in her room tonight. Let Runa and Ottar know.*

Lara: *Okay, we'll station another guard at her door, just for your peace of mind.*

Keller: *Thank you.*

Lara: *Don't be too hard on her, Keller.*

Keller: *Don't tell me how to handle my girl. Good night.*

I move over to my side of the bed, where I used to sleep before we were separated, and I set my phone on the night-stand before peeling my shirt up and over my head. I toss it to the ground, then sit on the bed, where I take off my shoes and socks, tossing them to the side as well.

While she finishes up in the bathroom, I lean forward, my arms bracing on my trembling legs. The adrenaline from the night starts to settle in my veins, making me feel sick to my stomach and full of energy all at the same time.

"Keller?" Lilly says from the bathroom door. I glance over my shoulder where she stands in only a nightgown. "What are you doing?"

"What does it look like I'm doing?" I ask.

"I thought we weren't supposed to sleep in the same room."

"Yeah, well that changed the minute you decided to slip out of the palace without your security detail." I turn and lift the covers so I can get my legs in. With my back toward her, I lie down on the pillow.

She turns the light off and slips into bed as well.

We lie there, silence consuming us, the moonlight coming through the partially open curtains. After a few moments, she turns toward me on the bed and scoots in close.

"Don't," I say.

"Don't what?" she asks.

"Don't touch me."

"Keller, can we talk about this, please?"

"You want to talk about this?" I ask as I flip to the other side, facing her. I lift on my elbow so I can look down at her. "Fine, let's talk about how I nearly lost my mind with worry as we searched for you, as I waited for Ottar and Lara to bring you back, and how I could do absolutely nothing to protect you because it's not my job anymore. Do you know how I felt? Helpless, Lilly. Fucking helpless."

"I . . . I didn't think it would be that big of a deal."

"Of course you didn't. You don't think about anything other than yourself."

"Hey," she says, her expression growing angry now. "That's not fair. I made a mistake, Keller. Don't go making assumptions about my character off one mistake. You've made them too. Pretty sure the reason we broke up in the first place was because of a mistake you made. You don't see me throwing that in your face."

"This is different."

"How is this different?" she asks.

"Because there are people out there who would give anything to hurt you, to hurt me, and you willingly put yourself in danger."

"We barely left the palace."

"It doesn't matter. You left," I say. "You put yourself out there, for anyone to take advantage of the situation."

She places her hand to my chest. "But—"

"You don't get it," I yell at her as I move my hand to hers and pin it up above her head, my body eclipsing hers. "Just because you didn't get hurt, doesn't mean you won't get hurt the next time."

Her breath catches in her throat as she stares up at me, those wide eyes filling with tears.

"Are you trying to make me mad? Is this your way of getting back at me for all this shit we've been through?" I ask.

"No," she says, shaking her head. "I was just trying to have some fun. My life has been a circus lately with engagements, fittings, wedding planning, couples therapy that—"

"It's not couples therapy. They're pre-wedding classes."

She rolls her eyes. "You know what I mean. It's all been very heavy. Timmy thought we could loosen up."

"Timmy has no goddamn clue the kind of pressure we're under or the threats being made."

Her eyes widen as a tear falls down her cheek. "Threats? What threats?"

Fucking hell.

Good job, Keller. You weren't supposed to say anything, and there you go, letting it fly off your tongue as a defense tactic.

"Nothing you need to worry about," I answer. "It's being handled."

"No." She tries to remove her hand, but I keep her pinned. "Keller, I want to know."

"There's nothing to know that will do any service to you."

She struggles against me, and I loosen my grip to let her free. She sits up in bed and says, "I deserve to know. This is my life, and I'll be damned if you shelter me from it."

"Why? Because the more you know, the more you'll be careful?"

She crosses her arms, clearly hearing the sarcasm in my voice. "Maybe if you told me earlier, I wouldn't have gone off to the bar . . ." She pauses and then tilts her head to the side. "Is that why you had a larger security detail assigned to me?"

"Yes," I answer.

"Keller," she yells. "You lied to me."

"With your best interest at heart," I say. "If we told you we've received threats about the wedding, that would have stressed you out more, and Theo was worried about you."

"Why don't people stop worrying about me and let me worry about myself?"

"Because when you worry about yourself, you ditch your security and go to sketchy bars, not even considering the people around you."

"I didn't think it was a big deal," she yells. "Jesus, Keller. I said I was sorry, what more do you want from me?"

"I want you to be safe. I don't want to have to worry about you."

"Well, I'm sorry for being such a burden to you." She turns away from me, and I grind my teeth together, trying not to lose my shit.

"You know you're not a burden to me."

"Really?" she asks as she flops on her back. "Because it seems like ever since we've gotten engaged, I've become a burden. Everything going wrong in your life right now is because of me. So tell me how that's not a burden?"

"Being in love with someone is not a burden."

"You sure make it seem like it is."

"Excuse me?" I ask as she tries to roll away, but I stop her and force her to face me. "Care to explain that?"

"Just leave it," she says, trying to turn away again.

"I'm not going to leave it when you say something like that. Ever since I met you, my days have been focused on supporting you, being there for you, making sure you've had a smooth transition into this new life. I've given up everything I've known, put myself in situations I'm not comfortable with because I love you, because I'm in love with you. I've sacrificed, Lilly."

"So have I!" she shouts, pointing at her chest as tears stream down her cheeks. "I've sacrificed so fucking much. I left everything I've ever known for a world that offers me a family history. I've been carted around all over this godforsaken country, learning the traditions and connecting with the people. I've given up my life to become queen so the people of this country aren't handed over to the enemy. So excuse me for wanting a fucking mental break for one goddamn night, Keller. I wasn't trying to disrespect anyone. I wasn't trying to cause issues. I was trying to take a deep breath from the insanity that has been our lives for the past month. Not everything is about you and how you feel, how it changes your routine, because guess what, Keller? Not everything can be compartmentalized for you. Life doesn't work like that, and it's time you realize that."

She turns away from me and rests her head on her pillow, curling into it.

"So is that it?" I ask. "You're just going to end the conversation on that?"

"I have nothing else to say to you. I apologized. What's done is done. And you don't need to stay here tonight. Trust me, I won't be going anywhere."

"I'm not leaving," I say.

"Do what you want, Keller. I really don't care."

"How am I the bad guy in this scenario?" I ask.

She turns toward me again and says, "There's no bad guy or good guy. The fact of the matter is, I'm drowning over here, just as much as you are. You chose to lie to me instead of telling me the truth about whatever threats have come in, and it came back to bite you in the ass. If I knew there was a true risk, I never would have left the palace. If you want me to make smart choices, then educate me on what's happening. Simple as that."

"You wouldn't have handled it well."

"Well, I guess we'll never know now." She goes back to her side of the bed and says, "Good night."

I flex my hands, my irritation not subsiding from our conversation.

She's right that I probably should have told her about the threats, but what she doesn't realize is even if there were no threats, she still shouldn't have left. So many things could have happened, so many bad things, and I'm not sure she'll ever understand that.

———

I WATCH Lilly slip on a pair of nude-colored heels, her hair and makeup done, the pair of light blue pants and white blouse looking beautiful on her. It's been an awkward morning to say the least.

We've said about two words to each other while Runa has made her way around the room, helping her get ready. I've stayed in the chair next to the window, observing, skipping my workout this morning, and trying to determine how to bridge the wide-open gap between us.

But it doesn't seem like it's going to happen.

Not now.

Lilly stands from where she's sitting and pushes down on her pants as she looks in the mirror, adjusting her blouse. Queen Pala and her daughters arrive today. I know she's nervous but also very much excited.

"If you don't need anything else, I'll check on the dress that I had sent down to the laundry," Runa says, clearly trying to give us some space. Can't imagine how uncomfortable she feels, especially since I haven't left the chair. I've simply observed Lilly getting ready.

"I'm good, thanks," Lilly says as she adjusts her necklace.

"Very well. I hope you enjoy the time you have meeting your family. I look forward to hearing about it later." And then Runa leaves us. Alone.

I rise from the chair, picking up my shoes and socks. I put my shirt on when Runa entered, because I didn't think it was appropriate for Runa to see me shirtless.

With my items secured, I move toward the bedroom door only to be stopped when Lilly says, "What kind of threats, Keller?" I glance over my shoulder, and I'm about to answer when she says, "If you don't tell me, then I'm just going to find out from someone else. Don't you think it would be best to hear from my future husband?"

Unfortunately, I know how she works. She will find out one way or another. It's who she is. And I want to tell her rather than have someone else. It's my job.

I turn to face her and say, "There was a letter sent a few weeks ago. It was targeted at me and the wedding."

She doesn't show any emotions, just stands there, her hands connecting in front of her. "In what way did it target you?"

"Whoever wrote it, stated that they were not happy about

me marrying the future queen and they weren't happy with who the future queen was. They said they would see us soon. We received a follow-up letter that taunted us in the same way. Ottar and his team have been looking into the threat, but whoever sent it was very smart not to leave any traces. We've shortened the parade route for the wedding so we don't compromise our security detail. We've increased security around you and me as well. Theo believes the wedding will be fine and is confident in our efforts to control the situation."

She nods slowly. "Is it serious?"

"Any threat is taken seriously, but given this group knows what they're doing, we're treating it with utmost importance."

"Okay," she says, walking by me. When her shoulder brushes mine, she mutters, "Was that so hard?" And then she exits the room, her anger clearly still intact from last night.

I'm right there with her.

But I'm still not sure I would have done things differently. Anger or no anger.

Chapter Twelve

LILLY

"Lilly, I'm so, so——"

I stop Timmy before he can finish by giving him a hug. "Don't even think about apologizing," I say as I take his hand and guide him to the dining room where breakfast waits for us. Normally, I eat in my room while getting ready, but since I have a guest, we changed it to the dining room.

Timmy wears a pair of high-waisted slacks and a black button-up shirt that he's dressed up with a sparkling sun brooch. His hair is combed to the side, and he has his signature spicy cologne on. He's dressed in his finest today.

"I feel awful."

"No need to feel awful. It was my choice to leave. Don't worry about it."

Whispering because staff is everywhere, he says, "Keller looked pissed. I don't think I've ever seen anyone that angry."

"He was," I answer, thinking back to the deep frown on his face.

The minute Lara tapped my shoulder in the bar, I knew I was in trouble. She quietly whispered in my ear that I needed to leave. She didn't make a scene and didn't draw any attention. I wouldn't be able to say the same if it had been Keller who'd found me. Ottar was outside waiting for us, and together, we walked back to the staff quarters, and that's when I was met with the tall, imposing monster at the end of the hallway. Hands clenching at his side and a frown deeper than the Grand Canyon. I knew at that moment it was not going to be an easy night.

And it wasn't.

I truly understand why he was so angry. I get it, but it was like going around in circles with him. I apologized several times, and he wouldn't accept it, and then I find out about the threats, the true source of his anger. I was done after that. Just add it to the list of things he hasn't told me since we got engaged. And no doubt one of the reasons he didn't tell me was because the threat was directed at him. Another thing he'll take the blame for.

Keller is so loyal and overprotective that it will be his downfall. He's still clinging to the past, to what his parents told him about his role in the castle. He's also so protective over me that he wants to shield me from everything . . . even himself.

It's not going to work . . . and that's not settling well with me.

None of this is, but because I don't have the luxury of sitting down with him and hashing this out or being able to just have a moment to myself to catch my breath, I have to push it all to the side. Put on a happy face and move on with my day.

"Are you guys fighting?" Timmy asks.

"Yes," I answer. "We barely spoke to each other this morning."

"Fuck, I'm sorry. This is all my fault. I never should have pushed you. This is the last thing you needed."

"It's fine," I reply, patting his hand with mine. "We'll work it out."

"Will you?" he asks. "From what you've said, it seems like all you two have been doing is fighting."

"I know." I take a deep breath. "We need to change the subject because I'm going to get emotional, and I can't be emotional right now. My makeup will run, and I won't have time to fix it before I meet Pala and her daughters."

"Okay, yes, let's change the subject." He pauses and asks, "Tell me about your dress . . . and did you settle on real horse-hair?" He cringes and that makes me laugh.

"Synthetic, despite age-old horsehair being prepared for me."

"Thank God for that."

———

STANDING NEXT TO KELLER, right in the entryway of the grand entrance, I try to keep my fidgeting to a minimum as a black SUV pulls up in front of the doors. Theo and Katla are outside, greeting Pala first. I thought it would be appropriate to give them a moment before I'm introduced.

Timmy is enjoying a tour around town with Henrik. Since Henrik isn't needed at the moment, he offered to take Timmy, and we thought it was a great idea, especially since this family reunion should be kept private.

I can't remember the last time Theo and Katla said they'd seen Pala or the girls, but I do know it's been a very long time, so it will be emotional to say the least.

"You good?" Keller asks, stiff as ever next to me with his hands clasped in front of him.

"Fine," I answer, leaving it at that. I can't talk to him. I can barely look at him without getting emotional, so keeping quiet while standing next to him is the best I can do.

A day ago, we would probably be holding hands right now,

but neither of us even offered. Married in three days and we can't even hold hands. What the hell has happened to us?

My bottom lip trembles . . .

No, stop thinking about it. Focus. Eyes straight ahead.

Make a good first impression.

Through the doors, I watch an elegant woman step out of the SUV, her hair streaked in gray, her aged face resembling that of my late mother's. *This is what my mother would have looked like if she was still alive.* It's such a blow to the stomach.

Breathe, Lilly, breathe.

Then it also hits me. This woman lost her sister. Has she missed my mom as much as I've missed her? Does she have any stories that Katla doesn't know?

And then her daughters follow them. One with golden blonde hair like me, long, past her shoulders and slender frame, while the other has deep red hair, thick and wavy, like Merida from *Brave*. They're stunningly gorgeous, poised, and as Theo scoops them up into his arms like the loving man he is, I can't stop the tear that falls down my cheek. Only a few months ago, he was without family surrounding him, and now . . . now it seems like his cup is full.

I swipe away at my cheek as the group walks in, Katla and Pala holding hands, something I love to see since they've had such a tumultuous relationship, but I know Katla has been working very hard at repairing it.

I step forward when they reach the entryway and don a wobbly smile.

"My dear," Pala says as she lets go of Katla's hand and walks up to me. Hands on my shoulders, her eyes well with tears as she says, "You're the spitting image of your mother. My God." And then she cries as she pulls me into a deep, long hug.

A hug that breaks through any wall I might have erected and touches my soul . . . because it feels so familiar. It feels just like my mom.

My emotions get the better of me as I lean my head into her shoulder, and I grip her tighter, a sob wracking my body. Her hand falls to my head as she lightly strokes my hair. *It's just like hugging Mom.* "Shhh," she coos. "It's okay."

I don't pull away. I simply can't. This hug seems so . . . *overdue.* It feels like my mom has come back from the grave to hold me through her sister with the strength and love that I grew up with. It nearly collapses me to my knees. *Oh, Mom, I miss you so, so much.*

The fights, the doubts, the anxious thoughts, not to mention the building anger between Keller and me . . . this is something I would have gone to my mom for. Advice. Support. *Unconditional love.* And somehow with Pala holding me, comforting me, it almost feels like my mom is right here with me. "Everything will be fine, sweet Lilly. You're not alone," Pala whispers, and that just brings more tears. That's *exactly* what my mom used to say to me. She was my rock. She always made everything better. It highlights that I've felt so alone for the past ten years. *Until I met Keller. And now that feels so strained.*

After a few more seconds, I pull away and wipe at my eyes. "I'm so sorry. I must look like a wreck."

Pala smiles and wipes her eyes as well. "I knew I should have worn the waterproof mascara. It's just so hard to get off at the end of the night."

That makes me chuckle. "My mom would have said the same thing."

"She would have." Pala puts her arm around me and turns us toward her daughters. "Lilija, my dear, I want you to meet your cousins. This is Isabella." The blonde steps forward, and I catch her bright blue eyes right before she envelops me into a hug.

"It's so nice to meet you, Lilija." And then she squeezes me tighter and whispers, "You're so brave."

Yup, that hits me right in the feels as another wave of tears falls down my cheeks.

"Gosh, I'm sorry." I go to swipe at them, but Keller steps up and hands me a handkerchief. When I glance up at him, surprised he'd have one, I realize that despite our fight last night, he thought ahead and knew this would be an emotional meeting for me.

That's Keller, though, always thinking about me.

Always putting me first.

It angers me but also makes me swoon at the same time, because he's just as important as me. I wish he would realize that.

"Thank you," I say quietly as I take the handkerchief. He fades into the background as well while the redhead steps up to me.

"And this is Marit," Pala says.

Marit with the bright green eyes and most beautiful head of hair I've ever seen.

"It's wonderful to meet you," I say as Marit pulls me into a hug as well.

"It's so great to meet you." She pulls away, and just from this brief glimpse, I can tell that Isabella is the more loving one, while Marit is the stronger one.

I just learned that they're twins, Isabella three minutes older, crowning her the heir of the throne of Marsdale. Three minutes separates sisters from the pressure of fulfilling a long history of lineage, and one being the support. I could not imagine the dynamic between them.

"Keller, of course it's so good to see you," Pala says as she walks up to Keller and pulls him into a hug. Keller lightly pats her on the back, his body size much larger than everyone else in the room with Theo coming in a close second.

"Queen Pala, always a pleasure," he says, and Pala pats his arm.

"Just Pala, we're family. No need for formality." She scans

him up and down and shakes her head. "The last time I saw you, you had about forty pounds less muscle." She chuckles. "I didn't think you could grow more, but here you are, proving me wrong."

"He eats eggs, whole, like Gaston," Theo says from behind, causing us all to laugh.

Keller then shakes Marit and Isabella's hands before Theo claps his hands together and says, "Shall we head to the sitting room and do some catching up?"

"I would love that," Pala says as she takes her girls by the hand and follows Theo and Katla. "I also planned on giving the girls a tour of the palace. Show them all the places where I got into trouble as a kid."

"Can I join you on that tour?" I ask as Keller walks next to me.

"We'd love that." Pala winks at me.

I might not know what's happening with my relationship with my fiancé, I might be at my breaking point, but this right here, this joining of families, this is what I needed at this moment more than I ever thought.

———

"THEY KEPT you at Harrogate while you trained?" Isabella asks. "Mum has told us about that place. She was terrified to stay the night."

After an hour of talking as a group, Theo, Katla, and Pala stepped aside to have their own conversation, probably to clear up any possible old feelings they might have, while I took Isabella and Marit to the other side of the room where we huddled like a bunch of teenagers to gossip. Keller left to meet Pala's security team. I heard whisperings that they could help with wedding day security.

"The first night I was there, I thought I was being haunted by a ghost. Scariest night of my life."

"I can't imagine," Isabella says. "I've grown up in our castle, and I still have moments when I'm absolutely terrified, especially when the wind starts whipping around."

"Don't say that to her," Marit reprimands while nudging her sister. "She might not come visit us if she thinks the castle is creepy."

I chuckle. "No need to worry, I think after spending time in Harrogate, nothing can bother me now."

"So Keller took you there and trained you? What was that like?" Marit asks.

I lean forward and whisper, "In all honesty, boring as hell." They both laugh. "I love Keller, but he's not the kind of professor who keeps you riveted in the teachings. Also, he was very distracting with his bulky size and built muscles."

"He is quite fit," Isabella says. "Handsome as well."

"Remind you of anyone?" Marit asks, a knowing gleam in her eyes.

Isabella shushes her sister. "How did you two fall for each other?"

"Wait, hold on." I hold up my hand. "Do you have a crush on someone?"

"Her bodyguard," Marit says, causing Isabella to full-on swat at her sister.

"Marit!"

"What?" Marit shrugs. "I thought we were sharing."

"Then share about your life, not mine."

"Is this a taboo thing?" I ask, confused as to why it matters.

Isabella sighs. "He wants nothing to do with me. I'm way too young for him, and he sees me as a job. That's it. Trust me, there is nothing there, just lust on my end. I'm sure I'll get over it. Now, back to you and Keller. How did things change from him teaching you to now being engaged?"

"Well, I told him I thought he was hot. He of course also considered me the job and wouldn't come near me. But slowly and surely, I wore him down. I knew he liked me, it was all over his expression and the way he treated me, but he wouldn't give in. So I helped him give in."

"And from there, did it just snowball?" Isabella asks.

"Yes," I answer, thinking back to the days in Harrogate. It seemed too easy back then, which is crazy because I was fresh from being plucked from everything I knew, living in a foreign country with someone I just met. And yes, it was so much more comfortable back then, when it was just us.

Now, everything is so complicated.

"I miss those days," I say honestly. "It was easier being with him. We didn't have to worry about being seen by the public, schedules, staff walking in on us all the time. We had a lot more privacy."

"Yeah, you aren't afforded much privacy when you live in the palace," Marit says. She knows from experience.

We spend the next hour talking, sharing stories, and joking around, and for the second time since I've come to Tors-kethorpe, it feels like I've found a home again. I click so easily with Marit and Isabella, so much so that they feel like sisters to me, which is surprising, given how we've been raised in such different circumstances. Born to reign, they feel so real, so down to earth, like . . . if I took them down to Miami, they wouldn't blink twice at hosing down people for a wet T-shirt contest.

And they know what I'm going through, which is the best part. They're the only ones I've met, my age, who know exactly how it feels to have the weight of the country resting on their shoulders, Isabella especially.

"Well, are we ready for that tour?" Pala asks.

The doors to the room pop open, and Keller enters. His eyes find mine, and he says, "We have our final meeting with Gothi Elias."

I sigh. "Do you think you could hold off on the tour until I'm done?" I ask Pala.

"Of course. It will give us some time to get settled in our rooms. Come find us when you're done."

"Thank you." I give them all a quick hug, and then I fall in line with Keller. He presses his hand to my lower back, and together, we walk down the hallway toward the ancestor room.

We're silent for a moment, but as we grow closer to our designated room, Keller quietly says, "Don't mention last night. It's a security risk. Nor do you mention the threat."

"I wouldn't," I say.

He doesn't say anything else, but I bet it's because he doesn't believe me. Not that I've given him much chance to believe me when it comes to keeping my mouth shut. Whenever I feel nervous or I'm in uncomfortable situations, I seem to ramble on about things, and this would be one of them.

When we reach the ancestor room, Keller opens the door for me and once again, with his hand on my back, he directs me into the room and toward the couch.

Elias is sitting on the couch across from us with a smile on his face. What maniacal shit does he have planned for us today? Our last session, my guess is, he's planned for an absolute doozy, which is great since our relationship is ready to snap.

Once I sit down, Keller unbuttons his jacket and sits next to me. Usually, his arm would drape behind me or he'd rest his hand on my thigh, but this time, he keeps to himself.

"How are we today?" Elias asks. "I saw that you got to spend time with family this morning and with your friend, Timmy. I'm sure you must be on cloud nine."

I would be if things weren't so strained with Keller.

But once again, I put on a happy face. "Oh yes, it's been overwhelming but also full of joy."

"That's great to hear." He looks at us. "Well, I know it's been a tough few weeks, but with the wedding a few days away, we're ready to walk down the aisle, don't you think?"

My initial response is to say no because Keller and I are

barely talking. How can we possibly walk down the aisle and confess our undying love for each other if we can't even look each other in the eye?

But because I want to be out of here as quickly as possible, I lie.

"Yes, so ready," I answer.

"And what about you, Keller?" Elias focuses his attention on Keller, and from the corner of my eye, I watch Keller take on a calm composure. Looks like we're both acting today.

"I've been ready since the day I asked her to marry me," he answers, his head straight, not glancing at me once.

"Good to hear. Well, our last session is just for you. I'm going to give you a half hour to just be with each other. I'm sure after the many directions you've been pulled, this is the thirty minutes that you need. When that half hour is over, I'll come back in, and we can discuss anything else that might be on your minds."

"Oh, okay," I say.

"I would like you to discuss the future and what you see it looking like. This is a conversation just between the two of you, but if you need me to facilitate any discussion, I'll be right outside the door." He rises from his chair and then walks out of the room. The soft click of the door indicating that I'm alone with Keller.

And for the first time being alone with him, I feel . . . uncomfortable.

I don't know how to talk to him. How to broach the subject of irritation between us.

He can barely look at me, and I can barely look at him.

He won't hold my hand, and I won't hold his.

This morning, instead of kissing me goodbye, he took off without looking back.

This is not how I want to spend the last days before our wedding.

Something needs to change.

Someone needs to break.

That someone is me.

Wanting to move past the elephant in the room, I turn toward him. "What do you think the future looks like?"

The muscles in his jaw tick as he leans back against the couch. "You tell me," he says. He turns his head to face me. "Do you even see a future with me?"

"Yes," I answer, my brow pinching together. And when he gives me a disbelieving look, I add, "But it feels up in the air right now."

He slowly nods. And I hate that confirmation from him.

I hate that we're both unsure of what's to come. It makes me physically sick to my stomach, because from the moment my lips touched his in Harrogate, I knew this was it. He was it. No man would ever be able to match up to him. No man would ever be able to sweep me off my feet like he does.

So why am I now even second-guessing the future with him?

"Can you face me, please? This will be easier," I ask, and he listens, positioning himself so he's leaning his side against the couch now, one leg curled up on the couch. "I don't know how to make things right between us. I'm lost, Keller."

"Me too," he answers.

"Tell me how you're feeling."

"You know how I feel. I don't need to repeat it. I've been saying the same damn thing for the last few weeks."

It's true, he has.

It was a filler question, something to keep the conversation going, but he's better than that.

"Well, are you having second thoughts about the future?"

He looks away, and my heart sinks. Keller tells it to you straight. He doesn't lie. He doesn't beat around the bush, so the fact he has to turn away when I ask him this specific question, means he's having the same thoughts as me.

"Are you?" I ask, placing my hand on his leg.

"I don't have second thoughts about my feelings for you," he says. "But fuck, Lilly. This isn't easy, and I don't know how to move past this unbearable tension between us. I don't know how to make things better. And even though I want to believe it will all be all right after we get married, I fear that it won't be."

I press my lips together as his words sink deep into me, tears welling up in my eyes because I've thought the same thing.

What if this tension doesn't change after we get married?

What if we can't ever work through these issues?

"Are you feeling this way because of what happened yesterday?" I ask.

"No," he answers, his eyes landing on me. "Yesterday . . . that scared me to my very fucking core, knowing you could have possibly been taken, hurt . . . lost." He swallows hard, and when I look into his eyes, I see just how much my decision tormented him yesterday.

I scoot in closer, and I place my hand on his. He rolls his hand so our palms connect and our fingers entwine. The uncomplicated touch warms up my cold exterior.

"I'm sorry, Keller. I'm sorry I made you worry. I'm sorry I made a decision that affected a lot of people, and I'm sorry I was so careless."

His eyes fall to our connection, and he quietly says, "Thank you."

"I won't do it again, Keller. I promise. I was naive to think that I could do something so frivolous. And now that I'm aware of the severity of my position, that not everyone in this country is a fan of mine, I'll be extra cautious."

He wets his lips and nods.

Unsure of where to go from here, I ask, "Can we just hold each other? I don't think there's much more talking I can do."

"Yeah," he answers as he lifts his arm, and still with our hands connected, I lean into his chest and he brings our hands to my front, his arm encircling me. He kisses the side of my head, and I melt into his chest.

"I love you," he whispers. "More than anything, Lilly. I would do anything for you . . . anything."

"I know," I say as a set of tears roll down my cheeks. "I love you too, Keller." I take a deep breath. "I still want to marry you. I want to live this life with you. I want to see where it takes us."

He once again leans down and presses a kiss to my head and then holds me tighter.

And as we sit there, letting the time run out on our session, all I can think about is how I told him I still want to marry him . . . but he didn't say it back.

Instead, he would do anything for me.

Anything.

What does that mean?

Is there double meaning behind it?

―――

"DID YOU HAVE A GOOD NIGHT?" Lara asks as she walks me back to my room.

"I did," I answer. "It was nice getting a tour from Pala and hearing different stories about my mom growing up and some of her favorite places in the palace. I think I've done my fair share of crying for the day."

She chuckles and bumps her shoulder with mine. "Are you feeling better?"

I let out a sigh. "Not really. I mean I've had a wonderful time meeting Pala, Isabella, and Marit, but things with Keller are still tense. During our last session with Gothi Elias today, we were supposed to talk about the future, but instead, Keller just held me. I don't know. I worry about him, Lara. He's so disconnected. It feels like there's an ocean between us, and I'm trying to swim closer to him, but the current is too strong. I don't know what to do."

Lara is silent for a moment as we pad through the carpeted halls of the palace and up the stairs to my bedroom.

"Keller can become consumed by his thoughts, especially when he's stressed or anxious. After his parents passed, it was really hard to get him not to bury deep into forgetting about the world and rather look up to see what's in front of him. I think . . . I think you need to try to get him out of his head."

"How?" I ask. "Talking is not accomplishing anything."

We pause at my bedroom door, and she speaks quietly. "I know you're not supposed to, but maybe . . . maybe find a way to be intimate with him without being fully intimate."

"Like . . . dry-hump?"

She chuckles. "I don't care what you do, but I think you need to break him out of the vicious mental cycle. Help him just forget for a moment. You have tonight, and then tomorrow it's the night before the wedding. You'll be spending that with Katla and your aunt and cousins, so if you're going to try to help him, now's the time."

I bite on the corner of my lip. "He'll push me away."

"Not if you make it impossible. This is Keller we're talking about. He's infatuated with you."

"I feel like he was. Now . . . not so sure."

"Stop that," she says. "He loves you, Lilly. Just remind him how good you are together, okay? That your physical connection, although not the main connection, is vital, and not having that has created its own challenges." I nod, and she squeezes my arm. "Good luck."

She walks away, but I say, "Hey." When she turns around, I whisper, "Do you think we'll be okay?"

A soft smile spreads across Lara's lips. "If I know one thing, it's that Keller has never, ever loved someone the way he loves you. He's loyal to his core, so when he says he's going to marry you, he will."

Chapter Thirteen

"Is everything in place?" I ask as Pickering sets a tray of tea in front of me.

He nods. "Yes. I received a call from Magnus's group. They're in position, ready. Undetected."

A smile on my face, I pour myself a spot of tea. "Excellent." With teacup in hand, I lean back in my chair and stare out my window. "Have they been able to trace anything back to us?"

Pickering shakes his head. "Not that I'm aware of. We have our top R-19 soldier gathering intelligence. It doesn't seem like they've been able to find any leads."

"Good." My smile grows. "Keller thinks he's so smart when it comes to protecting his country, his palace, and his king, but the man truly has no clue. Loyalty will only get you so far." I stir my tea. "How he thought he could climb into position and save the country from its demise is comical. Torskethorpe is a dead country with no hope."

"From what I've heard, Princess Lilija is very dependent on Keller. I believe your plan will work in our favor."

"I know it will," I answer. "And then Arkham will finally be in control, like it should have been all along."

Chapter Fourteen

KELLER

"Are you comfortable with that?" Ottar asks me as we look over the parade route one more time.

"Yes," I answer, counting the marksmen we have on every building. Thanks to Queen Pala and King Clinton of Marsdale, we have more troops to help with security and crowd control. Knowing we have that extra protection has been a huge weight off my shoulders. "And there will be officers walking the side of the carriage as well?"

"Yes," Ottar says. "And we've switched to the bulletproof glass carriage. The team has worked night and day to prepare it and ensure it's ready for the day. The crowd will be able to see you, but you'll be protected the whole time."

"Great." I let out a deep breath while dragging my hand over my face. "Fuck, I'm exhausted. I didn't get any sleep last night."

"Me neither," Ottar says. "And I just want to tell you, I'm

sorry again about the lack of focus from the guards in front of Lilly's room."

I shake my head. "Don't apologize. I don't think any of us were prepared for Lilly to slip out of the palace. She promised me she won't be as frivolous anymore." I clasp my hands together. "I told her about the threats. I didn't mean to, it slipped when we were arguing, but you were right. I think it was for the better. She seemed to take everything more seriously after that."

"It didn't freak her out?"

I shake my head. "Not like I thought it would. But then again, we were arguing when I told her, so I'm not sure it registered." I push away from the table. "I should probably get to bed."

"Are you sleeping in Lilly's room again?"

"Yes," I answer.

"Tomorrow night, you know you can't, right?"

"I know," I answer. "But tonight, I just need to make sure everything is okay. Lara will be with her tomorrow, but I want to watch over her one more night."

"I'll station one extra guard at your door."

"Thank you." I stand and, because I think he needs to know how much I appreciate him, I reach out my hand to Ottar and say, "Thank you for everything you're doing to keep us safe."

Ottar stands and shakes my hand. "Not only is it my job, but it's my pleasure."

And with that, I take off, my suit jacket slung over my shoulder, my hair a mess from pulling on it all night, and my body completely exhausted from the taxing stress I've put it through.

A couple more days, a couple more days and this will all be over.

A couple more days and I can focus on Lilly. I can put the tension, the anxious thoughts, the self-doubt all behind me.

As I make my way through the hallways, I nod at staff, making sure they know I appreciate everything they've done to help us get ready for this big occasion, and by the time I reach Lilly's room, I'm ready to pass out. But I quickly go to my room first where I strip out of my clothes, slip on a pair of shorts, and then brush my teeth.

For a moment, I stare at myself in the mirror, noticing the dark circles under my eyes and the lack of smile lines on my face. I'm drained. Running on empty and it's showing.

I lean over the sink, splash some water on my face, then dry it with a towel. Ready for bed, I turn off the lights and work my way out of my bedroom and down to Lilly's. I nod at the guards and then lightly knock on the door before opening it.

The light on her nightstand illuminates the vast space, casting shadows all around the room, but she isn't in her bed.

"Lilly?" I call out, not letting panic seep in just yet.

"In the bathroom," she calls out.

Relief washes through me, knowing that she's okay, so I walk around her room, checking to make sure the windows are locked. When I'm done, I move over to the bed and sit against the headboard, not yet getting under the covers. I let out a deep breath and lean my head back just as Lilly comes into the room. I glance to my side to catch her walking over to the bed in one of her silk robes.

My eyes scan her up and down, the way her creamy legs pop through the slit, and how her breasts press against the thin fabric, her pebbled nipples enticing me. I want her so fucking bad. It's been too long since we've been intimate, since I've been able to fall deep into her soul, to a point where we forget about everything around us, the world fading to black.

"Hey," I say as she moves past her side of the bed and rounds the foot of the bed until she's on my side.

"Hi," she says as she tugs on the tie of her robe. It loosens at her waist, and when she undoes it, the lapels of her robe fall open, revealing her naked body beneath the silk fabric. She doesn't take it off though, she leaves it on her shoulders as the open part displays her cleavage, her flat stomach, and her bare pussy.

Fuck.

Me.

"Lilly," I say softly, my voice catching in my throat as she closes the space between us and straddles my lap. My cock hardened the minute she walked into the room, so when her backside meets my lap, a satisfied look crosses her face. "What are you doing?" I ask her as her hands drag down my thick pecs.

"I need you," she says. "I need to feel close to you."

"We can't——" Her finger presses against my lips.

"We won't. We'll just play around. Theo said nothing about not playing around, just celibacy. In my mind, celibacy is the act of intercourse." She leans forward and places a few kisses along my neck, moving her lips up to my ear. "As long as your delicious cock doesn't sink deep inside me, we're good."

Christ, why did she have to put it like that?

Her lips trail back down my neck, across my chest and to the other side of my neck, hot, wet pleasure trailing along my skin. When she reaches my ear, she whispers, "Please . . . my king. Make me feel something."

My hands fall to her hips, and I dig my fingers into her side as I try to contain myself.

"Just make me come once," she says. "I need to get lost with you. Help me forget everything else." Her teeth bite into my neck, and I groan as I move my hands to the inside of her robe and up her rib cage, her soft skin like fuel to the flame that's lighting up inside me.

"God, you're already so hard," she whispers as her hips slowly rotate over my cock. "And I'm dripping . . . wet . . ."

Fuck.

I can't.

I can't sit here and not touch her.

Not kiss her.

Not bring her pleasure.

Not when I need this too.

Not when I need to get lost as well.

And just like that, my will snaps as my eyes fall to her beautiful body, my desire so overwhelming that I take what I want.

I place my hand on her slender shoulder and slowly slide down one side of her robe, so her shoulder is exposed and the fabric pools at her elbow. Pleased with the amount of skin at my disposal, I lower my mouth to her neck, reciprocate the kisses she was giving me, letting my teeth lead the way.

"Yes," she gasps just as I take one of her breasts in my palm and squeeze it. My palm full, I revel in the feel of her breast, in her sexy reaction as I move my mouth to the juncture of her shoulder and bite down, causing her to cry out. Her delicate skin easily fades into a shade of red with every pass of my mouth, every nibble of my teeth. The tension in my muscles that have been bunching at the base of my neck, creating headaches and unease, dissipates with every acute moan that falls past her lips.

Pleased with her response, I lap the same spot of her neck after every time I bite down. I keep my bite marks on her neck to a minimum, not wanting to make it too hard for her to cover up tomorrow, but also making my mark, wickedly reminding her who exactly she fell in love with in the first place.

"Yes, my king," she whispers as my mouth falls to her shoulder and my hand crawls up to her neck where I grip it possessively. I feel the gasp in her throat from the surprise of my grip, and then the sigh as I force her to move her head to the side.

"I've dreamed every night of possessing this beautiful neck," I say. "Of marking it, making sure no one else thinks they have even the slightest fucking chance to be with you. Because you're mine, Lilly. All fucking mine."

"Yours, my king," she says breathlessly. I drag my tongue along the column of her neck, all the way to her jaw where I pepper kisses up to her ear, keeping a strong hold on her neck the entire time. "I belong to you."

"Don't you fucking forget it," I reply as my hand slides to her jaw. My thumb digs into the spot just below her ear as I tilt her head back, giving me full access to her neck. My lips suck along the column, spending my precious time maneuvering over the spots that I know will make her wetter with need. Her hands scrape along my pecs, her fingernails digging into my skin like sharp, yet pleasurable knives moving over my nipples and down to my stomach, driving up my hunger for this woman.

My lips move to just the corner of her mouth that parts open on a heavy breath. She attempts to move her head to the side, to match my lips with hers, but I grip her jaw tighter, holding her in place only to lightly lick the corner of her mouth. Her body melts into mine, her breath catching in her throat as her fingers dig deeper into my pecs.

"You want my mouth?" I ask her.

"Yes," she answers breathlessly.

"This is all you're getting for now," I say as I run my tongue along her lips, but to my surprise, she pulls it into her mouth with a deep suck. All I can imagine is replacing my tongue with my cock.

I growl under my breath and remove my tongue before I tip her back on the bed. Her robe fans open, exposing her pink nipples begging to be sucked and the flush of her skin from my roaming hands and mouth. I lean over her, one hand on either side of her head as I bow forward to press the lightest of kisses on her cheek.

Her hand slides between us, and she cups me. I almost pull away for a second, but when she grips me tighter, a long hiss escapes my lips, and I let her play with me for a moment.

"You're huge," she says as her palm runs the length of my erection. "God, I miss your cock so much." She slips her hand past my waistband and cups my balls lightly before dragging her hand all the way up my length, sending a jolt of pleasure up my spine.

"That's enough," I say, feeling my body grow far too excited.

"But I want this cock," she says. "I want it inside me. I want it dragging over my skin. I want it on my face, in my mouth, coming all over me. I've never wanted something so bad in my life." The whole time she's confessing this, she's rubbing up and down my length. My stomach hollows out from the feeling, my pelvis slightly thrusting with her touch. That's how desperate I am. That's how much I want it too.

Fuck.

It feels too good.

So good that I let her stroke me a few more times, my balls enjoying every pass of her fingers, my body breaking out in a light sheen of sweat from the touch. It's been so goddamn long that I could get off just like this, her hand down my briefs, my pelvis slightly thrusting.

My teeth roll over my bottom lip, and just as my pleasure spikes, I dig my hands into the mattress and say, "Hands behind your back." A confused look passes over her eyes. "Now," I demand.

She removes her hand from my briefs, and I help her lift from the mattress by looping my hand around her back. After she places her hands behind her, I lay her back down on the bed carefully. In this position, her tits are more pronounced, her nipples pointed straight up into the air. She has zero control over the position, which is exactly what both of us want.

I back off the bed and keep my eyes on her as I lower my

shorts and briefs to the floor. My erection springs forward, and her expression morphs from happy to hungry as she takes in my length. The same feeling passes over me as I take in her submissive body, ready for my next command.

I bring my hand to her mouth and say, "Lick it."

She pokes that beautiful tongue out and laps at my hand a few times. Once it's really wet, I stroke my cock, letting her saliva act as a lubricant.

"Keller," she squirms, spreading her legs even more. She's so ready. Her pretty cunt glistens, begging for my touch, begging for my cock.

"Are you telling me what to do?" I ask her as I lower and slap my hand over her pussy. Not too hard, but hard enough for her entire body to seize and her eyes to water with pleasure.

"Holy . . . fuck," she breathes out.

"You like that, love?" I ask.

She nods, so I do it again. She moans louder, and I watch as she drips around her clit. Fuck, she likes it a lot.

My tongue passes over my lips, pleased that I've found a new way to pleasure her. Hand holding my cock, I slap her pussy again, but this time, my fingers drag over her slit after.

Her eyes squeeze shut as she murmurs, "I . . . I'm so close."

"Already?" I ask. "I've barely touched you."

"This is what you do to me."

Foolish pride surges through my chest. *This is what I do to her.* I own her. I give her exactly what she wants. She will never find anyone who knows her pleasure better than I do. And with that thought, I pull on her legs until her ass is at the edge of the bed. Her robe bunches up behind her, but I don't bother fixing it. In fact, I need to use it to my advantage.

"Sit up," I say.

Confused, she sits up, and I push the robe off her shoulders. I pull it from behind her and then whip the robe tie out of its loops. With the long silk tie, I lower to her legs and tie her ankles together, looping the silk thread a few times until they're secure. When I lift back up, I turn her on her back and bend her legs so her heels touch her butt.

"Give me your arms," I say. She moves them behind her, and I take her robe. I hold the ends out and whip it around until it's a thin rope, the perfect size to use as a tie. I maneuver the fabric, looping and crisscrossing until her hands are tied to her ankles, leaving her unable to move. I caress her back and ask, "Are you okay?"

"Yes," she answers.

"Nothing hurts?"

"Nothing, my king," she answers.

"Good." I turn her back over so she's kneeling now, her shins and knees holding her up, while her hands prop up her upper body, giving me access to her entire body without the interruption of her trying to touch me. "Tell me if you need a new position."

She nods as I bring my cock to her stomach. I drag the tip over her skin, around her belly button, and down to her pussy. She sucks in a sharp breath as I lower the tip to her exposed clit. Because her legs are spread for stability, I'm able to slide the tip of my cock right over her arousal.

"Oh fuck," she yells as I seek out her warmth. Never penetrating her, I stay on the outside, just teasing us. "Keller, it feels so good. Too good."

I pull away and slap the side of her ass, causing her eyes to widen in shock.

"You will address me appropriately."

"Sorry," she stammers. "My king . . . it feels too good."

"Better," I reply as I grip the back of her neck and bring her closer to me, offering her support in the uncomfortable position. I bring my mouth to her porcelain skin and mark it with my teeth, branding her shoulder, biting into her skin and then pressing kisses to the marred spot. With every nibble, she cries out in pleasure, her body turning more and more limp under my touch as she escapes to another world. I follow with her, dragging my mouth to her breasts where I suck in her nipples, my tongue sliding over her nipple rings.

I tug on them.

Pull.

Devour until she's practically crying in my arms, seeking her release.

I drag my tongue down to her stomach as well until I reach right above her pussy.

"Yes," she calls out. "Please."

I press a few kisses right where she wants them, but instead of using my tongue, I lift and slide my cock over her clit again. This time, though, I do it at a rapid rate, flicking the head quickly while I slide my hand behind her back to give her more support.

"Oh my God," she cries out. "I'm . . . I'm right there."

She is.

I can feel it in the tension of her body, in how wet she is, in how her jaw drops open, her orgasm on the precipice.

So I flick her clit harder.

Faster.

Her moans fall into the silent night.

Her teeth bite her bottom lip.

Her skin breaks out into a small sweat.

"Oh fuck . . . oh God." Her muscles tense. "My king, I need to come."

I almost tell her not to, but she's too far gone. There's no stopping her. Her orgasm is right on the cliff, ready to fall over.

"Come," I say, and within seconds, her body stiffens right before it shudders and convulses as she comes on the head of my cock.

"Oh my fucking God," she says through clenched teeth, her eyes squeezed shut. Watching her come apart like that is the most beautiful thing I've ever seen. It's so goddamn sexy that my cock swells in my hand. My orgasm so fucking ready.

I flip her to her stomach so she's lying on the mattress, and she turns her head to the right so she can breathe. Her legs and arms are connected at just the right position that I can slip my cock up against her ass. I spread her cheeks and fit my erection between them.

"Jesus," she mutters as I spank her, causing her ass cheeks to clench around me.

"That's a good girl," I say as I spank her again.

Her warmth surrounds me, squeezing me tight. The sensation feels so good that I do it again, leaving a bright red handprint on her perfect behind. Another way to mark her, another reminder that she belongs to me.

This time, when I spank her, I thrust my hips, so when she squeezes, I'm accompanied with the delicious sensation of friction.

I've never done this before, but fuck does it feel amazing, her tight warmth fucking me with every slap to her ass. It's so goddamn sexy.

I spank her a few more times, thrusting, seeking out my own release, and after the sixth one, I'm panting, sweat forming on my lower back, my legs trembling beneath me. I'm going to fucking come.

Instead of spanking her, I grip her legs, and I thrust back and forth. She squeezes her cheeks together anyway, holding me in place, and as my orgasm builds and builds, I pull away from her and slip two fingers inside her.

"Fuck, you're still wet."

"You spanked me, my king, of course I'm wet."

Jesus. I move my hand so I'm able to rub her clit with my pinky and curl my fingers inside her. She cries out as her walls contract around my hand.

With my other hand, I pump my cock, hard, from base to tip until my balls start to tighten up.

"Where's my good girl at? Are you close?"

"So . . . close," she says right before she clenches, and her body tightens again, her orgasm tipping her over the edge. That's all I need. I pump harder on my cock to the sound of her delicious moans and lean forward, and as my stomach bottoms out and my cock swells with my cum, I deposit right on her back, leaving one last mark for the night.

"Fucking . . . hell." I finish pulsing my hand inside her and drag my other hand over my length.

After a few moments of catching our breath, I release her legs and arms and then press my hand to her lower back, leaning forward so my lips are against her ear. "Don't move. I need to clean you up."

I move to the bathroom, find a washcloth, and wet it with warm water.

When I come back out into her bedroom and see her naked body marked by my handprint, by my teeth, by my cum, more pride surges through me. This woman who captured my heart months ago, she's mine, and I'm going to marry her soon.

All the stress has been washed away at this moment.

I move around her, wipe up her back and then wipe between her legs as well. I drop the washcloth to the floor and roll her to her back so she's looking up at me. I close the distance between us, grip her jaw tightly, and then press a kiss to her lips. She loops her arms around me and pulls me closer.

Our bodies melt together.

My chest to her chest.

My heart to her heart.

My nose to her nose.

Our breaths sync.

Our pulse thumps in rhythm.

And for the first time in a month, I feel reconnected to her.

After a few moments of staring into each other's eyes, she says, "I love you, Keller."

Those four words bury much-needed warmth into my cold veins.

"I love you, Lilly," I reply as I pick her up into my arms and bring her to her side of the bed. I lay her down and then go to her bathroom where I saw her pajama set over the tub. I take them into the bedroom and slip on the silk pants and then pull her to her feet so she can situate them around her waist. Next, I pull her top over her head before slipping her arms inside. With a kiss to her forehead, I lay her down on the bed and draw the covers over her body. I put my briefs and shorts back on before sliding into bed as well.

She turns her light off and slides across the bed so she's resting her head in the crook of my shoulder and arm. I bring my arm around her and slip my hand under the waistband of her pants so my palm is resting on her skin. She kisses my chest and sighs.

We don't say anything.

We just drift off to sleep, and for the first time since I was asked to stay in another room, I get the best night's rest I've ever had.

Not one nightmare.

Not one worry.

Just me and my girl.

It's all I'll ever need.

"GOOD MORNING," Runa says, coming into the room and opening a curtain.

Lilly groans and curls into me, clearly not happy about the wake-up call.

After last night, neither am I.

What I wouldn't give to spend all morning in bed with her,

holding her close . . . possibly having a repeat of what we did last night, but this time, slipping my cock all the way inside that delicious tight hole of hers.

"I see that we're in another fun mood today," Runa says as she moves about the room. "I'm going to pick out your clothes and rest them on the tub while you get yourself together."

Runa leaves the room, and Lilly curls into me. She drapes one leg over my waist and an arm over my stomach as her head buries deeper in my chest. She's so warm, so soft, that I allow myself this moment and pull her in tighter.

I kiss the top of her head, inhaling her sweet scent.

"Morning," I say softly.

"Good morning," she says as she kisses my chest, her lips soft and enticing. If Runa wasn't in here, I might have pressed her into the mattress and made out with her. "Tomorrow is the big day." She lifts up to look at me. "Are you excited?"

"I'm ready to be your husband," I answer.

"Good answer." She sighs and moves her finger over my chest as she says, "Today, I won't see much of you, so thank you . . . for last night and for staying in my bed."

I cup her cheek, her glittering eyes captivating me. "You don't need to thank me."

She leans her face into my hand and rubs against my palm just as there's a knock on the door.

"Come in," I call out.

Ottar appears at the door, his face neutral, but from the way he entered, I can tell he needs to tell me something. "Keller, can we have a moment?"

Lilly glances over her shoulder. "Is everything okay?"

"Yes," Ottar answers. "Just a change in the parade route that I want to confirm."

"Oh." She turns back to me and presses a kiss to my cheek. "Have lunch with me later?"

"Yes," I answer as I slip out of bed, my mind fixated on

what Ottar has to tell me. I grab my phone and head toward the door when Lilly calls after me.

"Are you going to kiss me goodbye?" she asks.

Fuck, right.

I move back over to the bed, lean forward, and give her a chaste kiss. When I pull away and she frowns, I smirk and grip the back of her head where I press my lips deeper against hers, parting her mouth with my tongue. She lightly moans, leaning into the connection, and even though Ottar waits, I take that moment to drive my tongue into her mouth. Her fingers dig into the back of my head, and before things can get carried away, I pull away.

Satisfied, she flops back down on the bed.

"Love you," she says, looking far too fucking beautiful with her hair splayed across the pillow, dreamy eyes staring up at me.

"Love you, Lilly."

I give her one more parting look before I head out the door with Ottar. We go straight to my bedroom where Ottar shuts the door and says, "We believe we've caught the person."

"Really?" I ask, spinning around to face him. "Who?"

"One of the guards was at the Crowned Cod last night and overheard someone talking about planting a bomb on the parade route, on the way to Norse Temple, and setting it off right before the wedding. They called us right away and we arrested them. It was someone from Arkham. What we expected. They're in holding right now and their apartment is being searched."

I push my hand through my hair and blow out a deep breath. "Fuck, really?"

Ottar nods. "Yes. But we're still holding steady with our original security plan, and the parade route is being swept for any explosives. This could be a decoy."

"Is that what you're leaning toward?" I ask.

"I think it's best that we keep all our options open at the moment. I'm not entirely convinced that this is taken care of." He glances away, and I can tell there's something that he's not saying.

"What?" I ask him. "What are you not telling me?"

He folds his arms at his chest and leans against the door. "Can I be candid?"

"Yes," I answer.

"I don't think the person we caught last night is the person sending the letters. I have this sick feeling something else is planned. I mean, why would this guy purposely go into the Crowned Cod, a place where numerous staff drink at the end of the night, and start spouting off about his plans? It feels too convenient."

"Yeah, it does, doesn't it?" I ask as I take a seat on my bed. "So what do you think it was all about?"

"I don't know, but I think whatever they have planned isn't about to be discussed in a public forum."

"Do you think we should call off the wedding?" I ask. "Because I fucking will. I'll call it off right now. I'll be damned if I let anything happen to Lilly."

"I don't think that's a good idea. I'm not sure it would look good for the country, for you."

"Fuck what people think about me," I say. "Do you really think I care about that? I would rather my girl be safe, protected. Who knows what this lunatic has planned."

Ottar drags his hand over his chin and says, "I just think it would look bad."

"Once again, I don't care how it looks. Has this been brought to Theo's attention?"

"Not yet. I went to speak to him, but he was taking a little longer to get out of bed."

"Is he okay?" I ask, my body on alert now.

"According to his esquire, Theo had a rough night last night and couldn't fall asleep, so he slept in longer."

"Well, let me shower and get dressed. Give me five minutes, we can talk to him together."

━━━

OTTAR and I are escorted into the king's private sitting room where he's enjoying a traditional Torskethorpian breakfast of oatmeal, Skyr with jam, and cod liver. I've never been into the cod liver, but Theo has always been a fan.

He glances up at us with a smile. "Hello, boys, to what do I owe the pleasure?"

"How are you feeling?" I ask him, just wanting to make sure everything is good physically with him.

"Great," he says. "My boy and my granddaughter are getting married tomorrow, nothing to complain about." He points his spoon at me. "Are you digging a sword up from a grave tonight?"

"Uh . . . no," I say.

"But it's tradition," he says with a sweep of his hand, truly in the jolliest of moods.

"I really don't feel comfortable breaking into a crypt to retrieve a sword."

Theo chuckles, a deep rumble lifting from his chest. "I get it. It was weird when I did it, and I felt haunted for months after." He scoops up a solid bite of oatmeal and asks, "What can I help you two with?"

I let Ottar take the lead as we both sit on the couch across from Theo. "We were informed last night of a man who was talking about his plans to ruin the wedding last night. He was captured at the Crowned Cod and brought into custody."

Theo's brows lift in surprise as he sets his spoon down and dabs his mouth with his cloth napkin. "Really? Well, that's great news. Why the morose faces?"

"Well, I'm to believe that maybe he wasn't the person we were after."

"Why would you assume that?" Theo asks Ottar.

"The dots aren't quite connecting for me. The man was from Arkham, but I'm not sure where the connection to Keller comes in. I just believe there's more to it," Ottar answers.

I continue, "And we believe that something bigger will happen, that this man was a possible decoy to throw us off."

Theo strokes his beard. "I see. But we have the best security out there right now. People are lining the streets. What do you suggest? To make it even tighter with protection?"

I glance at Ottar and then say, "Calling the wedding off."

"Absolutely not," Theo says, shaking his head. "That's not an option. Calling off the wedding would be terrible for this country. Not only because of the money we put into it but also because it would give the perception that our monarchy is crumbling, and it's not. It's thriving."

"I understand," I say in a calming tone. "But we don't know the grand scope of what could happen. Wouldn't you want to be better safe than sorry?"

Theo shakes his head. "If you need to call in more troops, shorten the parade route again, do it. Do what you need to do to secure the safety that would make you comfortable. But calling off the wedding will not be an option. Understood?"

"Yes, sir," Ottar and I say at the same time.

Theo picks up his spoon again. "Now, don't you have a final fitting you need to get to?"

"Yes," I say as I stand with Ottar. We both bow and exit the room. When the door is shut, I lean toward Ottar and whisper, "What the fuck do we do now?"

"Tighten up," Ottar says. "We have no other choice than to tighten up."

Chapter Fifteen

LILLY

"I can't believe you're getting married," Timmy says as I slip into my wedding dress behind a partition. "It was like only yesterday when you came up with the idea to sell bikinis out of the back of the truck and attract attention with a wet T-shirt contest."

"She did what?" Isabella asks on a laugh.

"Don't listen to him," I call over the partition as Runa buttons up the back of my dress. "He doesn't have the best memory."

Timmy laughs. "Girl, what are you trying to hide? Your personal life is out there for everyone to read with one Internet search."

"He's right," Marit calls out. "I just looked it up on my phone, and there's even a picture of you with the bikini truck."

I poke my head past the partition to look at them on the couch. "There are pictures?" I ask, horrified.

"No." Marit laughs. "But the look on your face is priceless."

I point at her. "I'm going to need to watch out for you."

"You are." She smiles at me before Runa pulls me back to finish up with the buttons.

Pala and Katla are having tea in the glass room, wanting to give me time with my cousins and Timmy. They said they'd see the grand reveal of the dress tomorrow. I thought it was a great plan because I truly want Pala and Katla to mend their relationship, which they've been doing. It's so great to see.

Once Runa is done, she strokes down my dress, adjusting any wrinkles, and turns me around. Her eyes meet mine, and a lovely smile crosses her face. "Princess Lilly, you look stunning."

"Really?" I ask as I glance down at the heavily laced dress with bell sleeves that hang perfectly down my arms.

Runa adjusts my hair and nods. "Keller is a very lucky man."

"Thank you," I say, feeling giddy.

"Let us see," Timmy calls out. "I'm frothing at the mouth over here."

Chuckling, I move from behind the partition and show them my dress. It fits like a glove, tailored specifically for my curves. The sleeves hang off my shoulders while the neckline dips down, providing a glimpse of cleavage but still maintaining a look of class. Runa was able to help me cover up my bite mark from Keller, thankfully. The bodice clings to my torso but relaxes at the hips, draping along my legs and giving me a very regal yet fairy-like feel.

"Wow," Isabella says as she clasps her hands together in front of her chest. "Lilly, that's gorgeous."

"I'm stunned," Marit says. "Absolutely stunned."

Timmy stands from the couch and walks up to me, tears in his eyes as he pulls me into a hug. "Dear God, Lilly, you're a vision."

I hug him back, tears welling in my eyes as well.

"I mean that," he adds as he pulls away and looks me up and down. "You've always been beautiful, but this, this wedding, this place, it brings out a piece of you I don't think I've ever seen before." He grips my hand in his. "You're happy, Lilly. You're truly happy."

"I am," I reply. "I'm so happy. I have family." I glance over at Marit and Isabella. "I have roots. I have the love of my life waiting to wed me tomorrow. I can truly say that at this moment, I don't think I've ever been happier."

Timmy pulls me into a hug, and I fit into the crook of his neck, holding him tight.

⬛

LILLY: *Where are you? I was able to bring lunch up to my room.*

Keller: *I can't make it.*

Lilly: *What do you mean you can't make it? You said we could have lunch today. It's our last time to be alone together before the wedding.*

Keller: *Something has come up. I'm sorry, Lilly.*

Lilly: *Okay. Well, when can I see you?*

Keller: *Probably at rehearsal.*

Lilly: *Can you at least save a moment for me at rehearsal? A moment to just be alone with each other?*

Keller: *Yes. I'll see you there.*

Lilly: *I love you, Keller.*

Keller: *Love you.*

⬛

"I HAVEN'T SEEN you all day," I say to Lara as we drive together to Norse Temple. I poke her leg. "You missed me in my dress."

"I know, I'm sorry. It's been a busy day today. How did it fit?"

"Great," I answer as I lean my head back against the car seat. "It felt so surreal, I can't believe I'm actually getting married tomorrow. Oh, and I did what you said last night, with Keller." I wiggle my eyebrows at her. "It worked."

"It did?" she asks, almost surprised at her own advice.

"Yes, it was perfect."

She nods and looks away. "So everything feels okay to you? Everything between you two?"

"Yes," I say, dragging my answer out because she seems skeptical. "What are you not saying?"

"Nothing." Lara shakes her head, but I know she's lying.

"Lara, what's going on?"

"It's nothing." When I poke her again, she adds on a sigh, "I just saw Keller earlier and he wasn't his normal self, that's all. I think he's just stressed, trying to make sure everything is in place."

"Is that what he was doing?" I ask. "He missed lunch with me, and I was sort of upset about it, but figured he had a good reason."

"Yes, well, they caught someone last night at the Crowned Cod who was planning to set off an explosive tomorrow."

"Really?" I ask. "Oh my God."

"I believe it shook him and Ottar. They're working on tightening everything, and I've spent extra time with the palace guard checking over their routes. We're on high security at the moment, so I'm sure that's what's keeping him preoccupied."

"Yeah, probably," I say. "Do you think he's going to be okay?"

"Yes," Lara answers. "Everything will be great."

She pats my hand, but despite her best efforts, my excitement has fallen, and dread has reared its ugly head. My mind falls to the past few weeks we've had.

The arguments.

The disbelief.

The doubt.

The loneliness.

The articles . . .

"He's going to show up tomorrow, right?"

Lara glances over at me. "He'll be there. Guaranteed. If he doesn't get there himself, Ottar and I will get him there."

"Now that's romantic, having the groom's security detail shove him down the aisle with brutal force. That's what dreams are made of. A true happily ever after."

"He will be there, Lilly," she reassures me.

"Okay," I answer as I look out the window.

For the rest of the drive, we're silent. Lara most likely is replaying her many responsibilities and checklists off in her head, while I take even, steady breaths, reminding myself of last night, the way Keller touched me, controlled me . . . loved me. Even how he held me last night, like I was the most precious thing in his life that he didn't want to let go.

Stop letting doubt creep into your head.

Stop letting fear slip into your bones.

Everything will be good.

He missed lunch because he's working with Ottar on tightening things. Nothing more, nothing less.

When we arrive at Norse Temple, guards greet us and open the door. Lara briefly looks around before moving to the side to let me out. Dressed in a white coat dress with my hair in curls, I look up just in time to spot Keller inside the arch of the door, waiting for me.

Perfect in a dark-blue suit, white button-up shirt with the top few buttons undone, he looks so dreamy as he stands there, his eyes set on me.

Smiling, I move past the guards, straight into the arch where he lightly moves his hand to my back and pulls me in close to him. He lifts my chin and lowers his mouth to mine for a chaste but perfect kiss.

"I'm sorry about lunch," he whispers.

And just like that, the fears are washed away and replaced with the same feelings I had last night.

Security.

Love.

Affection.

See, everything is perfectly fine.

"It's okay." I smooth my hand over his chest. "You missed a good time. I really went to town on a cucumber sandwich."

He chuckles. "Something I'll always regret missing."

Adela walks in, clipboard in hand with her assistant following closely behind. What's her name again? Cornolia?

I think that's it.

Her large glasses and bangs cover up most of her eyes, but they always seem to be downturned, like she can't gather enough courage to make herself known.

"There's the happy couple," Adela says. "How are we today?"

"Good," I say. "How are you? Busy, I'm sure."

"We are, but the good kind of busy with our final preparations. Everything has come together beautifully. Wait until you see the temple." She gestures her arm to the door that leads to the main temple.

Hand in hand, Keller and I walk through another arched doorway and into the vast main area, but instead of the impersonal space I initially saw, the stone walls are covered in dark green drapes and gilded in birch trees, extending toward the ceiling, almost giving the same feel as Frigga's Sanctuary. White and yellow flowers descend the aisle and up the pews, bringing a very vibrant, earthy feel to the space.

"Oh my God," I say, taking in as much as I can. "It's breathtaking in here."

"Do you like it?" Adela asks just as Katla walks up from the front of the temple. "We wanted to bring the sanctuary into the temple since you loved it so much."

"This is everything I could have asked for." Katla takes my other hand in hers and squeezes it tight.

"I'm glad you like it." Now from the front, Theo walks down the aisle, a cane in his hand as he slowly makes his way. Keller lets go of my hand and heads to where he holds his arm out to him. Theo just pats him on the shoulder and whispers something.

Together they join the group, and the whole time, I take in the sight before me. The two men who aren't connected by blood but have an unbreakable bond that goes further than any DNA. They have a mutual respect.

"This is beautiful," Theo says, raising his arm to the tall, fake trees. "Tomorrow will be a celebration to remember."

"It will be," Adela says. "I actually have a few things I need to go over with you quickly, Your Highness. Would you mind joining me?"

Theo shakes his head, and they walk over to his chair in front of the altar and hunker down for a conversation. I take that moment to drag Keller down the aisle, my arm threaded through his.

"I can't believe this. It's stunning. Did you know they were doing this?"

He nods. "It was a suggestion I made."

"Really?" I ask, looking up at him.

"Yes. I knew how much you loved Frigga's Sanctuary. I asked if there was a way to bring its ambiance to Norse Temple."

I turn toward him now and sigh as I reach my hand to his shoulder. "You're so good to me."

His hands loop around my back, pulling me into his chest. "I just want to make you happy."

"You have," I say. "You've made me happier than I could ever imagine."

"Good . . . because you're mine . . . forever." He leans down with a kiss, just as the front door to the temple opens,

Henrik hustling down the aisle. Keller frowns and asks, "Everything okay?"

Henrik adjusts his glasses. "Just some protesters gathering outside the temple."

"Protesters?" Keller asks as he releases my hand and moves past us.

"Ottar and Lara are handling them," Henrik says. "But I would like to get ahead of any press coverage."

Keller ignores him and goes to the front. I follow closely, and when he parts the door, we're flooded with a chant.

"Not our prince. Not our prince."

It's all we hear before Ottar steps up to the door and into the temple. "This is none of your concern. Go back to your rehearsal."

I glance at Keller and catch the telltale sign of his hardened jaw.

"Is it a threat?" he asks, teeth clenched.

"No," Ottar answers. "Just a small group trying to cause problems. It's being handled." When Keller doesn't move, Ottar stands taller and says, "It's handled. Go back to the rehearsal."

After a staredown that actually makes me shiver in my heels, Keller turns away, only to find me right behind him. "Lilly," he says, surprised.

"Don't," I say, taking his hand. "Don't let them get to you."

"I'm not," he says as he walks us back up to the head of the temple where everyone is gathered.

"Promise me," I say, growing nervous that his attitude changed so quickly.

"Promise," he says, squeezing my hand three times.

Three . . . times.

Our signal.

That's all I need. This will be okay. Everything will be okay.

REHEARSAL TOOK LONGER than I expected. Adela and Theo were finishing up some important details, traditions Adela wanted to make sure she got right, so when we arrive back at the palace, Katla gives me about five minutes to say goodbye to Keller before she whisks me away for the maidenhood rituals, something I'm still very much in the dark about. And you know what? I even tried to look it up on the Internet, but it seems to be a tight-lipped, royal family activity because I found nothing. Not one single piece of information to prepare me.

Knowing I'm expected up in my room right now, I turn toward Keller and rest my hands on the lapels of his suit jacket. "I hate that I won't be able to spend the night with you."

He rubs his hands up and down my back softly. "Me too."

"Nor will I see you until we're at Norse Temple. That's too long."

"The wedding is early, so you'll see me sooner than you think." He bends down and presses a kiss to my lips. "Have fun with the girls, and I'll see you tomorrow . . . my wife."

I smile up at him. "My husband . . . my king."

He tilts my jaw up with his thumb and steals one more kiss, this one is longer, deeper, full of promises and the future as his tongue swipes inside my mouth. I reciprocate the movement, getting lost in the way he possesses me. And when he pulls away, not putting much distance between us at all, he cups my cheek and softly says, "I love you, Lilly. You have my heart . . . forever."

"You have mine," I say.

Ottar walks up behind Keller and puts his hand on his shoulder. "Come on, you're with me."

Lara comes up to me as well. "I'll take you to your room."

"Take good care of her," Keller says, a slight worry in his eyes.

"I will," Lara says.

I point at Ottar and say, "You take good care of Keller too."

"He's mine until tomorrow, you can count on it."

"Good." I reach up and give Keller one more kiss. "See you tomorrow."

"See you tomorrow," he says. Lara takes me down the halls, toward my bedroom.

———

"NOW," Katla says, hands clasped together. "Strip down, it's time to wash the maidenhood off you."

Okay, so when I say I wasn't prepared for what tonight would bring, I was one hundred percent right because the moment I walked into my bedroom to find a large copper tub in the middle of the room and washcloths lined up with soap, I knew I was in trouble.

"Um . . . what now?" I ask as Katla stands before me, Isabella, Marit, and Pala behind her, all of them wearing robes.

With a pleased smile, Katla says, "It's tradition that the women of the family wash down the bride the night before the wedding. This is to scrub the virginity off you so you're ready for your new husband."

I nearly choke on my own saliva.

Scrub the virginity?

Yeah, that was scrubbed off years ago.

"So you want me to get naked in front of all of you, sit in that tub, I'm assuming, while you wash me? Like . . . do you scrub between my privates? Have me bend over for better access?"

Everyone laughs while Katla shakes her head. "No, dear.

A bathing suit awaits you. We just shower you with love, some essential oils, and then we will braid your hair while we chat. Runa has left a wonderful spread of crackers, cheese, and fruit for us to munch on as well."

"Oh . . . okay," I say, the nerves starting to fade away. "Because I know I used to be down for a wet T-shirt contest, but I don't quite think I'm ready to get naked in front of my newfound family yet."

"I don't think we are either," Marit calls out.

Katla pats my hand. "Go ahead, get changed. We'll be waiting for you."

Runa stands by the bathroom and guides me in. She helps me out of my coat dress, and when she turns me around, she says, "You know, I never said anything about the new marks on your shoulder." She raises a brow at me.

"Oh yeah . . ." I nervously laugh. "Weird, right? I bumped into a wall and blammo, bruised."

"Very weird," she says skeptically. "Because they look awfully similar to the bite marks Keller leaves on you."

"Hmm, what a coincidence."

Runa just shakes her head and helps me out of my stockings, bra, and underwear, then hands me the bathing suit. I don't mind being naked in front of Runa—everyone else is a problem.

"Take a seat," she says once I'm dressed.

I sit at the vanity in the bathroom, and she gathers my hair into a bun on the top of my head.

"I thought they said they were braiding it."

"They will, but first, the oil water has to be poured on you, and you don't want your hair mixing with that."

"Oh, makes sense." I look up at Runa through the reflection of the mirror and ask, "Have you done this before?"

"A few times," she says. "It's fun. A nice way to settle the nerves the night before the wedding." She finishes my hair and places her hands on my shoulders. "I'm very happy for you, Lilly. It's been my distinct honor serving you."

"Runa," I say, getting choked up. "Don't make me freaking cry."

She chuckles and pats my shoulders. "Come now, they're waiting."

Chapter Sixteen

KELLER

"Here," Ottar says, bringing a tumbler of whiskey over to me.

We're both in the kitchen—seasoned cod with roasted vegetables in front of us, thanks to the chef, and some fruit tarts for dessert. Not sure the whiskey will settle well with those, but we'll see.

"Thanks." I hold the tumbler up to him, and he clinks his glass with mine.

"One only, we don't need you hungover tomorrow. But one will help with the nerves."

I take a sip of the amber liquid, enjoying the initial burn down my throat. "I don't have any nerves about tomorrow," I say.

"No?" he asks.

I shake my head as I break into my cod. "No. I know Lilly is supposed to be mine."

Ottar nods slowly. "That much is obvious from the way you two look at each other."

I bump his shoulder with mine. "I would say Lara looks at you the same way."

Ottar shakes his head. "No, I don't think so."

"Why do you say that?" I ask, happy for the attention to be off me for a moment.

Ottar sets his glass of whiskey down and picks up his fork. "You're not the only one who's suffered through the planning of this wedding. The stress of security has taken a toll on us. We've gotten in quite a few fights."

"Really? Why haven't you said anything?" I ask.

"Didn't want to bother you. It's hard, being on the job and trying to date someone who works with you. We have different opinions on how to run things. We've just clashed, and I think we're working through that. We were supposed to go on a date the other night, but she canceled, said she wanted to focus on the wedding. I understood, but I felt she was avoiding me." Ottar shrugs. "Might be best. I know she struggled with Brimar."

"She struggled with Brimar because he didn't treat her right. He cheated on her and committed treason. He wasn't the man for her. I know she's moved on from that."

Ottar slips a forkful of cod in his mouth, and he chews while I stab a few pieces of broccoli. "I guess we'll see what happens after the wedding." He lifts his tumbler to his lips and takes another sip. "What a fucking whirlwind. If you truly look at what you've been through in the past couple of months, it's impressive."

"Yeah, I'm still trying to comprehend it all." I wipe my mouth with my napkin. "I still question if I'm going to be able to do this. I've spent a decent amount of time with Katla, going over the responsibilities as the consort to the crown, and I've spent countless years being Theo's right-hand man, but hell, I still have so much doubt in the pit of my stomach."

"That's the unknown," Ottar says. "You can study all you want and consume all the intelligence presented to you, but until you're actually put in the position, getting firsthand experience, you'll never truly know what it's like."

"You're right," I reply. "I just wish people didn't recognize my fear. That protest group today . . ." I shake my head.

"They were a bunch of idiots who had nothing better to do with their day. I wouldn't give it a second thought."

"I understand that, but it still makes me think . . . are they going to hate me? And sure, I probably don't care if they hate me or not, as long as they love Lilly, but a piece of me wants to make Theo proud. And if the whole country is against me, that doesn't really give him the impression that I was the right one to marry his granddaughter."

"You know all Theo truly cares about is that you and Lilly are happy. The country's love for you as a couple will come along, and given the spectacle that tomorrow will be, you'll prove to everyone that not only are you in love, but you're also ready to take on the responsibility."

"Thanks, man," I say, my voice fading as I focus on my meal in front of me.

We spend the rest of the night talking about the latest fisherman's report. Someone on the south coast caught a record-setting cod that will get him into the hall of fame. According to the people on the boat who were with him, they had to hold his legs down because he was being dragged overboard by the "beast."

We shared a few laughs, always enjoying a fisherman's tale, and by the time we walked back to my room, it was nearly eleven.

The light was out in Lilly's room, so I knew her "rituals" were complete. I was tempted to knock on her door, to see her one last time, but with Ottar by my side, escorting me to my room, I knew that wasn't an option, so in my head, I whispered good night to her and walked into my room.

"You good?" Ottar asks, standing in my doorway.

"I'm good."

"Okay. I'll be by tomorrow morning along with your esquire and breakfast."

"Sounds good," I answer, and with that, he salutes me and is out the door, shutting it closed behind him.

I move toward my bathroom where I peel off my clothes and rest them on the tub. I go to the bathroom and stand next to the sink. Wearing only my briefs, I stare at myself. The circles under my eyes remain, but there is also a lightness.

This is it.

Tomorrow is finally here.

This wedding, the threats, it's all going to be over.

It will be just me and Lilly. We'll be able to sleep in the same room again, we'll be on our honeymoon, and we'll be looking toward our future. Whatever it is . . . we'll deal with it together.

I squirt some toothpaste on my toothbrush and brush my teeth, my body exhausted from the events. When I'm done, I splash water on my face, dry off, and then turn the light off to my bathroom. In the dark, I walk over to my nightstand, switch on the light, and then pause . . .

My eyes narrow on a blue envelope addressed to me, that sits against my lamp. I turn my body, twisting behind me to look around.

Was that envelope there before?

I don't recall it.

It's the same blue as the other letters that have been sent to the palace, but this one, this looks like it was hand delivered.

Fear creeps up the back of my neck, making the hairs at my nape stand to attention. How the hell did it get here?

I glance over my shoulder again, my breath heavy in my chest as I try to slow my heartbeat and listen for any movement in the room. After I don't hear anything for a few short seconds, I pick up the letter and flip it over where the wax seal hasn't been broken yet.

It's a new letter.

Jesus fuck.

I drag my hand over my mouth and open the wax seal. It's the same thick cardstock as the other letters, and as I slowly reveal it, one sentence plain and simple comes into view.

Keller, the time has come.

What?

Dread falls over me. We were right, the bomb was a decoy. I need to call Ottar. Just as I reach for my phone, a blinding pain hits me between the shoulder blades, forcing me to my goddamn knees.

"Mother . . . fucker," I groan as my back is tased, rendering me a useless, lifeless puddle on the ground, twitching with the electrical shock flowing through me.

And then in a flash, my arms are pulled behind me, my face is shoved into the tapestry rug beneath me, and my legs are bound together.

"What the fuck," I say as my head is slammed against the floor, the taste of blood quickly slipping across my lips.

"Don't make him bleed, you moron. We can't leave any traces," a voice says.

My head is yanked back by my hair and a tissue is shoved up my nose before I'm released back to the floor, my body slamming on the ground from the lack of control I have over it. I groan from the onslaught of movement.

"Bring him to the desk."

Still lifeless, two men drag me to my desk by the window. In the middle of the desk is a single piece of paper and pen. That definitely wasn't there before.

"Clean up the blood on the floor. Use the bleach wipes," the authority says.

"What . . . what's happening?" I ask, feeling like my entire body has turned into liquid.

And then, in an instant, a cold, metal barrel is placed against my temple and the sound of a gun cocking back rings through my ear.

Fuck.

"Listen closely," a voice says. "You'll keep your goddamn voice down, or I'll end you right here, right now."

On a shaky breath, I nod.

"You have two options. You can do what we say and spare your bride from getting hurt, or we can press this button." He tosses a remote on the desk. "This will detonate a bomb right outside the princess's window, blowing up her room in seconds. Your choice."

I swallow hard, trying to get my mind on straight.

A bomb outside Lilly's room? There can't be because we've kept this entire place on lockdown. Then again . . . someone is in my room right now. There are at least three guards outside my room and all the windows lock from the inside. *How the fuck did they get in here?*

He could be bluffing, but if there's one thing I will never do, it's gamble on Lilly's safety, so I say, "I'm listening."

"Good choice," the voice says as he gathers the remote but keeps the gun at my head. "You need to write a letter to your bride. Word for word, you write what I say. If you try anything funny like escaping, I'll not only blow your brains out but your bride's as well. Got it?"

"Yes," I answer, my mind trying to commit this all to memory. The sound of his voice. The smell of his clothes. The type of gun being held to my head, but my mind is falling short. I'm still reeling from being tased and slammed into the floor. *How did they get the drop on me? I'm fucking trained for this.*

"Release his hand." My hand is released, and for a moment, I think about knocking the gun away, but I don't know who is behind me, how many men are in this room, and what other guns are pointed at me, so I make the smarter decision and pick up the pen. "Write this. 'Lilly.'" I start scrolling across the paper. Every word he says, my gut churning with every sentence, knowing when she reads this, she'll be absolutely devastated.

No, not just devastated.

Ruined.

Broken.

But what fucking choice do I have?

"Sign it," the guy says. "Sign it like you would any other letter."

Grinding my teeth together, I put a K at the bottom and then drop the pen.

"Tie him up," the man says, and my arm is whipped behind me again before I'm forced to stand. "Did you grab clothes for him?"

"Yes," another voice says.

"Then we're out."

Out where?

Not the window, we're up at least four stories.

Not out the door, unless they somehow got rid of all the guards. I'm about to laugh at them and wish them luck when the man with the gun walks over to the bookcase at the end of the room, pulls a green book, and the bookcase slides open, revealing a secret door.

What the actual fuck . . .

I don't have a second to think about it as a cloth is draped over my mouth and nose, and I'm forced to breathe in whatever is on the cloth.

The world around me turns black, and the last thing on my mind as I slip into a dark abyss, is Lilly and her beautiful, loving face.

Chapter Seventeen

LILLY

I stare at the dark ceiling above me, rumblings from beyond my door filling in the silence of my bedroom. Busy palace staff getting ready for the exciting day, fulfilling their tasks before they're welcomed to stand in at the joyous occasion that is my wedding.

"Holy shit," I mutter quietly, blinking a few times.

I'm getting married today.

Only months ago, I was in Miami, marriage not even on my radar, and here I am now, in a country that belonged to my mom, the love of my life a few doors down, waking up to walk down the aisle with me.

A smile spreads across my face, and like a giddy schoolgirl, I bring my blanket over my head, kicking my legs and arms about as I inwardly squeal.

It's been a journey, but we're here. Today is the day.

I flip my blankets off me, sit up in my bed, and adjust my top just as Runa comes through the door with a tray of tea and pastries.

"Oh, you're up."

"Making your job easy today," I say while she sets the tray down on my nightstand. "Ooo, chocolate croissant." I pick it up and take a huge bite.

Runa chuckles. "The chef made them specially for you today. He knows how much you love them."

There's a knock on my door, and Timmy pokes his head in. When he sees that I'm awake, he shrieks and runs to jump on my bed. "You're getting married today!"

I shriek with him. "It's so crazy." I offer him my croissant, but he reaches across me and plucks a raspberry scone instead. "Runa, can you believe it?"

"Hardly," she says.

Timmy sniffs the air and then leans into me. "My God, is that you that smells so good?"

Runa moves around the room as I turn toward Timmy, sitting cross-legged on the bed. "Yes. It's from the oils they used last night."

"Yeah, tell me more about that. Was it weird?"

"Slightly," I say in a hushed tone, not wanting to insult Runa or anyone who walks in. Even though the bathing thing was weird, it was still a fascinating ritual, a tradition. "The only weird part was when they made me lift my arms and they cleaned my armpits."

"Stop, they did not."

I nod and take a bite of my croissant. "Oh yeah. I giggled a lot because I was so awkward, which made them all giggle, so at least there was that."

"And they put the horsehair in?" he asks, tugging on my long braid.

"They did, and it's synthetic, remember?"

"Right." He nods. "What's the plan for today?"

"She must bathe again," Runa says. "And then the hair-dresser will start on her hair. It will take a while to style, especially with the additions of pressed flowers."

"Well, I'm here for it. I just need to shower and slip on my suit."

There's another knock on the door, and Lara steps into the room wearing a smile on her face. "Good morning, Lilly. How are you?"

"I'm doing great. Excited. Ready. What about you?"

"Ready." She gestures to her black-on-black pant suit with a few medals across her chest and a sash that signifies her importance.

"Is that what you're wearing?" I ask her.

She nods. "I might be attending in my heart as your friend, but in person, I'm your guard, so I have to dress the part."

"Shame, I would love to see you roundhouse kick any trespassers in a solid pair of heels and an evening gown."

"That would be hot," Timmy says.

Another knock and this time, it's Ottar.

"Good morning, Ottar," I say. "Ooo, black on black as well. I like what I'm seeing with you and Lara."

He barely acknowledges me with a smile and then whispers something to Lara. Her face scrunches up in confusion, and she holds up her finger to me. "Excuse me."

They're out the door of my room faster than Ottar entering.

"What was that about?" Timmy asks.

"No idea," I say, staring at the door. "Probably something to do with security."

"Does that scare you? Knowing someone is possibly out there trying to ruin the wedding?"

I shake my head. "No. We have the best team on the job. I know they'll take care of everything. Plus, if I worry, it will take over the positive energy I have for today. And I don't want that to happen. It's been a hell of a month getting to this day, and I won't let anything ruin that. Oh, which reminds me. I need to text Keller."

I set my croissant on my leg and pick up my phone to shoot him a text.

Lilly: *Good morning, my king. I hope you had a wonderful night's rest full of naughty dreams of me. I can't wait to see you later today in your handsome suit, waiting for me at the other end of the temple. I love you so much . . . you're mine forever.*

Happy with my text, I press send, just as Lara and Ottar come back into the room with blank looks on their faces.

Ding

I glance at Lara's hand where the sound came from, noticing she's holding Keller's phone. That's weird. Why does she have it? When I look up at her and notice the frown on her face, the crinkle between her eyes, and the slump in her shoulders, I swallow a gasp. *Something is wrong.*

"What is it?" I ask, my heart rate starting to pick up, the pounding of my pulse thrumming in my ears.

Ottar clears his throat and steps farther into the room, holding a piece of paper in his hand. My eyes float between the two of them, dread inching up my spine.

"Why . . . why do you have Keller's phone?" I ask.

Lara looks up at Ottar, who fidgets with the paper in his hand.

"Uh . . . Lilly," he says, but his voice gets caught in his throat.

"What?" I ask, standing now, my croissant falling to the floor. "What's happening? Why do you have Keller's phone?"

Ottar pinches his lips together, a grim expression in his eyes, and steps forward. "He . . . he isn't in his room."

"What do you mean he's not in his room?" I ask. "Did he go on a run? Is he lifting weights? You know he does that to relieve stress. Did you check?"

Ottar nods. "I did."

"Well, what about the kitchen? Maybe he's helping with

last-minute tasks. You know how he likes to help the staff. Did you ask around?"

"Lilly—"

"Did you ask around?" I shout, my hands trembling at my sides. "Because . . . he's around here somewhere. You just need to look."

Ottar wets his lips and takes another step forward. "We did look around. We still have people looking around, but . . ." He visibly gulps. "He left this."

To my horror, Ottar reaches his hand out, the one that's holding the piece of paper, and attempts to hand it to me.

"What's that?" I ask, my legs starting to shake beneath me.

"It's a letter . . . from Keller."

I shake my head, backing away. "No. No, it's not."

"Lilly." Lara steps up.

"Stop. No!" I cover my ears as I back up into my bed. "No. You need to go find him. He's here. The staff quarters, or . . . or Theo's office." Tears start to well in my eyes as I look at Ottar and Lara, pleading with them. "He's here, tell me he's here."

Timmy's arm goes around me, holding me tight as Lara squats in front of me, her hands on my thighs. "Lilly." She chokes up. "I'm sorry."

"No," I cry out. "Please, Lara, please tell me he's here."

Her eyes well up now as she shakes her head. "He's . . . he's not."

"Then he's at the temple? He's with the horses? Checking on the carriage?" Tears spill down my cheeks.

Lara grabs the paper from Ottar and holds it in front of me. "I'm so sorry, Lilly."

Eyes full of tears, I look down at the piece of paper in my hand and the first thing I notice is his handwriting.

This can't be happening.

Shaking uncontrollably, I bring the letter closer so I can read it.

From the desk of Keller Fitzwilliam.
Lilly,
I'm so sorry, but I think both of us knew this wasn't going to work. I'm not meant to be a prince. I'm not cut out for it.
K

Teeth rattling, I read it two more times before the paper slides out of my hand and floats to the floor. I stare straight ahead at my bedroom door, willing him to come forward, to walk into this bedroom and tell me this was all some miserable, sick joke.

But when he doesn't appear, when no one brings him forward, I know that this moment is real.

"Lilly, what can we do?" Lara asks as I sit there, catatonic from shock.

"Nothing," I say quietly. I swipe at my tears and then climb back up on my bed and under my covers. "There's nothing anyone can do."

I turn away and bury my head into my pillow as a wave of tears hit me all at once.

⊏⊐

"HOW IS SHE?" Katla says from my door.

Runa has been fielding visitors all day.

I've been in and out of consciousness since this morning, not bothering to lift my head from my pillow.

"Same," Runa says.

"Does she want to talk?"

"No, ma'am," Runa says. "She won't even talk to me."

There's silence and then she says, "Let me just try." Katla's footsteps cross the bedroom, and I feel her weight on the bed as she sits next to me. I keep my back turned away, tears still falling from my eyes.

Her hand presses against my back as she says, "Lilly, sweetheart. I just want to check on you."

My lip trembles, and I squeeze my eyes shut, not saying a word.

"I can't imagine what you're going through right now, but I want you to know, we're all here for you. Okay? Anything you need, please don't hesitate to ask."

More silence as my tears gather on the fabric of my pillowcase.

"And we're looking into Keller and his location. We're just as confused as you, and we want to reach out to him as well."

I want to tell her not to bother. I should have seen it coming. I could see it in his eyes last night. He said all the right things. He told me he loved me. He said he would see me tomorrow, but there was a darkness behind his pupils, a shaded fear that I believe only I witnessed.

He said he wasn't suited for the spotlight.

The people protesting outside Norse Temple.

His doubts of providing an heir . . .

He said it was fear. The same reason he left me the first time. But now I know better.

He's a coward.

And I don't want him anywhere near me.

He's weak.

And I want nothing to do with such spinelessness.

I should have learned the first time.

And then my heart wouldn't have been shattered into a million tiny pieces.

She rubs my back. "Okay, well, we love you very much. I'll come check on you later."

And with that, she walks out of the bedroom, leaving me with a silent Runa, just the way I want it.

Chapter Eighteen

KELLER

Fuck, my head.

It's pounding, searing with pain, thumping every goddamn second.

I move my body, but my arms are restricted with my back up against a cold surface.

Where the hell am I?

I open my eyes. Darkness surrounds me. I try to remember what the hell happened and why the hell I'm unable to move my legs and arms more than a few inches.

I blink a few more times, letting my eyes adjust to the darkness, and that's when I see a door, a millimeter of light filtering through the crack at the bottom, offering just enough visibility to help my eyes take in the rest of the room.

Dingy stone walls encompass what seems to be an eight-by-eight room, a stone-sized window up to the left, and only a pile of hay off to the side with a flimsy blanket as a bed. I attempt to move my arms again but notice they're chained down.

That's when it all comes flooding back to me.

Being tased and brought down to my knees.

Being tossed to the floor by men dressed in black.

The secret passageway in my room.

The note . . .

Fuck . . .

Lilly.

The wedding. I'm not there.

A surge of anger takes over my body as I pull on the restraints. The metal digs into my arms as I yank. *I need to get to her. I can't let her think that I left because I was scared.*

"Fuck," I shout as I pull again, yanking so hard that the metal cuts into my skin, tearing through the flesh.

"Looks like someone is awake," someone says from the other side of the door right before it opens. The light from the hallway blinds me, so when I look up, all I see is a shadow. "Well, hello."

"Where the fuck am I?" I shout, tugging on the chains again.

"Good idea chaining him up," the man says to another person who steps into the light. But because the backlight is so blinding, I can't make out any faces, just silhouettes. "He seems quite angry."

"I don't see why," the other person says. "We did him a favor. Torskethorpe wasn't ready for him to take over the crown. He wasn't well liked."

"Yes, I noticed that," the other voice says, so full of sarcasm that it makes me want to rip through these chains and wring their necks.

"Who are you?" I demand, which causes both of them to laugh.

"Oh, that's funny. As if we would tell him that."

"What do you want with me?" I ask.

"Isn't it obvious?" the main voice says. "Without you directing the new princess around, that gives us a world of opportunity."

"It does," the other voice says. "You see, from what we've seen, Princess Lilija lacks confidence when you're not around."

"Not true," I shoot back, forgetting all my training. I'm not supposed to be arguing with the enemy but rather attempting to befriend them, but the pulsing pain from my head, and the searing pain in my heart from knowing Lilly is alone, left without a groom, it's making me throw everything out the window.

"Oh, it's very true. And with her heart now broken, that leaves us with two options. One, she gives up on the stupid idea of being the next heir to the throne of Torskethorpe, which would be ideal. Or, after a decent amount of time to let her grieve, we show her that more than one man can take care of her."

"Don't you fucking touch her," I yell, pulling at my chains.

"Oh, we wouldn't," the main voice says. "But we have just the right man for the job."

"Which seems like the better option as we speak," the second voice says. "Look at the anger on his face. Think about the mental fuckery we could play on Keller Fitzwilliam, the almost king consort of Torskethorpe, forcing him to watch his girl fall for someone else. That sounds very appealing."

"Very appealing indeed," the main voice says.

"So what are you going to do with me? Kill me?"

"If we wanted to kill you, we would have done that already. No, we have plans to torture you, Fitzwilliam. You've overstepped your position in life, and because of you, our plans have been thwarted. You *will* pay for that, slow and torturously. Which reminds me, shall we introduce him to our friend Banamaor?"

"We should."

Banamaor . . .

Viking for killer.

Just then, a giant of a man steps forward, wearing a leather mask over his face, carrying a whip in one hand and a bludgeon in the other.

My eyes float up to his, right before he cocks his arm back and slams me in the face with the thick end of the bludgeon, turning everything back to darkness.

Chapter Nineteen

LILLY

The curtains part, and what little sun is shining filters into the room.

Runa steps up to the bed, and she takes a seat, resting her hand near me but never touching. "Princess Lilly," she says softly. "We need to bathe you."

Lips dry, mouth parched, eyes bloodshot, I nod but don't move.

Runa gently pulls down the bedcovers and takes my hand in hers. Together, she pulls as I lift from the bed. She helps me swing my legs off the mattress where she kneels before me and slips my slippers over my feet. When she stands back up, she helps me up from the bed.

It's been like this for the past week.

The first few days after the cancellation of my wedding, Runa periodically checked on me, bringing me water and food that went untouched. After what I assume was the third day—I can't be sure since time has stood still—Runa kindly asked me to allow her to bathe me and feed me. Feeling far too weak, I had nothing within me to fight her off.

Now, she does this every day to get me out of bed.

I recall Timmy leaving at some point, needing to get back to Miami, but my recollection on that interaction is minimal. I do know that he calls every day and speaks to Runa because I overhear their conversations. Runa always tells him I'm the same. The conversation is short.

"Princess Lilly, I'd like to get a little more food into you today," she says as she helps me to the bathroom, keeping one arm around my waist while the other holds my hand. "I have a protein shake that will be easy to drink. Think you can try it for me?"

I don't answer, I just mindlessly move into the bathroom and sit on the vanity chair, where Runa peels my top up and over my head. No need to wash my hair. She did that yesterday while finally taking the synthetic hair out as well. I cried the entire time.

I lift just enough for her to take my bottoms off, and then together, she helps me into the tub, the warm water breaking into my skin and relaxing my tense muscles. She dips a wash-cloth into the water and then runs it over my back. The monotony of my days lying in bed, nibbling on a little bit of food and sleeping, has become a treasured routine now. I don't have to think. I can mindlessly make it day to day without facing my reality, that the love of my life left me at the altar. Well, left me before I could even make it to the altar.

Runa runs a bar of soap over me and says, "Theo would like to see you today. He's going to come to your bedroom."

I haven't seen him since the wedding day. And at that, all I saw was his silhouette in my room. He didn't speak to me. Katla has been in and out of my room more than he has. And I can't be sure why he's avoided me, but I can only assume it's because he's in shock as well. He's mourning just like I am.

His "son" ran from not only me but his sworn responsibilities to his king. No doubt, he never saw that coming.

"I picked out a pair of fuzzy pants for you to wear and a long-sleeved shirt so you'll be comfortable. I also got more of those socks that you like, the ones that keep your feet extra warm while you're lying in bed."

I don't know where I would be without Runa. She has gently and patiently cared for me every second since the non-wedding. She's even worked extra hours, never giving herself a break, being a caretaker and thinking ahead of my every need.

If I didn't think I'd burst into tears, I'd tell her how grateful I am. But I can't seem to form the words, not without choking on my emotions.

It's best to stay silent.

It's best to remain catatonic.

Without thoughts.

Without feelings.

Then I won't have to hurt anymore.

She finishes bathing me and helps me out of the water before wrapping a large, warmed towel around my body. We spend the next few minutes getting me lotioned, clothed, and ready for the day. She braids my hair because since I lie down all day, it doesn't hurt when braided. She helps me brush my teeth because I'm too weak. And when she slips on my deodorant, I just stare at my gaunt eyes and the lifeless soul in the reflection of the mirror.

Arm around me, she brings me back to the bed and then goes to the curtains again, opening them even more, revealing a dreary day, a day that matches how I feel inside. A mixture of snow and ice pelt the window, streaking down in long, watery drops along the age-old pane.

"Here," Runa says, handing me a pint glass with a straw. The protein shake. "It's vanilla flavored."

Because I know it will make her feel better if I take a few

sips, I lean forward and suck on the straw, letting the cool liquid soak on my tongue before I swallow.

"Thank you," she says softly before smoothing her hand over my hair.

We spend the next ten minutes in silence as I slowly sip my drink, my stomach surprisingly grateful for the food. And when I finish it, Runa has a smile on her face.

"Wonderful," she says. "Would you like more?"

I shake my head and lie back down.

"Very well." There's a knock on the door, pulling Runa's attention away from me. "That must be King Theo."

She sets the empty glass on the nightstand and moves to the door where she opens it. I don't bother to look over to see if it's him, I keep my gaze fixated on a crack in the ceiling. The same crack that I've stared at for the past week. It's not very long, but at one end, it splits into two, and all I can think about is how the crack resembles Keller and me. At first, we were one—one solid line together—not letting anything come between us, and then, at the first sign of trouble, we're two. *Heading in opposing directions. How apt.*

"Let me grab this tray, and then I'll be out of your way," Runa says, moving around the room.

When the door clicks shut, I close my eyes, only to feel the bed dip next to me. "Lilija." Theo's strangled voice cracks, and just hearing the sorrow cutting through him causes tears to well in my eyes. He grips my hand, his warm palm covering my knuckles. "Talk to me. Please. I know you haven't talked to anyone, but I need to know how you are. I need to know how I can fix this."

My lip trembles as tears stream down my cheeks. I part my lips and let out a sigh as I close my eyes again.

"Please, my dear, please help me. I'm so sorry this happened. I'm still . . ." His voice comes out garbled. "I'm trying to make sense of it all. I'm sure you are as well."

I wet my lips, and when I open my eyes and meet his gaze,

I see how tortured he is. And even though talking is the last thing I want to do, I don't want to make him feel any worse than he already does. I know it wouldn't be good for his health, so I say, "I'm really, really sad."

Theo grips my hand tighter. "I'm sad too," he says.

I glance toward the window, another tear falling down my cheek, this one, I wipe away. "Devastated. I thought . . . I thought our love was more than this . . . this job."

"I thought it was too," he says, and his shoulders slump. "I put too much pressure on him."

"Don't blame yourself," I say. "This has nothing to do with you, and everything to do with him." I reach for a tissue on my nightstand and blow my nose. "This is all him."

Theo stares ahead as he says, "I wonder if we moved too fast. Would he have been more comfortable with a long engagement, one that gave him more time to adjust? I just . . ." He gets choked up again. "I'm just unsure how much time I have left on this planet, I want to be able to be there for your wedding."

"Don't talk like that."

He looks down at our hands, something passing over his features that I can't possibly read. Before I can ask him, he says, "How can I make this better for you?"

"I don't think there's much you can do," I say.

"I want to do something. I can't stand the thought of you in this room, day in and day out, that pretty smile no longer on your face, the energy you have dimmed by the shadow of Keller's evasion. It makes me physically ill." His eyes meet mine, and he says, "If you need to go back to Miami, if you need to leave here because it's too much, I understand. I just want you to be happy."

I look away and sigh. "The thought of leaving has crossed my mind," I say honestly. "It would be so easy to pick up and not look back. To put this all behind me and pretend it never happened." I dab at my eyes with a tissue. "But then I think about all of the people like yourself, Katla, and Runa who have given me your whole heart, your attention, your love, and I can't imagine abandoning the bonds we've formed because my life has been shattered."

"So what can I do?" he asks.

"Nothing." I shake my head. "There isn't anything anyone can do. It's just going to take time." My throat grows tight as I say, "Maybe one day I'll wake up, and I won't feel the need to cry anymore. Maybe I'll get the energy to go for a walk. But that time isn't now." I slink deeper into my bed and pull up my covers. "Now . . . I just want to be left alone."

He pats my leg and murmurs, "I understand." He moves from the bed, his cane giving him assistance. "Then I'll grant you your wish, but please, when the day does come when you don't feel like crying and you want to go for a walk, let me be the one who walks beside you."

I just nod, unable to vocally answer.

He leans down, hovering above me, and places a gentle kiss on the top of my head before taking off, leaving me alone. Now, if only the darkness would consume me again, then I would truly be in my happy place.

Three Weeks Post Intended Wedding Day

"PRINCESS LILLY," Runa says. "I need to change your sheets. Do you think you could sit on your settee for now?"

I roll my head to the side, looking up at her, my head feeling dizzy from lack of nutrition, lack of fluids.

"I can't," I say, my eyes blinking, trying to focus on Runa.

"Princess Lilly," she says, her voice growing more stern. "Are you okay?" She lifts my hand in hers, and it feels lifeless. I tell myself to grip her, to let her know that I'm okay, but I can't as my brain rolls in and out of consciousness.

"Lara," Runa shouts. "Get the doctor."

Feet traipse around me, and Runa lifts me, forcing me to look her in the eyes. "Lilly," she says, shaking me, forgetting all formalities. "Talk to me. Let me know that you're okay."

My head rolls to the side, my body limp.

"Diz—dizzy," I say. "Don't . . . shake."

Runa lays me down but peels the sheets and comforter off me, as her fingers go to my pulse at my wrist. I let her examine me, not thinking much of it, and when the doctor rushes in, she rattles off my symptoms, telling him I'm barely ingesting any food or liquids. That I'm in and out of consciousness all day.

He moves around me, checking my vitals, and issues an IV stat. That's the last thing I hear before my mind drifts off again.

A Month Post Intended Wedding Day

"THAT'S IT," Runa says as she scoops another spoonful of soup and lifts it to my mouth. "It's good, isn't it?"

I nod as I swallow the beef broth. "It is."

She smiles, helping me with another spoonful.

After I woke up again from a deep darkness, Runa told me that I was losing weight and fast, that I was dangerously dehydrated, and if I didn't do what I was told to do, I could easily lose my life. When she told me that and her voice cracked— Runa, my rock during this time, emotional—I knew I had to pull it together for her.

I still have an IV drip in, but I've been able to keep some

soup down, and even though I'm still in my bed, at least I'm not wasting away.

"Would you like some bread?" she asks.

"No, just the soup."

"Very well, but you will be eating that potato. I don't want to hear about it. After last week, I'm not taking it easy on you. I'll be damned if you turn into dust on my watch."

That makes me chuckle, startling Runa right out of her dress.

She drops the spoon in the soup and asks, "Did you . . . did you just laugh?"

"It was a mistake."

Runa smirks and taps her finger to my leg. "Oh no, you don't, that was a genuine laugh. I might be on my way to curing you after all."

"If anyone can do it, it's you, Runa."

<hr />

A Month and a Half Post Intended Wedding Day

"YOU LOOK WELL," Lara says as she walks next to me, down the long hallway of the palace.

I left my room for the first time a week ago and it was an ordeal. Like Theo said, he walked next to me while palace staff clutched at their chests, wishing me well. I cried several times, feeling so warm inside from the people here supporting me. Who are rooting for me. I didn't realize how upset people have been while I've mourned.

I can understand the relief. Their future queen had her heart destroyed, and she's been isolated in her room with some major health scares, so to see me out and about must give them hope.

Walking in my slippers and a set of green-and-blue-plaid flannel pajamas, I take it slow, still building up my stamina.

"Are you just saying that, or do you mean it?"

"I mean it," Lara says.

"Well, I would like to say the same about you, but it looks like you've been run over by a truck."

She pushes a stray hair behind her ear and says, "Some sleepless nights is all."

"Want to talk about it?"

She shakes her head. "I want to focus on you."

"I thought you would say that," I respond as I stop and take a deep breath. Lara waits patiently for me. "Runa told me that you and Ottar haven't been on speaking terms."

"We speak," Lara says.

"About anything other than the job?" I ask her.

"I'd rather not get into it."

I turn toward her and say, "Lara, what are you doing? You two were so great together."

"That doesn't matter," she says, looking down at the ground.

I start walking again, and she falls in line with my slow pace. "Does this have anything to do with Keller's disappearance?"

"No," she answers.

"Why don't I believe you?"

She sighs heavily and pauses, then she turns toward me. "Lilly, if you don't want me to talk about Keller, then please respect me when I say we're not talking about Ottar. We're keeping it professional, so let's leave it at that."

Sensing her need for this conversation to be over, I agree, and we start walking again, the afternoon sun draping through the stained-glass windows of the long hallway.

"Have there been any new developments about Keller?" I ask, surprised I can say his name out loud twice in one day, let alone five minutes.

From the corner of my eyes, I catch Lara shaking her head. "No. We heard rumblings that he's joined a team of fishermen on the south coast, but nothing concrete."

I slowly nod, letting that sink in.

On a boat, fishing.

That's what he'd rather do than be the man I need. And it's not like the requirements for the man I need are too big, too demanding. All he has to do is love me and stay by my side, that's it. That's all I've ever asked from him, yet he makes it seem like any other job, any other path in life is superior to the purgatory he'd experience with me.

"Well." I clear my throat. "I hope he catches some big fish and enjoys his time out on the open sea."

"Lilly—"

I hold my hand up. "It's fine. Let's move on."

He clearly has.

<hr/>

Two Months Post Intended Wedding Day

"I NEED TO LEAVE," I say to Theo and Katla as I sit in front of them.

Ever since I've heard about Keller the Fisherman, I haven't been able to get my mind off it. I haven't been able to think of anything else. And with each passing day, as I walk through the palace with Lara by my side, my strength growing with each step, I see Keller everywhere.

His bedroom down the hall.

The stairs where he once carried me up on the way to my room.

My bedroom where he fucked me on every surface.

It's playing over and over in my head, and I can't take it anymore. *I feel so suffocated.*

So I made a decision last night.

I have to leave.

Theo's eyes grow wide with concern as Katla sets her teacup down on the saucer in her hand. "Leave?" she asks. "Like, go back to the United States?"

I can see how they'd take that, so I reassure them. "No, this is my home." They both visibly relax. I learned a lot about Torskethorpe from Keller. I learned the traditions and expectations of being queen, too. Just because he fled his responsibilities—*betrayed me*—doesn't mean I should do the same. I refuse to abandon what I was brought here for. I refuse to bow to his cowardice. "But I need to get out of Strombly. I need a change of scenery. I need a second to breathe."

Theo nods in understanding. "Where would you like to go?"

"I don't know," I say. "I just need to get out of here. And please, not to Harrogate."

"We wouldn't send you there," Theo says.

"You know," Katla chimes in. "I was speaking to Pala last night, and she said if you ever wanted to visit, they would love to host you in Marsdale. Is that something that would interest you?"

Marsdale? With my cousins? With the woman who reminded me so much of my mom? *Yes.* That might be exactly what I need.

I vaguely recall the day they left Strombly. They each came in and kissed my forehead, but it's Pala's words I recall more clearly. They were the same words she'd said the day she'd arrived. Words to encourage me.

"Everything will be fine, sweet Lilly. You're not alone."

On that day, I'd felt very much alone. So cold. So sad. So angry. And as much as I could, I'd tried to latch on to her words, to feel desperately needed comfort. Perhaps spending time with Pala and my cousins is just what my broken heart needs. I just hope Theo and Katla don't feel disappointed in my need to leave Torskethorpe.

"Yes," I say breathlessly, the idea taking root quickly. "If you don't mind me going for a little while. Would Isabella and Marit be there?"

"Of course. I know they'd love to show you around. I can set it up if you'd like."

"I'd love that," I say, the idea feeling very right in my mind. When they were here, I bonded as if they were my own sisters, so spending more time with them feels like just what I need.

It would help me get my mind off Keller.

I could maybe find some joy again.

To get a reset.

I could also learn more about being queen, because that's my duty to Torskethorpe.

Yes, this might be exactly what I need.

Chapter Twenty

KELLER

Time is the most valuable commodity in this world.

You can never ask for more. You can never get it back.

Life rushes by you in a blink of an eye, time eating you up whole.

But the funny thing about being captured and held prisoner? *Time* is on your side.

You have a chance to observe, to take mental notes, to think about every second and how you would take advantage of your opponent's mistakes.

Time actually slows down, and if you're smart, you'll use every minute to plan for the precise second you'll seek your revenge.

And that's exactly what I've been doing.

Every sound, every scent, every word uttered, I've committed to memory. I've replayed words over and over in my head so when I get out of here, I'm ready to use my knowledge against them.

Footsteps clop down the stone hallway toward my door, indicating a visitor.

I crunch down in the hay, curled like a feeble ball, shivering and pathetic.

Metal skeleton keys unlock the door. Two clicks.

The wooden, metal-bound door creaks open, flooding my meager cell with light, casting a hollow spotlight on me.

"Pitiful as always," my keeper's voice says. He's the one appointed to take care of me. A peon with a distinct accent, the one who does the dirty work like feed me and empty the hole that is my toilet.

He's harmless but helpful. Because after listening to him for several weeks now, I've been able to narrow down exactly where he's from.

South Arkham.

"We need to hose you down. Fuck." He walks over to me and sets a metal plate of food on the ground along with some water.

I remain still, softly breathing, slowing down my heart rate. He toes me with his foot, pushing me a few times.

"You alive?" he asks.

I grumble something unintelligible.

"Good. The boss wouldn't want you dead." I feel him lean closer. "Has the blood dried on your back?" He shines a light on me, and I remain as still as I can while he checks the whip marks from last night.

The first time they sent Banamaor in, I radiated with pain for days. Pain delivered by his evil hands, and pain from being stolen from my girl.

Now the only pain I feel is the distance from Lilly. *Fuck, I miss her.*

However, I don't allow myself more than a few minutes a day to think of her. I need to remain focused.

Pain from missing her propels me forward.

This pain gives me strength.

"Fuck, you stink." He backs away. "The boss will be happy to know you're more pathetic than ever. He has you just where he wants you."

See, a peon.

Saying shit he shouldn't be saying to me.

"If it were up to me, I'd just get rid of you, but the sadistic side to the boss loves seeing you weak." He shakes his head and turns away.

When he shuts the door and locks it behind him, I sit straight up, only possible because the only shackles on me now are on my ankles. I glance at the plate of dry, stodgy oatmeal. Every day, the same thing, and every day, I eat every last drop. Not because I like it, but because I have plans.

Now that he's gone, I continue what I was doing by moving into a plank position, my hands firmly planted on the stone, and I resume my morning pushups.

I start with one hundred in the morning, finish the night with another hundred. I also work on wall sits to keep my legs strong, do squats, lunges, and shadow boxing. Luckily, they didn't bind my legs together. Instead, they put a shackle on each ankle chained to the wall, offering me plenty of slack.

I plan my workouts around when I know they're nowhere near my cell and they can't hear me. I did a thorough scope for cameras, and there are none. *Fools. How they've underestimated me.* And because I've portrayed myself as feeble with zero energy, they've lightened security.

There used to be a guard at my door, but not anymore. They also used to have my hands bound together. I'm just waiting for the moment where they unbind my legs. I know it's coming.

The boss might not order it, but the peon will do it. He's the one who unbound my hands. He's not as evil as the others. He will be spared.

When I'm done with my pushups, and my chest's on fire, I sit down on my hay and pick up my metal plate of oatmeal.

I've also noticed the peon has a soft heart from the portions of food he's been giving me every day. They've been growing. Today, there are at least two palmfuls of oatmeal. Just what I need for the energy I exert to keep strong. *And not much more.* But it will do.

I chew down the sticky, flavorless substance, sprinkling in some of my water to make it bearable, and stare at the door in front of me.

They will pay.

They have no fucking clue what I'm capable of . . . and what they took away from me.

I might be in Arkham, but the country is a mere vessel for my capture. King Magnus might be an accomplice, but he's not the one behind this. He doesn't know me. The letters that were sent to the palace were personal. They were about revenge.

And I will spend every waking hour figuring out who did this to me, and they will be brought to justice.

Chapter Twenty-One

LILLY

"We're so happy you're here," Isabella says as she takes my hand and squeezes it.

After a private flight to Marsdale, I was escorted through the capital in a black SUV. Lara accompanied me but stayed pretty silent. I stared out the windows, taking in the majestic, rolling hills covered in snow. I've never been to Scotland before, but I've seen pictures, and this is what it reminds me of. Stone walls throughout the valleys, crystal-white snow dotting the grounds, and sheep with their large wool coats making their heads seem whimsically small.

When I was reading about Marsdale, I appreciated that they take pride in their farming, just like Torskethorpe takes pride in their fishing. Best known for their barley for malting liquors, they also hold the sector in dairy production and fine cheeses, which I found quite interesting. A vast difference than freaking fermented cod cakes. Come on, Torskethorpe!

When I arrived at the palace, I was greeted by open arms,

given a tour—the palace layout is quite similar to Strombly—and then taken up to my room. A beautiful room to say the least. Decorated in whites, golds, and light blues, they filled the bright space with fresh flowers and everything I could possibly need for my stay. They went above and beyond to make this a comfortable spot for me. I'm grateful for it.

"I'm happy I'm here too," I say as I take a seat on the bed, instantly being molded into the plush mattress. "I needed this."

"Yes, I can't imagine what you've been through. If you ever need to talk, we're here," Isabella says just as Marit comes through the bedroom holding a tray.

"I figured we could sit and chat," Marit says. "Drinks are coming. I told Martha that we'd like to get started on the cookies." Marit sets them down in the sitting area of the bedroom. "And before you say you're not hungry, we've been given strict orders from Runa to make you eat."

With a chuckle, I move over to the seating area as well and pick up one of the Linzer cookies. "She's been on my case a lot lately."

"I don't blame her," Isabella says softly. "We heard about the health scare. I hope that's okay."

"It's fine." I take a bite of my cookie. "I figured Katla told your mom. I think everyone was scared there for a second, even me."

"I'm afraid to ask, but are you feeling better?" Marit inquires.

Am I feeling better? Can anyone really feel better after what I've gone through? At least not this quickly. I'm still heartbroken, which is swapped out for anger daily. I fluctuate from feeling debilitated to ready to riot against the man who I thought loved me. It's exhausting.

"A little. Each day feels like a new opportunity, and I'm trying to make the most of it while not taking on too much."

"That's really good," Isabella says. "And we're here to help you with moving forward. It's not as cold here as it is in Tors-kethorpe, so we have some fun winter activities we can do. We can also just lie about the palace and drink wine."

"Wine is always preferred," Marit says.

"Our chef loves giving cooking lessons. Marit and I take them often, so we can sit in on those. He's very patient."

"He also thinks Isabella is hot," Marit adds.

I lift a brow toward Isabella. "So the bodyguard and the chef? My, oh my."

"Marit is exaggerating. Chef doesn't like me, plus he's about ten years older than me."

"Keller was older than me," I say before I can stop myself. I pause and take a deep breath. "God, saying his name still hurts."

"I'm sorry." Marit pats my shoulder. "Maybe we can do some sort of cleansing ritual, you know . . . like how we bathed you and washed your virginity away? Maybe we can wash the Keller right off you."

That makes me chuckle. "I'll be damned before I hop in a tub again and have you wash my armpits with washcloths. Sorry, not going to happen. I'll never get the feeling of you scrubbing my underarms out of my mind."

"I did it extra hard just to make you laugh," Marit says.

"Yeah, it worked. Not sure Katla was too pleased."

"She was fine." Isabella waves me off. "Plus, how can you truly take that seriously? Washing the virgin off? We all know that was washed away many years ago."

"Too many to count."

⸻

"AND THEN YOU fold just like that," Chef Martin says. He's been giving us step-by-step instructions on how to make butternut squash ravioli. We'll be serving it to Pala and Clinton tonight. And the girls were right, he's incredibly patient, even when I added two times the amount of salt needed. "Perfect, Lilly, you're doing a wonderful job." We're also on a first-name basis because Princess Lilija just isn't sitting right here. And Isabella and Marit skip the princess formality as well.

"Thank you," I say.

"And then we take our pizza cutter and slowly cut out the squares," Martin says, giving us an example.

"Chef, could we see you in the bread room?" someone asks from the archway of the door.

"Yes, of course." He wipes his hand on the towel over his shoulder. "Excuse me, ladies." He touches my shoulder and adds, "Excellent. Keep up the great work."

When he leaves the room, Marit slowly turns toward me, mouth open. "Oh my God, you're stealing Isabella's man."

"What?" I ask, shocked. "No, I'm not."

Marit laughs, and Isabella swats at her. "Don't listen to my sister. She likes to cause trouble. Martin is just friendly."

"He's hitting on Lilly. She's the only one he's complimented, and frankly, our ravioli looks the same, if not slightly better. He's into her. You're old news, Isabella."

"Well, she can have him," Isabella says. "Although, I'd like to steal his Kringle recipe that he keeps locked in a safe. If I wed him, I bet he'd grant me access to it." She taps her chin. "Eh, I'll just demand it when I become queen."

"That a girl," Marit says. "Use that power in the right kind of ways. Kringle recipes."

I chuckle and finish cutting up my ravioli. "Are you nervous about becoming queen one day?" I ask her.

Isabella shakes her head. "No. We've been groomed our whole life to take on these roles, it feels normal at this point. We're already pretty much doing what our parents do minus the parliament-type stuff, but that's all show. The community outreach though, and the parties and hosting, that's as easy as it comes. Might seem scary to you, though, since you grew up in an entirely different environment."

"Yeah, it's more intimidating to me, but I've started to get the hang of it, although, I can't imagine what my first public outing will be like after this whole wedding fiasco. I'm dreading it, actually."

"I think the palace has handled the breakup well," Marit says. "At least from what I've read."

"I agree," Isabella says, placing her cut ravioli on the flour-coated butcher block in front of her. "They didn't go into detail, kept it classy, didn't place blame on any party, and asked for privacy. I don't think they could have handled it any better."

"I haven't looked," I say. Both of them glance up at me, winces in their expressions. "No, it's okay. I think it's good that we don't avoid the elephant in the room. It's been two months. I'm ready to talk about it."

"You are?" Isabella asks, just as Martin walks back into the kitchen.

"How's it going?" he asks, a bright smile on his face.

"Good," I say. "What do you think?" I show him my ravioli, and he comes up next to me, placing his hand on my shoulder.

"Incredible. Just beautiful."

I glance at Marit, who obnoxiously winks, causing me to have to keep in the snort that wants to fly out of me.

Okay, yeah, maybe he's favoring me more than the other girls, but I'm not going to complain.

⊏⊐

"THIS IS BEAUTIFUL," I say as I stare up at the snowy sky.

At the very center of the palace on the fourth floor is a large glass dome. Clinton had it set up as a loft filled with pillows and blankets for the girls. The first night I arrived, they took me to the loft, and we laid about, talking and drinking wine of course. Now it seems to be our nightly ritual.

We drink.

Talk.

Have a good time while wearing our pajamas.

They truly are the siblings I've always wanted, and with every day that passes, being here, I'm starting to find joy again. I'm finding laughter, I'm finding that the heavy weight that's been sitting on my chest is slowly loosening.

Isabella fills up my wineglass. "Our favorite time is when it snows up here. The snow never sticks to the dome, so we're always rewarded with the view of falling snow without being caught up in the cold."

I take a sip of my wine. "Still getting used to the cold and the snow. It's beautiful, especially when you're inside and warm."

"And drinking wine," Marit says while raising her glass.

The more time I've spent with Marit and Isabella, the more I've noticed just how different they are. Not just in their looks, despite being twins, but also their personalities. Isabella is more subdued. She can joke around and have a good time, but there's a sense of properness in her, regality. And Marit, she's looser, funnier, the jokester and instigator. But even with Marit's frequent teasing and high jinks, it's so obvious how much Isabella loves her sister. Isabella has said how lost she'd be without Marit, and I couldn't help but think that's how I felt with Keller.

"So." Marit flips to her stomach and eyes me. "The other night, while we were making ravioli, you said you were ready to talk about Keller. So let's talk."

"Marit, don't be too pushy."

"I'm not," Marit says. "She doesn't have to talk about him if she doesn't want to. I'm giving her the option, but the door is also open in case she wants to." She turns her attention back to me. "So do you?"

I swirl my wine in my glass, feeling the effects of it. "You know, I think I do want to talk about him."

"Oh yay." Marit sits up and crosses her legs. "Lay it on us. Tell us everything."

"Well, I'll tell you this, if he really is out there, fishing like Henrik's reports have said, if I ever run across him, I'm going to slap him across the face with a cod."

The girls let out a roar of a laugh.

"A wet, cold one. Right into the old cheek. Because really, giving up being with me and being a prince to live on a boat with a bunch of smelly fishermen? Spending your daylights floating around in the ocean, your body odor so atrocious that you actually scare the cods away . . . that's what he traded in for?" I shake my head. "He did me a favor because marrying an idiot was not on my list of things to do."

Isabella chuckles. "Seriously, that's what he's doing?"

"Yes, a few people have said they've heard he's out on the boats."

"That does seem stupid," Isabella says. "I mean, look at you . . . you're telling me being on the boat is better than being by your side?"

"That's what I'm saying." I lean forward, holding my glass of wine out. "And I have my nipples and clit pierced."

"What?" Marit asks, nearly falling off her pillow. "No, you don't."

I slowly lean against a pillow, nodding. "Yup. And he loved playing with them."

"Oh my God, I'm so envious," Marit says. "I've wanted my nipples pierced for so long."

"What?" Isabella asks, shocked. "Have you?"

"Yeah," Marit replies with a playful smirk. "I heard the sensation of having them played with is unlike anything."

"It's true," I add. "Feels amazing."

"We need to make this happen," Marit says. "Who can we call?"

"Uh . . . good luck getting anyone to come to the palace without Mum and Dad knowing about it. They check everyone. What are you going to say? Your friend Lance from the tattoo shop is visiting for a spot of tea?"

"Lance might like tea," Marit says.

"Is Lance a real person?" I ask.

"Fictional," Isabella says. "Just an example."

"Just because Lance has a bald head, countless tattoos, and wears leather chaps doesn't mean he isn't a man of the steeped beverage." Marit gulps a big drink of wine.

"Do you borrow his leather chaps?" I ask, enjoying the repartee.

"I wish," Marit says on an eye roll. "The crotch is too big, obviously."

"Obviously," I say on a laugh.

"What if Lance was my boyfriend?" Marit asks dreamily.

"Mum and Dad would murder you," Isabella says. "You wouldn't have a chance to share chaps because you'd be dead."

"They're not into tattoos and assless chaps?" I ask.

"Who said they're assless?" Marit asks.

"Honey, all chaps are assless, at least the good ones," I answer.

"The girl with the pierced nipples would know." Marit winks.

"Damn right." I lift my glass and take a sip. "Seriously, though, would they be mad?"

"Madder if Isabella was dating a Lance. They'd be disappointed in me," Marit says. "I have a touch more leeway than she does. Our parents aren't super strict, but tattoo man with chaps . . . yeah, that won't fly. He'd have to cover his whole body and wear a toupee if he wanted to join this family."

"Maybe Lance would want to," I say. "There are men out there who are willing to accommodate women like us, women in power. I mean, I might not have dated one, but there have to be men out there ready to slip on a toupee for the one they love."

"There has to be." Isabella lifts up. "Where are all of the Lances?"

"Yeah, where's my toupee-wearing, magnificent crotch of a man?" Marit asks.

"We deserve more." I lift my glass.

"We do." Isabella lifts her glass as well.

"And we're going to join a dating app and find them," Marit says as we clink our glasses together and take a long sip.

Finally, Isabella lowers her wineglass. "I don't think we're allowed to join a dating app."

"Dammit all to hell." Marit tosses her body backward.

Chapter Twenty-Two

LILLY

Two and a Half Months Post Intended Wedding Day

"My darling, how are you?" Katla says as she presses a kiss to both of my cheeks.

"I'm getting better, thanks," I say before we both take a seat.

Katla has come to visit me in Marsdale. She's only come one other time and that was when Pala got married. Isabella and Marit were telling me how happy their mom is that she's been able to reconnect with Katla, and the fact she's here speaks volumes.

"You look incredible." Katla takes me in, and her eyes start to water.

"Why are you going to cry?" I ask as I move closer to her.

"Because you really scared us," she says. "I know it's not

your fault and you were grieving a love, but we were truly worried there for a moment."

"I understand. I think I worried myself as well. But I'm doing better. Being away has truly helped."

"I'm glad."

"And being with Isabella and Marit has been a breath of fresh air. I truly love them as if they were my very own sisters."

"They are quite wonderful, aren't they?"

"They are."

"Are you talking about us?" Marit asks, walking into the room, Isabella close behind her.

"Just saying how wretched you are." I smile.

"Good, wouldn't want you telling our grandmum any lies." Marit and Isabella hug Katla. "We don't want to disturb your gathering, but we wanted to see if you'd want to stay an extra week or so."

"The reason Marit asks," Isabella says, "is because we're having our annual Winter Flurries party, and we'd love for you to be there."

"Martin will be cooking." Marit wiggles her brows, causing me to roll my eyes.

"Don't start on me with that Martin stuff again."

"Who is Martin?" Katla asks.

"Their chef," I answer.

Marit leans in and says, "It's been a real scandal. Once a loyal fan of our dear Isabella, Lilly came in and stole his heart. He made her mashed potatoes the other night, just the way she liked them, with chives. It was a spectacle."

"He asked me." I laugh.

"Meanwhile, the future queen of Marsdale over here"—Marit thumbs toward Isabella—"has to have cheesy potatoes. Talk about a slap to the face, especially since she loves chives in her mashed potatoes." Marit slaps the armrest. "Unheard of."

"Don't pay any attention to her. She had some sour gummies and is now on a sugar high," Isabella says. "And for the record, I love cheesy potatoes."

"Not as much as the chive." Marit taps her own nose.

"Will you stay?" Isabella asks, clearly ignoring her sister on a sugar high.

"Of course, as long as I'm not needed in Torskethorpe."

Katla shakes her head. "Take all the time you need. I'm just happy to see a smile on your face again."

"Then it's settled. Now, if only we can get Granddad to come as well . . ." Marit taps her chin.

━━

"NOTHING?" Lara whispers into her phone. "Okay, well keep me posted. Uh-huh . . . is he okay?" The hairs on the back of my neck stand to attention as I stay in the bathroom while Lara is in my bedroom. "What did the doctors say? Is he still coming? Okay, sounds good. Bye."

I slip out of the bathroom in a pair of leggings and a long-sleeved shirt, ready to do some mild, and I mean mild, exercises with Lara. Just something to build my stamina.

"Who was that?" I ask, not even bothering to mind my own business.

"Oh, uh . . . Ottar," she says.

"Uh-huh, and what were you talking about?" I fold my arms at my chest. "Anything to do with Keller?"

"Ottar hasn't heard anything from him if that's what you're asking."

"Even if he did, I don't think I'd want to hear about it." I nod at her. "What was the doctor comment? Is everything okay with Theo?" When she glances away, I know she's about to give me some sort of made-up comment to benefit me, so I stop her before she can start. "Don't lie to me."

She sighs and says, "The stress of the wedding, Keller, all

266

of that has been a little much on him. He's on bedrest right now."

"What?" I ask, standing taller. "What do you mean bedrest?"

"That's all Ottar told me, and that's why he won't be at the party tomorrow. It will just be Katla."

"Does she know?"

Lara nods her head. "Yes, she's known for a while. They haven't told you because they didn't want to stress you out."

"Wait." I take a step forward. "Is he going to be okay? Like he just needs some rest, right?"

"I don't know, Lilly. It might be more serious than that. I wasn't supposed to say anything, but I also can't stand here and lie to you either."

"I appreciate that." I twist my hands together, my mind racing. "So if he's not doing well, do you think I should go back to Torskethorpe?"

"That's up to you. Katla and Theo would never ask you to return, unless it was dire."

"Is it dire?"

Lara shakes her head. "Just cause for concern at this point, but he's working with the best doctors. We should know more soon."

"Okay." I lean against the doorway.

Silence falls between us, and I'm not sure either one of us knows what to do at this moment, because if something is seriously wrong with Theo, my role just became imminently more important.

———

LARA: *Have a good time. Don't think about our conversation from yesterday. After tonight, we'll figure it out.*

I stare down at her text just before I turn off my phone and slip it into my clutch.

"Are you ready?" Isabella asks, looping her arm through mine.

"I am but also a little nervous." I will be honest. It took a while to feel used to someone other than Runa getting me dressed and ready for tonight, but Ida, the lady-in-waiting Pala gave me while I've been here, has been so lovely. Gentle. Not quite as pushy or chatty as Runa, but quiet and efficient. I could *not* have gotten ready for this ball tonight without her. So, whilst I'm nervous, I know I *look* like a Torskethorpian princess.

"That's to be expected. This is a new experience for you, but I promise, you'll love it."

The curtains to the grand ballroom part, and a man standing next to us announces our arrival. Since we're both future queens, they had Isabella and me walk in together first.

The dance floor opens up as we walk forward, people moving aside to allow our entry. It feels like a scene out of *Bridgerton*, so regal and formal with a room decorated for royalty. Thousands of twinkle lights dangle from the ceiling while tall ice sculptures are dotted throughout the room. White trees from trunks to leaves scale the walls, casting shadows into the blue-lit walls from lights surrounding the floor perimeter. It feels like a winter fairyland in here, and for a moment, a weak moment, all I can think about is how fun it would have been to dance under these lights with Keller.

I wash that thought away quickly as Isabella holds on to me tightly, and we glide into the room.

I chose a light-blue formfitting gown with a high neckline and a dipped back that reaches the base of my shoulder blades. It's something I know Keller would have loved, and I think one of the reasons I chose it, out of spite. *God, why did he bail?*

I'm so sorry, but I think both of us knew this wasn't going to work. I'm not meant to be a prince. I'm not cut out for it.

I'm not cut out for it. *For fuck's sake, Keller, I wasn't even born in Torskethorpe, yet I'm trying.*

Enough.

Focus on this night. Focus on the beauty around me. Focus on my family.

I look at my beautiful cousin. We look so much alike, it's like we're sisters.

Isabella went with a classic white, bandeau neckline with rhinestones dripping off the fabric like teardrops. It's a gorgeous dress that I truly believe only she could pull off. And of course, she's wearing a tiara that was gifted to the monarchy by an ally country. She asked if I wanted to borrow one of their many tiaras, but I opted for a more Torskethorpian look and layered some flowers in my hair.

And of course, Marit, with her gorgeous long wavy locks, chose a midnight-blue silk trumpet dress that clings to every part of her body but flares at the bottom, giving her just enough space to walk and dance. I know this because she tested out her dancing skills while she was trying it on.

With my arm threaded with hers, Isabella takes me around the grand ballroom, introduces me to many people from all different social classes, and impresses me with her knowledge. One day, she's going to make a beautiful queen, dignified and composed. I can only wish to be like her.

By the time we're done making our rounds, the first song plays.

"Come dance," Isabella says, tugging on my arm, but I wave her off.

"Not sure I'm ready for that. I think I'm going to grab a drink and observe for a while."

"Are you sure? It's so much fun."

"Later on, let me get my feet wet first."

She winks at me. "I'm holding you to that." She heads toward the center of the room where she takes a man's hand in hers, and he starts formally dancing her around the room. Other couples join, reminding me of the 1800s.

Uh . . . not the kind of dancing I thought she was talking about.

Is that the waltz?

Hell if I know.

But let's just say, I probably won't be dancing later tonight unless that jumpity waltz turns into some club-like twerking, because that's all I know how to do. *Thank you, Miami nightlife.*

I move through the crowd, a few people stopping me to introduce themselves, and when I make it to the drinks, I put in an order of vodka and tonic with some lime. I might be in a better headspace than I was almost three months ago, but that doesn't mean I'm completely *mentally* ready for a party like this.

"What did you order?" a deep voice asks to my right. I glance over to find a tall man with blond hair and dark-rimmed glasses staring down at me. He's wearing what seems to be a military uniform, at least that's what I think it is from the plethora of medals pinned to his suit. His eyes are a unique deep green, and his square jaw is cleanly shaven, not a millimeter of facial hair on his face.

"I want to tell you water, so it makes me look regal," I answer.

"But really some vodka in disguise?" he asks, a raise to his brow.

"Possibly," I answer as I take the drink order from the bartender and thank him.

"I wouldn't judge you. These parties are hard."

"Yet you seem to be here. What would propel a man to come to a party that he's not looking forward to?"

"Parents. They think it's my duty as the future Lord of Sotherby to be here."

"Lord of Sotherby, well, that sounds fancy."

"Sounds like it, but it's just a title and presents expectations of who I'm supposed to marry."

"Ah, I see." I nod. "And what, pray tell, would those expectations be?"

"Someone with class. Someone with money. Someone with the personality of a dried-up crouton."

"You know, some might say a crouton is already dried up." I take a sip of my drink, the vodka stronger than I was expecting.

Holy crap that . . . burns.

I try to hold back my cough in front of this stranger, but it's no use. I let out a wallop as my mouth hangs open, searching for anything to eradicate this toxic liquid from my throat.

"No one warned you about the Marsdale vodka, did they?" he asks as he gently pats my back.

"Not so much," I say in a strangled voice.

"Don't worry, you burn your esophagus with your first sip, so the rest of the drink will go down like a breeze."

Chuckling, I say, "Good to know." When my coughing ceases, I look up at him and hold my hand out. "I'm Lilly, and I'm embarrassed to say I can't handle this liquor."

He takes my hand in his. "I'm Evan, my parents forced me to come here."

"It's nice to meet you, Evan, even though your parents forced you to be here."

"It's very nice to meet you," he says with a cheeky grin that's actually quite adorable.

"Are you from Marsdale?" I ask.

He clutches his chest. "Your Majesty, you wound me with your lack of knowledge. I'm the future Lord of Sotherby, after all."

"First of all, the *Your Majesty* stuff can be dropped right now. Hearing too much of that might break me out in hives, especially when I'm supposed to have a relaxed and fun evening. Second of all . . ." I lean closer and say, "I have no idea who the Sotherbys are, so help a girl out."

Laughing softly, he replies, "We live to the east of the capital."

"The capital? Wait, as in . . . Torskethorpe?" He nods. "Huh, so that means you have a general understanding of who I am."

"Perhaps," he answers as he lifts his drink to his lips.

"Let me ask you this . . . were you invited to the wedding that never happened?"

He rocks on his heels. "I was."

"Uh-huh." I nod. "And were you massively disappointed to know that you wouldn't be served a wedding vinarterta that night?"

"Cried myself to sleep."

"That would make two of us," I say as I take another sip of the toxic drink. And Evan was right, the second sip does go down easier.

Evan grows serious and says, "I'm sorry that it didn't work out. I won't ask you about it, so don't feel you need to go into details. I'm sure you're trying to forget it ever happened."

"I am, hence why I'm here."

"Well then, can I offer you some conversation to help you enjoy the evening?"

"I don't know." I look him up and down. "Are you a master conversationalist?"

"Master? Probably not. Interesting? Most definitely."

"Well then, show me the food so I can grab a bite before diving into this riveting conversation."

⸻

ISABELLA AND MARIT twirl around the dance floor, reminding me so much of Ana and Elsa from *Frozen*, enjoying the night under the twinkle lights. It makes me chuckle. And how they so willingly go from dance partner to dance partner. Poor Clinton, he has his hands full for sure. They are both boy hungry. From what I've learned, they're very inexperienced, pretty sheltered when it comes to dates—not knowledge—and all they want is to find someone to fall in love with. They don't get many opportunities, so they must be living out their dreams tonight.

"Tell me exactly why your parents found it necessary to fly here for a party?"

Evan pops a piece of cheese in his mouth, the blueberry goat cheese, and chews. When I tell you that Marsdale is famous for their cheese, they're not lying. I've filled up on so much dairy these past few weeks that I feel like I could milk myself at this point and create my own cheese.

"They had business to attend to. I have no idea, but they said my presence was required."

"And if your presence wasn't required, what would you be doing?" I ask.

"Building a stone wall."

I give him a disbelieving look.

"What?" He laughs. "It's true. I've been working on a stone wall."

"In the dead of winter?"

"The cold never bothered me."

"Are you a Disney princess?"

He chuckles. "Nah, but seriously, the cold really doesn't cut through me like I'm sure it cuts through you. You're from the beach somewhere?"

"Miami, Florida. And yes, the winter has nearly frozen off my limbs." I almost say nipples, but thanks to Keller's constant berating, I went with something more public friendly. *See, I have self-control and decorum.* Although, I'm not kidding about the nipple thing.

"Big culture shock. What else has been different since you've moved?"

"Uh, let's see. The love for cod. I'm not mad about it, but I've never seen a country so adamantly in love with a fish before. The weather, clearly. The seasons and daylight. The customs and traditions. Although I love them, they were different at first. And then of course, the restrictions that come with being the future queen. Oh, and I miss Target."

"What's Target?" he asks, nearly stabbing me right in the heart.

Who doesn't know what a Target is? Good God.

"Only the mecca of all stores. Come on, Evan," I say, exasperated. "Think of anything you might need. Bed sheets, deodorant, socks, fungal cream, strawberries . . . you can find it all in Target. It's a shopper's dream. One-stop shop."

"Wow. Yeah, we don't have those in Torskethorpe. I couldn't imagine what that might be like. Probably saves on time, rather than going to many small stores."

"I wouldn't know what that's like either. Not that I'm complaining, but I don't get out much."

"Maybe you should plan to have a day when you get back to Torskethorpe that focuses on visiting all the little shops along a main street. Might be a fun experience. Plus, the community would probably love to see you."

"That's actually a really good idea," I say.

"See, an interesting conversationalist. Aren't you happy you grabbed some cheese with me?"

"I think I might be."

———

"SO ARE you going to tell me about your medals?" I ask Evan. Our cheese is now finished, the vodka has barely been touched and replaced with a glass of wine for me, while Isabella and Marit are working the room, shaking hands, and taking a break from dancing. But I'm sure it won't be a very long break.

He glances down at his chest. "Just some shiny things that attempt to establish me as important."

"Well, are you?" I ask.

"Not as important as you," he answers with a charming smile.

"Debatable," I reply. "So were you in the military?"

"Secret operative actually," he says.

"Really?" I ask, standing taller. "Like . . . Tom Cruise in *Mission Impossible?*"

"Something like that." He chuckles.

"Do you still do it?"

He shakes his head and then lifts his beer. "No. Been out for a year. Now I'm training to be the next lord of the Sotherbys, remember?"

"Ah, how could I forget, your lordship." He chuckles. "From the tone of your voice, I'm guessing that's not something you want to do?"

"Not really," he says with a wince. "But it's what my parents want, and for some reason, I have this stark need to always please them, hence why I'm here in my military garb."

"Well, I might be bias, but it seems like you're having a good time."

His eyes scan me over, the green so deep that it almost seems black. After a brief perusal, he says, "Yeah, I am." He glances at the dance floor and then holds his hand out to me. "Care to dance?"

"Uh, I don't know any of the dance moves."

"This is just a simple slow song." He sets his beer down. "Come on, my parents will kill me if I don't dance at least once."

"Can't have parental homicide. Might not look good for the Sotherbys."

"See, you get it," he says as I place my hand in his and set down my drink.

As he guides me through the crowd, something feels so

unusual. It's not the environment or the glamour. It's not the music. I pause, wondering what feels so odd, and then it hits me. I'm holding another man's hand. *And it feels both odd and wrong.*

Evan is a nice guy and all, and he's handsome, fun to talk to, but an air about him is missing. The reason I was so transfixed with Keller was because he stole the oxygen right from my lungs. From his unruly disposition to the demanding scowl in his brow to the way he unraveled when it was just me and him. He commanded my soul with a single look.

And that realization makes me miss him all over again.

Fuck.

"Okay, just place your other hand on my shoulder," Evan says, knocking me out of my thoughts. "And follow my lead."

He lowers his hand to my waist, where he holds me tightly, bringing our chests to almost touching. I quickly inhale, taking in his sandalwood cologne, and glance up at his handsome face . . . and feel nothing.

Absolutely nothing.

It's so startling that I question if I'm dead inside.

Because here is a very attractive man, someone I'd consider my type. He's funny, he's charming, he's bulky in all the right places, and he's holding on to me, about to glide me along the dance floor. And for the life of me, I can't feel one freaking twitch, one jolt, one palpitation of my heart.

"Ready?" he asks.

"Ready," I say in response, with a smile.

Together, we move around the dance floor, dancing in time with the music. The room spins around us, the lights twinkling with every pass, and it almost feels like time slows down as another man holds me close to him.

For a moment, my eyes squeeze shut, and I can feel Keller holding me instead, his grip so strong that I know I belong to him and only him. His cheek pressing against my face, his rough five o'clock shadow marring me in the sexiest way possible. My emotions get the best of me as tears spring to my eyes.

God, don't cry, Lilly.

That would be humiliating.

Focus on Evan.

Focus on the cold, dark hole where your heart used to be.

"Oh no," Evan says, startling me again. "Don't look now, but my parents are watching. They're the couple over to the right. My mother is wearing the beehive hat on the top of her head, and my dad is the one with the foot-long mustache."

Pulling it together, I glance to the right where I see his parents, an ornery couple with eyes keen on us.

"That's one giant freaking mustache," I say, proud of myself for holding back my tears and clearing my mind of Keller.

Evan chuckles. "My mum combs it for him at night."

"Stop, no, she doesn't."

"She does," he says. "I walked in on them once. It was horrifying."

That makes me laugh, easing the growing tension in my chest. At least Evan can put a smile on my face. And at the end of the day, that's all I need right now.

⊏══⊐

"WHEN ARE you coming back to Torskethorpe?" Evan asks as we make our way back to the table we were standing at. A server brings around glasses of champagne, and Evan snags one for each of us, as well as some petit fours that have been passed around the room.

"Probably in the next day or so," I answer. I'd prefer to stay in Marsdale where I feel safe, where the memories of Keller don't flood me, but I also know that Theo is unwell, and that means I need to be there for him. Me being gone has probably added more stress to him.

"You say that as if it's a bad thing," he says. "Do you not love Torskethorpe?"

"No, I do," I say quickly. "But, you know, returning to a place where you've spent time falling in love with your ex-fiancé can pose obstacles."

He nods in understanding. "I get that. My girlfriend of five years broke up with me right before I deployed for my last mission. It was brutal coming back and reliving memories." *Five years. Does that make me a wuss, missing Keller so desperately?* We were only together months. Should I feel thankful that there aren't years of memories? *Perhaps.* I cannot imagine the pain Evan experienced, especially while he was serving his country so honorably.

"Did it get easier after a while?" I ask.

He nods. "It did. It took some time, just like every breakup, but it got easier. And you know what? Her loss, she could have been Lady of Sotherby." He smirks and picks up a pink square cake from the plate we're sharing.

"Huge mistake," I say. "Plus, the daughter-in-law to the grandest mustache in Torskethorpe. Ooof, what a missed opportunity for her."

"I'm glad you see it that way." The music dies down, and everyone starts clapping. "Looks like the evening has come to an end."

"Really? Well, that flew by."

"Always does when you're in good company." His smile spreads wide, and he really is quite attractive. "Which leads me to my question."

Uh-oh . . .

"What question would that be?" I ask, growing nervous.

"If you would like to have lunch some time, when you're back in Torskethorpe." Before I can answer, he holds up his hand and adds, "No pressure. I know things are complicated for you, but if you need some company, I'm there."

I mentally sigh, because thank God he added that.

"Thank you," I say as I stare at my champagne. "I'm just . . . I'm not sure."

"That's totally fine," he says, bending at the knees to catch my attention. "Just figured I'd put it out there. And if you get bored or need someone to walk the streets to see the *little* shops, I'm only a phone call away. Just ask for the future lord of the Sotherbys."

I chuckle and look him in the eyes. "I'll keep that in mind for sure. Thank you, Evan. And thank you for taking my mind off everything for the evening."

"Anytime." He bows before me and says, "Good evening, Princess Lilly."

And just as quickly as he appeared, he disappears, leaving me confused and sad at the same time.

It was such an easy night. There wasn't any drama, there wasn't any fighting, it was just simple conversation, and I honestly can't remember the last time I had that with Keller.

They are two very different men. Evan seems very relaxed, maybe a touch guarded, but I'd blame that on his profession. He wasn't here to command or control me, but to have a good time. If I had spent the night with Keller, he'd have reprimanded me for saying something inappropriate, he'd have worried about what people thought of him as the man who stood by my side, and even though he likes to control everything in his life, I would have relished in having him hold me against his chest as he moved me around the dance floor.

And why is that?

Was our relationship really based on our physical attraction to each other? Was that all it ever was? Because if I'm honest, our problems began when we entered the month of celibacy. When Keller wasn't *my king* and we didn't have that aspect of our relationship to fall back on. *To rely on. Would we have actually gone the distance if sex was what held us together?*

"There you are," Marit says as she and Isabella walk up to me. "You're finally alone." Marit playfully pokes me.

"Dancing the night away with Evan Sotherby, good choice," Isabella says.

"Did he ask you out?" Marit asks.

"He did," I say, causing them to squeal with excitement. "I turned him down, though, well . . . I actually told him I wasn't sure." I sigh and lean my elbow on top of the high-top table. "I don't know, just doesn't feel right."

"I get that," Isabella says. "But at least you took the first step tonight and allowed yourself to talk to someone else."

"Exactly." Marit takes my hand. "The first step is the most important."

Maybe it is.

———

"ARE you feeling better than when you first arrived in Marsdale?" Lara asks me as we make our way to the airport.

I said my goodbyes to Isabella and Marit this morning, and we promised to visit each other as much as possible. I also said goodbye to Pala and Clinton and thanked them for their hospitality. Chef Martin made me some fresh croissants and jam for the trip, which of course made Isabella and Marit smile knowingly.

"I am," I say. "I think I needed that time away."

"You did." She clears her throat. "And spending the whole night with Evan Sotherby, that was a turn of events I wasn't expecting."

"Okay, when you say whole night, you make it seem like he spent the night with me, and you and I both know that didn't happen."

"Fine, you spent the whole party with him."

"Better," I say with a smile. "And yes, he was nice to talk to. I enjoyed his company."

Lara nods and looks out the window, indicating she's hiding something. I know her too well at this point.

"What aren't you telling me?" I ask. "And don't say nothing, because I know it'll be a lie."

She rolls her head to the side, a smile playing on her face. "We need to distance our relationship; you're becoming too in tune with me." I laugh, and she continues, "It's just interesting that you ended up talking to Evan."

"Why? Do you know him?"

"I do," Lara says. "He's very well decorated and has immense clout in the government."

"Oh, so lord of the Sotherbys is actually something special?"

She chuckles and shakes her head. "No, that's just some silly title his dad likes to cart around. This is outside of his last name. He's worked very hard as a secret operative for Torskethorpe. Theo is a big fan of his."

"Oh," I say, surprised by that. "He didn't mention that."

"Of course he wouldn't. Evan is really humble. Great guy actually. I know he's out of a job now with his retirement, but he's an excellent resource if you ever need one who's not Henrik, or anyone in the palace for that matter. He's been through the ins and outs of government business with Torskethorpe. His parents are a bit much, but that's probably something you can look past."

"Why do you say that as if I'm interested in him? Because I'm not. I mean, sure, he's very attractive and charming and has a great sense of humor, but I can't fathom even thinking about dating anyone right now."

"I know," Lara says. "Just for the future."

And that gives me pause because it's the first time she's mentioned me moving on, or at least implied it.

Looking out the window, watching the rolling hills go by, I ask, "Do you really think Keller isn't coming back this time?"

Lara heaves a heavy sigh. "I'd be the first one to tell you to hold out, that he'll come back." Her fingers twist together in her lap. "But I don't think that's the case this time. There hasn't been any correspondence. Nothing. As much as it pains me to say . . . I don't think he's coming back."

"How do you know?" I ask, feeling my heart in my throat.

"Because." Her eyes meet mine. "The first time you two were separated, he checked on you every day, if not multiple times a day. This time . . . I haven't heard one thing." She shakes her head. "Not one damn thing."

Chapter Twenty-Three

KELLER

Footsteps make their way down the hall, halting me from my wall squats.

As quickly as I can, I slide to the floor, spread across the hard stone, and curl into a feeble ball just as the door to my cell opens.

"Well, he's looking rather pathetic today, isn't he?" a familiar voice says. I've been trying to place it, but for the life of me, I'm having the hardest damn time.

The first time I heard it was when I was brought to this cell. My mind wasn't functioning properly from being drugged and tased, so I didn't think too much of it.

But the second time I heard it, I realized I've heard the deep baritone before.

And now, hearing it again, I keep my breath still so I can listen closely for any tells, anything that would point me in the direction of figuring this out.

"And he smells foul."

Not my fault. They don't do anything but hose me down every once in a while.

No soap.

No deodorant.

Nothing.

Their problem, not mine.

The smell is actually working to my advantage. Banamaor doesn't want to stay in my cell for very long because I smell so bad, so it makes the torture even shorter.

"Well, shall we tell him?" the familiar voice asks.

I remain still, as still as I can be.

"I think we should."

There's purpose behind what they're about to tell me, meaning, they want a reaction. And that's not something I'll give them. I've come this far, playing the part of the nearly dead prisoner, I'm not about to lose all that work because of their predisposed plans of trying to rile me up.

Stay cool.

Stay calm.

It will pay off.

"It seems like the princess has found some freedom being newly single."

My breath pauses in my throat.

Freedom?

As in . . .

My nostrils flare as my teeth grind together. I was ready for them to tell me something that would anger me, something about Torskethorpe, maybe something about Lilly being brokenhearted, but I'm not fucking ready to hear about Lilly and her newfound freedom.

"Spent a month in Marsdale, just as we expected."

The familiar voice says, "And for a moment, we thought that she was still too hurt to even think about looking at another man, but she surprised us at this past Winter Flurries party held by King Clinton."

My tongue curls in my mouth as red-hot anger bursts through me.

Lilly with someone else?

No fucking way.

She'd never.

"I still can't believe she spent the whole night dancing and talking with Evan Sotherby."

What?

Evan?

What was he doing in Marsdale?

"She looked very smitten, didn't she?" the familiar voice asks.

"Very. Glad we set that up. Everything is going according to plan, wouldn't you say?"

"I would." Familiar voice comes up to me and kicks me in the leg. The pain is nothing at this point, but I groan just to make the asshole happy. "With this pathetic ass out of the way, we just have to take out Lilly, and Torskethorpe is ours."

"And once it's ours, we're claiming Birch Forest."

"Shut up, you nimrod," the familiar voice says. *The shrill of his voice.* Frustration creeps up my chest as I can't place him. "Come on. We have to speak to our contacts, see how the king is doing."

They leave the cell, locking up, and when I no longer hear their footsteps, I sit up, the cold of the floor still pressed into my chest, matching the cold seeping into my heart.

She's been seen with Evan Sotherby? Would she really move on that quickly? And how the hell did they set that up? Evan is as loyal as I am when it comes to his country and protecting the crown. He wouldn't be swayed by the enemy.

I drag my hand over my face, as I bend my knees to my chest, and try to figure out this goddamn puzzle.

Fuck, is she really seeing him?

I tug on my greasy hair, the strands much longer than I've

ever worn them now. Would she move on that quickly? *No, they're just trying to fuck with you. That's been their plan all along.*

Stay straight, Keller.

Don't let them get to you.

Focus on figuring out what you know so far.

Familiar voice.

Almost two familiar voices.

Definitely attached to Arkham, that much is true.

Wanting to take over Torskethorpe, overthrow Lilly.

Wanting the Birch Forest . . .

I press my hands to my head.

Fuck, what does it all mean?

Why would they want Birch Forest? That makes no sense to me.

And what the fuck do they have planned for Lilly?

They hate me. The first step was intended to make Lilly believe I didn't want her. But why not just kill her? If they want the throne, that's the most logical tactic. Why are they keeping me alive? *How does that work to their advantage?*

And who are their contacts at the palace?

Once again, there's a mole. But who?

Chapter Twenty-Four

LILLY

Next to his nightstand, the dim yellow glow casts a shadow over Theo's face as he rests in his bed.

"He's sleeping," I whisper to Katla. "I don't want to disturb him."

"He said the moment you returned he wanted to speak to you." Katla encourages me to step forward. "Please, dear, he wants to see you."

The entire flight home from Marsdale, I was dreading this, having to see Theo. I was worried what he might look like, how sick he might be, and from a brief glimpse, I can tell he's lost some weight, which is concerning. I tried to ask Katla how he was as we walked up to his room, but all she said was tired and excited to see me.

So I'm truly in the dark here.

Katla gives me a pat on the shoulder and then closes the door behind me, startling Theo awake.

He glances over at the door, and when he spots me, his

face lights up. "My darling, Lilija," he says, reaching his arm out.

My emotions get the best of me, hearing his comforting voice, and as I step up to him, tears careen down my cheeks.

"No, my dear, please don't cry."

"I'm sorry," I say as I sit next to him on his bed. "I just . . . I didn't know you were sick. I'd have come back sooner."

"Stop it." He waves me off as he sits up in his bed. I help him prop his pillows behind him and make sure he's comfortable. "I'm glad you went to Marsdale. Did you have fun?"

"I did," I answer. "I love Isabella and Marit. They were just what I needed."

"Good." He squeezes my hand. "And how do you feel about Keller?"

"Probably how you think I feel about him. Angry. Hurt. Confused." Especially now knowing that he hasn't even reached out to Lara to see how I'm doing. Something doesn't sound right about that, but clearly, I didn't know Keller as well as I thought I did. I honestly didn't think him capable of such betrayal . . . and then to simply not give a shit about me. *And the anger is back.*

He nods. "All valid reactions to the situation."

Feeling like I can open up finally, I say, "I just don't get it. I don't understand any of it. He told me he'd see me down the aisle, that we were getting married, that I was his forever. I just don't understand what changed overnight. What made him have such a one-eighty. And then go completely silent?" I shake my head. "I don't understand."

"I've been asking myself the same questions," Theo says. "I can't fathom a moment when Keller would do this. The only thing that makes me believe he'd do such a thing would be to protect you."

"What do you mean?"

Theo tugs on his beard and says, "I've been running through scenarios with Ottar, and our only possible conclusion is that he knew if the wedding didn't go through, then the threats we've been receiving wouldn't happen. Therefore, he was protecting you."

"Protecting me?" I ask, anger curdling deep in my stomach. "That's not protecting me. That's crushing my very soul. I didn't need a hero. I needed a husband."

"I'm not saying that's *what he thought*," Theo says. "But I also can't think of any other reasoning. But even with that reasoning, he should have talked to me, talked to Ottar before making that decision for everyone."

"And why make me believe we were getting married? It makes no sense. And also, not to have any communication with anyone afterward? As if we wouldn't care to hear from him? I know I'm not the only one hurting here. You and Katla, Ottar . . . Lara. Even Henrik. This has hurt all of us."

"It has," Theo says as he leans his head against the headboard. "It has truly taken a toll on my emotional health. I can't stand knowing that he's left us under circumstances that could have been controlled. I hate that he's out there, somewhere, alone. I hate that you have been hurt so bad it might be beyond repair." His eyes water up. "Will you even let yourself love again?"

My heart thumps heavily in my chest as I scoot closer. "Of course," I say. "Of course, I'll love again. I think it might take some time, but I'll get there."

He swipes at his eyes, then closes them, taking a few long breaths. "I don't know how much longer I'll be on this earth, Lilija. I don't want to know that you're going to take over this responsibility and have to do it alone. My heart can't bear it." He presses his hand to his chest. "I flipped your world upside down by bringing you here. I've asked more from you than any person should ever ask, and now . . . now you'll assume your role with no one by your side." He shakes his head. "It's not right."

"Stop," I say, bringing his hand between both of mine. "I

have plenty of people near me, and you're not going anywhere, okay?"

"We can't be sure of that," he says, being so evasive that it's killing me. "This is all my fault. I put too much pressure on Keller. To protect you, to be there for you, to make sure he helps carry on the bloodline. Of course, he fled. It was too much to ask of someone. *Again.* And look what it has done."

"Please, Theo, please stop." I grab a tissue from his night-stand and dab at his eyes. "This is not your fault. You were looking out for what's best for this country, and that's what a king is supposed to do. It's always been said, country first. As royals, we are humans, and we're allowed our feelings, but like you've said before, it's about the sacrifices we make for this country."

Theo silently shakes his head as more tears fall down his cheeks, the sight of him so distraught tearing a hole in my already battered heart.

I don't want to see him like this.

I don't want my misfortune to cause him any more pain or even worse, create a situation that he can't bounce back from.

After losing both of my parents and feeling so alone for so long, finding Katla and Theo has been like a reawakening for me. A chance to reconnect with my mom, and I've been so grateful for these past couple of months. I'd do anything for them.

Anything to keep Theo safe.

To keep him safe.

I'd *sacrifice* anything . . .

My words echo back into my mind: *It's the sacrifices we make for this country.*

Sacrifices . . .

Steeling my jaw, I tack on a smile. Theo doesn't want me to be alone, then I'll make sure he doesn't think I'm alone. He needs to get better, and if this will make him better, I'll do it.

"And you don't need to worry about me because I actually . . . uh, I actually met someone."

"What?" Theo looks at me, confused. "You met someone?"

"Yes, at the Winter Flurries party. We talked the whole evening and danced one dance. It was all very platonic, but he actually lives here in Torskethorpe, and we seemed to have clicked. He asked me out to lunch, and I told him I'd get back to him." I hide my unsteady hands that seem to involuntarily shake.

"Who is it?" Theo asks.

"Evan Sotherby."

"Oh." Theo looks surprised. "Good man. Has done a lot for this country. He was in Marsdale?"

"Yes, apparently his parents had some business to tend to, and they forced him to go with them. Something about always wanting to please his parents."

Theo nods in understanding. "Evan has a complex relationship with his parents. Lost his brother in a horrible boating accident off the coast. Evan wanted to leave the military immediately to be with his parents, to help them through the loss, but his contract kept him in the military for five more years. I believe, from what I've been told, Evan will do anything to make his parents happy. So attending an event like a Winter Flurries party, something that's out of character for him, is an event he'd take on if it meant making his parents happy."

"Yeah, I got that impression from him. He didn't speak of his brother, though. I know what losing a loved one is like."

"Yes, you do," Theo says. "We both do." Clearing his throat, he asks, "Are you actually ready to move on? It seemed that at the beginning of this conversation, you mentioned it taking time."

"It will take time, but at least I can get to know someone while I adjust my feelings."

"And what about Keller?" Theo asks. "If he ever came back, what would you do then?"

"Wouldn't matter." I shake my head. "We're done." And I mean that. I can't imagine a scenario where we'd ever be a couple again, not after all of this.

"Even if he had the best of intentions?"

"The best of intentions would have been walking down the aisle for me, threat or no threat. He should have trusted the security strategies he'd helped plan. Leaving me the morning of our wedding to deal with the humiliation and heartbreak of not marrying the person I thought would be there for the rest of my life . . . that's not something I could ever forgive."

Theo nods solemnly. "Then I guess that means it's time to move on."

"It does," I say while I look into his weathered eyes. "What about you? How can I help you get better?"

"You being here is all I need." He softly smiles, and even though he's saying that's all he needs, there's this niggling feeling in the back of my head that this is more serious than he's letting on. And if that's the case, I can't let him think that I'm not going to be okay, that I'm going to be alone. That I won't have someone by my side, helping guide me through the role of the queen of Torskethorpe.

The more stress I can take off his shoulders, the better.

Which means one thing. I need to find out how to contact Evan, the future lord of the Sotherbys.

———

STARING down at the number in my phone, I take a deep breath and write out a text.

You're doing this to move on.

You're doing this for Theo.

You're doing this for the country that has embraced you so lovingly.

Squeezing my eyes shut, I press send.

Lilly: *Hey Evan, it's Lilly. I pulled rank and got your number. I hope that's okay.*

I stand from my bed and pace my room, phone in hand. When I asked Lara for Evan's number, I felt like I was back in middle school, looking to score the hot guy's phone number from a friend. Lara of course had no problem finding it for me, but God, was it embarrassing. And when she handed it to me, she asked me if I was sure about this. She wanted to make sure I wasn't rushing into anything, and I told her I was more than ready, even though in the back of my head, I know that I'm not.

I'm still in love with Keller.

You don't get over that kind of love quickly. But I feel like I'm up against a wall right now. Theo isn't doing great, and seeing me upset, heartbroken, isn't helping him in any way. He needs to see me happy. He needs to see me functioning, not withering away in my room. I need to get back to my public appearances. I need to show him that everything will be okay.

And maybe, just maybe, if I show him I'm doing fine, he will get better. Because I'm not ready to lose him too. *I've only just found him.* I'm not sure how I'd cope if I lost both Keller and Theo.

I'm on my third round of pacing when my phone dings back with a message. I'm so startled that I nearly drop my phone.

I lift the screen and read the text.

Evan: *Pulling rank to get my phone number? I'm honored. Also . . . feeling slightly stalked. [Emoji: winking, tongue out]*

Okay, just as playful as the other night. See, I can do this. He's easy to talk to.

Lilly: *Perhaps, but some might call it using their resources.*

Luckily for me, he texts right back.

Evan: *There's a positive spin. So to what do I owe the distinct pleasure?*

Lilly: Well, I was doing some research on the Sotherbys when I got back to Torskethorpe, and you weren't entirely honest with me.

Evan: Are you accusing me of lying to the future queen of Torskethorpe?

Lilly: I am. This could bring you a grave deal of jail time and dishonor to your family.

Evan: Ouch. Please tell me what I lied to you about.

Lilly: According to Torskethorpian Wikipedia, the Sotherbys are actually in charge of one hundred acres of land. That's a lot of acreage.

Evan: Are you impressed with the Sotherby's acreage?

Lilly: More like concerned since you think the lord of the Sotherbys doesn't do much. Your father is in charge of land for the goats.

Evan: Ah yes, the goats.

Lilly: I'm sensing you're not a fan of the goats.

Evan: The goats don't really care for me.

Lilly: If the goats don't care for you, then how on earth are you going to be the lord of the Sotherbys?

Evan: Great question. I'd love to have lunch with you to discuss it. (I figured that's where this was heading, please correct me if I'm wrong.)

Lilly: No, you're not wrong. How would you feel about coming to Strombly for some lunch? Feel free to bolt past the guards any time the conversation gets boring to you.

Evan: Boring? With you? Impossible. And I'd love to come for lunch. Name the time and date.

———

"HE'S IN THERE?" I whisper to Lara, pointing at the door that leads to the green room.

"He is," Lara replies.

"Oh God. What am I doing?" I whisper so he can't hear. "This is crazy. I mean, I just got left at the altar, and here I am, going out to lunch with another man. People are going to think I'm a floozy. Am I a floozy?"

Lara grips my shoulders and looks me in the eye. "The

reason you told me you're doing this is because you said you're ready to move on, and you want to let Theo know you'll be okay. But if you've changed your mind, I'll go in there right now and send him home."

I bite the corner of my lip. "The prospect of you sending him home is very appealing to me at the moment, but I can't do that to him. It's just lunch, right? It's not like I'm going to slink to the floor and give him a blow job."

"Jesus," Lara replies, wincing. "Why would you say that?"

"I don't know. I'm nervous. I say stupid things when I'm nervous."

"Well, don't say that to him. Remember, you're still expected to remain somewhat poised."

"Yes. I know." I shake my arms out and bounce from side to side in my wide-leg trousers and black sweater. "I can do this. It's just lunch." I smile wide and get right in Lara's face. "Is there anything in my teeth?"

She leans back and examines. "No. You're good."

"Good, starting off on the right foot. That's great. Okay. Just lunch. I can do this."

"You can do this."

I head toward the door but then quickly turn around and grip Lara's arm. "I'm still in love with Keller though, so this is weird and I fear that I might tell him that and getting over Keller is going to take some time but I don't have time I need to do this now so please, for the love of cod, let me be normal in there and not mention that man who broke my heart into a million pieces."

Lara blinks a few times. "Uh . . . good luck?"

"Thank you." I turn away and then stick my butt out to her.

"What are you doing?" she asks.

"I need a solid slap to the ass. Like a go get 'em kid type of smack."

"You want me to slap your ass?"

295

"Yes. As a friend, I'm asking you to spank me."

Lara looks over my shoulder to the guards, then back at me. "Sometimes I truly wonder where you've come from." And with that, she slaps me on the ass, sending me on my way.

The guards open the doors for me, and I walk into the room where Evan stands from his chair with a large smile on his face.

Dressed in regular clothes this time, a pair of flat-faced gray chino pants and a forest-green shirt, he looks very handsome but also slightly nervous.

As I approach, he adjusts his glasses and bows. "Lilly, it's so nice to see you." I step up for a handshake, which he takes, then places a kiss on each of my cheeks.

"That was so formal," I say.

He chuckles. "Yeah, well it's not very often you're invited to a lunch date at Strombly. Consider me slightly shook."

I chuckle, and we both take a seat at the table while staff moves about the room, filling our glasses with water and setting a fruit platter on the table for us to pick at. "Funny enough, this is my first official lunch date at Strombly too, so we can take each other's virginity together." The moment the words leave my mouth, I wince. "I mean . . . uh, maybe phrasing that's classier than that."

He laughs. "I quite like the virginity thing." He pauses and then with a horrified expression, he says, "Uh, wait, that didn't sound right."

"No, it did not." I smile.

"Maybe we start this conversation over."

"Why? It's going so well already."

He smirks and it's quite cute. "You sure know how to make someone feel comfortable."

"Is that sarcasm?" I ask him.

He shakes his head. "No, it's not. Many people I've met in the higher positions in the government are pretty stuck-up, the king and queen excluded. If I said half the stuff to them that I've said to you, I'm pretty sure I'd be court-martialed."

"Well, have no fear, there's nothing stuck-up about me . . . other than the fact that I'm still trying to get used to the fermented cod cakes."

"That will take time. Just be happy you're not an honored guest at the fermented cod cake cook-off. I've seen many a judge lose their cookies at those events."

"Making mental notes to tell Henrik that I'll never take the job on."

"Very smart." He picks up a strawberry. "What made you change your mind about lunch?"

I shrug. "Just thought it might be fun. I had a good time the other night and figured why not allow myself to continue to have a good time. And in all honesty, when you asked me, I was caught off guard. It's so close to the wedding that I was second-guessing myself. But, you know, we're just talking and hanging out, that's all."

"Exactly. No promises, nothing like that. I really enjoyed our evening too. And if anything, I can now say the future queen of Torskethorpe stalked me."

"I expect you to put that on your résumé."

"Already did." He smirks again.

⸺

"I'M sorry you had to see that," I say to Evan, who quietly sips his soup across from me.

"See what?" he asks.

"Me sucking on this soup like it's life's nectar."

He lets out a laugh, his head tilting back, showing off the thick column of his neck. I've noticed that the thin fabric of his sweater has indicated that this man has a fit body. Not just fit . . . ripped.

The soft fabric clings to every contour and sinew of his

body from his pecs to his biceps. And with every move he makes, the sweater tugs and pulls across each muscle, momentarily distracting me. I might still be in love with another man, but it's hard not to stare at what Evan has to offer.

"It's good soup. I won't hold it against you."

I lean back in my chair and rest my hands on my lap while he finishes his soup. "You've bestowed some class on this lunch date. If it wasn't for you, this table would be hounded by rabid beasts."

"You being one of them?" he asks.

"Naturally, and the woodland creatures I keep in my purse."

"Aw, I heard a rumor about you carting around squirrels, but up until now, I just assumed it was a rumor."

"No, it's all true, they accompany me on outings and keep me on the straight and narrow."

"But not while eating?"

"No, we all lose our sense of decorum while food is in front of us."

He chuckles. "You know, you don't expect someone within the royal family to have such a great sense of humor, or at least you don't see it that often. It's refreshing."

"It's my downfall. Keller was always whispering under his breath to pull it together." I pause and then sigh. "Ugh, sorry. I didn't want to bring him up."

"It's okay," Evan says, his voice full of understanding. "Keller was a huge part of your life. You were going to be married."

"I know, but it's just weird. And probably really uncomfortable for you."

"No, it's not. I know him. I could see him saying that to you."

"You know him?" I ask.

He nods. "Yes, I've done some woodwork with him in the past. He's also been a part of the different medal ceremonies that I've participated in. You probably don't want to hear it, but he's a good guy."

"Yeah . . . he is," I say. Just can't stick around to marry me is all. "Just didn't have what it takes, I guess."

The servers walk into the room again. This time, they bring a three-tier plate of sandwiches and desserts while taking away our soup bowls. When they leave, I say, "This feels more like a tea party than a date."

"I like tea parties," he says while picking up a cucumber sandwich.

"Have you ever been to one?"

"Not really," he says, "but I've seen them on television, and they seem enjoyable." He takes a bite of his sandwich, and his expression morphs into shock. "Wow, this is really good."

"It's my favorite," I say. "I love a cucumber sandwich. So delicious."

"I was eating this first because I thought I wasn't going to like it." He examines the sandwich. "Now I regret my decision."

"What were you saving for last?"

"The cod cake."

I pluck the cod cake and set it on my plate. "Yeah, this is my first one."

He smiles. "Still not a fan?"

"Getting there. It's going to take time. Slowly but surely. At least this one is fresh, and it's not fermented. Those I struggle with terribly."

"At least you're honest."

I cut into my cod cake with a fork and dip it into my individual sauce bowl. The more the merrier. "Why did you join the military? I know that seems like an odd question, but I'm curious given who your family is."

He dabs his mouth with his napkin. "I wanted to feel something, anything," he says. "Growing up as a Sotherby, it just felt like everything was handed to us. My parents live among the upper crust, and they dragged us around from party to party. Mum would spend her evening with the women, trying to decide who would be the perfect match for her sons, and my dad would be in the parlor rooms, smoking cigars and making deals with the other pompous men in the room. I'd be stuck in the ballroom, watching everyone follow suit, and I hated it. I wanted so much more. I wanted to travel, feel alive, feel the earth, seek out way more than this world where we ate the finest food and sneered at the people who made way less than us."

"Wow," I say. "That's impressive. So you thought the military was the way to go?"

He nods. "Yes. I just felt like I'd be doing something, to make use of the breath I was given. And it was fine to leave because my brother was staying with my parents, and he'd take over, but then I lost my brother in a boating accident, and everything seemed to fall apart."

"Oh gosh, I'm so sorry," I say, reaching out and placing my hand on his. I run my thumb over his knuckles. "I lost my parents in a car accident. It was devastating. I can only imagine how you felt."

"Numb," he says.

"That's the perfect way to describe it."

He nods. "I was on contract with the military, so I had to remain on duty until the contract was over, but after, I promised to take care of my parents. They were suffering terribly from the loss. I know Dad made some bad deals, and Mum spent most of her days in her bed, weeping. It changed the dynamic of my family, and I'm not sure we'll ever recover." His lips twist to the side as he looks up at me. "Makes you really want to go out on another date with me, doesn't it?"

I chuckle and squeeze his hand. "I do. I like how real you are. But I do wonder, you know what my life is like here, right? It's very upper crust."

"I bet there's a big difference from my family to yours," he says. "You reach out to the community, raise money, do good for your people. That wasn't the case with the parties my parents attended. The exact opposite actually. They were more about trying to get involved with the wrong people so they could make more, have finer things, present themselves as the true lord and lady of the Sotherbys."

"Makes sense. Money and greed are a strange thing. Are they still like that?"

He shakes his head. "Like I said, they've changed. They rarely go to parties now. I was truly stunned when they wanted to fly to Marsdale for the Winter Flurries party. It's something they would have done in the past, but not something they'd do now. But I didn't question them. I can also add that they were quite taken with you and urged me to see if you were okay when they saw you standing by yourself."

"Really?" I ask. "You wouldn't have come up to me otherwise?"

He shakes his head. "No. Not because I wasn't interested, but because that's just not within my character."

"Well, you were pretty good at it and clearly made a good first impression."

"You made it easy."

My cheeks blush. "Good line." I call him out, making him laugh and shake his head.

"I see how this is going to go."

━━

"AND HERE ARE some pictures of old people who I'm still trying to learn about," I say as Evan walks right next to me on the tour I offered him.

"Fascinating. Your in-depth knowledge of Strombly has made this a magnificent tour."

"Thank you," I say on a laugh. "Pretty sure Henrik would keel over if he heard what I was saying."

"I've met him a few times, and I'd agree with you." Evan gestures to a large picture of Theo and says, "Do you know who this is?"

I laugh and push at his shoulder. "Of course. That's my grandfather, also known as the King of Torskethorpe."

"You got one right. Good job."

"I mean, I don't want to brag, but . . . look at me knowing things." I fluff my hair.

"When do you get your picture painted?"

"Oh, I already sat for it. I think they're just putting the finishing touches on it. Honestly, I have no idea what progress has been made since I've been sort of MIA. I should ask Henrik. Katla told me that the first painting she had done of her, the artist gave her an absurd nose. She was so polite that she wasn't going to complain about it until Theo saw the portrait and demanded the artist give her a nose job."

Evan laughs. "Did he say it like that?"

"He did."

"My assumption about the royal family isn't correct. You all have a sense of humor, but you just don't show it."

"For the most part, yes. And Theo, he seems so intimidating with his big beard and stern eyebrows, but he's the biggest, cuddly bear ever. He has so much love to offer. And Katla, she's very precise and regimented, but she also has a fun side, a loving, teasing side that feels motherly and also like she's a friend at the same time. I'm so glad I found them."

"You enjoy being up here? You think you'll stay? I know things with Keller could have rocked that a bit."

"It did, for a second, but this is home. Torskethorpe is home. I might still be learning about it, learning about the traditions, getting used to the cold and the fermented cod cakes, but I feel more at home here than I did in Miami. Once my parents died, I really didn't have anything to cling to there.

When I was brought here, it felt like my mom surrounded me. I saw where she grew up, and I was able to hold the linens she'd embroidered. I've been able to look into the eyes of her parents. It feels right."

"You have quite the story," he says. "I don't think anyone has the kind of tale that you have. Plucked out of a different culture and dropped into this one, into a family you didn't know existed. It's truly something to witness, especially since you've given up everything to make sure Torskethorpe remains led by Strom blood."

"It's an honor," I say as we come to the end of the hallway. "Well, I think that just about ends our tour."

"Probably the best tour I ever received."

I turn toward him. "I'm glad you enjoyed it."

"I enjoyed lunch too," he says. "If you're interested, I'd like to take you out somewhere. I know you'd need to talk to your security and all of that, but if you can carve out some time, I'd like to see you again. Maybe we can check out those shops . . ."

"I'd like that," I say, and I mean it. I had a good time with Evan. Could I see something growing with him, probably not at the moment. My heart is still attached to someone else, but then again, the more I hang out with him, maybe those feelings for Keller will fade away. Not to mention, this isn't just about love, this is about letting Theo know I'll be okay.

This is about making Theo better.

"Good." He takes my hand in his, and he brings my knuckles to his lips. He presses a soft kiss to them and then releases my hand. "I'll text you, and you can let me know what works."

"That would be great," I say, my smile feeling wobbly, because even though this wonderful man is standing in front of me, asking me out, all I can think about, all I can see, is Keller's face and what he'd have thought if he saw Evan kiss the back of my hand.

Chapter Twenty-Five

KELLER

Today is the day.

Today, I'm getting the fuck out of here.

I've played the peon and garnered his sympathy, so now I'm not chained to anything. He's offered me another blanket, and he's given me more food. I know this is against what his bosses are saying, but he seems to have a heart inside him.

I've built my plan in my head.

I've considered the possibility that if anything goes wrong, I can lose my life.

But that's a chance I'm willing to take because after yesterday, I can't fucking be in here anymore.

I stare down at the newspaper that the familiar voice dropped off yesterday. Told me it would provide me with some good reading material.

The minute he left, and I saw the headline, I wanted to scream.

Princess Lilly Finds New Beau.

Evan Sotherby.

How the fuck could she?

I didn't believe it at first, but when I read the article and saw the picture of them walking the streets of Torskethorpe together, I nearly threw up.

From what I've been able to figure out with scratches against the floor, under my hay spot, it's been a little over three months since the wedding.

Three fucking months!

And she's moving on?

Over my dead fucking body.

So today is the day.

I will not stand by and be fed newspaper after newspaper article about how my girl is dating someone else.

I clutch my hands together while I lean against the cold stone, my eyes set on the door in front of me.

Banamaor will be here today.

He's my way out.

And then when I'm free, when I get the hell out of here, I'm going to make it my life's fucking duty to find out who's behind this and make them pay.

Footsteps sound down the hall, right on schedule. I lift from where I'm seated and move behind the door. Now that I've played these fucking fools, they don't even bother with extra security. Banamaor lets himself in, fucks around a bit, hits me a few times, and then leaves. Nothing like when he first showed up. And if I planned this out right, I'll be able to take advantage of it. *Please, may this work.* I'll be able to take advantage of it.

The key to my cell is inserted into the lock, and it twists open, followed by the door.

Ready.

Fear and excitement creep up the back of my neck. *Don't fuck it up, Keller.*

I wait for just the right moment . . .

He steps into the cell, shutting the door, and that's when I pounce.

I cover his mouth with my hand to muffle any sound he makes, and with one quick yank, I snap his neck, rendering him dead on the spot.

With my foot, I shut the cell door, then slowly lower Banamaor to the floor.

I wipe the back of my hand over my nose and stare down at his lifeless form. "Fuck . . . you," I whisper.

Step one, complete. Now to follow through with the rest.

I move him over to the hay and then start peeling his clothes off him as well as his leather face mask. Thankfully, we're the same size and were once the same build, or else this plan wouldn't have worked. Where I was once muscled and broad, I'm now much more lean. *I'm stronger from this time apart from Lilly.*

Once he's undressed, I slip out of my rags and replace them with Banamaor's clothes, leaving the face mask to the side for now. Bigger on me, I adjust the pants on my narrow hips and fit the shirt over my chest. It will do for now.

I don't bother putting my clothes on him because they'd probably tear anyway. Instead, I drag him over to the hay, and I drape the blankets that were given to me over his large body and precariously cover his face so they can't tell it's him.

When I lift, I take a deep breath and calm my racing heart. Adrenaline will not do me any good right now. I need to remain focused and steady.

Just in case someone is outside my cell, I take the bludgeon and whack the dead body in front of me a few times, making a groaning sound after each whack. When I think I've put on enough of a show, I pick up the leather mask and fit it over my face.

From looking into Banamaor's face several times, I know that the mask covers everything, so walking down the halls undetected will hopefully be exactly what I need to escape.

I fasten the bludgeon to my belt as well as the skeleton key, and for the first time in three months, I step outside this cell.

The light shines brightly as I close the door behind me and fasten the door. My hands shake for a moment, and I take a few steadying breaths before I move on to my next step.

When I look to the side, there isn't a guard in sight—my plan has worked. It's taken three fucking long months, but slowly letting them believe I wasn't a threat was the best thing I could do for my plan to escape.

With no one in sight, I pocket the key and turn to the right, the way the footsteps would always come, and I walk down the hall, unsure of where the hell I'm going. I'll figure it out, because I have one thing on my mind—get to Lilly.

The minute they find out I'm gone, they're going for her.

She isn't safe.

I need to get to her.

Shoulders drawn back, trying to emulate the posture of a man who beats prisoners for a living, I move down the hallway, carefully listening for any sounds, any voices. When I reach a fork in the hallway, I glance to the right toward a set of stairs that lead down. To the left is another hallway, brighter and less dungeon-like.

I take a left just as I hear a voice.

I pause and hold my breath as I recognize the voice. It's the peon.

"Yes, Banamaor is in there right now." He must be on the phone. "Not great. He's pretty much lifeless. I gave him an extra blanket . . . because you don't want him dead. Not yet at least." He pauses. "When are we taking Lilly?" My spine straightens. I fucking knew they would. "Okay. Yeah . . . okay, bye."

I straighten up some more, and instead of heading back down the lighted stone hallway, I head toward the dark staircase. If luck is on my side, it might lead to an exit on the ground floor. Only one way to find out.

If they're going to capture Lilly, I don't have much time, which means I need to move fast.

Chapter Twenty-Six

LILLY

Marit: *Have you kissed him?*
Isabella: *Have you?*
Lying in bed, I stare down at my phone, excited to catch up with my cousins.
Lilly: *No. I think he knows that I'm still trying to recover from the whole wedding debacle, so he's been very respectful.*
Marit: *Do you want him to kiss you?*
Isabella: *Great follow-up question.*
Lilly: *Umm . . . I don't know. I mean, he's sweet. We certainly connect easily, but I just feel like something's missing. I enjoy his company, but I also don't feel right whenever he gets too close. Like, he held my hand for a second the other day, and my stomach twisted into knots.*
Marit: *It's probably because you never got closure with Keller, so it's hard to move on.*
Lilly: *Yeah, you're probably right. I'm just not there yet.*
Isabella: *So why push it?*
I pause before answering because should I really tell them?

I don't want Theo to find out the real reason I'm dating Evan, then get mad that I'm putting myself out there before I'm ready. Then again, it might be nice to talk to someone else about it. There's only so much I can say to Lara and Runa. I trust them with my whole heart, but I also know that they'd possibly let it slip to someone else about what I'm doing.

Feeling like I can trust my cousins, I text back.

Lilly: *Okay, what I'm about to tell you has to stay between us, like . . . absolute vault.*

Marit: *My lips are locked.*

Isabella: *You can trust us, Lilly.*

Lilly: *I know, I feel like I just need to reiterate the vault thing.*

Marit: *We got you.*

Lilly: *Thank you. Anyway, when I got back to Torskethorpe, I found out that Theo has been pretty ill, and he's heartbroken over what I went through and losing Keller—they were really close—and he was afraid that he'd leave me alone in this world. He was really troubled by it. I told him he didn't need to worry, that I actually met someone.*

Marit: *This makes so much sense.*

Isabella: *I was wondering why you were going out with Evan when you told us that you still had feelings for Keller. It was for Theo.*

Lilly: *It is. I want to reassure him I'll be okay so hopefully he won't stress so much. The doctors think the stress is what's getting to him.*

Isabella: *That's very courageous of you, Lilly, but you realize this is your life, right? We don't want you to be with someone just to make Theo better. He wouldn't want that either.*

Marit: *She's right.*

Lilly: *I know, and I'm hoping that I can take it really, really slow with Evan and see if feelings develop. Like I said, I enjoy his company. I think he's attractive, smart, sweet. He's nothing like Keller, which is a good thing because I don't think I could ever be with someone who was like Keller.*

Marit: *As in, you didn't like Keller's personality?*

Lilly: *No . . . how do I explain this? You know how when you lose a dog, there are people who don't want another dog that resembles the first* dog because it's far too painful? *That's what it's like with Keller. I can't have anyone like Keller ever again because it would be too painful for me. I'd miss him.*

Marit: *Ah, that makes sense. Also, love that you used a dog analogy for men.*

Isabella: *I enjoyed that as well. And that makes so much sense. So you're just going to see where this goes? What if Evan tries to move things along?*

Lilly: *I'll just have another conversation with him. He already knows that I'm struggling with letting go of Keller. I don't think it would surprise him if I tried to slow anything down. But for now, it's nice hanging out with him. He helps me get my mind off things.*

Marit: *I hate to admit it, but I was following your little outing the other day online. He's really hot.*

Isabella: *Marit!*

Marit: *What? He is.*

Lilly: *It's totally okay. He's hot. There's no denying it.*

Marit: *Have you seen him with his shirt off?*

Isabella: *Oh my GOD! She hasn't even kissed the man, so do you really think she saw him with his shirt off?*

Marit: *She could have. Maybe he was sweaty and lifted his shirt up to wipe his brow, and she caught sight of his abdomen. Did that happen?*

Isabella: *It's the middle of winter.*

Marit: *People still sweat in winter.*

Lilly: *I haven't seen him with his shirt off, but I could only imagine the abs on the man.*

Marit: *See . . . Lilly gets it.*

Isabella: *I think you need to go to bed, you're getting out of control.*

Marit: *Possibly, but at least one of us has a little bit of male attention. If things don't start becoming more active over here, I'm going to scream. Not even one date after the Winter Flurries, what the hell?*

Isabella: *Yeah, that was weird. We're good people. Attractive, have kind hearts.*

Marit: *And willing to perform sexual favors.*

Lilly: *HA! I was too, and look where that got me, on my wedding day without a groom. Trust me, be patient. The right guy will come along.*

Marit: *He better, because I'm not getting any younger.*

Isabella: *We're twenty-four! We have plenty of time.*

There's a knock on my door and then Runa comes in. "Princess Lilly, do you need anything before bed?"

I shake my head. "I think I'm good."

"Did you do your skincare routine?"

I chuckle. "Yes, and thank you for always making sure to keep me away from those mean old wrinkles."

"Tis my duty." Runa smiles, then comes farther into the room. "Shall I turn your sheets down?"

"You realize you don't have to do that, right?"

"And you know it's my job, so do we really have to go over this again?"

"No," I answer.

She plucks my phone from my hand and plugs it into the charger on my nightstand. Runa hates that I'm usually on my phone before bed. She always tries to get me to read. I haven't caught the reading bug just yet, but I'm working on it.

She adjusts my pillows as I lie down on top of them, then she brings my blankets up to my chest. "There," she says. "Comfortable?"

"Always," I answer, and before she leaves, I say, "Hey, Runa."

"Yes?"

"I don't know if I ever told you how appreciative I am for you and everything you did for me after the ruined wedding. If it wasn't for you, I don't think I'd have gotten through that first month."

"No need to thank me. Like I said, it's my job."

"You went above and beyond," I say in all seriousness. "And I'm indebted to you. Thank you."

She smiles softly. "You still being here is thanks enough." She pats my blankets. "Now get some good sleep. You have another date with Evan tomorrow, and you're going to want to get some good shut-eye."

"Are you saying I need sleep to be charming?"

"You need sleep to avoid saying something ridiculous."

"I don't care for what you're implying," I tease her.

She smiles and moves to the end of my bed, fluffing the blankets. "I believe I know you very well at this point and sleep is vital to your mood."

"If you know that, then why would you let Lara barge in here for early morning workouts?"

"Because those are good for your health."

I roll my eyes. "Who knew you were going to police every aspect of my life."

"More like make sure you're taking care of yourself the best you can so in return you can take care of us as a country."

I sigh. "Ugh, Runa, why do you always say the right things?"

"I'm wise of course. Now good night, Princess Lilly."

She starts walking toward the door, and because I truly want to know her opinion, I ask, "What do you think of Evan?"

Hands clasped together, she turns toward me and says, "I think he's a well-respected man who could offer you a safe, easy future."

"And why do I feel like that was the easy answer for you? What are you not saying?"

She glances to the side. "Keller was a challenge for you. He pushed you to be more, and I truly believe that was good for you."

"Probably, but Keller walked out. At least Evan has no problem acknowledging who I am and the role I'll play in this country. Evan wouldn't leave me on our wedding night with only a note explaining his reasoning."

Runa nods slowly. "Well, we don't know that. Your future with Evan would be an easy one. But that's a bridge you can cross when you get there. Now get some sleep."

Runa turns out my light, casting my room in darkness, and when the door clicks shut, I stare up at the shadowy ceiling.

Runa has a point about Keller, he did push me to be better. He was always challenging me while protecting me at the same time. He made me a better leader, a better person in general, but he also left me. He pushed me to be greater, but he didn't push himself.

Evan is different, and maybe when the time comes—

Creak.

I pause in my thoughts, my ears perking back. What was that? Was that a floorboard?

No, probably my bed. The damn thing became quite squeaky thanks to Keller and his unruly hips that would pound into me night after night. The age-old bed wasn't built for that kind of force.

Which reminds me, I think I need to ask for a new bed. Too many memories—

Creak.

Okay . . . okay, everyone, calm down. That certainly wasn't the bed. I know this because the first creak made me practically catatonic. That was a classic floorboard creak.

And now my anxiety is ratcheting up as my eyes fly from one side of the room to the other. Checking all the dark crevices for any goblins or monsters that might be lurking. When I see nothing, I question my sanity.

Am I hearing things?

God, it feels like the first night in Harrogate all over again. The wind blowing, a distant pounding in the background. But this time, it's a floor squeaking. In Harrogate, it was just Keller, maybe this is just . . . someone else.

It probably came from the hallway.

Yes, good thought, it came from the hallway. People are always walking about the palace at night. Just another human being, performing their duties.

But, you know, just to be safe, I sink further into my covers.

Everything will be just—

Creak.

Oh dear God! That one was louder, closer.

It was not outside my door. It was in this room.

Maybe it's a rat.

A giant, menacing rat looking for cheese . . . or fermented cod cakes.

Sorry, dude, we're all out in this room. Go home.

Creak.

Motherfucker son of a bitch. Fear screams down my spine, and I reach for my light. When this room illuminates, and I don't see a giant rat, possibly wearing one of my flower crowns, I'm going to scream.

I lean forward, almost there . . .

Please be a rat, please be a rat . . .

Just as my hand connects with the light switch, the bed dips behind me, and a large palm covers my mouth. It's so quick, so stealthy that it muffles my scream.

What the fuck is happening?

I thrash in bed, kicking and continuing to scream, but my limbs are pinned down to the bed, my stomach to the mattress by a large body, making me immobile.

Oh God . . .

OH GOD!

Panic rises up inside me.

Fear bursts through my mind, and as my hands are being tied together, I try to scream again, but this time, a cloth is placed over my nose, and that's all I remember before everything goes black.

———

THE DISTANT SOUND of a crashing wave startles me from my slumber, the sun nearly blinding me, making it impossible to open my eyes.

It feels like there's a jackhammer going off in my head, pounding uncontrollably. My stomach twists from the pain.

"Fuck," I mutter as I go to block the sunlight with my hand . . . *but realize I can't.* "What the hell?" I tug a few times, but my hands are strapped above me.

Concern pulses through me as my memory floods back to me.

The intruder.

Being pinned to the bed.

Everything going black.

I peel my eyes open, one millimeter at a time, the light so bright that it's hurting my head even more, and as my blurry vision evens out, I notice I'm in someone's bedroom.

Oh my God.

I've been abducted, and I'm in a stranger's bed.

What the hell am I doing in a stranger's bed, and what the hell are they going to do to me?

A blood-curdling scream flies out of my mouth as I attempt to rip the ties holding me down, but with every tug, every pull, the rope digs into my wrist, not letting up.

I try to lift from the bed to look around, but the way I've been tied, I can barely get my head up.

Okay, this is not good.

This is not good at all.

Panic is replaced by terrifying fear.

I've been abducted with no way of knowing where I am, who took me, and how to escape. Easily the scariest moment of my life, and as tears fill my eyes, I hear the distinct sound of feet moving around outside the bedroom.

Since I can't see anything, all I can do is listen carefully.

The feet come closer, fear ramps up in my chest, and when the door to the room creaks open, I can't hold back.

"I'm not who you think I am," I shout as I can't see anyone. "I know what you must think. I look like Princess Lilly, and I was technically sleeping in her bedroom, but I'm actually a decoy. The palace has used me to make it look like Princess Lilly has recovered from the cancellation of her wedding, so whatever plans you have for me, they won't work." Yes, this is good. This is really good. Run with the decoy thing. "Although, job well done on the kidnapping thing. I'll be sure to applaud you when I get my hands back. Which by the way, when will that be? I have an itch on my nose that's just unrelenting, plus . . . yes, you know, I think I have to go to the bathroom. Is that something you can accommodate, or is this one of those mattresses that can soak up pee? Just let me know my options because I don't want to pee on your mattress if it's something you care about, and also, the pee smell might make it unpleasant in here. Anyway, if you could just let me loose, I promise to pretend this never happened, and we can go our separate ways. How does that sound?" I tack on a smile and offer a thumbs-up, hoping my capturer will go easy on me.

But silence falls in the room.

Was there even a person near the room?

Am I hearing things?

Is this all some sort of weird dream?

I try to crane my neck to look toward the door, but it's useless.

Just as I give up, I feel a presence near the bed, then . . . "You fucking retained nothing when I trained you."

My body stills.

My heart stops.

And the blood in my veins freezes over.

Keller?

I lift my head up as high as I can, straining my neck just to catch the smallest of glimpses of a tall, broad figure standing in the doorway. Shaggy blond hair, a thick full beard, arms like boulders . . .

Holy.

Shit.

"Keller?" I ask.

He takes a step forward, coming fully into my view, and from the mere sight of him, an entire shiver works through my body.

"Why . . . where . . . I don't understand," I say, taking in his overbearing stature. He looks so different, not just because of his hair and beard, but he looks weathered, like he's seen hell and just returned. His waist is thinner, but his chest is broader, and his arms are chiseled. I can see every sinew of muscle, every vein working in his forearms. "Where are we? Why are you here? Why am I tied up?"

He doesn't say anything. Instead, he moves to the bed, his sizable stature eating up all the oxygen in the air as he undoes the ties on my legs, then works his way to my arms. The entire time, I take him in, a million questions running through my head.

The most important one being, *why the hell are you here with me?*

Once I'm released from the constraints, I sit up and scoot against the headboard like a scared animal, pulling my legs into my chest. His eyes roam me, sunken and lifeless. The man I once knew is nowhere to be found. He's been replaced by this cold, comatose human.

I'm scared.

His eyes remain on mine as he stands straight, the time away from him making me forget how tall and domineering he is. His fists curl at his sides, the ropes clung into his palms as he breathes nothing but silence.

I want to ask him where he's been.

Why is he here now.

Why was I tied to the bed.

But before I have the chance to formulate any sort of sentence in my head, he drops the ropes on the bed, turns on his heel, and walks out of the bedroom door.

I should be confused, but I'm surprisingly relieved, and I let out a long pent-up breath. I'm grateful for the second to gather myself. To make sense of this.

I make a quick glance around the room, taking it all in. The first thing I notice is the expansive window that offers a breathtaking view of the pristine water just outside the home. A beach separates the structure from the lapping water, but it almost feels like the house is right on top of it.

The next thing I notice is the theme of the bedroom. It's all white with white oak furniture. Not a note of personal decorations. Is this where he's been staying this whole time? While I've been suffering up in the cold, he's been hanging out in the tropics?

There's also no trace of someone living here. No clothes on the floor, not a single thing on top of the dresser, nor is there anything on the nightstands. It's a completely blank canvas.

Irritated, I move off the bed. *I've been changed into a pair of silk shorts and a matching tank top.* For some reason, that makes me feel violated. I know he was my fiancé, but he no longer has the right to see me without clothes or change me for that matter.

Wanting answers, I make my way through the bedroom door and out into an open floor plan. A white kitchen is off to the left near what I'm assuming is a front door, while to the right, there's a living area and dining room. Clean and crisp, the tile floors are made up of large cream squares. The walls are painted as well, with nothing to decorate them, leaving the view of the ocean to be the main feature.

And as I scan the humble yet modern furnishings, I notice one very important thing—Keller is nowhere to be found.

He's getting really good at the disappearing act.

Hands on my hips, I examine the clean sophisticated space that doesn't seem like it belongs to Keller because he'd never decorate like this. He's dark, a mystery. His place would be made up of furnishings as black as his heart.

I rub my wrist, which is sore from the ties, and make my way to the sliding glass door where I spot Keller on the beach, tugging in a boat by a rope. I open the sliding glass door and step out into the warm, sun-soaked air.

God, that feels good.

I've missed this kind of weather, where it feels like Mother Nature warms you from the tips of your toes to the top of your head. It brings me back to my days in Miami. Waves lap at the sand, casually crashing into the rocks on either side of the small beach. Seagulls squawk up above, circling a spot over the water, and the lightest of breezes flies through the bushes, rustling the branches together to offer a melodic soundtrack to the already beautiful setting.

Where the hell am I?

What the fuck is going on?

And then a manly, irritated grunt falls past Keller's lips, snapping my attention back to the here and now. He drapes the rope over his shoulder and walks toward me, the boat following him until it's finally on the shore. That's when he hops into the boat with impressive athleticism and picks up two large boxes, one with each hand. He jumps out of the boat and walks up to the house, moving around me as if I don't even exist.

Uh . . . what the hell?

Not one to back down, I storm right behind him, and when he sets down the boxes, he turns around but is met with me.

Hands on my hips, I ask, "What the hell is going on?"

His eyes fall to my chest, then to my legs, and all the way

back up to my face. His perusal is unwelcomed. "What do you think is going on?"

"Uh . . . I don't know," I answer, annoyed. "Seems to me like you brought me to the little fishing paradise you've been hiding out in."

He slowly nods. "That's what you think?"

"What else am I supposed to think? In case you don't remember, Keller, you left me on our wedding day. Left . . . me. So color me shocked that I'm standing in some beach house with you right in front of me."

"Good to know," he says, pushing past me and pissing me off even more.

I jog in front of him and place my hand on his chest, my hand colliding with what feels like stone. Well, someone was able to work out over the past three months.

"That's all you're going to say? *Good to know?* What the fuck, Keller? Why am I here?"

"You're here for a reason, a reason you don't need to know. So why don't you go back in the house, relax, and think about your boyfriend back home."

He moves past me again and walks up to the boat, leaving me dumbstruck.

"Really?" I call out. "That's what you're going to do? Spin this around on me? Well, first of all, he's not my boyfriend, and second of all, you have no fucking right to be jealous, Keller. No goddamn right," I shout. "You left me. You chose to leave because you were too chickenshit to fulfill the responsibilities of being by my side, so before you start shitting on me about seeing someone else, point the finger at yourself first."

With that, I turn away from him and head back into the house. The arrogant prick.

Think about my boyfriend . . .

Seems like he's been thinking about him enough for us both.

Chapter Twenty-Seven

KELLER

I grip the side of the boat, my fingers digging into the wood so hard that I hope for splinters, anything to take away this brutal agony ripping through me.

Why did I think when she saw me, she'd be relieved?

Why did I think when I saw her, everything would be okay?

Why did I actually, momentarily think she wouldn't believe the letter that was left on my desk the night before the wedding, that she'd give me the benefit of the doubt?

Fucking naive.

So fucking naive.

And for her to think the goddamn worst of me? After everything I've said to her. After the promises I made to her. Not for one second did she believe that something could have happened to me? That something could have pulled me away from her?

No, she just assumed I was . . . as she put it, too chickenshit to stand by her side. She assumed I wasn't man enough to walk down that fucking aisle.

She thought the worst of me, and that hurts more than everything I've been put through over the past three months. My love for her kept me alive. My belief in her, *in us*, kept me focused. *And for what?*

I heard what she said to Runa. I heard her comment on Evan being a good fit. *She. Moved. On.* Because she had absolutely zero faith in me. Well, if that's the case, then she can be with fucking Evan.

I'll fulfill the promise I made to myself, figure out who kidnapped me, and I'll end them. After that, Lilly is on her own.

From my pocket, I pull out the burner phone I picked up, and I type in Theo's personal cell phone number. Very few people have it. I don't want him to worry, but I don't trust anyone else. So I send him a vague text.

Keller: *Gisla is safe. Mole in the palace. Will report. – Rogue*

I press send, knowing he'll read the text and know exactly what to do.

He'll pull Ottar and Lara into a secure room and explain to them what's going on. Hopefully, he'll connect me with Ottar on a private line so I can communicate with him about what I know. Until then, I'll wait.

I move into the boat and pick up the two other boxes of supplies and carry them into the house.

When I was planning my escape from Arkham, I knew exactly where I'd go with Lilly if I found out she was in trouble. Theo's private island would offer security, the perfect escape, and all the resources we might need. After I escaped the palace in Arkham, which proved to be a lot easier than I expected, I stole a car and drove out of the city to the coast where I boarded a boat for free in exchange for my labor. I worked hard enough to earn my free fare and some clothes.

When we arrived in Torskethorpe the next day, I was glad

for the beard and shaggy hair, because it helped me walk through the streets without being recognized. From there, I followed the passageway that my kidnappers took that led right up to my room and rummaged for clothes and anything I might need that I could fit into a backpack, then I quietly washed myself down in the sink, not wanting to make any noise, and changed into all black. Sneaking into Lilly's room wasn't difficult since they took the guards away. I'm not sure why. That's something I need to talk to Lara and Ottar about. From there, it was seamless. Took my seaplane that Theo gifted me a few years ago and flew it down to the island.

And now that I have my supplies, I can get started on my important work of keeping Lilly safe and figuring out who's responsible for all of this.

I set the boxes down in the living room where Lilly is sitting on the couch, cross-legged, looking really fucking pissed, but I ignore her and start unpacking the fresh food and non-perishables. We have enough to last us a few weeks.

"Went grocery shopping, did ya?" she asks in the same snarky tone she used when she was pissed at me in Harrogate. "Buy any fish? Oh wait, you probably have plenty from all the fishing you've been doing."

I ignore her and stock the shelves.

"You know, if you were thinking about reinventing yourself after walking out, the beard and the shaggy hair aren't working for you."

Yup, she's digging in deep. Don't know why I forgot about this side of her.

"And what were you planning on doing to me, all tied up to your bed? You realize how insane that was? Kind of creepy, Keller."

I pause with a carton of oatmeal in my hand. I glance over my shoulder and say, "I didn't want you waking up and fleeing."

"Fleeing where?" she asks, extending her arms out. "We're

on an island. Pretty sure I'm not about to go swim in the ocean."

"You never know with how fucking insane you are," I mumble as I slam the cupboard door and turn back to the next box that has fresh fruits and veggies in it.

I open the fridge and start stocking it up.

"So you're really not going to tell me why I'm here?"

"No," I answer.

"Why not?"

"Because I don't need you getting in my way," I shoot back at her.

"Ah, you don't want me getting in your way, so you just go out of your way to perform a very elaborate kidnapping and bring me to an island where it seems like we're the only two people here. Very intelligent."

I close the door of the fridge and turn toward Lilly. "I suggest you don't piss me off more than you already have."

She points at her chest. "Me piss you off? How? You're the one who left. How is this my ordeal?"

"Because I wasn't gone for long before you found someone else." I grip my hair, tugging on the strands. "Jesus Christ, Lilly, did I really not matter that much to you?"

"Excuse me?" She walks up to me, anger pounding in her every step. "When you left, I was devastated, Keller. *Devastated.* You have no fucking idea what I went through to reach where I am today, able to stand on my own two feet and go out in public."

"And you have no fucking clue what I went through either," I snap back at her before snagging an empty box and moving past her.

I should tell her. I should throw it in her goddamn face.

Tell her exactly what happened and use it to hurt her the way I'm fucking hurting right now, but that won't do any good.

She's moved on, so I need to move on.

Telling her will only garner sympathy, and I don't want her goddamn sympathy. I want her. I want all of her. I don't want to share her with fucking Evan Sotherby . . .

And what the hell is he doing, moving in on her?

That's not the kind of man he is. So why now? It almost feels connected in some way.

All of this feels connected, but for the life of me, my brain can't figure it out. Not when I've been tortured for the past three months. I'm still recovering. Still trying to rehydrate. Build up my protein intake to build strength, and get to a point that I can mentally function better.

Until then, I'm going to keep to myself because arguing with Lilly won't do any good.

———

I PICK up the bowl of ramen with sautéed veggies I made for dinner and take it to Lilly who is sitting on the couch, legs crossed, in total silence.

When I hand it to her, she looks up at me, skepticism in her eyes, but takes it. "Thank you," she says, her voice pained having to utter those two words to me.

She curls up on the couch and brings the bowl up to her mouth, twirling the fork through the noodles as I take a seat at the dining room table.

My bowl is much bigger than hers, but then again, I've been so fucking hungry for the past three months that I'm stocking up. I even added some tofu to mine. Anything to help me bulk up some more and fill my stomach.

I shove a forkful of noodles in my mouth and look up at her. *Fuck. I hate Lilly's tears.*

Mother.

Fucker.

Inwardly groaning, I look away. No, don't let that fucking affect you. It's one lonely tear, it will not crumple your facade of indifference. She's probably just missing her boy toy. Focus on what you need to focus on, getting healthy and figuring out who's behind this.

I take a sip of my water, but my eyes land on her again, just in time for her to wipe a tear off her cheek.

Goddammit.

I clench my jaw, and not able to stop myself, I ask, "Why are you crying?"

"None of your business," she shoots back, turning away from me.

"You are my business," I say to her.

"Oh fuck off, Keller." More tears stream down her cheeks. "You can't say shit like that to me anymore. You don't have the right."

"If you're the future queen of my country, you will always be my business."

"No, matters of the crown are your business, my personal feelings are not."

She sets her bowl of food on the table and moves out to the beach where she sits on the sand, pulling her knees into her chest.

It's dark. The moon reflects off the ocean in front of her, and the porch light illuminates her back so I can keep an eye on her as she finds some peace . . . from me.

I grip my jaw and drag my hand down.

Fuck.

Why did I think this would be easy?

Fucking naive thinking. That's what it was.

There's so much anger, so much hostility between us.

We might have pretended everything would be fine before the wedding, but we were both angry and frustrated in our own rights. And now, that anger and hostility has just grown exponentially. I want to scream the words *I never would have left you by choice. I love you.* But I can also barely fucking look at her because while I was barely surviving, she was moving on.

Looks like Theo was wrong. Lilly could and *would stay in Torskethorpe without me.* To think I could have walked away like I'd first suggested. *Would my attackers have simply taken Lilly instead?*

Focusing back on my food, I finish up my bowl, inhaling it quicker than expected, grateful for flavor, then go to the kitchen to clean up.

That's when she walks back into the house, bypasses her food, and goes into the bedroom.

Dish towel draped over my shoulder, I lean against the doorway of the bedroom and spot her rummaging through her dresser drawer. "Are you going to eat your food?"

"Not hungry," she says.

"Lilly, you need to eat."

She whirls around. "And you need to learn not to tell me what to do," she cries out. "What the hell am I supposed to wear to bed?"

I grip the back of my head. "Clothes?"

Her eyes narrow, and I realize that was the wrong answer. But in all honesty, I wasn't really thinking about pajamas when trying to get her out of her room.

"Clothes." She nods. "Wow, thanks." She goes straight to the bathroom where she shuts the door.

Well, more like slams it.

Knowing there's nothing I can do, I put her meal in some Tupperware and stick it in the fridge. I'll eat it tomorrow if she doesn't. We're not wasting one bit of food.

I finish cleaning the kitchen, then make my way around the small cottage, securing the windows and doors, locking them with devices that will alert me if they're shifted or moved. I can't be too cautious about security, especially after what I've been through.

Satisfied, I move to the bedroom, exhaustion taking over me, just as Lilly pops out of the bathroom wearing a towel around her torso. "What are you doing in here?" she asks.

"What do you mean what am I doing here?" I sit down on

the bed and pull my shirt up and over my head. Her eyes immediately fall to my chest. "I'm getting ready for bed."

She doesn't hide the fact that she has no problem checking me out as her eyes peruse for a few more seconds. Clearing her throat, she says, "Do you think you're sleeping on this bed?"

"Yes, I do," I answer, standing now.

"It's far too small for us both. Take the couch."

"I'm not sleeping on the couch, and I'm not sleeping in a separate room than you."

She rolls her eyes. "Keller, we're not together—"

"For safety, not for anything else," I answer, my voice terse. "I don't make a move on a woman who's with someone else."

Her nostrils flare, and I can see the stubborn side of her immediately fall in line, ready to war. "Fine." She smiles brightly. "Sleep in the room, not like I care."

"Fine," I say as I move past her, our shoulders bumping. I head toward the bathroom when she gasps.

"What the hell happened to your back?" she asks.

Oh . . . fuck. How could I forget about the scars and scabs on my back from Banamaor and his whip?

Shit. Keeping my back toward her, I wince while saying, "Fishing line accident."

She thinks I was out on a goddamn boat all this time, might as well ride with that lie.

"Oh . . ." she says, her voice a touch softer but still having an edge. Not wanting to elaborate, I move into the bathroom and shut the door behind me.

I grip the counter in front of me, taking a few deep breaths, my mind returning to that first night when Banamaor was ruthless with his whip, striking me so hard that I thought I'd throw up. After that, he didn't do much with the whip, and I'm grateful for it, just a few slashes here and there.

I push off the counter and turn so I can see my back. At least eight gashes, deep enough to leave scars, strewn across my back, the barely healed skin puckered and purple. They are ghastly to look at, so I don't blame Lilly's reaction. I could put a shirt back on, but I don't want anything, and I mean anything, to distract me from my sleep, including a shirt getting tied up around me.

Even the idea of sleeping in a bed has me itching to climb in. And how I've missed the luxury of cleaning my teeth. They've felt furry for so long now, I'd forgotten what freshly cleaned teeth felt like. *Heaven.* I nearly cried when I took a shower earlier. *I'd never take these things for granted again.*

Once done, I turn off the light, entering the bedroom just as Lilly drops her towel, revealing her completely naked and gorgeous body.

Fuck . . . me.

She braided her hair, so it's gathered to the side and over her shoulder. Her pert nipples are puckered from the evening air, and her nipple piercings glitter under the moonlight, making my mouth water. Fuck, I can't remember the last time I had those in my mouth. And her waist, it looks thinner than before, causing a jolt of concern to run through me because she was already small as it was.

"What, uh . . . what are you doing?" I ask her.

"Getting into bed," she says. "There aren't any pajamas to wear, so I'm just going to sleep naked." She then lifts the blankets and slides into bed.

Well, fuck. How the hell am I supposed to sleep now?

My fists clench at my sides as I try not to show how much this is affecting me. She isn't going to make this easy on me. I strip out of my shorts, leaving me in just my briefs, and I slip into the bed as well. When my shoulder presses against hers, I realize just how small this bed really is.

Christ.

"You're touching me," she says.

"I realize that," I reply.

"Told you the bed was small."

"Do you want a goddamn reward?" I ask.

"Actually, yes, I would."

From under the covers, I smack her ass hard enough to feel the sting on my palm and for her to squeal out. "There you go, your prize. Now don't touch any windows or doors, everything is locked up and the alarm will go off if you do. Get some sleep."

She rolls to face me and props her head up on her hand, looking down at me. Maybe we have an inch of space to work with. What is this bed? A full?

"Don't fucking touch me like that," she says.

"Like what?" I ask, knowing exactly what she's talking about.

"Like you own me. Because you don't."

That makes me laugh. "Lilly, I'll always fucking own you." I look at her now. She's furious. "You can try to move on to someone else, but you know in the back of your mind, when you spread your legs for another man, it will be my cock you're thinking of."

Her nostrils flare with anger. "You're so fucking arrogant."

She turns away from me, and for some reason, maybe because I'm fucking furious with her, or because I miss her, or because I'm so fucked in the head right now, I decide to push her further.

Either way, I've lost my goddamn mind as I turn toward her.

Under the blankets, I smooth my hand up her back and to her hip as I lean closer, talking directly into her ear. "You can't deny it, I'll always have a grip on you."

She turns so my hand slides over her stomach. Her eyes meet up with mine, our mouths pretty close. If I leaned in just a few more inches, I'd be able to taste her again. "So why are you the one touching me, and I'm the one turning away?" she asks.

"Never denied not wanting you. You're the one who moved on."

"For good reason," she says.

"And what reason was that?" I ask as my hand slides up her stomach, my thumb just below her breast.

Her breath hitches, the subtle movement giving me all the goddamn power I need.

"You left me, remember? Why would I stay with someone who doesn't want to marry me?"

"I said I would. I promised." My thumb swipes at the edge of her breast, and her teeth fall over her lip . . .

Fuck. What I wouldn't give to own that mouth again. To grip her jaw and show her exactly who owns her with my lips and with my cock.

"You didn't wait for me," I say, my hand lowering back down her stomach, right past her belly button.

She sucks in a sharp breath.

"Don't, Keller," she says, her mouth saying one thing, the spread of her legs telling me something else.

"Has he played with your clit piercing?" I ask. "Or does he not even know you have one?" I slide my hand down another inch, my finger passing over her pubic bone once, causing her head to tip back and her chest to lift, the blankets falling past her breasts. Her nipples tighten from the exposure to the air. I'm so goddamn tempted to take one into my mouth. "Answer the question, Lilly."

"He . . . he doesn't know," she responds as her legs spread more.

"He doesn't know?" I ask as my finger slides down another inch. "He doesn't know that you have the sweetest, most addicting pussy I've ever tasted?" My finger is at the cleft, and if she moves, my finger would slide right in.

I desperately want to slide into her warm heat, to feel that clit piercing and play with it. To claim her as mine and no one else's. But the moment I give in—*the moment I break*—I'll fucking regret it.

She's choosing to see where things go with him. *She's so fucking loyal . . . until she believes she's been betrayed.*

How loyal has she been to him? Has he taken those perfect lips of hers? Does he know what it's like to hear her moan softly as he drives his tongue into her mouth? Does he understand the feral feeling of when her mouth parts just enough to tease you, but not give you everything you need?

The thought of not knowing nearly chokes me as my body stiffens. Because right now, I know she doesn't belong to me. Question is, though . . . does she belong to him?

So I retract my hand, causing her to cry out in frustration. That little cry, it's just enough confidence I need to retreat. When her eyes open to mine, questions swarming in them, I say, "See, you will always fucking be mine."

And with that, I turn away from her and grip my pillow with my hands, swearing not to move, not to even look her way, because if I do, I won't be able to keep my hands to myself this time.

Chapter Twenty-Eight

"What the fuck do you mean she's gone too?" I bellow as I slam my hand against my desk, startling Pickering back.

The moment it was reported to me that Keller had not only escaped but had killed Banamaor and simply walked out of the castle without anyone turning their goddamn head, I threw my glass of whiskey against the wall.

How?

How the fuck was that possible?

The man was a pile of flies on the floor. He could barely lift his head when we saw him in his cell. How did he have the ability and strength to escape, find his way to Torskethorpe, capture the princess, and take her away? *How the hell was that possible?*

"We severely underestimated him," my brother says from the chair where he sits with a tumbler of Scotch in his hand. "And are we positive she's gone?"

Pickering nods his head. "That's what our palace source just said. They're not releasing that information to the public, because they don't want to create worry."

"Do they know where he took her?" I ask.

Pickering shakes his head. "No. They've heard nothing.

The only reason we know it was Keller is because we're assuming. They didn't believe Fitzwilliam was back from his fishing trip."

"Jesus Christ," I say, dragging my hand over my face. "They still believe he went fucking fishing? I swear, the people there get more stupid with each passing year." I take a deep breath. "Does Magnus know yet?"

Pickering shakes his head. "No. It hasn't been reported to him. He's currently on vacation. Won't be back for a week."

"Then we have a fucking week. Call the Sotherbys and see if they know anything, if Lilly has tried to contact their son. Reach out to our source at the palace too, see if they've heard anything. Dig for any information. Any lead." Pickering nods. "Now get the fuck out of here."

Once the door is shut, my brother says, "Told you, you should have kept him chained."

"He was too goddamn weak to make it to the bathroom with the chains, he was pissing all over himself." I drag my hand over my face. "The point wasn't to kill him."

"What was the point?" my brother asks.

"To drive him mad, like he drove us mad. To take over his precious fucking country, destroy the forests he so proudly protected. To use every last inch of that moss as biological solar and sell it to Magnus. And while we give him the keys to the country, Fitzwilliam would rot away in his cell for eternity. That was the goddamn plan."

He takes a sip of his Scotch, then lowers his glass. "Seems like you have a week to fix it."

"No, brother, *we* have a week to fix it. Because I'm not going down without you. We're in this together."

Chapter Twenty-Nine

LILLY

Desire will make you do some really foolish fucking things . . . like let your ex-fiancé nearly finger you when you shouldn't even allow him to touch you.

The only way to describe last night was charged.

Anger.

Tension.

Frustration.

Confusion . . .

Those scars on his back, they were brutal—*horrifying*—and I didn't want to make him feel bad, but my shocked gasp popped out of me before I could stop myself. I've never seen such angry, purple scars before. And from fishing line? What happened on that boat? Is that why he's no longer there?

Does it have anything to do with why I'm here with him?

I wish he'd just talk to me. It's so infuriating.

And what's even more infuriating is that I woke up this

morning without getting much sleep and completely unsatis-fied but turned on thanks to him.

For me, the bed is perfectly fine, but put his broad body in it, and it felt like we were sharing a twin. I'm glad I slept naked or else I'd have been way too hot with his body heat pouring under the covers.

And of course, he woke up early, probably to work out or something. Not sure there's any equipment around here, so he's probably out on the beach lifting rocks. Scooping sand for bicep curls, possibly whipping seaweed up and down like ropes. Who knows.

When I got out of bed, I pulled on one of his shirts, then stared out at the water for a while, contemplating how I want to handle the situation with him moving forward. I'll tell you right now, I'm still clueless. I don't know where to go from here. Clearly, Keller doesn't want to talk to me about anything. He thinks I'm some floozy who can set aside the love we had and go for someone else. He thinks the worst of me.

And I think the worst of him. *Looks like he did us both a favor by walking away from our marriage. Lust, we understand. Trust, we clearly don't.*

Shaking my head, I move into the main part of the house where a note has been left on the counter. I walk up to it and read his slanted handwriting. At least this note isn't life-altering.

Out on a walk. There are croissants in the pantry. Eat one. Don't go anywhere.

Still freaking demanding even when he's not here.

But thanks to my lack of dinner last night, I'm starving, so I go to the pantry and spot the croissants in a Tupperware bin. I pick one up, then rummage around for a plate. I look in the fridge for any jam, and lo and behold, there is some.

That's infuriating.

Do you know why that's infuriating? Because he knows how much I like croissants, and he knows how much I like . . .

yup, strawberry jam on them. See, that's what's going to freaking break me. Him making dinner last night, taking care of the house, keeping it safe, buying me freaking strawberry jam. Doing all the little things that matter when, in reality, a much bigger problem hangs over us.

I reluctantly put the jam on my croissant, grab some coffee that he made a pot of and kept on a warmer—because he knows I need some coffee in the morning, damn him—and then move out to the back of the house and take a seat at the dining room table outside.

It's not that warm out yet, probably high fifties, but compared to what I was living in a day or so ago, it feels like a tropical vacation. And I have to admit even though he kidnapped me, scaring the living hell out of me in my own bedroom, where he took me isn't so bad. It's actually quite gorgeous here.

Too bad I can't enjoy it with him like we were supposed to on our honeymoon.

Too bad we have so much bad blood between us that while we're here, for however long, we won't be able to truly enjoy it.

Well, fuck that.

If he won't tell me why we're here, at least I can ignore him and enjoy myself.

Like . . . take a dip in the water naked.

Lie on the beach . . . naked.

Walk around the house . . . naked.

Do all the naked things, because there is never a time when I can do that, not in the palace with staff constantly popping in and out. If it drives Keller crazy at the same time, seeing me naked, then it's a win for me.

From the corner of my eye, I see movement, and for a heart-stopping moment, I think it's an intruder, but then Keller comes into view, wearing low-hanging shorts that dip past the indented V in his hips. His chest glistens with a sheen of sweat, the light bouncing off every sinew of muscle wrapping around his bones, and there's more than I remember. It's almost as if he's lost every ounce of body fat, leaving him as skin and muscle. His body is insane. My eyes travel up to his now trimmed beard, only scruff lines his jaw, and he's fastened some sort of hairband that pushes his hair out of his face. It's ridiculous for a man to wear a hairband the way that he is, but Jesus Christ, it makes my mouth water. He looks so incredibly hot that I squeeze my thighs together, reminding myself that we're mad at him.

He hurt you.

He damaged you.

He left you.

Remind yourself that every time you catch him looking so delicious that you would do anything to lay your tongue across his stacked eight-pack.

When he looks up to find me sitting at the table, wearing his shirt, eating, he doesn't change his expression, he just nods and keeps moving forward . . . with a gun in his hand.

Dear God.

"Why do you have that?" I ask, pointing at his gun.

"Why would anyone carry a gun?" he mumbles.

"Don't be smart, Keller. Why do you need it if we're clearly on a private island?"

"Because if anyone finds out we're here, I need to protect you."

"Uh-huh, and why exactly would people be looking for us? You failed to mention that. Also, you realize you kidnapped the future queen of Torskethorpe. That might mean jail time."

"Theo knows you're here with me," he answers, moving past me and into the house.

"Wait, what?" I ask, getting up from my chair and leaving my croissant to follow him. "What do you mean he knows I'm here? Was he on board with the kidnapping?"

He goes into the bedroom and grabs a notebook from his nightstand drawer as well as a pen. He sits on the bed and writes something down.

"Uh, hello?"

"Can you stop for a goddamn second?" he says. "I need to write something down."

His brow creases as his hand flies across the paper. I try to catch a glimpse, but I don't want to be too obvious. When he's done, he shuts the notebook and puts it back in his drawer.

Noted.

There'll be snooping later, and before you get up in arms about it, a girl has to do what a girl has to do.

When he stands from the bed, he moves past me again. This time, he takes a seat on the couch and presses his hand to his forehead as he leans against the back of the couch. Once again, I shamelessly peruse his body, unable to comprehend how much his body has changed. The muscle surrounding his ribs is ridged, looking like a ladder leading up to his thick, pronounced pecs sprinkled with light chest hair, something he's shaved in the past, but seeing it unshaved just makes him more rugged. Sexier. What would he do if I just walked over to him, sat on his lap, and started giving him a lap dance?

I know what he'd do. He'd grip my hips and enjoy it.

Because that's what we're good at. We're good at sex. Never had a problem with that. Ever.

Even if it was angry sex.

"Are you going to answer my question?" I ask just as I see a white flash of movement to the right. I glance to the side, a startled gasp coming from my mouth, causing Keller to leap to his feet just in time for both of us to watch a seagull land on the table and pick up my croissant. "Hey!" I shout as I run out to the patio, but I only scare him away, croissant in claw. "Come back here! That was my breakfast, you fucking thief!" I wave my fist in the air, but it's no use. It's a freaking bird, as if it knows English.

"Forgot to tell you, your food can get stolen if you don't pay attention," Keller mumbles as he takes a seat back on the couch.

"No shit," I say as I walk back into the house. "What's your deal? Did your walk tire you out?"

"Dehydrated," he mutters. "Massive headache."

"Oh . . . well, then lie down or something."

"Can't," he says.

"Why not? Have some gardening you have to take care of? Maybe some accounting I don't know about? Have to report all of those fish?"

He pries one eye open to sternly look in my direction.

"Funny," he answers dryly. "I need to make sure everything is taken care of." He lets out a deep breath and closes his eyes. "Fuck," he grumbles.

Okay, so it actually looks like he's in a lot of pain, which is annoying, because I can't just stand here and let him wallow in it.

Urgh . . .

"Get up," I say to him, causing him to look at me again with one eye.

"What?"

"I said get up. Go lie in the bed. I'll grab you some water, and I'm assuming there is Ibuprofen in this house?"

"I can get it myself," he says as he goes to stand. He pauses, his legs wobbly beneath him, and within seconds, I watch him start to tip forward, so I rush to him and press my hand to his chest, righting him up.

"Jesus, Keller." I keep him steady. "You need to fucking lie down."

"Just give me a second."

"No," I yell. "You've clearly pushed yourself too much. Now lie down." I put my arm through his and move him toward the bedroom. This time, he doesn't put up a fight and follows me.

"Only for a second," he says.

I move him through the house at a slow pace, and when we get to the bed, I lay him down carefully. And because I can't ever let anything go, I lean forward and say, "I want it to be noted that not only was I able to catch you but also drag you to the bed. So next time you're asked to do the trust exercise with me, don't judge a book by its cover, you anus."

There.

If I have to take care of him, at least I can tack on a cup of petty with my treatment. Makes it easier.

"Now, tell me where this first aid kit is."

"Bathroom, under the sink," he says, his bulky arm draped over his eyes.

I locate the first aid kit and open it up. One side is full of bandages, antiseptic spray, and gauze. The other side is filled with medicine. I pluck out four Ibuprofen for him, then go to the kitchen where I locate some black tea. That'll have to work for caffeine, and I'll pump him with water.

When I bring back the Ibuprofen, he's no longer on the bed. I'm about to yell at him when I hear him from the bathroom . . . throwing up.

Oh God.

"Uh, you okay?" I ask him, unsure of what to do.

He just groans.

I set the medicine and drink on the nightstand, then go into the bathroom where his arms are draped over the toilet, his shoulders slumped. Feeble, that's how I'd describe him right now, as if he just ran a marathon for three days straight and is now feeling the effects of it.

I squat next to him and place my hand on his back, gently rubbing it, the puckered scars bumpy under my palm. "Are you done?" I ask.

"Yeah," he murmurs.

"Okay, stay there." I go to the sink and pick up his toothbrush. I wet it and line it with toothpaste, then bring it over to him. He's now leaning against the wall, his eyes closed, his posture sunken. That's when I notice a few new scars on his chest. They're small and almost look like burn marks. Scars I've never seen before. Scars I don't think were there before.

No, I know for a fact they weren't there before. I've licked every inch of this man's body, and he didn't have those before.

Where did they come from?

What has he been doing?

And why is he so dehydrated?

I grip his cheek and say, "Open your mouth." He doesn't have enough strength to fight me, so he opens his mouth, and I brush his teeth for him. "Spit in the toilet," I say, helping him lean forward.

Once I finish up, I rinse his toothbrush, then I help him up from the ground, carrying his body weight.

"I'm . . . sorry," he says, his voice in an immense amount of pain.

"It's fine," I answer just as I help him back into bed. "I need you to take this medicine and drink some of this tea, it will help the medicine be more effective."

He sits up just enough for me to place the medicine in his mouth. I bring the bottle to his lips and he sucks some of it in before swallowing.

"Good," I say. "Just a little bit more. Two more large gulps."

He listens, then I set the drink on the nightstand. He lowers down on the pillow, his arms hanging by his side.

"Just try to get some sleep," I say as I stand from the bed, but he grabs my hand.

"Don't leave," he says quietly, so quiet that my heart nearly breaks from the desperation in his voice.

"Keller—"

"Please," he says.

I squeeze my eyes shut, my body screaming yes, my brain

telling me not to fall for it, not to get caught up in this man all over again.

"Lilly," he murmurs and fuck me, I can't stand hearing his voice like this, like all of the wind has been sucked from his lungs and he won't be able to go on without me.

I squeeze my eyes shut, willing myself to block out the sound of his voice, but for the life of me, I can't.

"Let me close the curtains first," I reply, defeated. I move around the room, closing the curtains to cast the room into darkness. Then I move to my side of the bed and slip in. Immediately, he curls into me, his hand going directly under my shirt and straight to my stomach where he pulls me in close and just holds his warm palm to my skin.

I take a few deep breaths, calming my nerves, telling myself that this is just for comfort and nothing else. This doesn't mean anything. He's sick and needs this moment to get himself better.

You're not letting him penetrate the wall you've put up around your heart.

You're not going to let him hurt you again.

I bite my lower lip, steadying my trembling lip, as my eyes start to water. His head nuzzles into my hair, and he physically relaxes, as if my presence is all he needs to be better.

And I hate that.

I don't want him to need me.

I don't want to be the cure to his pain.

I don't want to have this overwhelming sense to crawl right into his hold and never let him let me go.

Because he's hurt me too many times.

But with every deep breath, every rise of his chest, my heart hammers harder and harder for him.

"HOW ARE YOU FEELING?" I ask Keller as he shifts behind me.

I'm not sure how long we slept for, but now that he's awake, I slowly slide away, his fingers dragging over my skin as I pull to the edge of the bed.

"Okay," he mumbles in a gruff voice. But he doesn't sound okay. He still sounds pained.

"You need to drink some more liquids," I say as I hop off the bed. "Let me grab you some water. Can I get you anything to eat?"

"I can get it," he says, starting to move.

"Keller, stop." When he glances at me, his eyes so incredibly weathered, I can't help but wonder, why? Why does he look so defeated? So worn out? "You're not getting up. I'm grabbing some water."

When in the kitchen, I grab a few bottles of water as well as some pretzels, in case he wants some food, and I bring them back to the bedroom where he sits up a little on the bed. I take a seat next to him, and I offer him the water, making sure to uncap it first. "Does your head still hurt?"

"Yeah," he answers as he brings the water to his mouth and starts drinking.

"Why are you so dehydrated?" I ask him.

"Wasn't paying attention to my body," he says in a simple answer.

"You always pay attention to your body," I say.

"Things change," he answers as he finishes his bottle of water.

"Yeah, that much is clear," I say and uncap another bottle for him, but he doesn't drink it right away. He just holds it, holding the bottle on his thigh while he rests his head, his eyes shut. "Why do you have all of these little scars on your chest?" I ask.

"What scars?"

I point at one on his pec. "These?"

345

He glances down and shrugs. "Who fucking knows." He slinks farther down and takes a deep breath. "Give me a moment, then I can make you lunch."

"Have you lost your mind?" I ask him. "You're not making me lunch. Jesus, Keller. You just threw up hours ago because you're clearly not doing well. You're no use to me if you're not taking care of your body. I mean, why would you even go on a walk this morning if you weren't feeling well?"

"Needed to make sure it was secure," he answers almost absentmindedly.

"You need to chill," I reply. I lift the pretzels and hand them to him. "Here, eat these. I'll grab some fruit and cheese if your stomach can handle it."

"I'm fine, Lilly. I don't need you waiting on me."

I take a deep breath and in a steady voice, I say, "Stop trying to be a prideful hero. Just give me today to get you back to where you need to be, and you can do whatever the hell you want to do tomorrow. But Jesus Christ, Keller, just take a moment to fix your body." And with that, I leave for the kitchen.

If he follows me, I'll scream. I don't understand men sometimes, particularly Keller. Doesn't he know that every human shows weakness at one point or another? No one is perfect.

It's infuriating.

I look through drawers and cupboards, and when I spot a few bottles of Gatorade, I grab one and bring it into the bedroom. Instead of sitting up and drinking, Keller is once again curled into his pillow, sleeping.

Well, that took a few seconds.

I'll leave him like that for now.

I go back to the kitchen and find the dinner he made me last night. I decide I can have that for lunch, so I heat it in the microwave and turn on the TV, keeping it low. There are no channels, but there's a DVD player and some DVDs of old shows. I go with *I Love Lucy*, because at least I can keep things light around here.

Sitting on the couch, cross-legged, I eat my lunch and focus on the show, rather than letting my mind wander about Keller.

⊏====⊐

"LILLY, don't . . . no, don't take her," Keller says from the bedroom. It's been another hour since he last went back to sleep. Is he dreaming?

I move to the door and prop it open.

"Don't fucking take her," he says again. "Please . . . no . . . Lilly!" He jackknifes off the bed, startling me so hard that I bang my head against the doorframe.

I grip my head and watch the confusion in his eyes move from terrified to realization that he's in this cottage, with me.

"What . . . what happened?" he says, glancing around, his chest sweaty.

I rub the back of my head and say, "You were dreaming."

"Is there anyone here?" he asks, panic in his eyes.

"No." I shake my head and walk over to the bed. "Just you and me."

"I need to make the rounds." He goes to move, but I press my hand to his damp chest to keep him still. His heart is beating rapidly.

"Keller, everything is fine. I locked up the house, so there's nothing to worry about. We're safe."

He falls back on the bed, shoulders slumped as he scans me. "It . . . it was a dream," he says, as if he's trying to convince himself.

"Yes," I answer.

Slowly, he lowers back down and brings both of his hands to his face as he takes a few deep breaths. His hands shake, and my heart breaks.

I hate his nightmares. They overtake his mind and body, and it's hard for him to calm down after them. I realized this the first time he had one in Harrogate.

I move in closer and press my hand to his stomach. "Do you need a second? I have some Gatorade if you want some."

"No," he whispers. "Just . . . lie with me."

Not again.

The first time was because I felt bad for him after throwing up, the pleading in his voice foolishly tricking me. But this time? How can I allow myself to fall into his arms again when I know with every touch, every hold, I can easily fall back into old habits with him, despite the way he broke me the day of our wedding.

"Please," he says in a strangled voice that cuts right through me.

I suck in a sharp breath, hating myself.

Hating him.

Hating this entire situation. I was making it work without him. I was moving on, finding joy in the little things, finding little moments of hope to keep me distracted from the gut-wrenching pain.

And then, here I am, all over again, in a situation where my heart goes out to him, aches to help him when he appears to be so weak. So damaged.

I bite the corner of my lip and move to my side of the bed. On a deep breath with a reminder to my soul that this is nothing more than comfort for him to get better, I slip under the covers. He slides against my back and moves his hand under my shirt again and presses his palm to my stomach.

"You're not wearing anything other than my shirt," he whispers.

"I was lazy," I say.

"I like you like this." His voice almost sounds dreamy, like he's about to drift off to sleep. "I've missed you," he says so softly that I have to bite on the inside of my cheek to stop myself from crying.

Because there was a time, a few months ago, when I'd have done anything to hear him tell me that. When I'd have given anything to be held like this by him again. To feel his strong presence behind me, melting into my very marrow.

But as the time went on during those three months, I grew more and more bitter.

So now, instead of melting into his touch, I form a ball of anger in the pit of my stomach, a ball that twists and pulls, making me angrier and angrier.

Because this isn't fair.

Because if he really missed me, then why did he leave?

CRASH.

I spring up in bed, the darkness of night covering the room, making it hard to see.

I pat Keller's side of the bed but come up short. I glance around, not seeing anything but light coming from the other room.

"Keller?" I call out.

The bedroom door opens, and he appears. "Fuck, sorry. I didn't mean to wake you up. I dropped a pot."

"What are you doing?" I ask, wiping my eyes, while trying to calm my pulse that just skyrocketed.

"Making some dinner."

I groan and get out of bed. "What did I tell you?"

"I was hungry." He returns to the kitchen, so I follow him and see a bunch of empty bottles on the counter. Wow, he drank all of that?

"Are you feeling better?" I ask.

"A little," he answers as he cuts up some chicken but takes

a second to breathe heavily. Behind him, there's a pan on the stove, looking like it's heating up.

"I can do that," I say.

"So can I," he answers stubbornly.

"Back to a fun mood, I see." I take a seat at the island, watching him run his finger along the breast, the sight of it oddly erotic.

He glances up at me, his brow perched. "I'm acting normal. Not like I'm going to throw a parade, is that what you want?"

"No, but you don't have to be such a dick to me after I took care of you."

"How am I being a dick?" he asks. "I'm making you dinner."

"It's the way you speak to me."

"I don't know what you want me to do, Lilly. I don't know how to talk to you right now. And you just caught me in a really fucking vulnerable mood today, I'm . . . I'm embarrassed."

"Embarrassed to show me your vulnerability?" I ask him. "You realize that makes you human, right?"

"Three months ago, I wouldn't have cared." He slices the chicken. "Now . . . now I care."

"I see," I answer. "So is this how it's going to be while we're here? You're just going to shut down?"

"I'm trying to figure some shit out, and the sooner I can get you out of here, the better. Trust me, I don't want to be here either."

Wow. Okay then.

Any sympathy I was feeling for him a few hours ago, completely vanished. This was the exact wake-up call that I needed.

"Lovely." I push off my chair and walk over to the couch. Before I sit down, I fold my arms and turn toward him. "You know, Keller, for a second, I actually felt bad for you today."

"Don't," he says. "Don't for one goddamn minute feel bad for me."

I shake my head and turn away from him.

Good. I don't.

I go back to watching my *I Love Lucy* episode, because at least that will keep my mind off the infuriating man in the kitchen.

You would think he'd be grateful for today, but nope, he's back to his regular self, guarded, not letting anyone in.

That's fine.

I can do the same fucking thing.

Chapter Thirty

KELLER

I stare down at my notebook, my notes feeling like complete nonsense.

If only I could connect these dots, but my mind still feels like mush. I didn't know how much I was damaged over the past three months up until now.

Not to mention, I can't stop thinking about Lilly.

How she took care of me.

The look of concern in her eyes.

How she let me hold her.

It's swarming my brain and making me . . . feel.

It's making me want to lean on her, lean into her, let my heart wrap around the comfort and safety of her warm body.

Just tell her, you idiot.

Tell her what happened.

Tell her everything.

But . . . will she believe me?

Will it even matter?

She doesn't want me like that anymore.

And more importantly, I don't want her to feel like she has to come back to me because of what happened.

I want her to want me for no other reason than she never stopped loving me and will never be able to let me go.

But we know that's not the case.

From the nightstand comes a buzzing sound.

The cell phone.

Lilly is still watching shows in the living room, so I shut my notebook and open my nightstand, where I pull the phone out. It's from Theo.

Theo: *No mole found, any leads? – Torch*

It's from Ottar. Relieved to hear from him, I type back.

Keller: *Arkham involved. Familiar male voices. Used secret passageway in Strombly.*

Theo: *Any recollection of voices?*

Keller: *Negative.*

Theo: *Passageway in Sapphire?*

Keller: *Affirmative.*

Theo: *Any suggestions on mole?*

Keller: *Look into anyone new. There is a source.*

Theo: *Roger.*

I set the phone back in the nightstand and lean my head against the wall just as the TV is turned off and Lilly walks into the bedroom. She glances in my direction and says, "I'm taking a shower." She tears my shirt off her body and places it in the hamper before shutting the door behind her.

I squeeze my eyes shut, hating every goddamn second of this.

After dinner, I cleaned up, then slipped into the bathroom myself where I took a shower. I changed the bed sheets, afraid that I made them sweaty with my nightmare. I also drank two more bottles of water. From the combination of the protein and greens as well as water, I'm feeling halfway like myself, which is better than this morning.

I hate to admit it, but Lilly was right. I need to focus on taking care of myself. If I push myself too hard, I won't be able to take care of her. I might have been able to push through when in the jail cell, but I also think I was running off adrenaline. I hit a wall today, a hard one. It was life telling me to slow the fuck down and recover. So I'm taking the warning seriously.

While she's in the shower, I go over my notes again, trying to write down a list of suspects, but all I have is Brimar and Magnus.

That's how fucking fried my brain is.

We checked, Brimar is still in jail, and I'd have recognized his voice. Magnus . . . the king of Arkham, has been trying to take Torskethorpe for years now. I know he wasn't happy when Lilly came along, but what does that have to do with me?

I pinch my forehead.

Fuck, this is irritating.

Not wanting to develop another headache, I return my notebook to the nightstand, then stand. Since it's late, I should lock up and make sure everything is secure. Tomorrow, I'll set up motion cameras around the island so I have eyes on every corner just in case anyone finds out where we are. I'll feel much safer once I have those set up.

Once I feel good about the house, I move back into the bedroom where Lilly rubs lotion all over her body. *It must have been in the bathroom.* I avert my eyes and go to the bathroom where I take care of business and brush my teeth. My eyes fall to the scars on my chest.

Those were from when Banamaor decided to press his cigarette into my chest as if I was his own personal ashtray. I should have known walking around with my shirt off would result in questions, but I've been restricted from comfort for the past three months. I deserve the freedom. That's what happens when you've been chained to a wall for a long period.

I need the freedom so I don't go crazy.

So my mind doesn't drift back to those lonely nights.

To the sound of Banamaor breathing heavily with pleasure as he tortured me.

I turn off the bedroom light and crawl under the covers of the bed.

"Did you change the sheets?" Lilly asks.

I don't look in her direction, not able to take her just standing there naked.

"I did."

"These are silk sheets," she says.

"It's all there was."

"Naked on silk sheets? You realize how horny that's going to make me?"

"Then put clothes on," I say. "Borrow one of my shirts."

I glance and catch her side-eye me. "Did you do this on purpose?"

"Change the sheets? Yes, I did. I felt how sweaty I was today, and I didn't think you wanted to sleep on sweaty sheets. I'm happy to pull them from the hamper and change the bed again."

She grumbles something under her breath, then slips into the bed next to me. The smell of her lotion infiltrates my space, and my cock grows hard from the thought of that smell being spread all over her body.

Jesus Christ, maybe the silk sheets are making me horny as well.

She scoots back, her bare butt hitting my thigh.

"Am I in your way?" I ask her.

"Yes. There isn't any room on this thing with your big body."

"There was room earlier."

"Yeah, well, that was different. I let you cuddle into me because you asked nicely."

I turn on my side and rest my hand on her bare hip. "What if I asked you nicely now?"

"You can go to hell," she says, nearly making me smile. "You're not going to wind me up like you did last night, then just leave me throbbing." She pushes my hand off her side.

"Throbbing?" I ask.

"Yes, throbbing, and before you start puffing your chest, it's been a long time for me."

"It's been the same amount of time for me," I say, my resolve slipping for a second. I blame the lotion. I blame the coolness of the sheets. I blame the fact that she parades around here naked.

It has nothing to do with my inability to have any protective barrier around my heart where she's concerned.

"Glad to know we've suffered celibacy together. Something we at least have in common."

"We have more in common."

"Oh yeah?" she asks on a laugh and turns toward me. "Like what?"

"What we enjoy in bed."

She rolls her eyes. "Elias was so right. Our entire relationship was built on sex."

"Nothing wrong with that."

"Everything is wrong with that, Keller."

"So are you telling me you have more in common with Evan than me?"

Her lips twist to the side as she studies me, and I can tell she's choosing her words wisely. "He's easy to talk to. Fun. Knows how to make me smile when I hadn't thought smiling was an option anymore."

Well if that doesn't fucking piss me off.

"He didn't growl at me," she continues. "He didn't reprimand me. And he didn't feel embarrassed walking next to me."

"I never felt embarrassed walking next to you," I say

through clenched teeth. "If anything, I didn't think I was good enough because you are so goddamn beautiful and smart and made for the role that you're in. Never once did I ever feel ashamed being next to you. It was a fucking honor."

Her lips press together, and she looks past my shoulder, not able to look me in the eyes.

"And he was easy to talk to because it was most likely shallow conversation." I tilt her chin so she looks in my eyes. "Our conversations weren't easy because they were deep. Because there was purpose behind them, meaning. I don't have the need to charm you with laughs and jokes. I wanted the person under all of that. I wanted the Lilly that suffered through losing her parents. I wanted the Lilly who was terrified to take on the crown. I wanted the Lilly who nearly drove us off a cliff in a car, showing me how proud of herself she was at learning a new skill. If it's easy, it's not worth your time. The hard in a relationship is what bonds you."

Her nostrils flare. "Then why did you hide yourself before we got married? If it truly is the hard that bonds us, why were you running away?"

She got you fucking there.

"There's a lot more behind it that you don't know."

"Clearly," she says. "And it seems like I'll never know. That's why I went with easy, because I tried hard and that clearly didn't work out for me."

She turns away from me, and I clench my teeth, fury running through my veins. She's trying to get under my skin and it's fucking working. Evan is a good man, but I also hate him with everything inside me, because I could easily see Lilly and Evan together. I could see the mass appeal. I could see how they'd get along so well and charm the country. Would they share the same kind of love that Lilly and I shared?

Never.

But then again, it doesn't seem like she's looking for that.

She was looking for someone to fill the role, and she found him.

And that's a goddamn knife to the heart. *It shows just how easily replaceable I am.*

It doesn't settle well.

It actually lights a flame of anger deep within me, so much so that when she shifts uncomfortably next to me, I snap, "What?"

From the tone of my voice, she pauses and glances over her shoulder. "I can't get comfortable. You going to be pissed about that too? You're the one who brought me here and is intent on sharing a bed, deal with my discomfort."

"We're sharing a bed because I'm not about to leave you unattended."

"The living room is like two feet away."

"More like twenty. And I'm not sleeping on a fucking couch when this room contains a perfectly fine bed."

"Fine is an exaggeration. There's no space." She pushes at my legs with her feet. "Stick to your side."

"There are no sides. It's just a bed. Deal with it."

She huffs. "This must be so much fun for you, sleeping next to a naked woman in silk sheets, almost as if you planned it."

Clenching my jaw, I say, "If I planned this, you wouldn't be pushing me away."

"Oh please," she scoffs, pissing me off even more. "You're resistible, okay? I have no problem keeping to myself. You're the grabby one."

"Is that right?" I ask, "You think you can resist me?"

"Yes. You're not the be-all and end-all when it comes to sex, Keller."

I work my jaw to the side, my mind whirling with stubborn thoughts. She really thinks she can resist me? She thinks I can touch her and she won't feel something? Not give in?

I'd LOVE to fucking see that.

My silence falls between us as I figure out how to handle this. How to prove her wrong. Because that's exactly what I'm going to do. She thinks she can throw Evan in my face, tell me it's easier being with him, piss me off, then emit a bald-faced lie like I'm resistible to her?

No fucking way.

She shifts again, grumbling under her breath, and I take that opportunity to loop my arm around her and plaster her up against my bare chest.

"What the hell are you doing?" she asks.

"Making you more comfortable. That better?"

Her ass is snug against my crotch, and her bare skin smooths against mine. It's a whole lot better for me.

"No. Worse," she says, removing my hand and scooting toward the edge of the bed.

So fucking stubborn.

"You're a fucking liar," I say as I pull her back into my chest, but this time, I flip us both to our backs so she's resting between my legs and her back is against my chest.

"What the hell, Keller." She swats at me, but I pin her arms down, which causes the sheets to slide down her front, exposing her breasts.

Leaning forward, so my lips are close to her ear, I say, "You're telling me, right now, you're not turned on?"

Her chest rises then falls as she wets her lips, her body leaning into mine from the way my lips are so dangerously close to her face.

"No," she answers, but there's desperation laced with her answer.

"You're lying to me again," I say. "Why are you lying to me?"

"Because I'm mad at you," she says, her voice full of disdain. "You broke me, Keller."

"I didn't want to," I say as I slide my hand up her stomach, my thumb brushing her breast.

"Doesn't matter, you still did. You leaving . . . it was painful. The only reason I'm still here is because of Runa, who never left my side. Because she took care of me every fucking second you were gone." My thumb swipes at her breasts, and she rolls backward an inch, giving me better access.

"Every second I was gone, I thought of you," I say, my thumb inching to her nipple.

"I don't want to hear that," she says as her chest rises.

"Then what do you want?" I ask her, sliding my hand down her stomach right above her pussy. I linger my fingers there, slowly dragging them from one hipbone to the other. She wiggles beneath me, the friction she's creating rubbing against my hardening cock.

"Nothing from you."

"Lying again," I say as I move my finger to her slit where I toy with her, dipping lower.

Her legs spread, and I feel the first touch of her arousal.

Satisfied, I say, "If you want nothing from me, then why are you wet?"

Her head presses against my shoulder, her fingers curl into my thighs, and her pelvis tilts up just enough for my finger to slide deeper.

"Fuck," she whispers as she pulls her hips back, then lifts them again, my finger sliding farther this time.

With my other hand, I drag my fingers up her stomach, to her breast where I circle her areola.

"God," she cries out in frustration. "I hate you for making me want this."

"Then tell me to stop," I say as her hips move again, and my finger rubs along her clit.

Warm and wet. Fuck me I want to bury my face between her legs.

I still want her more than fucking anything. I never deserved her, I know that, but fuck, I want her. I hate that I hurt her. I hate it. *And it feels too late to tell her the truth. She's made up her mind about me now.*

"I . . . want . . . to." She breathes out heavily, and I take that moment to solidify what she actually wants. I cup her breast, my mind turning murky with confusion as I'm transported back into a time where she was mine. Where her body belonged to me, and I could do anything I wanted and she loved it.

I squeeze her breast, letting my thumb roll over her nipple and getting lost in the feel of her rocking against me, her body rubbing against my strained cock, her wet cunt begging for more.

"Fuck," she whispers, her breathing picking up.

Her legs fall apart and her eyes stare up at me, desperation clouding her pupils. I know that I can't fucking deny her what she wants, not when she looks at me like that, not when I want to claim her, show her why we were so good together. Why she trusted me in the first place.

I remove my hand from her pussy and adjust the pillow behind me so I'm more comfortable, but from my release, she tenses beneath me, then says, "Goddammit, Keller, don't taunt me."

"Taunt you?" I ask as I kick her legs apart with mine, making her curl them around my shins. Then I take her hand and move it right over her pussy. "Is this taunting you?" I lower my mouth right to her ear and whisper, "Finger yourself."

She lets out a long, drawn-out "fuck" right before she slides her finger along her clit, my mouth watering with jealousy.

Taunt her, no, that's not what I'd do.

Show her what she's been missing in her life, what she'd never get with Evan, now that's a different story.

I run my fingers up her stomach, watching her skin light up with goosebumps, and cup her breasts gently, just enough to show her my intentions, but not enough to give her what she wants.

Her head tilts back against my shoulder, her hair rubbing against my chest, her pleasure already starting to make her lose control, to drop the facade and just enjoy. With satisfaction, I watch her every move, from the way her finger moves over her clit, to the rise and fall of her chest, to her mouth parting open as I twist her nipple piercings.

"Yes," she whispers, her response exactly what I want.

"Smooth one finger over your clit," I say. "Slowly."

She wets her lips, then I watch carefully as her finger disappears between her legs and, at a snail's pace, runs along her clit piercing that I've spent many hours licking.

"Good girl," I say as I continue to twist her nipple piercing, never touching her breasts, just moving the metal through her nipple, the pebbled nubs becoming harder and more desperate with every second.

She's so responsive.

Even when she hates me . . .

"How wet are you?" I ask.

"Very," she answers.

"Let me taste," I say, my mouth parched for her pussy.

From her pause, I don't think she's going to do it, but then to my satisfaction, she lifts her hand, and I lean forward to suck her fingers into my mouth. I lap at them with my tongue, then slowly draw them past my lips until they pop out. "Fucking delicious," I say.

Her back shifts against my chest as she hums in the back of her throat, enjoying this just as much as I am. And when she goes to move her hand back between her legs, I stop her.

"What are you doing?" I ask.

"Touching myself," she answers as if it's the most obvious thing ever.

"I never said you could touch yourself again. Rest your

hands on my thighs." When she doesn't listen right away, I pinch her nipple, hard.

"Fuck," she hisses as her hands move to my thighs.

"That's my good girl," I whisper right before I cup her breasts. "Spread your legs wider." She does, and I lock her ankles with my foot so she can't move them. Firmly in place, I pinch her nipples with my forefinger and thumb, rolling the hard nubs to pull a long, delicious moan from her lips.

Besides my cock pounding into her, there's nothing she loves more than nipple play.

She loves the torture, the pleasure, the bolts of lust sent straight to her pussy with every pinch, every tweak.

That's how she'll come tonight. She will find her release from my hands.

"Take a deep breath for me."

Her chest rises as she sucks in sharply, then lets out her air slowly.

"Again," I say. "Slower."

This time, her body relaxes more as she exhales. I lightly pass my thumbs over her nipples as she does this.

"Again."

This time, her chest rises longer as she sucks in air, and when she lets go, I press down on her nipples. A moan falls past her lips along with her breath.

"Again."

This time, as she inhales, I circle her areolas with the tips of my fingers, and when she exhales, I press down on her nipples.

"Fuck," she whispers.

"Again."

"Keller, I'm already throbbing."

"I said, again."

Her teeth fall over her bottom lip, and she takes a shaky deep breath. I circle her nipple, and when she exhales, I flick her nipples rapidly.

"God," she cries, her legs shifting, but I hold them still. "I need to touch myself."

"No, you need to listen to me. I know what's best for you, best for your body." I pause, then say, "Again."

Shakily, she takes in a deep breath while I squeeze her breasts, and when she exhales, I pinch her nipples and lightly pull up. She cries out in ecstasy, her hands gripping my thighs with a deathly grip.

I welcome the dig of her fingernails. *It makes me feel alive.* Something I haven't felt in months.

When she inhales this time, she shifts her body and her ass gently rubs against my erection, and fuck, does it feel good. Christ, what I wouldn't give to just flip her over right now and bury my dick so far into her pussy that she can fucking taste it.

But this isn't about me. This is about her.

This is about showing her how no matter who she tries to date, she will always belong to me.

I move away from her breasts and drag the backs of my fingers down her sides, to her waistline, then press the pads of my fingers against her skin as I bring them back up. I repeat the process but bring them closer to her pussy with each pass, then back up to her chest where I circle around her areolas.

It's slow.

It's formulaic.

There's a purpose.

To drive her wild with need. To beg for her release.

Her body undulates against my touch, her chest rising and falling, her stomach hollowing out, her pelvis tilting up, and I allow it. With each pass, I grow closer and closer to exactly where she wants me until I reach her breasts again, and this time, I twist her nipple rings.

"Fuck, Keller." Her nails dig deeper into my thighs and my cock surges from the pleasure of it, knowing I have her right where I want her.

"Are you close?" I ask her.

She nods as her mouth drops open and her chest rises into my hands. I flick her nipples now, fast, just like I'd flick her clit with my tongue. Her breasts press against my fingers, her head rolls from side to side, her moans grow louder and louder.

She's so fucking close.

Her pelvis rocks back and forth, her entire body seeking pleasure but being completely controlled by the way I play with her nipples.

It's so fucking hot that I can feel my balls start to draw up, my impending orgasm climbing just from the way she's pressing against my cock and watching her react to my touch.

"Fuck . . . let me touch myself," she finally says.

"No," I say. "You will come from my fingers, not yours." I move my fingers to her areolas, then start squeezing, pulling her nipples up into the air on a pinch just loose enough it doesn't cause her pain, but tight enough to make her scream.

"Mother of fuck," she cries out, her fingers scraping up my thighs. "Oh fuck, Keller."

I do it again, this time pinching longer, and just as I reach the tip, her fingers turn into claws as her back arches and a feral sound falls past her lips.

Loud.

Sexy.

Uncontrolled.

She cries out my name as she comes, her orgasm wracking her harder than I expected as her moan draws out, her entire body convulsing under my touch until she finally relaxes and her death grip on my legs eases.

"Such a good girl," I say as I gently pass my fingers over her breasts, let her fully relax until she's limp against my body. I lift her up and move away from her, my erection slipping past the waistband of my briefs, the tip full of precum.

I lean back against the headboard, pull my entire length out, and use my precum as lubricant as I pump feverously. It takes me about two seconds to get to where I need to be, and I don't prolong it. I grip my cock harder and pump until I swell in my hand and my body stills as my orgasm rips through me, cum flying up my stomach.

"Shit," I grumble as I slow down my strokes to the point that my hand is barely passing over my cock. That's when I glance to the side and catch Lilly staring at me, her eyes hungry.

I release my cock and drop my hands to my side as I catch my breath. "Fuck," I mutter.

I stare up at the ceiling, unsure where to go from here. Technically, she's with someone else, and I just made her come. What does that mean? I know I told her she's always been mine and always will be, but where does she truly stand with Evan?

I roll my head to the side to talk to her, but she heads to the bathroom, her mouthwatering body swaying with every step.

I pinch my brow, disappointed in myself, but also fucking satisfied that I could make her come just from nipple pleasure.

What the fuck are you doing, Keller?

She appears in the doorway of the bathroom, and when I glance in her direction, she tosses a wet washcloth at me and says, "Clean yourself," before disappearing.

"Christ," I mutter, as I wash my stomach.

What did you just do, you fucking moron?

IF I THOUGHT she hated me before last night, I was fucking wrong, because Jesus Christ, does she want to murder me today.

After she came out of the bathroom from cleaning up last night, she went to her side of the bed, gave me her back, and didn't say a word. The entire night, she must have put up some sort of invisible wall, because she didn't accidentally bump into me one time. It was as if I was diseased, and she made it her mission to cling to the edge of the bed.

And when I woke up this morning, she was already out of bed, clanking around in the kitchen and making such a ruckus that it was impossible to get back to sleep.

When I approached her in the kitchen, she sarcastically asked if she was too loud, then clanked a pan against the stove. I just moved around her, took the pan, and made us some eggs with spinach and mushrooms. She ate out on the patio.

I ate at the dining room table.

And now, she's out on the beach, basking in the sun naked, while I sit on the couch, watching over her, wondering how the hell I navigate this mess.

She's mad at me.

I'm mad at her.

And there doesn't seem to be a platform to bridge the gap.

I lean back on the couch and push my hand through my hair, frustrated, tired, mentally exhausted. This would be so much fucking easier if my mind was sharper. If I didn't feel like I was constantly trying to solve the world's hardest problem when it comes to simple tasks. I never realized how much I've been running on adrenaline and sheer willpower until now. I'm fucking shocked I was even able to fly a plane down here because my mental clarity is shit.

The sliding glass door opens and Lilly appears, a towel around her torso, hair loosely in a messy bun on the top of her head, a few tendrils framing her face.

Fuck, she's so goddamn hot.

My mind immediately transports back to last night, with her between my legs, playing with her nipples until she came. It never gets old, seeing her come apart like that from just my hands. I'd do that every night if I could.

"Stare much?" she says, breaking into my thoughts.

I meet her gaze. "I did bring you clothes, you know."

She lets her towel drop to the floor and walks over to the kitchen. "Yes, but walking around naked irritates you, so why would I put clothes on?"

"It's not smart to irritate me, Lilly."

"Why?" she asks as she bends over, her ass and pussy on full display as she reaches for a drink in the fridge. When she stands and faces me, those delicious nipples of hers hard as stone, she says, "It's not like we're a couple or anything. It's not like you have the right to sit there and tell me what I can and cannot do."

I run my tongue over my teeth, knowing she's trying to get under my skin. *She's doing a perfectly good job at it.*

"Let me ask you this," she says as she walks toward me. "When you were out fishing on your boat"—she stands in front of me and my hands itch to reach out to her—"did you even consider what I might be feeling?" She places one foot on the couch next to me, her legs spreading, drawing my eyes down to her pussy.

"When I was away, I thought about you every second," I answer as I wet my lips.

She moves in closer and places one of her hands on the back of the couch, right next to my head. I go hard immediately.

"Yet you left this," she says just as she straddles my lap. I lace my hands together behind my head as her palms fall to my chest.

"Well, you didn't mourn for too long," I say as she moves her pelvis over my length.

"What did you want me to do? Believe that you were going to come back, kidnap me from my room, and take me to a remote island and be happy about it?" She lifts her chest and rubs her nipple over my lips. I part them but she pulls away, not letting me suck on the little nub. "You moved on, so I had to move on."

"You could have waited," I say as she twists on my lap so

her back is now against my chest. She loops her hand around the back of my neck, anchoring herself in place as she undulates her ass over my erection. It feels so fucking good. Her pace is perfect, and the softness of her ass passing over my cock is the perfect combination of friction and pressure. She's building me up slowly despite the hate she has for me.

"You left me once," she says as I unlatch my hands and cup one of her breasts lightly. Her body tenses before she moves my hand away. "You could leave me again. Why would I wait?"

"Because I told you I loved you," I say.

That makes her turn back around to face me, and the movement causes my cock to slip past the shorts I'm wearing. Noticing, she pulls it all the way out of my shorts, then plasters her clit against it, moving her hips harder, grinding her arousal into me so I get lost in how wet she is.

"If you loved me, Keller, you never would have broken me the way you did."

Her hands loop around the back of my neck and her hips move faster, her head falls back, exposing her beautiful neck and, if we weren't in the middle of some serious hate sex at the moment, I'd run my tongue along the column, all the way up to her mouth where I'd claim it.

"Who's to say I broke you on purpose?" I ask as her breath catches in her throat and her head falls forward, her body tensing against mine. She's close.

"Fuck," she whispers as she forgets to respond to me and focuses on her pleasure, creating such a delicious friction between us that I feel my mind falling to our connection and the thrust of her hips, the soft moans falling past her lips.

Her fingers dig into my skin and her thrusts become frantic as her head falls back again, her lips parting.

"Uhhhhh . . . oh . . . God," she moans just as her body convulses, her orgasm ripping through her like a bolt of lightning, so fast I wasn't expecting it. Seeing her fall apart, right here in front of me, sends me over the edge as well in surprise.

I push her away a few inches, grip my cock, and pump as I come quickly between us, my cum once again hitting my stomach.

"Jesus," I mutter, not expecting to have such a fast release.

I don't think she was either, because when her eyes meet mine, they seem confused but with a slice of anger.

Once I catch my breath, I say, "Was that what you wanted?"

She pushes off me, standing before me now. "No, what I wanted was to marry you, what I got was a broken heart and a shattered soul."

She takes a step back as I drop my hand to the side. "Then why bother fucking me if your soul is so shattered? I'd think you wouldn't want to be around me."

"You're right." She walks over to where she dropped her towel and picks it up. "I don't want to be around you. This"— she motions between us—"this was a mistake. Last night, that was a mistake."

"Is that how you truly feel?"

"Yes," she answers and wraps the towel around her. She heads to the bedroom. I quickly wipe up my stomach with a wet paper towel before following her.

"If this was all a mistake, then why let me touch you again?"

She keeps her back to me as she answers, "Because despite hating you and what you did to me, I can't deny the fact that my body still wants you." She looks over her shoulder. "But that doesn't mean I don't hate you . . . because I do." Her eyes well with tears. "I hate you, Keller. I hate what you did to us. What you did to me. I hate every second that I have to be in this stupid cottage with you for God knows what reason, probably you trying to get me to fall for you all over again." She grips her towel tighter. "Well, it's not going to happen. I'm not going there again." She tilts her chin up. "This was a momentary lapse, won't happen again."

I work my jaw back and forth, anger pumping through me. She fucking hates me? Really?

"Life isn't as it always seems, Lilly. Best you remember that as you move through this cottage with me."

"And this body, it doesn't belong to you," she says, cutting me deep. "Best you remember that." She heads toward the bathroom, pauses, then turns to face me. "It took every ounce of strength I had to get through the past few months, and I'll be damned if you set me back again. I'm moving forward, and you're not in the picture."

I nod slowly. "Let me guess, Evan is?"

"He's a hell of a lot more in the picture than you." And with that, she slams the bathroom door behind her, leaving me in a silent bedroom.

Fuck her.

I push my hand through my hair.

Fuck.

Her!

This is exactly why I haven't told her what happened, because she thinks the worst of me. Why the fuck would I even try to be with someone who doesn't have a shred of doubt that maybe . . . just maybe I didn't leave her on our wedding night?

Elias might have been right all along. Our relationship was built on sex . . . and sex alone. We didn't resolve conflict unless you call shouting and angry sex resolution. It isn't. It sates you momentarily, but that's it. *We were destined to fail, our fate inevitable.*

AT THIS POINT, I don't know which is worse, sitting in that dank cell, all to myself, chained to the wall, or having to share a bed with an angry, naked Lilly.

The cell is looking pretty damn good at this point.

At least when I was there, I had hope that maybe she was still thinking of me, maybe looking for me, doing anything to preserve the relationship we had.

That's not the Lilly I have to deal with now. She's volatile, and the sooner I can figure out who was behind all of this, the better. At least once I figure it out, it will give us a second to breathe . . .

Then again, if I give her time to breathe, she's going to lean into Evan, and the thought of her with him makes my skin fucking crawl.

I sit up in bed, unable to sleep, and I reach into my nightstand for my notebook and pen as well as my mini light that clips onto my notebook. Lilly shifts next to me, but I keep to myself as I flip it open and go to the back where my poems and sketches are hidden.

I stare down at the paper, at the poem I wrote today after my fight with Lilly.

I owe the stars my life.
Glistening.
Singing.
Lighting the way to your arms.
They gave hope.
They gave freedom.
They gave me you.
Yet the stars have faded,
Broken.
Shattered.
There is no you, only me.

I scroll the pen over the sketch of Lilly's face, deepening the lines in her pupils, leaving a white spot where her eyes used to shine while looking up at me. Just like the day before our wedding, after waking up with her in my arms that morning. She looked up at me with so much love, like I was her entire goddamn world.

Now, they feel lifeless, like the soul has been sucked from them. Just like mine—

"Are you drawing me?" Lilly says, her voice startling me.

I snap my notebook shut and turn off the light.

"I thought you were sleeping," I say gruffly as I set my notebook on my nightstand.

"Hard to sleep when there's a light shining in the bed."

"I didn't think it was that bright," I mumble. "Sorry." I slouch down in bed and stare up at the ceiling, my heart racing from being caught.

Fuck, did she read the poem?

"You didn't answer me," she says. "Were you drawing me?"

I bite down on the inside of my cheek to keep myself from growling in frustration. Of course, she's not going to drop it. When has she ever dropped anything?

"What did it look like?" I ask.

"It looked like you were drawing me. And I'm wondering why?"

"I don't know, Lilly, maybe because despite the apparent hatred between us, I still think about you constantly."

That leaves her silent for a moment. I'm about to turn on my side, away from her, when she says, "Why do you say things like that, Keller? You know it only hurts me."

"Me saying I still think about you, hurts you?" I ask, bewildered.

"Yes," she says, sitting up on one elbow to look at me. When her beautiful face comes into view, I have this primal instinct to close my hand behind her head and bring her mouth down to mine, to erase all of the bad energy between us. "It hurts me. It confuses me. It makes me believe that there still could be a you and me."

"There still could be," I say. "There very much could be a you and me, but right now . . . there's a you and someone else."

"Is that what you're really tied up on?" she asks.

"Yes," I nearly shout. "Jesus Christ, Lilly. Yes! You chose to go out with someone else. When I saw the news that you were with another man, it gutted me." My throat grows tight, so I take a deep breath, trying to calm myself down. "Seeing you walking with someone else other than me is an image that will be burned in my brain, forever."

A confused look passes over her face as she says, "Then . . . then if you cared so much, why did you leave, Keller?"

I bite down on my lower lip and stare up at the ceiling. "Sometimes, we don't have a choice in the matter."

I turn away from her, tucking my pillow under my head and trying to get comfortable, even though I know it will probably be another restless night.

"What does that even mean?" she asks.

I don't answer.

I don't know how to answer without getting into everything, and honestly, I'm too fucking raw right now to get into it.

I know the moment she gives up, because she shifts on the bed, turning away from me. I can tell from the way the bed dips. Once again, she's up against the edge, and for the first time since we've shared this bed, there's actually room, because both of us are trying to keep our distance as much as we can.

She's keeping her heart at a distance, which is the very reason I'm keeping the truth at a distance. Until I have that heart of hers back, I can't possibly earn her love back through sympathy.

I want it because that's how she truly feels about me, no other reason.

"MORNING," Lilly says from the bedroom door, where she stands, wearing one of my shirts again. I'm surprised she's even talking to me right now after how things went last night.

"Morning," I say from the kitchen, cup of coffee in hand.

She saunters into the kitchen and lifts onto the counter, where she takes a seat, her legs dangling against the cabinets. I lift my cup of coffee to my lips as I take her in. Her shoulders are slumped, and she twists her hands in her lap before she glances up at me.

"I don't know why you left the night before our wedding. Not sure you'll ever tell me, but I want to tell you this." She takes a deep breath. "I've never felt the depth of pain I felt the moment I read your letter. That pain will be greater than anything I ever experience in life, greater than the day I lost my parents, greater than the day I'll lose Theo and Katla. My heart chose you, Keller, and when you left, you ripped my heart out with you." She speaks softly, without anger, just clearly so I understand.

I set my coffee down, and I place my hands behind me on the counter, gripping it tightly. When I glance up at her, I catch the emotion in her eyes, the damage I've done.

"I'm . . . I'm sorry, Lilly," I say. Even though it was completely out of my control, she still deserves that apology.

She just nods, then hops off the counter, moving over to the coffee pot right next to me. Her hair brushes up against my chest as she pours herself a cup. I'm tempted to grab her by the waist and pull her into my embrace, to run my lips along her jaw to her mouth, to let her know how sorry I am that she was hurt.

Because despite being mad at her, I still can't help but love this woman. Seeing her in pain guts me.

She grabs the creamer I got just for her from the fridge, and she pours it in her coffee before stirring. When she's done, she brings the mug up to her lips and looks over the rim at me. She's so close, a few inches away. With her gaze matching mine, she quietly says, "For the record, I didn't want to date him."

Date him?

What is she talking about?

"Huh?" I ask, confused.

"Evan. I didn't want to date him. I wasn't ready."

My brow pulls together. "Did he force you?"

She shakes her head. "No. He was nothing but a gentleman."

And then with that, she turns on her heel and heads toward the patio, but I push off the counter and move in front of her, stopping her. "Wait, what do you mean you didn't want to date him?"

Still speaking softly, she says, "I met him at a party in Marsdale. I talked to him the whole night, but it was just conversation. He asked me out, and I said no."

I swallow hard as her truth falls past her lips, the truth I wish I'd have known so much sooner. *I agonized over her being with someone else.*

Continuing, she says, "I found out the next day that Theo wasn't doing well. I rushed back to Torskethorpe, and when I saw him in his bed, I nearly lost it."

"What?" I ask. "Is he . . . is he okay?"

"He was heartbroken," she says. "From losing you, from me losing you, from what he considered his own failure. He was afraid I'd be left alone, that I wouldn't have anyone by my side, and it was stressing him, causing his health to deteriorate. So that day, I chose his health over my well-being. I found out Evan's number, and I asked him out to lunch."

My breath picks up as the pieces start falling into place. She didn't date him out of spite or because she actually liked him. She went out with him because of Theo. Fucking hell.

"It was harmless," she continues. "We never kissed. We

were never intimate, not even close." What? My heart nearly rips out of my chest . . . he never . . . he never tasted her. Holy fuck. "It was more companionship than anything. We went out three times, then you took me." Her eyes meet mine. "There was no way I was getting over you. I even told him that. He understood."

My heart is beating so fucking rapidly that I almost can't get out my words as I ask, "He never touched your lips?"

She shakes her head, her eyes so earnest that I can feel her answer to my very core.

"Why are you telling me this?"

"Because I didn't want you to think that getting over you was easy. It wasn't. It isn't. I still struggle with it. Every day, I wake up and tell myself, this is the day I'm not going to think about you, that I'm not going to think about what we had, but it's impossible because every breath I take, every heartbeat in my chest is propelled by the love I felt for you . . ." Her eyes shift up to mine. "The love I still feel for you. You said you will always own me, and you're right." She takes a step back. "I hate to admit it, but it's true. You will forever and always own me, Keller."

And then she turns on her heel and walks back into the bedroom, shutting the door behind her.

I drag my hand over my mouth.

Fuck.

<hr />

LILLY LIES out tanning naked in the middle of the beach, and as I set up my last camera, I can't stop staring at the way her skin glistens in the heat.

I spent the entire morning chastising myself, running our morning conversation over and over again in my head until I drove myself crazy.

I should just fucking tell her. *She hasn't moved on.*

She's still very much in love with me.

So what now? Do I lay it out for her? Do I ask for forgiveness? Do I explain the whole story?

From the corner of my eye, I watch her lift from the towel and stand. She spots me staring at her and calls out, "Going to rinse off."

"Okay," I say, gulping as I watch her perfect ass walk away from me.

When she's out of sight, I take a seat against a rock and drag both my hands over my face. I can tell her tonight.

I'm not sure what will come from it, but she told me the truth, so I should give her the same courtesy. That's the logical thing to do, so why does that realization make me physically ill?

Because I'm afraid of what she might think.

That she might not believe me . . .

I bow my head and squeeze my eyes shut.

It's Lilly. She'll believe you.

If anyone will believe you, it's Lilly.

Just feels so fucking farfetched, even though it's so goddamn real.

I let out a deep breath, then finish setting up the security camera. When I check it out on my receiver and see it's working, I walk back to the house for another bottle of water. I've been outside for a good deal of time, and even though I've been drinking the whole time, I want to make sure I'm never in a position like I was the other day.

When I grow closer, my eye catches movement through the master bedroom window, and I spot Lilly sitting on the bed, her head tilted down . . . reading.

What is she . . .

Is that my notebook?

Fuck!

I run into the house and charge into the room just as she looks up from my notebook. Shit.

"What the hell is this?" she asks.

I walk up to her and rip it out of her hand. "I told you not to fucking read this."

Her face morphs into shock as she stands in her towel, fresh from the shower. "It was on the bed, I wanted to look at the picture you drew of me."

"That's . . . that's not for your eyes." I shove it into the nightstand and slam the drawer.

And then she holds up the phone that was in the nightstand as well and says, "And what's this?"

"Did you actually shower, or are you just in here snooping?"

"I'm wondering why the hell you have a list of people on a piece of paper with some other nonsense, and a phone that you never told me about. What the fuck is this?" she asks, holding her hands out. "You say Theo knows that we're here, but there's no rhyme or reason to our days. You say you're setting up cameras for protection, but are you setting them up just to make sure I don't get away? Was this all because you saw me with another man? You had his name circled in your little notebook. Like, what the actual fuck, Keller?"

"Do you really think I'd just kidnap you for the hell of it?"

"I don't even know at this point, Keller. Like . . . what the hell is going on? You tell me you don't want me, that you don't want to touch me, but then you need to cuddle with me to feel better. You tell me that I'm with another man, but then you make me come so hard that I actually forget why I'm here. So what is it? Why am I here?"

"Because someone is trying to fucking kill us," I say, unable to hold it back anymore.

"What?" she asks, startled. "The same person from before the wedding?"

Fuck, not the way I want to have this conversation.

I didn't ever want to have this conversation. I wanted to protect her from the truth. I don't want her on this island, worrying that someone is out to get us, but I can't hide from the truth any longer.

It's time.

I move over to the dresser and pull out one of my shirts. I toss it at her and say, "Put this on."

Confused, she stares at me for a few seconds before she drops her towel and slips my shirt over her head. When she's dressed, I sit on the bed and lean against the headboard. I then take her hand and pull her onto my lap so she's facing me.

"What are you doing?" she asks.

"Trying to talk to you about something I've been avoiding." My hands fall to her thighs, gripping them gently. "And I need to . . . I need to hold you when I tell you."

"What's going on?" she asks, now looking scared. "Does this have to do with the threats we received before the wedding? Is that why you left? To distract them? Make them think that the wedding was off so they didn't hurt us?"

I shake my head.

"So then you just left . . . no reason other than what you wrote? You really couldn't handle being with me?" Her eyes well up, and I smooth my hands over her thighs.

"No, Lilly. I wanted to marry you. I was dead set on watching you walk down that aisle toward me."

"Then why didn't you?"

I take a deep breath. Here goes . . .

"That night, I went to get in bed, when . . . when something struck me from behind."

"What?" she asks.

"I was tased. The electric shock brought me down to my goddamn knees. Then a few men came up behind me, one held a gun to my head, and they forced me to write that letter to you."

"Wait." She sits back, her expression trying to make sense of this. "But we had guards at your room. Ottar was watching over you. How could a bunch of guys sneak in? That makes no sense."

Fear creeps up my spine because she's right. It makes no goddamn sense, yet it still happened.

I want her to believe me.

I need her to believe me, so in a controlled voice, I continue, "There are secret passageways throughout Strombly. There was an inside source working on the job who must have told them about the passageways because they came through one in the sapphire room and dragged me out of it."

She sits still on my lap, staring at my chest, her brows pinched together as she tries to comprehend all of this. "You didn't leave me because you weren't ready to marry me?"

"No," I say, cupping her cheek, but she pushes my hand away and gets off my lap. Fuck . . . "Lilly."

Seething now, she stands in front of me, her chest heaving. I can't tell if she believes me.

All I can see is the raging anger pumping through her as she stares at me, her hands clenched at her side. Finally, she says, "Then why the *fuck* didn't you say that the minute you saw me?"

"Because I thought you were with someone else. I thought you moved on."

"Then you don't fucking know me at all." She pounds her hand against her chest, tears forming in her eyes. "Jesus Christ, Keller. I thought I wasn't worthy enough to give up everything." She shoots her arm out to the side. "I thought that the love of my goddamn life just walked out on me because I wasn't worth the time and aggravation and complications. I withered away into nothing on my bed because of it. I had to be brought back to life by Runa, and you bring me here and make me believe that you were on some fishing trip or just living the good life down here on the island. You should have told me immediately. The minute I opened my eyes, you should have told me."

381

"I didn't want your sympathy," I yell at her as I stand as well. "I was fucking taken, Lilly. I lived in a stone-walled cell, chained to a goddamn wall. I was whipped, beaten, and burned for the hell of it." Her eyes widen as her hand covers her mouth. "I was tortured every goddamn day knowing that you were left behind, that you thought I didn't want to marry you. And to top it off, I had newspaper clippings dropped off in front of me to read about how you were with another fucking man. So yeah, I didn't tell you right away because I wanted you to want to be with me for no other reason than you wanted me."

Her lip trembles as tears spill over her eyes and onto her delicate face. "I've always wanted you, Keller. Always." She wipes away the tears with the pads of her fingers, and without another word, she walks out of the bedroom and out to the back patio, shutting the door behind her.

Chapter Thirty-One

"What do you want?" I ask Pickering when he comes into my office.

"King Magnus is on the phone, and he's not happy."

"Fuck," I mutter. "Where's my brother?"

Pickering shrugs. "Last I saw him, he was smoking a cigar on the balcony."

"Well, get him in here, immediately." When Pickering doesn't move, I scream, "Now!"

He startles, then heads out of my office and down the hall. Imbecile.

Calming my voice, I take a few deep breaths and pick up my phone. I clear my throat and say, "Magnus, to what do I owe the pleasure?"

"Care to explain to me why the hell the security detail from Torskethorpe is calling me on a conference call with the security detail from Marsdale, asking what my involvement has been with the disappearance of Keller Fitzwilliam and the future queen of Torskethorpe?"

Shit.

I clear my throat again, nerves etching up my spine. "The, uh . . . the princess is missing?" I ask. "That's news to me."

"It shouldn't be fucking news to you," Magnus bellows. "You should know every goddamn thing going on in that palace. Especially after I helped you plant a contact in there. The princess should not be missing. She should be out on some ridiculous date with that Sotherby kid. That's what we planned. So where the hell is she?"

My palms go sweaty, and for a second, I consider telling him we lost Keller, that he escaped and we're now on the hunt, but if Magnus finds out that we lost Keller, he will never let us live another day. Not when he's being questioned by other countries.

And why is he being questioned?

Because of Keller.

He has communication with the palace. Don't know how, don't know how much, but the longer he's out there, connecting the dots, the more our lives are on the line.

"I've heard there's been negative press surrounding the princess and her willingness to jump to another man so quickly," I say, making this all up. "I'm sure this is a ploy for the palace, hiding her from the public eye."

"That doesn't explain the fact that two countries are coming to me, asking about my involvement."

He's right, that gives about zero explanation.

"Well, my source did say that they've asked all of the ships across the shores and checked on Fitzwilliam's passport. No one has seen any sign of him, so they're starting to ask around, looking for him. My guess is they're checking off their boxes, trying to scare you."

"I'm not scared. I'm pissed. This was supposed to be easy. Torskethorpe is supposed to be mine. You didn't believe Princess Lilija would take the throne without Fitzwilliam, that she'd slink back to her own country. Blackmailing the lord and lady of the Sotherbys was the new plan, yet that has seemed to fail as well. So what now? You want your payday, don't you?"

"I do," I say, pinching my brow. "It's just become more complicated than I expected."

"Am I going to have to step in and take charge? Because if it was up to me, we'd kill Theo, and with the princess missing, we'd therefore claim the country, just like we talked about. You're relieved of your duties, and I get exactly what I want."

"We can't kill Theo," I say, my voice growing terse.

"I thought you didn't have an attachment to him?" Magnus asks.

"I don't," I say quickly. "But if we kill him, Lilly will come back for sure. She has devoted herself to him. We need to brainwash her into thinking she can't handle this, that this isn't the life that she wants. Removing Fitzwilliam should have done that." Also, it was fucking working until Keller got away, dammit.

"Well, it didn't work, and now I have two countries breathing down my neck. You realize the power Marsdale has? We can take down Torskethorpe, but not Marsdale, and certainly not both. So you need to figure out what the fuck is happening, find a solution, and get me that country, or else it's your head that's on the chopping block."

I go to reply, but the line goes dead.

"Fuck," I yell as I hang up the phone, just in time for my brother to walk into my office casually.

"Troubling news?" he asks, one hand in his pocket.

"We need to find Fitzwilliam. Now. He has Lilly. We need them both dead."

He scratches his chin. "I might have a few ideas as to where they might be."

"If you say Harrogate, I'm going to lose my shit. They wouldn't be there, that would be the last place they'd hide."

He shakes his head. "They're not there." He sticks his hand back in his pocket. "Marsdale . . . or the island."

"We have people watching over Marsdale, so I can check with them. Does Keller know about the island?" I ask.

"No clue. I need to call your contact at Strombly."

"Well, fucking call her. We'll send out teams one by one if need be. We need them dead. Or at least Fitzwilliam."

Chapter Thirty-Two

LILLY

I bury my head in my hands as tears spill past my cheeks, my mind unable to process what Keller just admitted.

He didn't leave me.

He wanted to marry me.

And he didn't tell me because he didn't want my sympathy?

I don't get it.

And the fact that he was tortured . . . whipped.

Those scars.

My stomach rolls as my mind goes to what that must have been like. To be chained to a wall, unable to do anything but take the pain delivered to you. All for what? Because of me? Because of our love?

My teeth chatter, my body shivering from the mere thought of it all.

Why . . . why didn't he want to tell me? I thought we established trust . . .

"Lilly." His voice comes out strangled as he walks up behind me. I don't say anything, I just keep my legs pulled into my chest as I sit on the blanket I laid out earlier. He walks up right behind me and sits, his legs on either side of me, his arms wrapping around me in a warm, comforting embrace.

Keller wrapped around me—it feels like being transported back home, and it's all I need to fully lose all of my emotions, to break me down to just about nothing. A sob wracks my chest, and I curl into a ball as he pulls me in closer. His lips find my neck, gently kissing me, whispering that it's okay.

But it's not.

He was tortured.

He has the scars to prove it. And somehow, someway, he was able to escape, and the first thing on his mind was to save me.

Jaw chattering, I turn into his embrace and rest my hands on his chest. "You . . . you came for me."

"Always, love," he says softly. "I've said it from the very beginning, and I'll say it until my dying day, you matter most." He lifts my chin, and my watery vision takes in his handsome, weathered face.

And at that moment, everything starts aligning.

How his body looked like it didn't have an ounce of fat on it, probably because they starved him.

His long hair, his beard, the dark circles under his eyes.

His need to hold me when he wasn't feeling well.

The dehydration. The need to keep me safe.

He has truly been to hell and back for me. And I know, deep down in my soul, if he had to do it all over again, he would, because that's how much this man loves me. That's how much this man would do for me.

I reach up between us, and I cup his cheek, my thumb running across the small scar near his lip. My eyes search his, and I say, "You didn't want my sympathy, but I don't want to give you any sympathy for what you went through." I stare deep into his eyes. "I can only offer you my undying love." My thumb strokes his rough cheek as my voice catches in my throat. "You are the love of my life, Keller. Until my dying day, forever and always, I'm yours."

His eyes water as well, his grip on me growing tighter as I tilt his jaw down and lift my mouth. When he inhales a sharp breath, I close the space between us and press my lips to his.

"Fuck," he mutters against my mouth just before he cups the back of my head. There's nothing rushed or forceful about his kiss. It's soft, it feels . . . *grateful* as he lets me take the lead. I slide my lips over his, reveling in the feel of him, in his taste. Tears stream down my cheeks as I realize just how much I've missed this. Missed him.

Needed him.

He's my everything.

And now that he's here, holding me, I can't ever let him go again.

I part my lips, and he does the same. We don't use our tongues, not yet. Instead, we just fall deep into the feel of each other, in the way our mouths match up so perfectly, how our lips glide against each other, opening, closing, signaling to our hearts that this connection is unbreakable.

He leans back, bringing me with him, and I lie on top of him, cupping either side of his face while I continue to move my mouth over his. Both of his hands slide up my shirt, bringing the fabric with him to the point that I just lift, and he pulls the fabric off before rolling me to my back and propping himself up so he can stare down at me. His eyes are misty, and when I reach up to touch his dewy cheek, he leans into my touch.

"I want to hold you forever," he says softly. "Never let go. Never be parted from you."

"Never," I say as I push his shorts down. He helps me, and when he's fully naked, he presses himself into my thigh.

He brings his mouth back to mine, and this time, when

our mouths part, our tongues collide. His demands grow with every stroke, his needs transported through the urgency in his mouth. The fire of his touch and the hunger in his groans light the fire between us.

I spread my legs and reach down to his erection. I stroke it a few times before placing it against my entrance.

He breathes a heavy breath, then breaks our kiss just enough to meet my gaze as he enters me.

My teeth roll over the corner of my lip as he slowly fills me up until he completely bottoms out. "Jesus," he whispers as his breath catches in his chest. "I've never loved anything in my life more than you, Lilly. No one compares to you. Never will be."

My lips press together as a new wave of tears fill my eyes. He kisses them away before bringing his lips back to mine. I wrap my arms around his neck, and I hold him close, getting lost in his mouth, allowing my mind to focus on the feel of his tongue swiping against mine, on the gentle way he cups one of my breasts, and the tenderness in his touch, something I've never experienced from him before.

I want to commit this to memory.

Burn it into my brain.

Never, ever let go of this moment when we're giving each other ourselves, completely, unfiltered, raw, just the way we are.

And as he slowly moves his hips, pulling his cock almost all the way out of me only to so damn slowly insert himself back in, my hands stroke down his back, my fingers running against the puckered skin of his scars. He tenses for a moment, but I kiss him harder, trying to show him that I love him, I love everything about him, even his battle wounds—the wounds he acquired for loving me.

After a few seconds of letting me explore, I become possessive over the fact that this man is mine.

His heart.

His mind.

His soul.

No one else will be able to feel him the way that I do.

No one will have access to his mind like I do.

And no one will ever be loved, protected, or feel the safety in his arms like I do.

"Make me come," I say softly.

With that, his kisses grow hungrier, the undulation of his hips more intense, and when he bottoms out inside me three times in a row, the tingling sensation of my impending orgasm climbs up my spread legs.

"Nothing will keep us apart," I say, and he drives harder into me. "Nothing will ever come between us."

"Nothing," he says through a clenched jaw. He props up, his hands digging into the blanket below us, giving him better leverage. I slip one of my legs over his shoulder, presenting him with a different angle, and we both groan when he goes an inch deeper with each stroke. I can feel him all the way in the pit of my stomach. And with every pulse, my body grows closer and closer to the edge.

"I'm right there," I say to him.

"Me too," he says, his hair falling past his headband and over his forehead. "Fuck, Lilly . . . right there."

He pumps faster, his mouth now focused on making us both come as he drives his tongue forcefully in my mouth. I match each stroke, spurring on the sensation of ecstasy in my body, bringing me to the hilt, until my pussy spasms, my body shivering all the way down to my toes.

"That's my good girl," he says. "Come for me."

He drives into me a few more times, heightening my senses, and I hold on. I don't let go, and I don't let myself fall over. I want to feel this sensation forever. I want this burning, numbing, explosive sensation to last until the end of time, but as he starts to swell inside me, I can't hold off any longer, and I fall over. A feral moan falls past my lips just as he comes, his body stilling and tensing at the same time.

"Fuck!" he yells as his body shakes, my pussy clenching around his cock for what feels like forever.

And while we both ride out our orgasm, his lips find mine again, and he kisses me senseless. Never letting me take a second to breathe, and I don't want to. I want to be consumed by him. I want him to be the one who gives me life.

"Jesus," he finally says as he lifts and presses a kiss to my cheek. Then he slips out of me, lowering my leg to the ground.

Completely infatuated, I stare up at him, so in love with this man that if something were to happen to me at this moment, I know that I'd die a happy woman . . . because I'd die knowing I had this man's love.

He brushes his knuckles over my cheeks and smiles down at me. "I've missed you."

I smile up at him. "I've missed you more."

"Not sure that's possible."

THE HEAT of the sun feels like a warm blanket, swaddling us in the daylight. The waves crash into the shore just in front of us, and the occasional squawk of a seagull filters through the serene air as Keller and I lie naked together on the beach.

Propped up on one elbow, I run my finger over his chest, trying not to press too hard on his new scars but also wanting to explore them.

"Lilly, don't," he says as my eyes tear up again, probably for the tenth time in an hour.

"I just keep thinking about you in that cell, chained up, helpless."

"There was nothing helpless about me," he says as he captures my hand in his. "Not at any point while I stayed in that cell did I ever consider myself helpless. I had all the power to make a change. And I did."

"How?" I ask, impressed and turned on by his attitude. I knew Keller was on another level, but escaping a prison, finding his way back to me, and flying us down to a remote island? That's some Tom Cruise, *Mission Impossible* kind of stuff.

"Remember the training we went over when we were in Harrogate?" he asks.

"Yes," I answer. "You were supposed to listen, to give in, to make a connection with your captor. Is that what you did?"

"With the captor? No." He shakes his head. "But there was a guy who was in charge of me, of my food and things like hosing me down, shit like that. I didn't speak to him, but I did find that he felt guilty. He had a soul. Because the more I pretended to be wounded, unable to move, the more he eased up on me. He let me out of my chains finally. He brought me more food. More water. He didn't want me to die, and I took advantage of that. Every time he came to check on me, I'd act weaker and weaker. He took mercy on me."

"Were you weak?" I ask.

He shakes his head. "There was nothing I could do about the beatings. They were simply sustained beatings to make me meek. Downcast. However, I worked on not losing too much muscle tone and strength. I wasn't fed much, but I knew I was getting out of there, so I had to find a way to keep my strength up. Morale. So I did pushups, squats, wall sits, anything to keep my muscles from atrophying. And when the time came, I was ready."

"What did you do to escape?" I ask, still in awe of his story. It doesn't feel real. It doesn't feel like this is something that could actually happen.

He tucks a strand of hair behind my ear and says, "The guy sent to inflict pain, his name was Banamaor. He was about the same size as me. Dressed in leather and wore a leather mask. I'm not sure if he took mercy on me, or if they told him not to kill me, but as time went on, our sessions became simpler, easier to stomach, and I realized that he was the key to my escape. When I knew the time was right, I hid behind my cell door—"

"Because you weren't chained to the wall anymore?"

"Correct. Because I was able to fool them into thinking I was barely holding on. I hid behind the door, and when he came in, just as he was shutting the door, I walked up behind him and snapped his neck."

My hand flies to my mouth. "Oh my God."

"I lowered him to the floor, shut the door, and thankfully, since I didn't pose a threat anymore, they no longer had guards at my door. I quickly undressed him, laid him in my sleeping spot, and draped blankets over him. Then I put on his clothes and his mask—"

"Oh my God," I say, gripping his shoulder. "You walked right out of there, didn't you?"

He nods. "I did. And from there, purely on adrenaline, I was able to bargain and make my way back to Torskethorpe. When I secured you and finally made it down here, I think it all hit me in one day, and that's when I practically collapsed."

I shake my head in disbelief. "I'm in awe, Keller." I smooth my hand up his chest. "You're so strong. I never would have survived anything like that."

"I believe you could have."

I shake my head. "No, I nearly died from a broken heart." His brow pulls together. "It was really bad there for a month. I owe everything to Runa. She never left my side." I bite down on the inside of my cheek. "I hope she's not worried."

"I'm sure Ottar has looped her in. She'd be a valuable source for him."

"I hope so."

The wind blows, a cold burst of water spraying at us and

causing me to shiver in response. "Let's get you inside," he says as he moves.

"I want to stay like this, with you."

"Love, I'm not going anywhere." He lifts and helps me put my shirt back on, then slips his shorts on. He stands and takes my hand. "But we both need some fluids after being out in the sun, and I don't want you getting burned either." He pulls me up and links our hands together as we move back into the house. "You hungry?" he asks.

I shake my head as he goes to the fridge and grabs drinks for us. He uncaps the water for me and hands it to me.

"Are you sure?" he asks.

"Yeah, I don't think I could eat anything right now."

He glances over at me, his bottle halfway to his mouth. "Why are you looking at me like that?"

"Like what?" I ask.

"Like you don't know if you should cry or devour me?"

"Because that's how I feel," I answer. I step up to him and take his hand in mine. I pull him toward the bedroom and push him down on the bed.

"Lilly," he says softly as I set my water bottle down, then pull my shirt up and over my head. His eyes roam my body as I move in front of him, where he places his hands on my hips and leans forward, his lips pressing against my stomach.

"I want to explore you," I say as I press my fingers to his chest, forcing him to lie down. I set his drink on the nightstand as well and tug his shorts off, leaving him naked, his powerful thighs flexing in anticipation as I run my hands up them. "I want to kiss away the pain that you suffered." I look up at him as I start to crawl over his body. "Will you let me . . . my king?"

His eyes turn dark, my name for him feeling so right as it falls off my tongue for one of the first times since we've been split from each other.

His Adam's apple bobs as he swallows, then nods.

Pleased, I press my hands up his thighs, past his growing erection, and up to his chest where the burn marks are scattered over his pecs and his ribs.

One by one, I press my lips to the damaged skin, and with each kiss, his cock grows harder.

"Did these hurt?" I ask.

"Barely," he answers. "I was numb by then."

I move from one pec to the other, taking my time, giving him all the love that I can. When I reach his nipple, I run my tongue around it a few times, his hands flexing at his sides in response. I move over to his other nipple, and I do the same thing. Pleased with his reaction, I decide to pluck at his nipple, and when his pelvis thrusts up, a wave of wet, hot lust whips through me.

"Keller," I whisper, happy with his response. "This makes you hard?"

"You make me hard. Anything you do." He takes a deep breath. "Pinch harder."

So I do.

I roll his nipples between my fingers and watch his stomach contract, his abs rippling beneath me as his cock rubs against my body.

"Fuck yes, that feels amazing."

I bend down and replace my fingers with my teeth, pulling the hard nub between them and nibbling.

A hiss escapes him, and his hand falls to his cock where he starts pumping.

I don't mind. I actually want him to do whatever makes him feel good, and if that's it, then he can pump all he wants.

"Shit. Again," he moans, the muscles in his neck flexing.

I move to his other nipple and do the same thing. With every nibble, I can feel him pull harder on his cock until he starts moving more rapidly under me as if he's getting close, so I pull away.

He groans but doesn't protest. Instead, he removes his

hand from his cock and lies still, waiting for my next move, his chest heaving.

I lift and catch a glimpse of his threatening length, stretching up his stomach, looking for release. It's so sexy that I almost forget what I'm doing.

Kissing away his pain.

"Roll over," I say.

"Lilly, no," he says.

"I want to see them, explore them. Love them. Please?" I ask.

"They're ugly."

"They mean the world to me," I say. "They're battle wounds for our love. Please, Keller."

With a sigh, he turns over, revealing his back. I've looked at his scars a few times now, but never this close. I smooth my hand over the top one and whisper, "Does it hurt?"

"No," he answers.

So I lean down and press a kiss along the long, thin scar. His back tenses, but he doesn't say anything, so I do the same to the next and work my way down his back until I reach the very bottom. Then I work my way back up, his back growing less and less tense with each pass.

When I reach the top, I say, "Can you get up on your knees?"

He doesn't ask what I have planned, doesn't even question me. He lets me take the lead and that only makes this so much hotter for me.

When he's up on all fours, I work my way behind him and spread his legs wider. His balls hang right in front of me so I rub my thumb along the seam between them. A harsh hiss passes through his lips as his cock jolts from the touch.

"I've missed playing with you, my king," I say as I palm his balls and gently roll them with my fingers.

"You're such a good girl, knowing exactly what your man wants. But harder, love."

"I will," I say as I move under him, between his legs, which he spreads just a bit more to accommodate my shoulders. His cock moves in front of my mouth, so I lightly blow on it while I grip his balls tighter.

"Yes, Lilly," he says. "Just like that." I press a kiss to the very tip of him, precum running across my lips as I smooth one finger over his seam and to the spot right behind his balls, and I press down on the sensitive flesh. "Fuck," he says harshly, his pelvis jolting. "Open your mouth."

"I thought this was on my terms."

"Open your goddamn mouth," he says, making me smile because he wouldn't say it unless he needed it.

I open my mouth and guide him in as I continue to pulse my finger against his perineum, pleasuring the sensitive spot and urging his pleasure to spike with each press.

His hips move so he's lightly fucking my mouth. I suck down on his length while he makes the movement, keeping it so I'm only sucking the tip, but from the shake in his body, I know he wants to go farther.

"Open wider," he groans while I tug on his balls just enough that I know I'm bordering pain and ecstasy for him. "Fuck me," he mutters and presses deeper into my mouth, causing me to gag.

"I'm okay," I say before he can ask.

"Fuck, I need to go deeper. Open your mouth wider, Lilly." Relinquishing control, I open my mouth, breathe through my nose, and he pulses deeper, hitting the back of my throat. "Motherfucker," he says as he does it again, and again, but then gives me a moment to relax. When I open my mouth back up, he does the same thing.

The next time he pulls out, I run my finger over his soaking cock, gathering the wetness, and when he goes to pulse back inside me, I run my wet finger to his behind and slowly insert it.

He freezes.

Relaxes.

And then I slip it in farther.

He remains still, letting me adjust until I'm fully inserted. He takes a few deep breaths, his abs constricting so tight that it has to be one of the sexiest things I've ever seen.

I take his moment of pause to bring the tip of his cock back to my mouth where I swirl my tongue around in a circle, then suck him hard. With my other hand, I reach up to his nipple, and while I suck him hard and push my finger against his prostate, I pinch his nipple.

"Ahhh fuck . . . me." He tenses. "Fuck . . . fuck," he says, his entire body clenching. He's right there, so close, so I do it again, this time running my teeth along his cock, and that's all it takes. His stomach hollows, his balls draw tight, and he's yelling my name as he comes into my mouth, the force of his orgasm so strong that I have to swallow quickly right before he pulses twice and stills, his entire body stiffening.

"Your fucking mouth," he says out of breath. "Jesus, fuck." He falls to his side, and I move up on the bed, giving him room.

When he lies flat on his back, I smile down at him right before leaning forward and pressing a kiss to his nipple. He grips my hair, pulling my head back, and presses a kiss to my lips. It's aggressive, and I love everything about it.

I smile against his lips, then stand from the bed. I glance behind me just to see him lift a brow in question. "Where the fuck do you think you're going?"

"I was going—"

He doesn't let me finish before scooping me up and pinning me against the wall right next to the bathroom door.

"Keller," I say breathlessly right before he lifts me higher and moves my legs so they drape over his shoulders. My back is against the wall, and my hands fall to his head just as his mouth finds my clit.

"So fucking wet and you smell like fucking heaven," he says as he flicks out his tongue.

"Oh God," I say, unsure what to do as my head nearly touches the ceiling.

His entire mouth opens wide and smothers my pussy, almost as if he's making out with my clit, and it's the most intense, most erotic, sexually charged moment of my life. Because this man is eating me out as if it's his last goddamn meal. My entire body lights up in seconds, and in order not to fall over, I thread my hands through his hair and grip tightly as his mouth continues to press against me, licking, sucking, flicking. He's rabid, never stopping, creating such a bundle of heat in my stomach that it releases through my veins with each suck, each vibration of his tongue flicking against my clit. My breath catches, and my head falls back against the wall.

"Oh my God, Keller. Oh fuck, Keller. I'm going to . . ."

He pulls away just in time to edge my orgasm so hard that my body seizes on me, holding me right there on the edge.

He tosses me down on the bed. "Hold your legs wide."

I grip my knees, pulling back hard, and he brings one hand up to my throat. He clamps his fingers around it and whispers, "Mine," before slipping two fingers inside me. He starts thrusting with such brutal force that I have no control over my body.

The combination of him holding me, claiming me, and the feel of his fingers curving up and hitting me in just the right spot gets me to a point of no return.

And my arms and legs fill with pins and needles, my mind goes blank, and then my orgasm rips through me with such force that for the first time in my entire life, I squirt. The sensation is so strong, so powerfully charged with raw eroticism. My body convulses for what feels like minutes until I'm finally able to catch my breath, only to feel Keller press his lips up my body and to my mouth. His hand that's gripping my neck remains still, but his thumb strokes my jaw.

When my eyes open, he stares down at me. "You're such a good girl."

The praise settles into my heart, wrapping me up in a wave of warmth that I've been missing for the past three months.

"I'm glad I can please you, my king."

He smiles down at me. "You could never disappoint."

Chapter Thirty-Three

KELLER

"Why are you always up so early?" Lilly asks as she strolls into the kitchen, her hair a total mess from how I was tugging on it last night. She's wearing one of my shirts, and her eyes are barely open. She stumbles toward me, arms open, head down, looking for some comfort. I pull her in and lean against the kitchen counter.

"I've always been an early bird."

"I know, but you leave me in bed, all alone and cold." Her head rests against my chest. "I want to wake up in your arms, warm and snuggly."

I kiss the top of her head. "I'll remember that." I rub her back and ask, "Do you want some coffee?"

"I'll just drink yours."

"I'm having tea."

"Ugh," she groans. "Fine, I'll have some of your tea."

"I can make you coffee."

"No, that's okay. I really just want to cuddle. And listen to the waves."

"We can do that," I say before picking her up and placing her on the counter.

"Dear God," she says as she lifts her ass and hisses.

"What?" I ask, looking around.

"The counter is cold," she says as she takes a deep breath and settles down.

"Sorry." I chuckle, and her eyes snap up to mine in surprise. "What?" I ask.

Her expression softens as her hand finds my chest. "I don't think I've heard you laugh in a very long time. I've missed it."

I smooth my hands up her thighs. "It has been a long time. But it's also been a long time since we've truly been alone. I'm at my best when I'm able to be with you."

"Then we need to make sure we make that happen more," she says as she cups my cheeks and leans in for a kiss.

I could easily get lost in her mouth right now, spread her across the counter, and bury my head between her legs, but she wants to cuddle and listen to the ocean, so I'll give her exactly what she wants.

Reluctantly, I pull away and move over to the coffee machine to make her a cup.

"I said you didn't have to make me coffee."

"And I know you have better mornings when you drink some coffee." She sighs behind me, and when I start her coffee, her foot pokes me in the back. When I glance over my shoulder, she smirks. "What?" I ask.

"You're really hot."

Forgetting the coffee, I move between her legs and grip her waist. "Yeah?" I ask, then bring my lips to her neck, reveling in her warmth. "Even with all of these new scars?"

"Even more so," she says as I work up to her jaw. "They're a reminder to me of how much you love me."

I take a second to pull away. "How so?"

Her finger drags over the burn marks on my chest.

"Because you were bound, chained, and abused, yet still found a way to not only pull through but to find me again. You went through hell, Keller, and the whole time, you were thinking about me." She purses her lips. "Makes me feel like shit that I even considered going out with someone else."

I grip her chin and force her to look me in the eyes. "You were trying to help Theo," I say. "And Evan meant nothing to you, right?"

"Nothing," she says. "I was so distraught from losing you. I honestly don't think I would have been able to open myself up to someone else."

"Good," I answer. "Because nothing was stopping me from finding you and claiming you all over again."

She smirks. "That much is obvious."

I chuckle again, then fill up her cup with coffee. I grab her favorite creamer from the fridge and make her coffee just the way she likes it before turning toward her, catching her eyes scanning me up and down. Just the way that I like it. I always want her eyes on me. I always want to be her man.

I nod toward the couch. "Want to sit?"

She nods and hops off the counter. I set our mugs on the coffee table and go to the sliding glass door where I open it all the way up, letting the fresh air into the house. When I go back to the couch, I sit, then I pull Lilly onto my lap before reaching for our mugs.

"Thank you," she says when I hand her, her drink. She blows on the steamy liquid, then leans down to take a sip. "Why is it always better when you make it?"

"Because I'm great at everything."

She rolls her eyes. "Walked right into that one, but glad to see you have your sense of humor back. I feel like it's been missing. You were Mr. Stern Face throughout our wedding planning." She sips her coffee. "Which is actually something I want to talk about."

"Okay," I say as I rest my hand on her thigh. "What do you want to talk about?"

"I think we need to have an honest conversation about what's going on between us, what our future looks like, and everything that went sour between us."

"Yeah, I think we do too." I rub my thumb over her soft skin. "But I do want to say something first." I look her in the eyes so she understands how genuine and serious I am. "I'm sorry, Lilly, for everything that happened leading up to the wedding. I should have been more open with you. I shouldn't have shut down as many times as I did." I wet my lips and continue, "I had a lot of time to think about it when I was in my cell, and my biggest regret was how I handled you and our communication."

"I wish I handled it better too. It just felt like we were being pulled in two different directions and never had a chance to pull back together, you know?"

I nod. "Yes, I know exactly what you're talking about because I felt that hard. Between the nightmares, not being able to be near you, the bad news from the doctor, and Elias trying to pry deep into a part of my life I only want few people knowing, I felt like I was unraveling. I should have leaned on you, and I didn't. I just didn't want to put more on your plate than you already had."

"I appreciate that," she says, then places her hand on my cheek. "But, Keller, without you communicating with me, all it felt like was you were pulling away, which was more scary than anything. I know you say I matter most, but can we change that phrasing? Because what I realized is that I'm nothing without you. I don't want to walk this life without you by my side. So no, I'm not the one who matters the most. *We* are. We matter most."

I shift my head and kiss her palm. "Okay," I say. "We matter most."

"Thank you," she says softly. She sets her mug on the table

and takes mine as well. Then she straddles my lap and rests her hands on my chest. "So can I assume that maybe, once this is all figured out, we might have another chance at walking down the aisle?"

"I'm a man of my word, Lilly. I asked you to marry me because I'll be damned if you're not my wife. I have every intention of making sure you're mine forever."

"Good answer." She smiles. "Which means, if we must go through the entire process again, you'll communicate with me this time? You'll work on your humility and not being so hard on yourself to be so freaking perfect all the time?"

I nod slowly. "It will take me some time, but yes."

"And whenever you feel like you're inferior or something is sitting heavy on your chest, you will talk to me, no matter what?"

"Yes," I answer.

"And whenever we get back to Strombly, and I have access to a vibrator, you'll let me peg you?"

My brow rises in question, and she tilts her head back and laughs. "Nice fucking try."

Still laughing, she asks, "Why not? You liked the slip of my finger yesterday."

"Yes, you know I like that, but I'm not about to bend over and let you fuck me in the ass with a strap-on. Sorry, I'm the one who does the fucking in the ass."

"Ooo, promises, promises." She runs her thumb over my nipple. "What about getting your penis pierced? Think you would do that?"

"I would, but I also wonder how the hell you'd find someone to pierce the future prince's dick so the future queen can have more pleasure."

"I'm sure Ottar can find someone." She waves her hand.

"He'll need a pay raise."

"I'm willing if you are." She wiggles her eyebrows, and

fuck, she's so cute it makes me want to spread her across the couch and fuck her right here and now.

"I'm willing to do anything you want." When her brow lifts, I add, "Besides the pegging."

"Ugh, what a shame." She lets out a deep breath. "I actually have one more thing to talk to you about, but this is serious."

"Okay, what is it?"

"The whole future baby thing." I nod in understanding. "I know it'll be tougher for us, but I still want to try. I want to give us some time and figure out if it's something we can do ourselves. I mean, we have enough sex for the entire palace combined. I feel like a sperm is bound to make its way through to my eggs."

"Romantic," I say.

She chuckles. "You know what I mean. But I say we give it a timeframe, and if we can't get pregnant, then we try other options. But at least let's give it our best effort. Are you open to that?"

"I am," I say. "I'll do anything for you . . . besides the pegging." She chuckles, and I grow serious as I cup her cheek. "If we have to use someone else's sperm, then that's what we have to do, but no matter what, I'll love that baby just like it's my own. That's not something you ever have to worry about."

"I wouldn't," she says. "I know you're going to be an amazing father when the time comes because you are the most protective, loving, caring man I know."

That hits me hard.

Harder than I expected, because I've never thought of myself as a dad. Before I met Lilly, I was resigned to the thought that I'd forever serve the crown. I wouldn't marry, I wouldn't have a family, I'd just do my duty. But everything changed the moment Lilly came along, and I'm still trying to wrap my head around that.

"That means a lot to me, Lilly. More than you probably know."

"I believe in you, Keller." She leans in and presses her lips to mine, and this time, I don't let her get away with a peck. I slip my hand behind her head, threading my fingers through her hair, and I hold her tight, showing her through my kiss just how much I appreciate it.

⸻

"WHERE ARE YOU GOING?" I ask as I prop one arm against the sliding glass door, watching my naked fiancée walk toward the ocean water.

"I haven't gone in the water yet. It's been calling my name."

"It's cold."

"Can't be that cold," she says as she dips a toe in the water and turns around, her jaw dropped. "Holy fuck, Keller. That's cold."

I let out a roar of a laugh. "I told you."

"How can it be that cold when it's warm out?"

"Because it's still winter, and even though it feels warm out on the sand, it's still cold water."

"Well, that ruins my plans to go swimming." Hands on her hips, she stares at me. "What am I supposed to do now?"

I could think of a couple of things.

Like sitting on my face.

Although, she's probably worn out by now. It's probably best to let her rest, even though I don't want to.

"You can lay out," I offer even though that's what her main activity has been.

"What are you doing?" she asks.

"I'm going to take a shower, then go around and check the cameras, make sure everything is secure."

"Can't you tell by looking at the monitor?"

"Yes," I answer. "But it doesn't hurt to check either."

"You're so thorough and meticulous, it can be incredibly frustrating at times." She rolls her eyes.

"Is that your way of saying you want me to spend more time with you? What do you want me to do?"

She shrugs and walks back up the beach. "You don't seem like the kind of guy who would lie on the beach naked, soooo . . ."

"Not so much."

"Fine," she complains. "You go take your shower and check your cameras."

Very convincing.

I don't move. Instead, I ask, "Do you want me to lay out with you?"

She shakes her head. "No. I know how important it is to keep your mind at ease. Take your shower, check your cameras. Then maybe we can play a game or something. I saw some board games in the cabinet."

"Are you sure?" I ask. "Because you know I'll do whatever you want me to do."

"I know, and that's why I'm telling you to do what you want to do. Take your shower and check your cameras, but then the rest of the day is all mine."

"Okay," I say as I push off the doorway and head into the bathroom. I strip out of my shorts and briefs and turn on the shower to let the water warm before I step in.

The talk I had with Lilly this morning, although emotional and tough, was necessary. I'm glad she asked to have it because if she didn't ask, I was going to suggest it. She was right. Everything felt off between us before the wedding, and we were being pulled apart. No wonder she believed the letter, because leading up to that point, it almost felt inevitable.

Like the whole process was supposed to be driving us apart.

Like I wasn't supposed to walk down the aisle with her.

I step into the shower and stand under the raining water, letting the warmth wash down me. Eyes closed, I take in the feeling of a warm shower, not something I'll ever take for granted again. That or soap, a warm meal, plenty of fluids, and the feel of my girl's arms wrapped around me.

For three months, I suffered without them.

Never fucking again.

As I push my hands through my hair, the bathroom door clicks shut, and I open my eyes just in time to see Lilly step into the shower with me.

"Jesus," I mutter, my heart rate pulsing rapidly.

"Did I startle you?" she asks.

"Yes." I take a deep breath. "I'm sorry, I'm just a little jumpy."

"It's okay," she says as she steps up to me and palms my balls. "I'm sorry I scared you. How can I make it up to you?"

My eyes flutter closed as she massages my balls just the way I like it. Just hard enough that it borders painful.

"You can suck my cock," I say.

When I open my eyes, she drops to her knees. She picks up the soap that's on the ledge and runs the bar up one leg, over my stomach, then down the other leg. Avoiding the spot where I want her hands. Then she rubs the bar between her hands, creating a palm full of suds, and places her hands around my cock, gripping it tightly as she brings the soap over the head, then down to my balls.

"Fuck," I groan, feeling the strength in my legs diminish from her touch.

Her small hand squeezes tight as she drags the soap up my hard length, over the tip, and back down, past my balls and to the other side. I place one hand on the tile, steadying myself as she stands and turns on the shower wand, only to bring it between my legs and rinse me off, the whole time, she's stroking me.

And when she pulls away, I think she's about to turn off

the water. Instead, she grabs the soap and lathers up her tits, her pebbled nipples drawing my attention until she brings her hand between her legs. Then she rinses off as well.

"I thought you were going to suck my cock," I say.

"Wouldn't you rather fuck me?" she asks just as she turns off the shower and steps out, her beautiful ass enticing me.

Yes.

Yes, I would.

I snag my towel from the hook and make quick work of drying off while she does the same. Before she can even set her towel down, I pick her up and toss her on the bed. I then grab a belt from the dresser and walk over to her.

"Hands," I say. "In front of you."

A lustful expression crosses over her face as she lifts her hands in front of her. I wrap the belt like a figure eight around her hands until it's secured tight. I lift her wrists up to my mouth and press a gentle kiss to them. "How does this feel?"

"Perfect," she says.

"Good," I answer before pulling her to her feet and bringing her over to the hook on the wall where she hangs her robe. I toss the article of clothing to the side, then lift her arms over her head, looping her hands over the hook so she must remain in place. "Comfortable?" I ask her.

"Very," she says while spreading her legs. "And already wet."

"Good," I say as I sit down. I lean back on one hand, and I stare at her as my legs spread and my other hand falls to my cock. I grip the base and squeeze hard.

"What are you doing?" she asks.

"Getting myself off," I say.

"But . . ."

"No talking," I snap at her as I squeeze my cock harder, then drag it up to the tip. Not satisfied with how it feels, I stand and ask, "You're wet?"

"Yes," she says in a breathless tone, so I walk up to her,

kick her legs apart, and slide my dick along her pussy, dragging her arousal over my length until I'm fully satisfied. When I pull away, she groans in disappointment. "Keller."

"I said no talking." I get back into position on the bed, run my hand along my cock, and this time, my hand slides easier. Pleased, I bring my hand up to my mouth and lick my palm, watching her eyes widen from the gesture. "You always taste so fucking good," I say as I continue to stroke myself, my eyes fixated on her body. "You have the sexiest tits, Lilly. Puff them out for me."

She arches her chest, and my cock grows harder.

"Good girl. Now, tell me what you want."

"Your cock," she says, her eyes trained on it. "Your cum. I want you so deep inside me that I can't walk tomorrow."

My lips curve up. "You want to be fucked senseless."

"Yes," she breathes heavily, but I remain on the bed, my hand pumping faster.

My palm rubs over my tip, then descends to the base where I squeeze and pull up hard.

"Fuck, yes." I do that motion again.

And again.

And again.

Until my chest is rising and falling rapidly, my legs shaking.

I edge myself to the point that my orgasm ramps up at the base of my spine, ready to explode, and that's when I let go, placing my other hand behind my back, and with her eyes fixated on my cock, we both watch as it twitches, seeking out relief, relief that won't be found until I'm buried deep inside her.

"I'm throbbing," she says.

"Does my good girl need to be touched?"

"Yes," she says in desperation. *Good, because given how hard I am, I need her now too.*

With my cock jutting out, I stand and move my hands

under her ass and lift her, her hands unhooking. Once she's pressed against the wall, and her arms are looped around my neck, I place my cock at her entrance and then let her slide over my length.

Both of us suck in a sharp breath.

"You're so thick," she says as I thrust up into her. "Harder."

I grip her hips and lift her, then slam her back down, eliciting a hiss from her. As I do it again, her fingers dig into my nape, and she leans forward, biting down on my neck. The pain from her teeth sends me into a frenzy, and I slam her against the wall, causing her to gasp. I'm about to ask if she's okay, but she bites down on me again. *Fuck, yeah, she wants more.*

Not getting the angle I want, I move her over to the bed where I lay her down on her side. I press her legs together, then position them into a ninety-degree angle before lowering myself down and pressing my tip at her now narrow entrance.

It feels so fucking incredible.

With one hand on her hip and the other one holding her arms down, I pulse my hips into her, knowing damn well this angle is way more pleasurable for me than her.

"Take my cock. Make me come with that greedy pussy." I spank her hard enough for her to arch her back and her pussy to clench around me. "Fuck . . . yes," I groan, spanking her again.

"Oh God," she moans.

"More," I say. "Drain me."

I spank again, and this time, her moan is long and drawn out. I pulse a few more times until I pull out, my cock jolting forward, seeking pleasure. I grip her top leg and lift it so her legs are spread now, and she's on her back. I lower to my knees and pull her to the edge of the bed, only to bring my entire mouth to her pussy, smashing my lips, eating her so hard that her hands are now pulling on my hair.

"Oh my God, Keller," she yells, her legs shaking next to me, her chest rising and falling. "Oh fuck . . . oh fuck . . ."

"Don't come," I say, lifting and turning her to her stomach.

I prop her up on her hands and knees, and she shakes beneath me as I slam my cock inside her.

"I can't . . . I can't hold on."

"Finger your clit. I want you drenched."

"I am."

"Do it," I say as I hold still inside her, my orgasm nearly ready to rip me in two.

She moves her hand between us, leaving her to lean on her shoulder and tilt her head to the side. Her fingers press against her clit, and I let her massage a few times before I rear back and drive into her again.

"I want to hear you moan," I say before spanking her. "I want your voice cracking." I drive into her, then spank.

"Oh . . . God," she cries out as her body tenses.

I keep up my relentless pace, never giving either of us a second to catch our breath. Sweat climbs down my back as she starts to constrict around me.

Smack, the crack of my hand against her ass echoing louder than her moans.

Thrust, my pulse jolting the entire bed to the side.

Smack . . . "Fucking fuck, Keller," she yells.

I can't hold out any longer, and she can't either.

"Come for me, Lilly."

"Thank . . . God," she cries out as her pussy convulses, squeezing me so tight that I explode with her, stilling my hips as my cock spasms with pleasure deep inside her warm, wet cunt.

"Jesus Christ," I say as I grip her ass and catch my breath.

Fuck, that was . . . that was incredible.

I lean forward and press a kiss to her back before reaching under her and undoing the belt holding her hands together.

I pull out of her, then flop down on the bed, my hand to my chest as I try to gracefully fall from such a fucking high. She curls into me, and I loop my arm around her shoulder.

"You okay, love?" I ask her, smoothing my hand over her back.

"Perfect," she practically purrs.

"Can I get you anything?"

She shakes her head. "No, I'm good. I just want to stay here, with you, and not have to worry about—"

Buzz. Buzz.

My spine straightens just as Lilly asks, "What's that?"

"The phone," I answer. I sit up and reach into the nightstand, grabbing the phone. *It's not the scheduled time.* "It's from Ottar."

I click on the message and feel all of the blood drain from my face.

Ottar: *Get out. Now.*

"Fuck," I yell as I stand. The phone buzzes again.

"What?" Lilly asks, standing as well.

Ottar: *Head to Harrogate.*

I toss the phone on the bed. "Get dressed. Now."

"What? Why? What's happening?"

"Lilly, please, no questions, just get dressed."

She must hear the desperation and tension in my voice because she doesn't ask another question. She starts pulling out clothes from the dresser.

"Your warmest clothes. I know there isn't much," I say.

I throw on some clothes, my hands shaking. I try to calm my rapid breath so as to not scare Lilly, but my mind whirls to worst-case scenario. Ottar said now. What kind of time does that mean? Do we have hours? Do we have minutes? Seconds?

Either way, I move around the house, packing my backpack with supplies.

First aid kit.

Drinks.

Non-perishable snacks.

My notebook.

The phone.

The security monitor.

"Move, Lilly," I say as she comes into the living room in a pair of leggings and a long-sleeved shirt. "Shoes, now." We both slide on our shoes, and I go to the cabinet where I kept my runaway bag that contains maps, the keys to my plane, a gun, and a few knives.

I strap on my backpack, take her hand in mine, and I head out the front door, no time to lock it.

"Keep quiet." I can feel her tremble next to me. To reassure her, I squeeze her hand three times, and she shakily squeezes back.

The house now behind us, we stay close to the rocks, and I realize I'm walking around unarmed, so I stop us, reach into my backpack, and pull out my gun.

"Oh my God," Lilly whispers, her voice terrified.

"I got you," I whisper back. "Stay close, watch where you step."

Still holding her hand, I work her around the bend that leads to the rocky cliff. The water crashes into the rocks at a dangerous speed, startling us both. A yelp pops out of her mouth, and I grip her even tighter. This is exactly why I used the boat to transport the boxes of supplies, because I wasn't about to carry them up the slippery stones.

Knowing only one way to the boat, I guide her down the steep stones.

"Careful, Lilly," I say as I move us down some makeshift stairs and into a shelter covered by ivy. "Wait here." Gun out, I move it past the ivy and point, looking for anyone who might be hiding in there. When the coast is clear, I pull the ivy to the side and say, "Hold this."

She grips the curtain of vines tightly. I work my way

behind my small seaplane, and I push it out into the opening, struggling as I keep slipping on the wet rock. Once I get it out, I open the door and hold my hand out to Lilly.

She pauses, fear consuming her eyes, causing them to water.

"Trust me, Lilly. I've got you." The plane rocks violently with the water. "Love, we don't have time, please trust me."

She nods, and on shaky legs, she makes it the rest of the way down the rocks, slipping briefly, but I catch her in my arms.

"That's it, Lilly," I say calmly, even though my heart is racing. I open the door to the plane and help her into it, relieved when she's sitting.

"Buckle up." Her face is ghost white as she does what I say. "I have to push the plane some more. Stay put."

She nods, and before I shut the door, I lift her hand and kiss her knuckles.

A single tear falls down her cheek just as I shut her plane door, and I catch her wiping it away. Moving to the back of the plane again, I give it a hefty push, my muscles screaming at me, my feet slipping against the wet rocks. I don't give up until the plane is in a position where it's clear to start the engine.

Thankfully, I filled it up with gas before I hid it, knowing there could be a chance we'd need to make a fast getaway just like this. I step over the floats to get to my side and hop into the plane. Once I have the keys from my backpack, I set the gun down on the console in front of me, ready to prepare for takeoff.

"Keller," she says, her voice trembling while I start the plane. "I'm terrified."

"Love, I won't let anything happen to you."

I slip on my headphones, flip the switches, and the propeller turns on. We'll be flying into the wind, best conditions for a seaplane. *Thank the gods.* I retract the water rudders and hold the yoke back, and we start moving across the water. Once we reach its maximum nose-high altitude, I relax the back pressure on the yoke and return it to neutral. There's considerably less drag with only the floats touching the water, as we plane across the water on the step. And then we're lifting off the water. Once we're fully clear of the island, I feel a lot safer. *How close was the threat? How did they know we were there?*

"Oh God," Lilly says as she brings her legs to her chest and rests her chin to her knees.

"Hang in there, Lilly," I say as I pull up, and we soar into the sky.

The wind creates significant turbulence as we take off, Lilly making scared sounds with every bump along the way. Once we're in the air and the plane evens out, I push her legs down and place my hand on her thigh. "It's good, Lilly. We're good."

And then with that, she bursts into tears.

Chapter Thirty-Four

LILLY

"Come here," Keller says as he puts his arm around my shoulder, and I lean into his chest, tears streaming down my cheeks. "Shhh, it's okay."

The adrenaline from the rush and unknown fear has drained from my body, leaving me a shivering, shaking, emotional mess.

The moment I saw the panic on Keller's face when he read the text on the phone, I knew whatever he was reading was dire. I did my best to keep it together, not ask him the millions of questions running through my head, and I got ready. But when I say a crater-sized pit formed in my stomach when he pulled out his gun, that would be an understatement. Terror took over, my adrenaline spiked, and I blacked out until we were up in the air.

"What's . . . what's happening?" I ask, my teeth chattering from the fallout.

"Our position was compromised. Ottar told us to get out immediately. We're headed to Harrogate now."

"Harrogate? But won't that be an obvious place to look for us?"

"Ottar said to meet at Harrogate."

"Are you sure it was Ottar?" I ask, and he pauses for a second. I glance up at him, and he's questioning himself. "I didn't mean to confuse you. I'm sorry——"

"No, it's a solid question. And I'm sure it was from Ottar. The only person who has that number is Theo, and Theo gave it to Ottar."

"Okay. So how would our position be compromised? I didn't think people knew about the island."

"There has to be an inside source communicating with whoever is trying to take us out," Keller says. "I believe Ottar is trying to figure it out. We should know more when we get to Harrogate. Until then, just try to relax."

Try to relax, ha!

Easier said than done.

My fiancé was kidnapped. Our wedding was ruined. I was kidnapped by my kidnapped fiancé, and now we're flying in the freaking air in a tiny seaplane that my fiancé is flying—I had no idea he could fly, well . . . I suppose Katla did mention his pilot's license, but . . . still—so color me shocked.

Yup, relaxing isn't quite on my to-do list at the moment.

What kind of freaking life is this anyway?

I was selling bikinis earlier this year, I was in a happy place where wet nipples showed through white T-shirts. There weren't people trying to kill me, and I didn't have a fiancé who knows how to wield a freaking gun like he's some secret operative ready to strike.

Not to mention, a fiancé who can FLY A PLANE!

Maybe focus on that.

Might get your mind off spine-chilling things.

Check out the way the veins in his large hands twitch as

he grips the yoke. Or his powerful thighs spread, so his fore-arms can rest on them. Or how incredibly hot he looks wearing his headphones with the little microphone in front of his mouth.

Huh.

That seems to be working. The tension slightly eases from my chest as I say, "You're good at this."

"Good at what?" he asks.

"Flying," I say. "Protecting. This whole James Bond-type personality I never knew you had."

That lifts the corner of his mouth. "James Bond not so much."

"Keller, you were able to survive torture, twist some guy's head off, walk out of a prison undetected, and then fly around a plane as if it's just an everyday thing for you. I thought I was marrying some Torskethorpe historian know-it-all, not the next greatest assassin."

This time, he chuckles. "Not an assassin, nor did I twist a guy's head off. Just snapped his neck."

"Oh right, sorry. *Just* snapped his neck. My mistake."

He chuckles again. "Being close to the king, it was my responsibility to know how to protect him if needed. Lara, Brimar, and I took the classes at the same time. Self-defense, strategy. I took flying lessons as well as boating. Lara special-ized in target shooting, rescue, and of course strategic hostage techniques. When I tell you I planned on dedicating my life to the king, I did. And I made sure of it with the classes I took and my education."

"Well, it's oddly hot."

"Oddly?" he asks.

Trying to keep it light, because if I think too much of what's really happening to us right now, I might hyperventi-late, I say, "You're not supposed to fall for the bad boy carrying a gun, but here I am, head over heels in love with you."

"You fell in love with me before you knew about this part of me."

"I mean, I knew a little bit about it. You showed your colors when we were in Harrogate, and Lara threw that broom at me, striking me in the head. I can still picture you in your briefs, the panic on your face. And then when the window crashed open, and you thought someone would steal me. That's the first time I got to taste you, and I liked it."

He glances over at me. "I liked it too."

I smirk and snuggle in closer to his chest. "But now, it's like you graduated from some secret spy class, and you're showing me everything you have in your arsenal. It's very hot."

"Glad you see it that way." He leans in and presses a kiss to my head. "I just want you to feel safe."

"I always feel safe with you," I say. "When you held me for the first time, it was like I finally found my haven."

"Same," he says just as we fly through a cloud. The visibility is impaired, but I just close my eyes, take a deep breath, and let Keller take the lead, because that's what he does best.

⸺

"WE'RE GOING to land on the water?" I ask as we approach the ocean beneath us.

"That's what seaplanes do," he answers.

The flight was much longer than I expected it to be. We stopped once to refuel and for Keller to stretch. I was asleep when we landed, so I have no recollection of the event. We shared some snacks and didn't discuss the reason we were running. We kept conversation light and fun. But now that we're approaching the midnight water beneath us, I'm freaking out.

"How can you see?"

"We've already done this once. Why are you freaking out now?" he asks, his eyes fixed ahead.

"Because it's super dark now, the water looks choppy, and I was asleep then."

"It's fine," he says as he brings us closer and closer.

I close my eyes, grip the handle next to me, and as we bump against the water, a little shriek passes my lips before we are solidly floating in the ocean. Unharmed.

"Are we there?"

"Yes," he says, moving the plane close to the shore just as a light flashes toward us.

"What's that?" I ask, glancing out the window.

"I don't know," he answers. "But stay here and stay low."
He pulls his gun out and opens the door to his side.

"Wait, you can't just leave me in the floating plane." I grab at him, but he's out before I can stop him. "Keller," I whisper-shout, but he doesn't stop. He moves along the plane, and I catch him, rope in hand, hop to the rocks where he ties the rope into a knot around a boulder.

Okay, so I won't float away, but still . . .

He crawls up the rocks, staying low and holding his gun out. The light flashes again, and fear creeps up my back.

This isn't hot anymore. This is scary. I don't want him getting shot, hurt, or taken again.

I duck down low but also lift just enough to see through the window. Keller starts army-crawling against the grass, the light becomes brighter, closer. It flashes up to my window, and I screech while ducking. Oh God, did the person see me?

I remain hidden just as I hear voices.

Please don't be killers, please don't be killers.

Footsteps approach, the light shines on the plane . . .

Where's Keller?

And then . . .

"Jesus fucking Christ," a booming voice says. A voice I know. "Keller, you scared the shit out of me."

Is that Ottar?

I poke my head up, and sure enough, Ottar and Lara are standing by the rocks, Keller now beside them.

"Just making sure it wasn't someone else," Keller says, and I watch as Ottar pulls him into a hug.

Feeling that it's safe, I open my plane door just as Ottar says, "Fuck, man. How are you?"

"Good," he answers, then I watch Lara pull him into a hug, her head pressing against his chest. Keller wraps his arms tightly around her, and they stay like that for a few more seconds. When they pull away, Lara punches Keller in the chest. Keller rubs his chest. "What the hell is that for?"

"Scaring me. Worrying me. Making me care far too much about your stupid ass."

Keller chuckles, then walks up to the plane. He sticks his gun in the waistband of his pants and says, "Grab my bag for me, love."

How can he possibly be so calm? Sheesh.

I grab his bag and backpack, then he helps me out of the plane and up the rocks to Ottar and Lara.

Immediately, Lara pulls me into a hug. "I'm so glad you're okay."

Oh my God, I've missed her. My heart is pumping fast. Given I hadn't known we were in danger on the island, and despite the emotional roller coaster with Keller, I've survived being away from Lara. Being away from home. But I wasn't aware how scary this all was until today, until I was rushed off the island, up into the air, and now, standing here holding one of my dearest friends. No wonder I'm shaking. *Talk about an adrenaline rush.*

"I'm good. A little shaken from the past twenty-four hours, but good."

She releases me, and to my surprise, Ottar pulls me into a hug as well. It's brief, but it's very unlike him. "Glad you're both safe. Let's head into Harrogate. You two must be exhausted."

"I don't know, I have some adrenaline pumping through me," I say as Keller walks up to my side and links his hand with mine. Lara takes in the gesture, and a smile crosses over her face.

Not sure how much they know, but it seems like we're about to have a download.

━━━

LARA SHAKES HER HEAD, her eyes teary. "I can't believe you were able to make it through that," Lara says. "Keller, I'm . . . I'm so sorry. I thought such shitty things about you. I should have known. I should have considered your sudden departure more. I just . . . I just wrongfully assumed you didn't want to go through with the wedding."

"So did I." Ottar hangs his head in shame. "Fuck, I'm sorry."

We're all sitting in the living room, a fire blazing in front of us, thank God, because the moment I was able to take a breath, the cold seeped back into my bones. It feels odd and also amazing being here again. Harrogate was a safety blanket for me when I first came up to Torskethorpe. It's where I learned about my mom, my grandparents, my country. And it's where I fell hopelessly in love with Keller. It's also where he proposed to me. Now, it's part of my enchanting homeland. *Mine.*

"Don't apologize. I didn't make it easy for anyone to believe otherwise." I curl into his side, holding him tighter. He kisses the top of my head.

"When you left, you knew you had to get Lilly because if you didn't, the people who kidnapped you would?" Ottar asks.

Keller nods. "Yes. I heard one of the men talking when I escaped my cell. They were going for her next. I wouldn't let that happen, and since they obviously had an inside source, I didn't want to attempt tipping you off."

Ottar nods. "Well, the palace is on lockdown right now."

"Really?" Keller asks.

Ottar nods. "We planted a few spies at the Crowned Cod, trying to hear anything that might be going on. One of our spies heard someone mention the king's island. They didn't hear much, but the person was asking questions, seeing if anyone had heard of it. Immediately, I knew you had to get out of there."

"But why bring us here?" I ask. "Won't this be obvious?"

"Yes, that's why you should come here. The palace isn't safe right now with an inside source leaking information and the secret passageways that we're working on closing up. Queen Pala and King Clinton's staff are protecting Theo and Katla in Marsdale. And Henrik and a team have everyone who's been involved over the past four months being held at the palace and questioned. No one is allowed in and no one is allowed out, not until we figure out who's behind this."

"But Theo and Katla are okay?" I ask. "Did he look better?"

Lara nods. "He actually started to look a bit better once he heard from Keller." Her eyes find Keller. "He was terribly distraught over losing you. I went to visit him once to see how he was, and he held my hand and wept." Lara takes a deep breath. "He was so happy to hear that you were okay. I'm not sure how much we tell him you went through, but—"

"Everything," Ottar says. "We need to tell him everything. It might hurt to know, but Keller deserves the accolades and recognition of bravery."

Keller shakes his head. "No, that's not necessary."

Ottar's eyes narrow. "No way in hell am I going to let this slide under the table." Ottar leans forward. "What you did to survive, to make it through three months of hell only to come out of it and save the future queen from harm, that deserves to be recognized."

"He's right," I say. "And if you don't tell him, I will."

Keller looks between us and shakes his head. "I survived for Lilly." He gestures at us. "I don't need you all ganging up on me."

"Deal with it," Lara says.

"Yeah, deal with it," I say, poking him in the stomach, bringing out that sexy smile of his.

"Now, can I ask something that I probably shouldn't ask, but I just need to know in order to get any sleep," Lara says.

"Sure," Keller says.

"Can I make an assumption from how you're holding each other that everything is good between you two?"

"Yes," Keller says. He brings my hand up to his mouth and presses his lips to my knuckles.

Lara claps her hands, the giddiness unlike her, but I appreciate it. "Does that mean there will be a wedding when this is all over?"

"Yes," Keller answers again, not even taking a second to think about it. "Lilly will be my wife, and nothing will stop that from happening."

He's right . . . nothing.

After a few more minutes of talking, I can feel Keller start to grow tired, so I stand and tug on his hand. "We should get you to bed. You're still not one hundred percent, and it's been an adrenaline-filled day."

"She's right," Lara says, standing as well. Ottar lifts from his chair and places his hand on Lara's lower back. I raise a brow at her, and she smiles. "What?"

I motion my finger between the two of them. "Uh, what's going on here? Are we back together?"

Ottar looks down at Lara as she looks up at him. "We're taking it day by day," Lara says.

But then Ottar shakes his head and says, "No, we're back together."

I chuckle. "I like Ottar's answer better."

Lara leans into him. "I like his answer better too."

"Congrats," Keller says, then lifts his backpack. He pulls out the monitor from the house. "In case anyone heads for the island, you can see it on that. Let's focus our efforts on figuring this all out tomorrow."

"Already planned on it," Ottar replies.

With that, Keller urges me toward the stone steps that lead to our old bedrooms.

"This feels all too familiar," I say as we climb up the stairs, his shoulders drooping.

He must be exhausted. Not only did he push his body hard for three months, but he also stayed up late and woke up before me every morning on the island. He never truly took a break besides when he collapsed from dehydration. He's worn out and deserves the sleep.

I wonder what room we'll sleep in, mine or his, but he doesn't give me much time to think as he pulls me toward his room.

Thankfully, Lara and Ottar brought us everything we might need including toiletries and clothes. Most likely packed by Runa. I remind myself to ask Lara how she's doing tomorrow.

Once Keller and I are ready for bed, me in a silk pajama set and him in his briefs, he brings me over to my side of the bed and pulls down the covers for me. He helps me into bed, always doing everything for me, then he moves over to his side. When he lies down, he lets out a deep breath and then curls into my back, holding me close to his chest.

"Do you feel better that you have Lara and Ottar here to help you keep watch?"

He nods. "I do."

"Think you'll sleep tonight?"

"Yes," he answers and then buries his head in my neck. "I love you, Lilly."

"I love you, too," I say while closing my eyes, feeling a wave of peace wash over me.

———

"IS KELLER STILL SLEEPING?" Lara asks as she hands me a cup of coffee while I sit at the kitchen table.

The stone kitchen with old wood accents holds so many memories, so many dear ones, that it brings a smile to my heart. Keller would not let go of me last night. Not sure if he was tired, grateful, or simply needed me close, but he took full advantage of the comfort of having friends present to help keep us safe, hence why he's still sleeping.

"He is," I answer. "I slipped past him and came down here, not wanting to wake him up. I honestly don't know how much sleep he's gotten since he was kidnapped. I feel like more happened while he was there, but he's saving me the gory details."

"I'm sure of it." Lara takes a seat and lets out a deep breath. "I can't think about him chained up, all alone in a stone cell. It makes me physically ill."

"Same," I say. "And when we were on the island, he didn't sleep much either. He actually ran his body ragged until it gave out on him. I had to nurse him back to health. I don't think I've ever seen him like that before, so weak."

"Even if he was, he'd never show it unless he couldn't hide it anymore. There's no doubt in my mind that he pushed until he couldn't push any longer. I'm glad he's getting some rest now."

"Me too." I sip my coffee and then ask, "Where's Ottar?"

"Setting signal detectors around the perimeter as well as some out in the fields. It will signal to us if anyone is headed our way."

"I'm sure Keller will be appreciative when he wakes up to find out he did that."

"Yes, he will." Lara nudges me with her foot. "How was it, seeing him again? I feel like it must have been wild."

"Uh, to say the least. He knocked me out with something.

I woke up tied to a bed, and I've never been more scared. And then he showed up in the doorway. Seeing him took my breath away. His beard was longer when I first saw him, but I'm pretty sure my heart stalled in my chest. Relief and anger both flew through my mind."

"How long did it take for you to work things out?"

"A few days," I answer. "The people who captured him showed him articles of me and Evan together."

Lara cringes. "That must have killed him."

"It's what spurred him on to get out of the cell quicker. But he didn't tell me about being taken right away."

"He didn't?" Lara asks, surprised. "I assumed that would be the first thing he told you."

I shake my head. "He was pissed about Evan and kept making jabs here and there about how I moved on. I finally told him that I didn't. That Evan was nothing, he never even kissed me, and it was for Theo. After that, Keller told me what happened, and let's just say I cried a lot."

"I can imagine." Lara shakes her head. "I honestly can't believe all of this is happening. I swear to you, nothing has happened like this in Torskethorpe. There were minor infractions here and there, but for the most part, it's a quiet, loving country. So I have no idea why this is all happening. I don't want you thinking this is normal."

I chuckle. "I didn't think it was normal at all. It has to do with me. Whoever is behind this is not happy that I'm here."

"Good morning," Keller's deep, scratchy voice says from the entry of the kitchen. I glance over my shoulder to see his hand pulling on his neck, his wild hair in all different directions, and a pair of sweats hanging low on his narrow hips.

God, he's so fucking hot.

"Jesus," Lara says. "Keller, your body."

He glances down at it and then back up at Lara. "What about it?"

I chuckle. "I think she's thinking what I am . . . how is it possible to have that many muscles."

"It's true," she says. "I've known you for a long time, and I've seen you work out, but this is another level."

"That's what happens when you're starved for a few months," he says while moving over to the coffee pot. "And then all you have to eat is oatmeal and some slop they throw together and call soup."

Lara cringes. "Sorry, I didn't mean for my shock to sound insensitive."

He shakes his head. "It's not. I can understand the shock. First time I saw myself in the mirror, I had the same reaction."

"Did you flex and say to yourself, looking fine, Keller?" I ask, adding some light to the conversation.

"Twice," Keller says, holding up his fingers and making me laugh. It's rare he cracks a joke, so when he does, it's so freaking cute.

"Oh, he's coming in with a sense of humor," Lara says. "I like it."

"He's lightened up a bit. Maybe he won't chastise me for talking about nipple piercings in public now."

His eyes narrow on me. "I'll always chastise you for that. Those nipples are my private property. I don't need other people hearing about them."

"It was a good effort," Lara says.

I shrug. A girl has to try. Keller sits next to me, then reaches for my hand and pulls me onto his lap, looping his arm around my waist and kissing my cheek.

"Where's Ottar?" Keller asks as he brings his drink up to his lips.

"Setting up signal detectors," Lara says. "And before you think you need to help him, don't. We all want you to take it easy. It's been a tough couple of months, let us handle everything."

"Please listen to her," I say quietly to Keller, and thankfully, he nods.

"Okay," Keller says, but I can tell it makes him slightly uneasy. He likes his control. I learned that very quickly.

"He started early anyway," Lara says. "He should be done soon."

"Do you want me to check on him?" Keller asks.

Lara and I both say, "No," at the same time, causing Keller to grumble.

"Seriously, Keller. Take a second to breathe. What you just went through is extremely traumatic. Just . . . relax. Spend the day not worrying, sitting on the couch with Lilly, maybe play a game or something. You have me and Ottar. We have everything covered."

"You know it's not in me to relax, right?"

"Yes," Lara says. "But I think it's time that you learn how to do it, because I think not relaxing got you tangled up on the wrong path before the wedding . . . right?"

"She's right," I say, my arm around him.

"You know, you two need to stop talking to each other. I don't like this two-against-one bullshit."

Lara and I chuckle. "Get used to it," Lara says. "Your hero days are over. Now, you need to be the prince who shakes hands, smiles for the cameras, and tries not to kick little schoolgirls."

"I didn't kick her," he groans just as the door to the castle opens.

"It's me," Ottar calls out. He works his way through the living room and into the kitchen. Decked out in all black, he's wearing a shoulder holster carrying two guns, and his hands are carrying two monitors.

My oh my, Ottar.

I catch Lara's quick perusal and the small pull of her lips in approval before she says, "Everything set up?"

"Yup. I secured the perimeter and was able to drive a mile

out each way and set triggers. I checked to make sure every-thing was working. We should be good to go."

"Anything on the roof?" Keller asks.

"Yes," Ottar says. "All four corners. We're covered."

"Thank you," Keller says, relief in his voice.

"Did you get some good sleep?" Ottar asks. "You looked exhausted last night."

"I did," Keller says. "It's good to be back here."

"It is good to be back here," I say. "Maybe we can do some more carving or history lessons in the back room."

"If you want some more history, I can bore you just as much as the first time," Keller says with a pinch to my side.

"Actually, I barely survived the first session. Not sure I can do another."

Ottar pulls a phone out of his pocket. "Theo texted this morning. He wants to FaceTime with you. Are you up for it?"

"Yes," I say, reaching for the phone. I prop it against my cup of coffee on the table and then say, "Oh wait, who do I call?"

Ottar chuckles and then picks up the phone. He dials Theo and places the phone back against the coffee cup as it rings.

It takes two rings before he answers.

"Hello? Oh, good heavens." Theo comes into view and places his hand on his chest in surprise. Instead of lying down on his bed, he's on a couch, holding the phone in front of him. He has color to his skin and is more lively than the last time I saw him.

Thank God.

"Theo," I say, my eyes welling up.

"My Lilija . . ." Tears spring to his eyes. "Keller, my boy."

"Hi, Theo," Keller says, lifting his hand in a wave.

"I briefed them this morning," Ottar says out of courtesy.

Katla comes into view as well, and she lets out a deep sigh. "My God, Keller." Her hand moves up to her mouth as she shakes her head. "Our dear boy. How are you? Are you okay?"

Keller rests his chin on my shoulder and nods. "I'm good."

Theo glances back and forth between the two of us, and with a shaky voice, he asks, "Are you two . . ."

"Together?" I ask. "Yes, we are. We're all good. Everything is good."

"Well, not everything," Keller says. "We still need to figure out who's behind all this."

"Yes," Theo says. "Priority number one. Henrik briefed me this morning about the process over at the palace. They're narrowing it down." He wets his lips. "Rumors have been circling about two people."

"Who?" Keller asks.

"Cornolia, the wedding planner's assistant, and . . . Gothi Elias."

"I fucking knew it," Keller says, his hand slamming on the table. "I knew something was wrong with him. The moment I met him, I felt uneasy, like he wasn't trustworthy."

"But he's a gothi," I say, confused. "He's supposed to be trusted."

"Trust no one," Keller says. *Oh Keller. I hate that this ordeal has confirmed that people can't be trusted.*

"We've discovered that he has a sordid past, which we suspect is what the Arkham people have exploited. His betrayal came as a grave surprise. He's been loyal to the throne for many years, so we also suspect he's not handling his guilt well. They'll be interrogated, but we're fairly certain they were contacted anonymously."

"Why would they think that?" Ottar asks.

"Henrik has been able to dig into Cornolia's and Elias's background, and they're actually related. Cornolia is Elias's niece. That's how she got the job with Adela, through his recommendation. It's why we're pulling them in together. As far as we know, they don't have any connection to Arkham. So we're trying to get more details."

Keller nods. "Okay, we're going to have a download here and try to connect some dots."

"But first, we're going to take a moment to breathe," I say, cutting in.

"Lilly," Keller says. "The quicker we figure this all out, the sooner this can be over. We don't have time to take a break."

"Keller, you're running yourself ragged. You're no use to me if you're not healthy."

"She's right," Theo says.

"I won't be doing anything other than talking," Keller says. "I've already been told I can't help around here."

"Good," Theo says. "Please keep them safe."

Ottar comes into view and says, "Don't worry, nothing will happen to them. I would like to ask Keller a few questions, though, if that's okay? I fear once whoever is searching for Keller and Lilly find they're not on the island, we won't have a lot of time after that. They might come to Marsdale. That's the hope at least with placing you there."

"And I've spoken to Clinton. They're ready if they do."

"Good," Ottar says. "Then if it's okay, I'll ask my questions and maybe figure some things out."

"Yes, but I also require him to take it easy, both of them."

"We will," I step in. "And you're feeling good?"

Theo nods. "Much better, especially seeing you together. What are your thoughts for the future?"

I smile and press a kiss to Keller's cheek. "When this is all over, we want to give Torskethorpe the wedding they were waiting on."

"That's everything I needed to hear," Theo says before relaxing against the couch.

Katla takes the phone and presses her hand to her chest. "I'm so happy you're together. The girls have been worried sick." She points the phone toward Isabella and Marit, who wave frantically.

"We miss you," they say together.

"Miss you too. Once this is over, we need to have another visit."

"Count on it," Marit says. "Glad to see you're okay, Keller."

"Thank you," he says with a nod.

Katla brings the phone back to her. "We'll let you go. Please keep us updated, and we'll do the same."

"Sounds good. Love you all."

"Love you both," Theo says before hanging up.

———

"HOW ARE YOU FEELING?" I ask Keller as I take a seat next to him on the couch.

"Good," he answers, but I know he's lying. I can see it in his wince and slow movements. After we got off the phone with Katla and Theo, Ottar made us breakfast, and I watched Keller carefully. I noticed how he grew more and more quiet. I thought that maybe he was trying to process the conversation with Theo, maybe trying to recollect everything he wanted to tell Ottar, but when we went upstairs to take showers and he sat on his bed, taking deep breaths, I realized that maybe it wasn't him being lost in his thoughts.

I sat between his legs and asked him what was going on. He told me his head was hurting again and that he just needed some Ibuprofen and more water. It didn't settle well with me, but I helped him take a shower, got him dressed, and then walked him downstairs to the living room with his note-book in hand.

"You don't look fine." I stand from the couch and say, "Stretch out, lie down."

"I'm good, Lilly," he says quietly as he squeezes his eyes shut.

"Keller, I'm not going to fight you over this. Lie down."

Grumbling under his breath, he stretches out along the couch, and I help prop him up against a throw pillow. When he's settled, I move the coffee table closer and sit on it.

I drag my fingers over his stomach and say, "Is it just your head? Is anything else hurting?"

"Just the head," he says as he takes a deep breath.

"As bad as when we were on the island?"

"Yeah," he answers as he drapes his arm over his eyes.

"Everything okay?" Lara asks as she walks into the living room.

"No," I answer. "Can you please grab four Ibuprofen and some sort of caffeinated drink for Keller?"

Her brows turn down, concern lacing her eyes. "Yes."

"Please don't make a big deal," Keller says, his voice heavy.

"This is the second time this has happened in a week. I'll make a big deal if I want to," I reply. "This is serious, Keller. This isn't just dehydration. You took some brute force while in that cell, so there could have been internal damage we don't know about."

He takes a few deep breaths and then swallows. "Fuck," he says and then twists to the side. "Move."

I get out of the way just in time for him to throw up on the coffee table. The sight of his body wracking from the force scares me senseless. Keller is never one to show weakness, but in this last week alone, he's shown it twice, and it's startling.

"Oh my God," Lara says as she walks in, taking in the scene in front of her.

"What's going on?" Ottar says, following her. "Jesus." He runs up to Keller and places his hand on his back. "Lara, grab some towels."

Lara runs off to the kitchen while Keller's body convulses,

and he throws up on the table again. I stand there useless, fear filling in the pit of my stomach, because something isn't right. Something isn't right with Keller, and we're going to need more than some water and Ibuprofen to help him through it.

Lara rushes in with towels and the garbage can. She quickly starts wiping up the puke while Keller slowly lowers back down to the couch. Ottar glances up at me, the same concern in his eyes, and I can tell he's thinking the same thing as me.

"Here," Ottar says, handing Keller some water. "You okay, man?"

"Yeah," he says breathlessly, eyes closed. "The pain . . . really intense."

"No need to explain," Ottar says. "Just take a few sips and when you're ready, we'll get you to take the Ibuprofen."

Keller doesn't say anything. He just takes a few sips, his eyes closed the whole time.

"We need to get him up to his room," Ottar says. "We need the darkness to help with the migraine."

"No," Keller barely says. "Stay . . . here."

"It will be dark soon enough with the sun going down," I say. "Maybe we can stuff pillows in the windows to break down what little light we have."

"That works," Ottar says. "I'm going to collect pillows. Lilly, stay with Keller. Lara, when you're done, come help me with the pillows."

"I can finish cleaning up," I say, but Lara shoos me away.

"Just grab me the disinfectant spray under the sink in the kitchen."

I glance at Keller, who is lying lifeless on the couch, his chest rising and falling deeply, my concern growing. After retrieving the spray for Lara, I sit on the couch, right next to Keller, and I place my hand on his stomach. His hand covers mine and he squeezes three times. For some reason, the gesture makes me far too emotional than I care to admit, and tears spring to my eyes.

"Stay with me," he says quietly, showing his vulnerability in front of Lara.

"I'm not going anywhere," I say as I scoot closer.

Lara finishes up and then goes off to help Ottar gather pillows and supplies.

When we're alone, I say, "Keller, I'm worried. These headaches seem to come out of nowhere."

"Just stress," he says, but I know that's not the case. There has to be something else. Something underlying.

"Did, uh . . . did that Banny guy—"

"Banamaor," Keller says.

"Yes, did he hit you on the head a lot?"

"Probably," Keller says. "Can't remember."

That's concerning as well, that he can't remember much. And he's been having a hard time putting the pieces of all of this together, which doesn't seem like him either. He was telling me on the flight here how he's struggling with figuring out who's behind the kidnapping, but I just assumed that maybe it was because he didn't have enough information. I never considered the fact that maybe . . . maybe something is wrong with his head.

Lara and Ottar pop into the living room with a bunch of pillows and some duct tape. They start covering up the windows, casting the living room into darkness. Lara switches on a distant floor lamp, which offers minimal light, just enough for everyone not to trip over each other.

"Okay, let's try to get some medicine into you," Ottar says while coming up to Keller. He helps lift him gently, and I hand him the tablets while helping Keller navigate his water bottle. Once he swallows everything, we lay him back down, and Lara brings over a blanket. We cover him up, make sure he's comfortable, and then Ottar nods toward the kitchen to have a conversation.

When I start to rise from the couch, Keller says, "Don't leave."

"I'll be right back. I promise," I say before placing a kiss on his head. "Right back."

He sighs and lets go of my hand, allowing me to leave.

I slip into the kitchen where Lara and Ottar wait. Quietly, Ottar says, "Is this what it was like on the island?"

"Yes," I whisper. "It came out of nowhere and took him out. He threw up then as well. While you were getting pillows, I asked him if the man who tortured him hit his head a lot, and he said he can't remember, he blacked out." My teeth pull on the corner of my mouth as I look back at Keller on the couch. "I think something more serious is happening to him, and I'm really concerned."

"Same," Ottar says. "Let me call Theo and see what he says. We can have Runa bring supplies as well as the palace doctor. I want to make sure Theo would be okay with that first since it's bringing someone from the outside in."

"We can trust Runa," I say. "She would never do anything to cross us."

"I know," Ottar says. "That's why I suggested her, but since the palace is on lockdown, I just want to make sure we have all of our bases covered."

"I understand."

Ottar slips past us and into the back room where Keller and I did our studying sessions. When the door shuts, Lara turns toward me. "I hope he's okay."

"Me too," I say as I twist my hands in front of me. "He's been struggling. Been really foggy. He told me it's really frustrating that he can't figure out who is behind all of this. That the voice that spoke to him was familiar, but he couldn't place it. It's almost like his brain isn't fully functioning, and that's scary, Lara."

"I know. He took notes, right? Maybe we can look at his notes and see if we can figure everything out."

"He did. He brought his notebook down to discuss with you, but then all of a sudden, his head started really hurting him and then, well, you know what happened after that."

"Let's see what Ottar says and then we can figure this out because the sooner we do, the sooner we can relay it to Theo, and he can decide what to do. He's been working closely with King Clinton on a plan of attack. If Arkham is involved, it won't be pretty for them, especially since Theo is working on joining the ITO."

"I know I should know this, but what is the ITO?"

"The Icelandic Treaty Organization. It's made up of fifteen countries that all pledge military allegiance to each other. Arkham is not a part of it, nor is Torskethorpe because we've never had a reason to join. Like I told you before, Torskethorpe has always been a peaceful country. But now with these threats, Theo wants to join, and King Clinton is assisting in the process, one of the reasons he's also in Marsdale."

"I get it." I glance over at Keller and ask, "Why aren't we in Marsdale? It seems safer there."

"With the source of the threats still undetermined, Theo won't have the current monarch and future monarch in the same place."

"Ah." I nod. "That makes sense."

Just then, Ottar walks back into the kitchen while pocketing his phone. "Theo wants a doctor sent out here immediately. I've contacted Runa, she's already pulling together supplies and gathering the doctor. She's been briefed on the conditions."

"Was Theo worried?" I ask.

Ottar nods his head. "Very. We considered taking Keller to a hospital, but once again, without knowing the threat, it could prove more dangerous. We're best hiding out for now."

"Are we sure we can trust the doctor?" I ask.

Ottar nods. "Yes, he's been cleared."

"Okay," I say. "When do you think they'll get here?"

"Late today or tomorrow depending on when Runa can meet up with the doctor."

"Well, I hope it's late today," I answer.

"Me too, but for now, why don't you go sit with him? I'm going to look up some home remedies that might help with migraines. Let's not bother him with questions until the doctor gets here."

"Agreed," I say and then take a deep breath. When I look up at Ottar, I say, "I'm scared."

He gently rubs my shoulder. "It's okay. We'll take care of him. Nothing will happen."

"Okay," I say. "Thank you." I offer them a soft smile and then walk back into the living room where I take a seat next to Keller.

When he feels my presence, he says, "Come here." He holds out his hand, and I slip my palm against him. "Lie on me, love."

"I don't want to hurt you."

"You're not. Please, I just want to feel you."

Knowing this is what he wants, what he needs, I position myself on top of his large body and rest my head on his chest. The moment I'm settled, he relaxes into the couch as his arm goes around me.

"Are you okay?" I ask.

"Better now," he answers.

And that's how we stay for the rest of the afternoon, me on top of him, him holding on to me like a lifeline. I wish it meant that I felt calmer, but if anything, with so many unknowns in the air, stress is still my friend. At least I'm no longer alone.

Chapter Thirty-Five

KELLER

"Lilly," I say softly. "You don't need to feed me."

Lilly holds a bowl of soup in one hand and a spoon in the other. She hasn't left my side since I pulled her on top of me. She's remained quiet, she's kissed my chest every so often, and she's helped me drink my water. The only time she's gotten up is to go to the bathroom or to help me to the bathroom.

Now that the migraine has eased up enough that I feel like I can breathe without pain, I'm sitting up on the couch, attempting to settle my stomach with food. Well . . . Lilly is.

"It's okay, I don't mind," she replies.

"Well, I do," I say. "Have you eaten anything besides breakfast?"

"I haven't been hungry," she answers as she dips the spoon in the soup.

I take the bowl from her, drop the spoon in the soup, and then set it on the coffee table in front of us. I turn toward her and say, "I need you to take care of yourself as well. That means eating."

She straddles my lap and smooths her hand over my chest as she says, "I've been worried sick, Keller. My appetite isn't there."

"Doesn't matter, you still need to eat," I reply as I place my hands on her thighs.

Lara and Ottar are in the kitchen, which is where Lilly's eyes fall to before she turns back to me. "Ottar said Runa and the doctor won't be here until tomorrow. I'm worried about you, okay? It's turned my stomach upside down and I . . ."—her lip trembles and she takes a deep breath—"I can't lose you again, Keller."

"You're not going to lose me, Lilly," I say as I cup her cheek. Her velvety skin leans into my palm, and she closes her eyes. "It's going to take me a while to get better from what I went through. I'm sure the doctor will be able to help that."

When I learned there was a doctor headed to Harrogate with Runa, I wasn't too happy. I was worried about the safety and word getting out, but Ottar assured me Runa was taking every precaution and wasn't letting on to what she was doing. And she would meet up with the doctor at an undisclosed location. He also stated that the doctor suggested to come tomorrow, as to not tip anyone off.

It still creates concern for me, especially since we aren't any closer to catching who's behind this.

But I have to agree with Lilly about her concerns. I'm concerned as well. I'm not sure how many times I was hit in the head when I was in the Arkham cell, but what I do know is that these migraines aren't normal. They come on so quickly and take me out within seconds. I've never experienced anything like it.

"I just need you to get better," Lilly says.

"I know, love. But I need you to stay healthy for me as

well. So will you go get some soup, and we can eat on the couch together?"

She nods, and before she gets off my lap, she leans forward and presses a soft kiss to my lips. She then rests her forehead against mine and says, "I love you, Keller."

"I love you, too," I say and then press one more kiss to her lips.

She stands and then hands me my soup. "I'll be right back."

After she heads into the kitchen, I bring the soup spoon up to my mouth and take a mouthful, exhaustion hitting me again. I seem to be going in these spurts, where my adrenaline picks up, I'm able to accomplish what I need to do, but then I crash, and I crash hard. I know I'm not where I need to be physically and mentally—I'm pretty shot—which is why I'm so fucking grateful to be here in Harrogate with Ottar and Lara. If I have to put my trust in anyone to keep us safe, it's them.

Lilly comes back into the living room with a tray. A bowl of soup, bread for two, and drinks.

"I brought some bread in case you wanted something a little heartier."

"Thank you," I say as she takes a seat next to me with her bowl of soup. She rests her head on my shoulder and heaves a heavy sigh. "Can we talk about what we're going to do after this is all said and done?"

"Of course," I say, glancing back toward the kitchen. "Are Lara and Ottar joining us?"

Lilly shakes her head and sits up so she can eat her soup. "No, I asked them to give us some privacy." She turns toward me now, sitting cross-legged, her legs right up against mine. "So, dream with me. Tell me what you want to happen."

I give it some thought while taking sips of my soup. "Get married would be job number one. I don't want to go another day without knowing that you're my wife."

"Agreed. I want you to be my husband."

"Then after that, some sort of honeymoon where we spend the entire time indoors fucking."

She chuckles. "That sounds fantastic. Maybe we can head back to the island, but this time . . . bring toys." She wiggles her eyebrows.

"I thought what we had to work with did the job."

"Yes, but if we bring toys, you can fuck me while a vibrator is in my ass, and I think that's something we would both be interested in."

I chuckle and sigh. "If the people of Torskethorpe only knew their future queen the way that I do."

"They would erect statues around the country for me."

"Yeah . . . something would be erect, that's for sure."

She smiles and pokes me in the side. "Don't turn me on with your humor. It's not fair."

"Why isn't it fair?"

"Because clearly we can't do anything about . . . my horniness," she whispers. "Not with your head and Lara and Ottar downstairs."

"Didn't stop us the first time when Lara and Brimar were downstairs."

"That was a different time. I was blinded by the need to have your cock in my mouth."

I shake my head. "Jesus, Lilly."

"It's true, but we're getting off topic here." She lifts a spoonful of soup to her mouth, sips, and then says, "Okay, honeymoon with toys, check. What about after the honeymoon?"

"After the honeymoon?" I ask, while picking up a piece of bread and dipping it in my soup. The warm liquid's making me feel better with every mouthful. "I would like to talk to Theo and Katla about moving."

"Moving?" she asks, surprised. "To where? Like out of the

country? Out of the capital? That seems sort of counterproductive, don't you think?"

"Moving out of Strombly," I say. "I know Strombly is the main palace, but the monarch also owns Astfangin Castle."

"Astfangin?" she asks. "What does that mean?"

"It means to be in love," I answer, causing the most beautiful smile to pass over Lilly's lips. "It's a property about two miles west of Strombly. The capital gardens surround it actually. It's slightly larger than Harrogate, more modern, and is the perfect place to start a marriage. It will offer us privacy, which I could use with you, at least for now, and maybe one day, it could be where we start our family."

"I love that," she says softly. "And I would love the privacy as well. Would we move into the palace or stay there when . . . you know, it's time?"

"Move into Strombly," I answer. "Astfangin is actually where Theo and Katla spent the first few years of their marriage. And when it was time for Theo to take the crown, they moved into Strombly. Pala was supposed to live in Astfangin but forfeited it to Sveinn when she married King Clinton. It was empty for a while, but when Sveinn married—" I pause . . . the mention of Sveinn's name triggering something in my head.

"Is everything okay?" Lilly asks, placing one hand on my thigh.

"Holy fuck," I whisper as I set my soup down and go to stand, but Lilly stops me.

"Keller, no standing, you're taking it easy. What's going on?"

"Get Ottar and Lara. Now."

Sensing my urgency, Lilly sets her soup down as well and vacates to the kitchen as I reach for my notebook that's on the coffee table, thankfully untouched by my vomiting episode this morning. I flip it open just as Ottar, Lara, and Lilly come into the living room.

"What's going on?" Ottar says.

I review my notes, my mind swirling over the Birch Forest, the accents, the prospective names. It fucking hits me like a ton of bricks. Slowly, I look up at Ottar and say, "It's Rolant."

"What's Rolant?" Ottar asks.

"Who's Rolant?" Lilly adds.

"The person behind this. It's Rolant," I answer. "It was his voice."

"Wait, is there another Rolant other than my uncle?" Lilly continues.

"You think it's Lilly's uncle, right?" Lara says as she takes a seat.

"Wait . . . you think my uncle, Theo's grown-ass child, the one who got exiled for drunkenly rolling on the thousand-year-old moss, you think he's the one behind this?"

"I don't think," I say slowly. "I know."

"Okay, walk us through it," Ottar says as he takes a seat on the coffee table.

"Wait, I don't want to make his head worse," Lilly says while sitting right next to me and placing her hand on my thigh.

"I'm fine," I say, lacing my hand with hers. "I promise. I need to get this out now."

Her concerned eyes connect with mine, but she just nods, giving me the go-ahead.

"The first time I heard his voice, I knew it was familiar, but I couldn't place it, and the more and more I heard it, it drove me nuts. The peon who was helping him, it was obvious he was from Arkham in the way he spoke, but the other two . . ." And then it dawns on me. "Jesus, fuck."

"What?" Ottar asks.

"There were two of them. Rolant and . . . and the other had to be Sveinn. They sounded very similar, and now that I'm piecing it together, I can almost count on it."

"Sveinn?" Lilly asks. "I thought he was lost at sea."

"Must have found his way to Arkham," Lara says. "But what would they want with Torskethorpe? I can understand Rolant wanting vengeance, but why wouldn't Sveinn just come back and claim his title?"

"Yeah, why wouldn't he come back and claim the title?" Lilly says.

"Rolant could have convinced him not to," I say as I glance down at my notebook. "They mentioned something about Birch Forest. Taking that over. And if Sveinn claimed his title, he wouldn't be able to do anything with Birch Forest. But if Arkham takes over . . ."

"Why would Arkham want Birch Forest?" Ottar asks.

"Isn't that where the hundred-year-old moss is?" Lilly asks.

I nod. "Yes, acres and acres of it."

Lilly's lips twist to the side. "Can't moss be used for electricity?"

"What?" Lara asks. "I've never heard of that."

"Me neither," I say.

"Hold on, someone give me a phone." Lilly holds out her hand, and Ottar gives her his phone. She types something into the search bar and then pauses to read before saying, "Yup, there are early studies that moss can be used to generate energy during photosynthesis, it creates surplus electrons. It's still at the early stages of testing, but with the quantity of moss Torskethorpe has, I wouldn't put it past them to want to harness the wealth behind that."

"And Arkham has been struggling economically as of late," Ottar says. "This would be the significant boost the country would need, especially if it's green energy they're looking for."

"They are," Lara says. "Their government has been going through a housing crisis and their main crops of wheat didn't bring in enough revenue this past year. They're struggling, and King Magnus is on record saying he's looking to help boost the economy. If they're looking into Birch Forest, I wouldn't put it past them."

"Jesus," I say, pushing my hand through my hair. "But why would Sveinn and Rolant be involved?"

"Because they're on the outside looking in," Ottar says. "The country has moved on without them, they don't have anything to go back to, so they most likely cut a deal with Magnus. Insider information to take over Torskethorpe. Rolant probably thought it was a done deal when Sveinn disappeared, but then Lilly came along."

"You think they've planned this for a while?" Lilly asks.

"Probably thought Torskethorpe would be handed over to Arkham," Ottar says. "And then Keller found you. Probably one of the reasons they attacked Keller. If they had insider information from Elias and Cornolia, they probably knew how important your relationship with Keller is, so they took advantage of it."

"Have we heard anything about Elias and Cornolia?" I ask.

Ottar shakes his head. "Not yet, but this realization needs to be reported to Theo."

"Won't it hurt him, knowing his sons might be behind this?"

"It's something he needs to know, despite how hurtful it might be," I say and then take the phone from Lilly. "And it needs to be told now so King Clinton and his team can help find Rolant and Sveinn." Lilly silently agrees with a nod, and I dial Theo just as there's a loud beeping sounding off in the kitchen.

"What's that?" Lilly asks.

"The security cameras from the island," I say.

Ottar stands and heads into the kitchen just as Theo answers the phone. "Hello?"

"Theo," I say, looking into the phone. "We need to chat."

"Okay," he says, his face turning serious. "Give me a

moment."

He stands from where he's sitting and asks King Clinton if he can borrow the office just as Ottar comes back into the living room, holding the monitor from the island.

"The island house is being invaded," Ottar says, holding the monitor out to me.

Men in black outfits move past the sensors, holding guns out in front of them, the scene painfully scary. *We could have been there.* If it wasn't for Ottar telling us to flee, we could have been held up and there's nothing I could have done to help Lilly. The thought makes my head pain rear up in anger all over again.

"Oh my God," Lilly says, her hand to her chest.

"What's going on?" Theo says over the phone, and when I glance at the screen, Theo and King Clinton come into view. Theo sits in a desk chair while King Clinton rests against the back. No need to ask if Theo is comfortable sharing this information with King Clinton because it'll have to be shared anyway.

"The island is currently being invaded," I say.

"Jesus," Theo whispers. "Thank God you're not there."

"Yes," I say on a tough swallow because, we could have been there. I thought we were safe. Hell, I think we're safe here. "That's not why we're calling, we believe we figured out who's behind this," I say just as another beeping sounds off. "What's that?"

Ottar's brow turns down. "The perimeter sensor for Harrogate. It's been breached."

"What?" I ask.

"What's going on?" Theo asks, and when I glance at Lilly, I can see the apprehension in her eyes.

Ottar moves to the kitchen where he has his monitor for Harrogate and checks it out. "It's a palace car," he says while glancing up at me. "Was Runa able to come out tonight?" He turns to Lara. "Did you hear anything?"

Lara shakes her head as she stands from the couch and pulls a gun out from her leg holster. "Can you zoom in on the person driving?"

Ottar touches the screen and then nods. "It's her."

"Sorry," I say into the phone. "We had the security sensors go off. Runa came tonight with the doctor rather than tomorrow."

"Good," Theo says. "I want to make sure you're okay."

Yeah, it's probably good because right now, my migraine is making things fuzzy again.

Lilly must notice, because she places her hand on my thigh. "You okay?"

I swallow, wetting my lips, but I have to shut one of my eyes, because a piercing feeling pulses through my head. Fuck.

"We can deal with this later," Lilly says, taking the phone from me. "Theo, can we call you back?"

"Of course," he says as I go to protest, but Lilly hangs up.

"Lilly—"

She shakes her head. "No, you're not feeling good, and this is something we can handle after speaking to the doctor. What's most important is making you better. I'm not going to push you harder than you can handle."

She stands up. "Where are you going?"

"To go meet Runa and the doctor." She pushes past Lara and Ottar, who glance at each other.

"Don't let her go out there by herself," I say.

"I was thinking the same thing," Ottar says.

I start to stand, but Lara gives me a look. "Stay, Keller. She's right, you need to get better."

"I'm fine," I say, as pain shoots through my skull, causing me to squeeze my eyes shut and wince.

Fuck.

"Real fine." She rolls her eyes and then takes a seat in front of me. "You're going nowhere."

Chapter Thirty-Six

LILLY

"Lilly, wait, let me clear the car first," Ottar says, coming up behind me.

"Clear the car?" I ask. "For what? It's Runa and the doctor. I'm going to help them unload. The quicker the doctor can see to Keller, the better."

"Just let me clear it first," Ottar says as I take a step outside, the car's bright lights shining on us both.

Ottar must flip a light on to the outside because the front of Harrogate lights up the circular driveway.

The car comes to a park, and I see Runa in the driver's side, a man in the passenger, and . . . are those two men in the back?

"Get back," Ottar says, standing in front of me. "Get back in the castle."

"Ottar, stop," I say just as Runa opens her car door and stands. "Runa!" I wave, and I move past Ottar to go give her a hug, but I'm snagged by the wrist just as the back two car

453

doors open and two tall men stand, both of them holding a gun.

What on earth is going on?

"Move it," the man next to Runa says, pushing her forward so she nearly stumbles to the ground.

"Lilly, back in the castle, now."

"She moves, and Runa gets her head blown off," the man says, pushing Runa forward more, the barrel of his gun pointed at her. My stomach bottoms out as the men come into view.

Broad shoulders. One with a beard, the other with a mustache, but eerily familiar in looks, both with the same eyes as my mom . . . as me.

Rolant and Sveinn. *Keller was right. Fuck.*

The doctor steps forward as well, a gun to his head.

"Drop the gun, Ottar," the older one says, who must be Rolant. "Now."

Hands in the air, Ottar lowers to the ground, dropping his gun, and then rises back up, his movements very slow, very purposeful.

"Who else is in the castle?" Rolant shouts.

"Just Keller," Ottar says, loud enough that I'm pretty sure Lara and Keller can hear.

"Get him out here."

Keeping his hands up, Ottar replies, "He's in bad shape."

"I don't fucking care. Get him out here, now." He shoves his gun at Runa's head, causing her to start crying.

Her lip is shaking, and I can't stand seeing her like this, so I call out, "Keller, I need you out here."

And I pray that only Keller comes out, not Lara.

"Tell him unarmed, or Runa is the first to go."

I swallow and yell, "Unarmed, Keller. They're going to shoot Runa if you don't."

There, that should tip him off, hopefully.

After a few seconds, Keller appears at the arch of the door, arms up as well, moving slowly, but he appears and stands next to me, if not slightly in front.

"There he is," Rolant says. "The bane of our fucking existence." He pushes Runa forward, and Sveinn does the same with the doctor, coming fully into view. "You realize the shitstorm you've caused us?"

"I'm sorry," Keller says, his voice strained. "I was just trying to get to my girl." It's odd, hearing him sound so subdued, because in a moment like this when guns are involved that could be pointed very easily at me, he would normally be growling, ready to pounce. But he's also a smart man, and antagonizing Rolant and Sveinn wouldn't be the smartest plan.

"Your girl." Rolant shakes his head. "I've never seen someone sleep their way to the top like you. Quite impressive, don't you think, brother?"

"He's been wanting into this family from the very beginning, when Papa took him under his wing, treating him like a son he never had, when in fact, he had two fucking sons. And then you slip into the role of his personal secretary. How many decisions did Papa make that were actually your brainchild?"

Keller clears his throat and says, "None."

"Bullshit," Rolant says. "When Sveinn left, you went straight to find the next replacement, you didn't even give him a moment to come back."

"Why didn't you come back?" I ask, knowing I should probably keep my mouth shut, but I'm curious.

Sveinn glances at me. "My brother is the one who brought me back, brought me in. Instead of searching for me, my parents searched for you. Why would I go back to a place where I'm unwanted?"

"You were wanted," Keller says. "Theo was desperate to have you back."

"Shut up," Rolant says, now pointing his gun at Keller,

causing my entire body to seize with fear. "Don't lie to my brother to make him feel like our parents cared, because they didn't. They never did."

I want to shout that's not true. Theo and Katla are loving and kind, and some of the most warm and welcoming people I know. If Rolant didn't feel that energy with them, that's his fault, not theirs.

"Why are you pointing the gun at Keller?" Sveinn asks, looking nervous.

"Because he's the reason we're here. This was supposed to be easy," Rolant says. *Man, this guy is unhinged.* Which makes this even more terrifying. "Blackmailing Elias was simple; give us the information we need, and we won't tell anyone about how he gambled away some of Mama's prized jewels. Looping in Cornolia was even easier because Elias had dirt on her. They gave us the information we needed and helped put a dent between you two." Rolant motions his gun between me and Keller. "Kidnapping Keller was a breeze, especially since you didn't take any precautions with the hidden passageways in the palace, something Elias was able to inform us about. But here is where the problem was. Taking Keller was supposed to devastate Lilly, make her leave Torskethorpe and forfeit the crown to Arkham, but to our surprise, it seems like Keller cares more for her than she does for him." Again, I want to shout that's not true, but I surprisingly hold my tongue. "That's why we brought in the Sotherbys to force their son to talk to the future princess, but Evan was too much of a goddamn gentleman to make the move we needed. And then you have to go and fucking escape." Rolant waves the gun at Keller. "Just tell me one thing, were you faking it the whole time?"

Keller shifts notably to the right, partially in front of me. His hands are still up in the air as he says, "No."

"Then how the fuck did you get out?"

"He's still weak, look at him," Sveinn says.

"He is, isn't he. Might as well end him now."

Rolant cocks back the gun, and I shout, "No!" I try to step forward but Keller doesn't let me. I hold my hand out past Keller. "Wait, please, there has to be something I can do that will make this better. What do you want? I'll do whatever you need. Please don't hurt him."

Rolant chuckles and glances over at Sveinn. "Maybe we were wrong. Maybe she does care about him more than we thought." He motions for me to come forward, but Keller doesn't move. "Unless you want your dick shot off, move so she can step forward."

"Keller, listen to him," I say, and reluctantly, he steps to the side, allowing me to move forward. "What can I do? Do you want me to leave? Go back to Miami?"

"No," Rolant says. "That seems too easy at this point."

"And we can't guarantee that she won't come back."

"Exactly, brother," Rolant says. "Which means we need to keep her around."

"And use her to our advantage. Make her do the work we were hoping to do," Sveinn says.

"Anything," I say with feigned desperation. "I will do anything."

"Anything?" Rolant asks. "She's a lot more willing to please than her mother ever was."

The mention of my mother from his mouth nearly makes me charge after him, but like Keller taught me, I remain as calm as I can.

"Much more pleasing," Sveinn says. "Which means, I bet she would give us access to Birch Forest."

"If she knew Keller was safe if she did, I bet she would."

"For energy, right?" I ask, taking a shot. I'm also hoping the conversation will distract them so Lara can work out a tactic to take them out. "The moss acts like a biological solar panel."

Rolant's brows pull together. "You know about the moss?"

"It's something I've been looking into. Theo is totally against it, but I don't see why we can't be careful and use it properly. It's not like anyone is even allowed near it to see just how old the moss is. Seems like a wasted resource."

"It is," Rolant says slyly, his eyes traveling up and down.

"I don't trust her," Sveinn says. "Keller trained her, so she knows exactly what to say in this kind of moment."

"You know what, you're right," Rolant says, an evil gleam in his eyes. "You're absolutely right. We went through crisis training, so we know every trick of the trade, and look at them following it with precision. Well, we're not falling for it." And then, he moves the gun, points it at Ottar, and shoots.

A scream falls past my lips as Ottar falls to the ground, blood spilling out of his leg as he clutches it.

"Why did you do that?" I ask as I look up at Rolant.

"So I can do this." He points his gun at Keller.

Time stands still as I watch evil overpower the look in Rolant's eyes. Pure, unadulterated anger and disdain, oozing from every inch of his body as he smirks . . . right before pulling the trigger.

I don't have time to think, I don't have time to question what's going on, all I have time for is basic instinct as the trigger is pulled.

I leap in front of Keller just as the most intense pain I've ever felt pierces my body.

Chapter Thirty-Seven

KELLER

"Nooooo," I cry out just as Lilly hits the ground, face down, blood pooling around her. I fall to the gravel beneath us just as two more gunshots ring out. They don't come from Rolant or Sveinn, but rather from Harrogate.

"They're down," Ottar calls out.

But I don't bother to look. Instead, I turn Lilly over and see the gunshot wound pooling over her heart.

"Fuck," I cry. "Help . . . fuck . . . help now!" In a state of panic, I stare down at Lilly and her lifeless eyes, pale face, my stomach flipping in fear. *Where was she shot?* There's so much blood. "Lilly, love, stay with me," I say just as the doctor comes up next to me with his kit.

"Stand aside," he says.

"I can't . . . I can't lose her," I say, my throat choking up. "Please, do something."

"Keller," Runa says, tugging on my arm. "Give him space."

"We need to take her to the hospital, now," the doctor says as he presses gauze against her chest. When I don't move, he yells, "Keller, now."

"Okay," I say standing, unsure of what to do. That's when I glance around and see Ottar on the ground, his leg bleeding. Fuck.

"Pick her up," Runa says to me. "I'll drive."

"I'll hold the gauze, you bring her to the car," the doctor says. "Quickly."

Panic and fear rip through me as I bend down and lift Lilly's limp body into my arms, giving the doctor enough room to press against her chest. "Ottar," I call out.

"I'm fine," he says.

"I got him," Lara says, coming out of Harrogate with a sheet for a tourniquet. "We'll be right behind you."

Glad that Ottar is taken care of, I move Lilly over to the car where Runa opens the back seat for me. I bend at the waist, sitting down first so the doctor can keep his hands on Lilly's chest, and then I scoot backward until I'm on the other side of the car, the doctor right next to me, applying pressure. Runa gets in the front seat and starts the car.

"Do you have a phone?" I ask her.

"Yes," she says as she turns the car around.

"Call the police, give them our location, tell them we have the princess in the car with a gunshot wound and to meet us with an escort."

"Got it," Runa says, moving with precision while under pressure. She presses on the pedal and propels us forward, flying down the road while she makes the phone call.

I stare down at Lilly, the pounding in my head a distant memory as I quietly say, "Stay with us, love. Please . . . please stay with us."

Tears cloud my eyes as I watch the doctor's hands fill with blood and watch as her chest rises and falls slower and slower.

"Hang in there, Lilly," I plead, my tears falling onto her. "Please hang in there . . ."

———

SIRENS ECHO off the buildings around us as we navigate the narrow streets of Houndsburg, the closest city with a hospital, about half an hour away.

It wasn't long before the police caught up with us and cleared a path while Runa drove dangerously fast, cutting our time down by ten minutes. She loops into the emergency room entrance where at least a dozen nurses and doctors stand by with a gurney, ready to take over. When the car comes to a stop, the door is whipped open. I scoot out the back, holding Lilly, and deposit her on the bed, only to be pushed out of the way. Before my eyes, they wheel her away and into the hospital. I stare off at their retreat, my fucking heart being ripped out of my chest as more and more distance is put between us.

My adrenaline drains out of me, weakening every bone and muscle in my body, causing me to crumple to my knees. With my clothes soaked in Lilly's blood, I kneel on the asphalt, tears streaming down my face as my breath rapidly escapes my lungs. Runa comes up next to me, her hand on my back as she kneels.

"She'll be okay, Keller. She has to be okay."

"Why . . . why did she step in front of me?" I ask, my voice choking on a sob.

"Because that's how much she loves you, Keller. She would take a bullet for you to make sure you go unharmed."

"That . . . that should be me," I say. "Not her. She's not supposed to get hurt. I'm supposed to protect her, not the other way around."

Another car pulls into the circle, and Lara calls out for help. I glance over at the car where Ottar is being pulled out, his limp body placed onto a gurney and escorted into the hospital.

"Fuck," I say as I attempt to stand, but my legs give out on me.

"Are you okay?" Runa asks.

"Yes," I say, feeling dizzy, my head pounding at such a rapid rate that my stomach starts to revolt.

Fuck, not right now.

Please not right now.

But it's no use. The pain catches up to me, and before I know it, I'm turning to the side, my hands on the asphalt, and throwing up.

In the distance, Lara calls for help again as my stomach convulses, and I throw up once more.

In seconds, I'm lifted from the ground and gently placed on a gurney while Lara speaks to someone about my head and gives them a quick rundown of what I've been through.

"Lilly," I say, my voice sounding garbled to me. "I need to be with Lilly."

But as I'm wheeled away, I just feel like I'm being pulled farther and farther away from her.

———

"HOW IS HE?" a female voice says.

"Good, we reduced the pressure on his brain during surgery. We feel positive about the outcome."

"Thank you," the voice says.

When the door clicks shut, I tell myself to open my eyes, but my body isn't listening for some reason.

"Oh Keller," the voice says as they take my hand. "What you've been through, it . . . it makes me so sick to my stomach. You don't deserve this. You didn't deserve any of this." My hand is lifted to their mouth, and a light kiss is pressed against my knuckles. "You need to pull through for us, okay? We need one of you to pull through."

One of you?

What does that mean?

Who is one of . . .

Lilly.

Fuck, Lilly.

Is she okay?

Did she not pull through?

My mind screams for my mouth to talk, for my voice to come through, but nothing happens. *Fuck.*

"We need you now more than ever," the voice says just as they rest their head against my chest and wrap their arm over me.

Why me . . . what about Lilly?

<hr />

"THERE WAS A FRESH SNOW TODAY," someone says next to me. "It's covered the rolling hills, and when it's sunny out, it almost looks like a layer of glitter. It's beautiful."

My head lolls to the side, and the person next to me shifts.

"Keller, can you hear me?"

"Mmm," I mumble, my brain feeling like fog.

"Oh my God, Keller, you can hear me." She takes my hand in hers. "It's Lara. Can you open your eyes?"

My mouth is so fucking dry, I feel like my tongue is plastered to the roof. "Wa-water," I say as my eyes start to blink open. Fuck, it's bright.

A straw is brought up to my mouth, and I take a few sips, the cool water refreshing my mouth and allowing me to free up my tongue to talk.

"Lilly," I say. "Where . . . where is she?" I'm able to blink my eyes open just enough to catch the troubled look on Lara's face.

"Keller . . ." she says, her voice tight.

"Don't," I say. "Don't fucking . . ." My voice catches in my throat. "Don't tell me something went wrong."

Her lips twist to the side. "She's . . ."

"She's what?" I ask, my pulse picking up.

"She's not . . . she's not doing well."

I try to sit up, but it feels next to impossible as my head pounds with pain again. I wince, and then rest my head back down. "Fuck . . . just tell me . . . is she alive?"

"Right now . . . yes. But she's coded twice. She's on life support. It's not looking good."

My stomach churns with nausea, and Lara must notice, because she quickly hands me a vomit bag and I throw up into it, the pain from my head so fucking intense.

After I dry heave a few more times, I hand the bag back to her and say, "Take me to her."

"Keller, you just had brain surgery. You can't go anywhere."

Eyes shut, leaning against the pillow, I breathe out heavily. "She needs me. Take me to her."

"Keller—"

"Please, Lara." Tears pool in my eyes. "Take me to her."

She grips my hand and says, "Let me see what I can do."

━━━

WITH NURSES and a doctor surrounding my hospital bed, I'm wheeled down the stark white corridors of the hospital, a few onlookers stopping to bow their heads to me. Lara told me they were willing to put us in a room together, but I told her that wasn't good enough. I wanted to be in the same bed. According to hospital protocol, they can't allow that to happen in case something drastic happens to the patient, they need full access to both. I told her again, that wasn't good enough, and then I heard Theo step in.

He demanded we share a bed and didn't care if it went against hospital protocol.

Once the hospital staff went to figure out how to make this happen, Theo came into the room and sat next to me. He didn't say much, but simply held my hand and told me how much he loves me. I fell asleep after that.

"Right over here," one of the nurses says to me.

I'm wheeled into a warm, tan-colored room with green drapes. Flowers fill the space. The aroma is so powerful that it takes over the sterile hospital smell that seems to have planted itself in my nose.

I try to lift my head to get a look at Lilly, and when she comes into view, my entire heart trips and falls to my stomach.

A tube is pushed down her throat, wires are hooked up everywhere, and her face is a pale, almost ghostly color as the lone beeping sound of her heart monitor fills the air. Resting in a large, almost full-size-looking bed, they've moved her to the side, making just enough room for me.

"Lilly," I whisper as my bed is wheeled up next to hers. "How . . . how is she doing?"

"She's stable for now," the doctor says.

"What does that mean?" I ask.

"It means she's fighting." And that's all I get from him before the sides to my bed are lowered and I'm helped up to my feet, two large men flanking my side to help me into her bed.

"Be careful of her cords. We can't afford for anything to be unplugged," the doctor says.

Earlier today, I was informed that I suffered from many concussions during my time in the cell, which led to bleeding on my brain. The doctor told me that he was baffled that I was able to fly a plane with the amount of blood applying pressure to my brain. It's also why I had such a hard time trying to pinpoint who was behind all of this. And that I should feel very lucky that I'm alive and didn't have a stroke.

Luck . . . what a funny thing, because right now, I don't feel lucky at all. Not when my Lilly fights for her life. Nothing about me is lucky.

I should be the one in her bed, fighting.

I should be the one with the bullet wound.

Not her.

I settle into her bed, and with my arm that has the IV attached to it, I drape it carefully over her stomach and then I move my head in close to hers.

"Please be careful," the doctor says.

"This is my goddamn life in this bed," I say to him. "You don't have to tell me to be careful."

His lips seal shut as he nods. "We'll be back to check on you. Ring the button if you need us."

The hospital staff leave the room, shutting the door behind them and leaving me alone with Lilly.

I press my lips softly to her cheek and whisper in her ear. "I'm here, love. I'm right here with you and I'm not going anywhere." I press another kiss to her cheek. "Just you and me. We can get through this. You can get through this, because you're a fighter, you're so strong." My voice chokes up. "The strongest person I know. Stronger than I'll ever be."

I nuzzle into her, her body feeling cold, stiff . . . like she's teetering on life and death. The lack of energy, enthusiasm, cheerfulness—it's debilitating to see her in such a state when she's always the brightest in the room.

"Please stay with me," I whisper. "I need you, Lilly. I can't . . ." I bite on my bottom lip as a sob catches in my chest, and tears fall past my lids and down my cheeks. "I can't walk this earth without you. Please."

And when she doesn't respond, when the only sound in the room is of her heart monitor beeping, I let my fear and heartache take over, and I cry.

As my tears flow, I beg and plead with whoever wants to listen . . . God, angels . . . her parents.

Please, please don't let her leave this earth.
It's not her time.

⊏⊐

"DO YOU NEED ANYTHING?" Ottar asks me as he stands next to Lara on a pair of crutches.

He was shot in the leg, in his left quad. Lara was able to fashion a tourniquet that helped staunch the bleeding to get him to the hospital. He had to have a blood transfusion, just like Lilly. And after a few surgeries, he regained consciousness and was discharged from the hospital when Lara promised to supervise him.

"I'm good," I say as I adjust the jogger pants Lara brought me.

Yesterday, I was cleared by the doctor and told to take it very easy. There's a list of recovery tasks I need to do daily, but those are the least of my concerns at the moment. All I care about is Lilly. Lara brought me some clothes to change into, along with many well wishes from people all around the country. A pile so high that it's intimidating to even consider reading.

Theo officially addressed the nation a few days ago, telling them about Rolant and Sveinn. From what Lara has told me, he has been absolutely sick about the entire ordeal as well as devastated about the men he thought he raised. Not to mention . . . mourning. I can't imagine what he must be going through, knowing that his sons betrayed him and his country, tried to take the life of his granddaughter, and then had to accept that to save me and Lilly, his sons had to be killed. The fact that he was even able to address the country is shocking to me.

He spoke the truth, though, from the very beginning. He spoke about the threats, the kidnapping, about how Elias and Cornolia betrayed the country. He spoke of my three months

467

in the cell and how I was able to escape to try to save Lilly. He spoke about Ottar and Lara and their heroic efforts to keep us safe, and he spoke of how Lilly took a bullet for me . . .

He honored the doctor who kept pressure on her chest, Runa's expert crisis management, and the hospital staff taking care of all of us.

He asked for our well wishes and to keep Lilly in their thoughts.

And they have.

Every night, a candlelight vigil is held outside under the Northern Lights. Wishes and hopes for the princess to get better have been placed outside her window. I've made sure to wave to them every night that I've been in her room, thanking them for their positive energy and thoughts. I've told Lilly about the signs that have been outside, the people who have shown up for her, and every night, I've kissed her, held her, and begged her to return to me. But with each passing day when she doesn't move or respond to my touch, I fear the worst, that maybe . . . maybe she's not coming back to us.

I even heard the doctor pull Theo to the side where they had a tough conversation about the probability of Lilly coming back to us. Theo responded that we do everything to save her, no matter the odds or how long it might take.

It would have been my same response.

We keep trying until she stops fighting.

She's still fighting. Every day, she's still in this game.

"Okay, well, let us know if you need anything else," Lara says.

"Thank you." I put away my clothes in the dresser provided in the room. I don't plan on going anywhere. They left my hospital bed in here in case I wanted another place to sleep, but I haven't used it. I've been plastered to Lilly every night because I know that's what we both need.

"Oh, we also spoke to Runa," Ottar says. "And about the night of . . . of the shooting."

"You did?" I ask, standing tall. "How did they find her?"

"Rolant and Sveinn cut them off on the road. Saw the palace car and held them at gunpoint. Threatened to take out the king if they didn't let them in the car. Runa assumed since we were at Harrogate, that we would be able to help take them down."

"I just wish I had acted quicker," Lara says.

"You acted quickly enough," I say, reassuring her. "We were trying to gain the truth. We didn't know they were going to shoot. I honestly didn't think they had it in them."

"You didn't?" Lara asks. "After everything they put you through? You didn't think they would shoot?"

"They never did the dirty work. They just gave the word." I drag my hand over my face. "Although, Rolant did look unhinged." I shake my head. "I still can't believe it was them. What has come of Arkham?"

"The ITO has been talking about going to war."

"Really?" I ask. "What about all of those innocent people?"

"That's what they're trying to figure out. It's complicated, but there will be repercussions. Elias has been very cooperative in giving us as much information as he can, as well as the Sotherbys. It all points at Magnus, Rolant, and Sveinn."

"What about Evan?" I ask, curious about where he lands with all of this.

"Had no clue," Ottar answers. "He was trying to please his parents. He wasn't a part of the deception."

"Do we trust that?" I ask.

Lara nods. "Yes, he's actually resigned from his position in the Sotherbys and is helping Marsdale with the investigation. He wants everyone to be brought to justice. He's been a valuable resource."

I nod. "Okay."

"Hey." Lara forces me to look at her. "He wants nothing

more than to watch you two walk down the aisle once Lilly wakes up. Okay?"

"Yeah . . . okay," I answer.

Ottar yawns and wobbles on his crutches, giving Lara concern. "Time to get you home." She pats his back.

"Where are you staying?" I ask.

"In an apartment down the road. We're close, so truly, if you need something, let us know."

"I will. Thanks. And, Ottar, don't push yourself too hard."

"I'm going to say the same thing to you." He sighs. "It's over. All of it. Focus all your attention on Lilly now."

"I will."

We say our goodbyes, and when they're out the door, I walk over to Lilly's bed, and I slip under the covers with her, wrapping my arm around her, and once again, I kiss her cheek, the side of her head, anywhere I can get my lips on that doesn't disturb the wires she's hooked up to.

"Come on, love," I say softly. "Come back to me. This isn't how we end. There's so much more of our story to be told. For one, we need to get married. I need to see you in your wedding dress, staring up at me with that gorgeous smile of yours. We need to go on our honeymoon where we spend every waking hour in each other's arms. And when we return, we have to move into our own place, where we can start a family." I run my nose over her jaw. "You're going to be an amazing mum. Our kids will know what a fighter you are, how strong you are, how you've never given up on anything, even this." Again, tears fill my eyes. "They will know how you've overcome the odds and how you came back to me, because we're supposed to be together, Lilly. You and me. Like you said . . . we matter most." Tears fall down my cheeks. "We matter most, love."

LARA: *How is she?*

Keller: *Same. The only thing that's keeping me sane is the fact that she hasn't gotten worse.*

Lara: *Did the doctors say that could happen?*

Keller: *Yes. They are pleased she hasn't declined.*

Lara: *That's good. If you need to leave the room, let us know, I can sit with her.*

Keller: *I'm not leaving.*

Lara: *It's been three weeks, Keller.*

Keller: *I'm not leaving, Lara.*

Lara: *Okay, well the option is there. We care about your health too.*

Keller: *I'm fine. Lilly needs me. I'm not leaving.*

Lara: *Okay, well, we will be by later. Let us know if you need us to bring you anything.*

Keller: *I will.*

———

THERE'S a knock on the door, and I glance up to see Theo walk into the room with Katla by his side, both looking grim.

"How are you, son?" Theo walks toward me with his cane. I stand, and he pulls me into a large hug. I hug him back, hanging on a while longer, because fuck, I need the comfort. Every day, I plead for Lilly to move, to twitch, to do anything that indicates she's coming back to us, and every day where nothing happens, my hopes slowly fade away.

"Okay," I answer truthfully.

Theo lets go of me, and Katla takes me into a hug as well. "You're looking thin, Keller. Have you been eating?"

"As much as I can," I answer as I pull away. Hands on my hips, I say, "It's been hard."

"We understand," Katla says. "We've struggled as well." They glance toward the bed, and I can see they have something on their mind as they take a seat on the couch up against the window. I take a seat on the chair next to Lilly's bed and carefully take her hand in mine.

"We spoke with the doctor," Theo says. "He has some concerns."

"Like what?" I ask.

Theo clears his throat. "He's glad she hasn't declined in health, but he's also worried that she hasn't made any progress in a month. He's worried that . . . that the machines she's on are keeping her alive, keeping our hopes up, but there—" His eyes well up, and he stares up at the ceiling. I glance at Katla who is dabbing her eyes with a handkerchief.

"Whatever you're about to say, the answer is no," I interrupt. "We are not giving up on her."

"I don't want to give up on her," Theo says. "I will do everything we can to make sure she stays with us, but I think . . . I think we need to talk about what happens if she doesn't."

"No," I say, shaking my head. "Respectfully, no. I understand your position as the king and the pressure you're probably getting from outside sources to figure out what's going to happen if she doesn't come through this, but I'm going to tell you right now, I have no doubt in my mind that she'll wake up. She's a fighter, and she might be taking her time, but she'll wake up."

"Keller," Katla says softly.

"Please," I say, my voice strained. "Please believe me. Please . . . please hope with me. Please don't leave me hanging out here, by myself, being the only one who thinks she will pull through. Please." I look up at them, my sorrow hitting me harder than I expected.

I know what everyone is thinking.

She's a lost cause.

The machines are the only reason she's still breathing.

We should move on and think about the future of Torskethorpe.

But she's the future.

She's it.

She will pull through this.

She has to, because . . . because I don't know what I would do without her.

Theo nods. "Of course," he says, his throat choking up. "We are here with you, Keller. She will pull through. I believe it."

Katla nods. "I believe it too."

"Thank you," I say, wiping my eyes.

—————

"WE LOVE YOU, Princess Lilly. We can't wait to see you back at our school again. Get better soon,'" I say, reading one of the several cards delivered today. "You know, I think that was from the girl I kicked. And yes, I said kicked, because sure, I might not have meant to, but did it happen? It sure did."

I set down the card and reach for another one.

"Oh, this is from the same class. I think this is the kid whose lap she fell into." I take Lilly's hand, rubbing my thumb over her knuckle. "He says, 'Princess Lilly, I like your hair. Get better.'" I stare at the card and set it down. "Compliments all around." I glance at her. "I love you, but man, if the kid saw your hair now, I don't think he would be singing your praises. I spoke with a nurse, and they're going to wash it today and possibly braid it. We will see."

I grab another card. This one is purple. "'Princess Lilly. I hope you feel better soon. I hope you like the cod I drew you.'" I flash the card at her. "This guy is showing off for you. I would say an accurate portrayal, might need a little help on the—"

I pause, and my eyes immediately go to where I'm holding her hand.

Heart stilling, breath catching in my chest.

Wait . . .

Did . . . did her thumb just move?

My heart rate picks up, and I drop the card, focusing all of my attention on her hand.

"Love . . . did you . . . did you just move your thumb?" I pause, waiting to see if anything happens.

Am I imagining it? Am I that fucking desperate that I'm feeling things now?

"Lilly, if you can hear me, move your thumb, your finger, anything."

I pause again, the distant sound of her machines the only noise filling the air. When she doesn't move, my heart crashes all over again.

Fuck.

"God, I really thought you moved for a second. Jesus Christ." I take a few deep breaths. "If that cod brought you back to me, I'd frame that godforsaken picture. I was being kind. It wasn't that great."

I move to the next card, and as I start reading, her thumb passes over my knuckle again. An actual chill races down my spine as I stare down at her connection.

"Lilly, love, can you hear me?"

I wait, my breath stilling in my lungs.

Please . . . please show me any sign that you're here with me.

Anything.

And then . . . her thumb moves again. I sob as I bring her hand up to mine and kiss it.

"Fuck, love, you're . . . you're here. With me." I crawl up the bed and wrap my arm around her, bringing my lips to her cheek, to her neck, to the side of her head. "Lilly, my girl, you're here." I press another kiss to her head, then ring the call button multiple times. A rush of staff come into the room all at once, and through a cloud of tears, I say, "She's moving her thumb."

SITTING on the edge of her bed, I watch carefully as Lilly's eyes move under her lids, the heaviness making it hard for her to open. Katla and Theo stand to the side, Lara and Ottar are by the couch, and Lilly's doctor and nurse are to the right, watching carefully.

"That's it, Lilly," I say softly. "Take your time. We're here, waiting for you."

Her lashes flutter and then, for the first time in over a month, her eyes open, and I'm met with the most beautiful pair of irises I've ever seen. A quiet gasp falls over the room as I reach up and cup her cheek.

"That's it, Lilly. Just like that." Tears stream down my cheeks as I lean in closer. "There's my beautiful girl."

The doctor steps forward. "Hello, Princess Lilija. Your throat might feel sore from your ETT, so take your time."

When she first started moving, the doctor checked Lilly to see if she'd pass a CPAP test. Once they were convinced Lilly required minimal oxygen supplementations and could breathe above the ventilator's breathing rate, they extubated her. It was such a relief to see her breathing tube gone and to know she could breathe on her own. My hopes rose even more then.

Lilly looks around, her eyes blinking a few times. They glance over my shoulder to Katla and Theo. And then by the window where Ottar and Lara stand. And when they trail back to me, I watch recognition pass over her as she quietly says, "Keller."

That one whisper of a word is all I fucking need. I lean forward and press my forehead against hers. "I'm here," I say. "I'm here."

Epilogue

LILLY

"Keller?" My throat's still so sore.

"Hmm?" he asks, his body pressed up against mine, his arm draped over my stomach.

"Are you mad at me?"

He lifts up to look me in the eyes. "Mad at you? What the hell for?"

It's been a day since I've opened my eyes, and I feel like I've been hit by a truck and dragged a few miles, but seeing Keller, being in his arms, it's everything I need to get through this confusion and pain I'm feeling.

According to the doctor, I barely made it. I died twice, and they were able to revive me. The bullet nearly hit my heart, just a few millimeters away. If it wasn't for Dr. Johansen applying pressure and Runa's expert driving, I probably wouldn't be here.

I shift my head to the side to get a better look at him. "For moving in front of you when Rolant shot you?"

His brows turn down. "That's not something we need to talk about."

"I want to," I say before coughing. Keller hands me my drink, and I take a few sips.

"Lilly, save your voice."

I shake my head. "No, I want to talk to you about this." I take a deep breath and continue, "All I can remember at that moment is if I lose him again, I won't be able to move on. It was instinct, and I jumped."

"Lilly—"

"I'm not done," I say. "I can't imagine the excruciating pain you've gone through, the fear, the unknown clouding your vision, but I will say this, for as much as I put you through by stepping in front of that bullet, I would do it all over again to make sure you weren't hurt."

His thumb rubs over my cheek as he shakes his head. "Lilly, it's my job to protect you."

"That's where you're wrong. It's both our jobs to protect each other. You mean everything to me, Keller, which means I would do anything to make sure you're never harmed."

He leans forward, pressing his forehead against mine. "No one has ever loved me the way that you do." He sighs. "Thank you for protecting me, Lilly . . . but for the love of God, don't do it again."

I chuckle and cough a few more times. Once I gather myself, I say, "Yeah, I'm pretty sure that stunt earned me a lecture from Theo."

"You think?" he asks. "Christ, Lilly. I'm pretty sure Lara, Ottar, Katla, and even your cousins are ready to give you a lecture on the proper protocol of jumping in front of a bullet, especially when you're the last fucking heir to the throne."

"Yeah, I didn't think about that. I only wanted to protect you. We've been through so much. I couldn't lose you again."

"But I almost lost you," he says quietly, his eyes watering.

"I don't know what I would have done if you didn't wake up. I can't even think about it."

"Then don't. Let's think about what the future looks like."

"Recuperating," he says. "Getting you back to where you need to be . . . then walking you down that aisle."

"Then honeymoon," I say. "With the toys." I wiggle my brow, causing Keller to chuckle.

"Can't forget the toys."

"Never." I sigh. "Is it really all over? Like . . . everything is going to be okay now?"

"Yes," Keller answers. "Rolant and Sveinn are dead. Rolant's assistant, Pickering, basically sung like a canary once he realized he was an accessory to kidnapping and attempted murder. He was able to provide phone call logs and is willing to testify against King Magnus, who he overheard several times consorting with Theo's sons. The ITO handles international crime for their countries, so they're currently interrogating King Magnus. It's doubtful he'll ever see freedom again. Pickering led detectives to where I was held, and they are slowly collating all the evidence to put the king away. Theo had Torskethorpe enter the ITO, which offers us more protection. We're no longer a sitting duck in the middle of the ocean by ourselves. And we are much stronger with Marsdale by our side as well. I can't promise you there won't be inane threats here and there, protestors against the monarchy, but what we just went through won't happen again. It's over."

"Thank God," I say as I press my cheek into Keller's palm. "I know I signed up to be the queen of Torskethorpe one day, but I didn't sign up to be kidnapped and shot in the chest. I'm just here for the fermented cod cakes."

"Are you really, though?" Keller asks with a raise to his brow.

"Oh yeah, love those fermented cod cakes, can't get enough of them."

"Good, I'll be sure to have the nursing staff bring some in."

I point my finger at him. "Don't you dare."

He chuckles and brings his lips to mine and kisses me. It's light, nothing too sexual, nothing too deep, just enough of him to let me know that he's mine. Through thick and thin, this man will always be mine.

<hr>

KELLER

THERE'S a knock on my door, and when I turn around from adjusting my tie, Lara stands in the doorway. Her eyes soften as she looks me up and down in my wedding suit. I have a few medals that I've added to my suit since the initial fitting. Medals awarded to me for bravery, courage, protecting the crown—some of the highest honors awarded in Torskethorpe.

Once Lilly was released from the hospital, we brought her back to Strombly and started working on her rehab. It took quite a few months to get her back to her normal self. She sustained a lot of nerve damage as well as muscle atrophy whilst in her coma, among other things.

But thankfully, she's doing well. During that time, we did one interview, which was broadcast all over the world. We told our story, what happened with the wedding, and why it was canceled—because I was kidnapped. They went into detail about what I suffered through despite not wanting to put that out there, and they connected all of the dots in a detailed timeline of what Rolant and Sveinn were planning. It was one of the most watched interviews ever aired.

And now . . . now the country is chomping at the bit for today, our wedding day. Not only is Torskethorpe excited, but the wedding is being aired on TV all around the world too. Tourism has spiked—strangely—and the country is thriving now more than ever, with Lilly and me being held in high regard. Not that I needed the acceptance of the country, but it feels pretty damn good to know they approve of me.

Doesn't mean I won't spend every day trying to still earn their acceptance. I just know it won't control how I feel and who I am.

"You look so handsome," Lara says, walking into the room wearing her typical black suit with black shirt. Her hair is slicked back into a tight bun, but there is one addition to her that seems to be bringing a smile to her face more than ever recently, and it's the engagement ring on her finger. Both Lara and Ottar never discussed their own falling out—faithful to a fault—but thankfully, all is resolved. My best friend is happy, and that's the best thing.

A month ago, Ottar proposed to her in the courtyard of the palace. We were able to watch from afar, and seeing my best friend from childhood find the love she so rightfully deserves, I've been filled with more joy than I expected.

"Thank you," I say.

"Are you nervous?"

I shake my head. "Just anxious. I want to be married already."

She chuckles. "Well, you both are overdue at this point. I'm actually in here because Lilly has asked to see you."

"She has?"

Lara nods her head. "Yes, she's in her room. She wants to see you before you leave for the temple."

"Everything okay?"

Lara smiles. "Yes, everything is great."

"Okay." I glance in the mirror one more time to make sure my hair is in place, then follow Lara out of the sapphire room —which I've been getting ready in, not spending the night.

Nope, I've been staying with Lilly every night. Theo threw all the traditions and rules out the window after we returned from the hospital. We knew that we didn't need to be separated to ensure our relationship was built on more than sex. Our sexual compatibility was never called into question. But our true faith in each other was. We both know we're so much stronger now. We've endured so much and are better as a result. We both didn't love the journey, but the results speak for themselves.

When Lara and I reach the room, I push through and find it empty.

Her cousins aren't present, nor is Timmy.

Instead, Lilly stands in the middle of the room, in her wedding gown, her gorgeous hair curled and draped over her shoulders, a flower crown placed gently on her head while flowers cascade down the tendrils of hair framing her gorgeous face.

My mouth goes dry as I fully step into her room, Lara shutting the door behind me.

"Lilly," I say, taking her all in, my eyes roaming, my heart rate speeding up with every new thing I notice about her dress, about her hair, about her makeup. She's so gorgeous, and to see her like this, waiting for me to take her hand, makes a grown man want to fall to his knees in thanks. "You look . . . you're stunning."

She smiles and walks up to me, looking like a goddamn floating angel. "You look unbelievably handsome," she says as her hand finds the lapel of my suit.

I chuckle. "Don't get any ideas."

Her fingers run up my chest. "Why not? Today is a cause for celebration."

"Yes, but let's get married first and then celebrate."

"That's not the kind of celebration I'm talking about," she says.

"What do you mean?" I ask.

My hand in hers, she walks me over to her nightstand and hands a box to me. It's the size of my palm and long.

"What's this?"

"It's for you. I thought I would give you a little present before we walk down the aisle."

Confused, I give her a look that just makes her laugh and poke me to open it. So I lift the box, push back the tissue paper, and when I see what's inside, my stomach falls to the fucking ground.

"No," I say, tears springing to my eyes.

She nods.

"No, this is a joke."

She chuckles. "It's not, Keller. You're going to be a dad."

I run my hand over my mouth in awe as I stare down at the positive pregnancy test. "This is for real?"

"Very real," she says as she takes the box from me and sets it back down on the nightstand. "The doctor confirmed it last night."

"But . . . how . . ."

"Well, there was the multiple times in bed, the multiple times up against the wall, the time in the bathtub, oh, and when we were in the stairway . . . remember that night? But if I really had to pin it to something, I think it was when we decided to have a quickie in the kitchen. The whipped cream you sucked off my tits really made a baby."

"Jesus," I mutter, making her laugh. "I didn't mean like that."

"I know, but it's fun pressing your buttons." She stands on her toes and kisses my jaw. "The doctor just said this kind of thing happens all the time."

"So we're really having a baby?"

"We are," she answers.

A large smile crosses my face before I lean down and capture her mouth with mine, my hands holding her jaw.

This woman has given me so much.

From the day I first met her, she's challenged me and pushed me out of my shell. She made me realize there's more to my life than just serving the crown.

I can be loved.

I can be cherished.

I can dedicate my life to the country I love.

I can be a husband.

I can be . . . I can be a father.

She's shown me what it's like to live, what it's like to fall deeply in love, and what it's like to live life after tragedy.

I once believed we were royally in trouble, that our lives were diverging rather than converging. But through those trials we learned so much about each other. We also found strength within that we had no idea existed.

With my beautiful Lilly alongside me, there's harmony even when there's chaos. There's joy even when there's trouble.

If I've learned one thing, it's that a *well*-loved life becomes a *well*-lived life. And that's my plan forevermore.

Made in the USA
Middletown, DE
26 July 2023

35784263R00269